WALKING EARTH – Reviews

"Walking Earth is a gripping read, well written and informative. Although difficult for a non-Navajo, Greg Sagemiller has infused the tone and ambiance of Dinetah into the contemporary mystery genre, and then provided layers of substance with his own archaeological expertise. I could almost smell the sagebrush and fry bread!"
Jackie Bralove, Alexandria, VA, Adjunct Lecturer in Religious Studies; Former Consultant to the Bi- Lingual, Bi-Cultural curriculum philosophy, Dine College (formerly Navajo Community College).

"From start to finish, Greg Sagemiller's novel Walking Earth is one hell of a wild ride."
Rick Collignon, Taos, NM, "The Journal of Antonio Montoya".

"Walking Earth, a novel about looters of archaeological sites...provides intrigue with actions of several governmental agencies for the importance of preserving the past for the future. The remote setting on Cedar Mesa, Utah...and the religious beliefs of the Navajo provide additional insight into the geology and landscape of this region."
David Kirkpatrick, Archaeologist, Las Cruces, NM

"I really enjoyed the book. The plot was amazing with many twists all the way to the exciting conclusion. My favorite part of the book was your wonderful description of the Cedar Mesa environment. I could easily visualize all of the action on the Mesa as well as the surrounding areas. I loved the good archaeological information, ranging from migration theories to laboratory analysis, which runs throughout the book. We continue to deal with looters who destroy our Country's heritage and Native American sacred sites. Quite often these looters are supported by wealthy collectors."
Paul Williams, Archaeologist, Taos, NM

WALKING EARTH   Greg Sagemiller

To Belinda ~

Enjoy your journey Through majestic Southwest Landscapes and rich cultures.

BesT~

WALKING EARTH

A novel of mystery and espionage

Greg Sagemiller

AUTHOR'S NOTE

Numerous local, state and federal government agencies are mentioned in this novel. They are real entities, but all references to them, their employees or policies are the sole interpretation and imagination of the author. Any resemblance of events or characters to actual events or persons, living or dead, is purely coincidental. Furthermore, any errors of fact concerning Native American ceremonies, traditions, legends or archeological interpretations thereof, are entirely the author's. Lastly, certain archaeological site-sensitive names and locations, including specific archeological ruins, are fictionalized in the spirit of site stewardship, preservation and recognition of Federal and State laws governing cultural resource protection.

To all

Aficionados of Ancient Civilizations

ACKNOWLEDGMENTS

Several people need to be thanked for their support, encouragement and research guidance. My wife comes first. Rebecca Sagemiller selflessly persevered more than five years of my antics to remove the story clamoring in my head into words on paper. She awarded me broad personal and spatial boundaries to research and to write; yet came very close to forming a local twelve step group for spouses of writers. Andy Dennison, creative writing instructor, University of New Mexico-Taos, waded through several chapters and entire drafts. My sounding board and mentor, he encouraged me to see my story to its end and not give up. Lois Coyle, my mother-in-law, donated her beachside Vancouver Island condo for two weeks of intensive, round-the-clock writing. Indeed, a writer's paradise, the beach could well have been 1,000 miles away, since I wrote in a timeless vacuum, succumbing only to brief episodes of starvation and exhaustion.

The comprehensive tour of Navajo Generating Station by George L. Watson, O & M Manager, and his assistant, Regina Lane, paved the way for action scenes in the final chapters. Thomas M Kliewer, Highway Maintenance Supervisor, Arizona Department of Transportation, Page, Arizona, furnished valuable highway information and insights into Navajo roads ("trails"). Rock climbing expertise beyond my neophyte level was provided by my good friend and skilled rock climber, Jonah Salloway. Mr. Andy Gilliland, National Fleet Manager, Pemberton Truck Lines, Knoxville, Tennessee, nearly a brother to me, provided technical expertise in chassis modifications and inherent dangers therein. David M. Brugge, Honorary Trustee of Hubbell Trading Post National Historic Site, Ganado, Arizona, friend and archaeological associate, author of fourteen Navajo and Hopi Nations books, assisted me with the Navajo language. Susan Thomas, Curator, retired, Anasazi Heritage Center, Dolores, Colorado, granted me extensive access to the museum's archived collection of prehistoric feather holders excavated from the Colorado Plateau.

The unique cover photograph and design was created by my editor, Brigitte Barlos, a Taos New Mexico-based translator, photographer and artist who proved to be a supremely competent editor and wizard of word selection and technical jargon. She molded my dreams into reality, greatly enhanced my writing skills, built my website www.walkingearthseries.com and launched me into social networking and electronic publishing.

"Whenever a civilization perishes there is always one

condition present.

They forget where they came from."

Carl Sandburg

ONE

It was hot – a blazing 97 degrees. The temperature seemed unbearable, even beneath the shady cottonwoods lining the San Juan River. Some call this place the High Desert, others refer to it as canyon country. It was both hot and arid. Neighboring Monument Valley, geologists acknowledged, was a misnomer. It was no more a valley than was Mount Everest. It was actually a Navajo Tribal Park. A parched highland stretching across an area of 20 by 30 miles; strewn with picturesque mesas and sandstone spires that had been forged by a geologic time machine. World renowned Mitten Buttes, two hand-shaped monoliths, could be seen from 75 miles away. Hollywood shot Westerns amid its grandeur.

Two friends cooled themselves in the shade. They leaned against a Bureau of Land Management pickup truck. It was parked in the gravel lot of the Anasazi Café in the sleepy little town of Mexican Hat, Utah. The San Juan River ran silently in the deep, ten feet away. Below where they stood, it flowed into the dizzying labyrinth named Goosenecks of the San Juan, twisting beneath 1,000 foot canyon walls. Forty miles downstream, it widened and spilled into the upper reaches of Lake Powell.

Semlow Wheeler was employed by the Bureau of Land Management as a law enforcement ranger. He was headquartered at a remote outpost on Cedar Mesa known as Kane Gulch Ranger Station. He stood in a relaxed pose, forearms resting against the truck's tailgate. Howie Parker, a skilled rock climber, ex-Marine and adventurer extraordinaire, propped his arms against the passenger-side gunnel. He was living out his dream in Utah's canyon-land playground. Far too often, career was relegated beneath climbing and archaeological pursuits. He'd often drive off-road into a canyon to go bouldering or spot new climbing routes. Much like a golf fanatic playing hooky at the office to squeeze in a round.

Parker's 6'1", 175-pound frame was lean and sturdy. The Corps had honed it perfectly when he was a 20-year-old soldier serving in the Persian Gulf War. He maintained it as though he'd never left. His mass was better proportioned than Wheeler's 192 pounds, whose midsection was capped with a firm 35 inch waistline. Yet, he was a tightly kneaded hulk of muscle stuffed into his 5'11" frame. Both men were potent forces. The type someone wanted on their side if ever in a tight spot. The men stared into the bedliner. Ribbed nothingness reminded Parker of a tilled pasture.

"I swear this is the best use of a pickup," said Wheeler. "Where else can men talk so freely?"

"I hear you. I'll take this outdoor conference room over a stuffy indoor one any day. Pity the folks confined to smoggy cities and office jobs. Truck-side philosophizing clears the cobwebs. Yields profound solutions. "

"Nothing wrong with talking around a kitchen table is there? Or a restaurant booth?"

"You and your culinary metaphors. Let's go inside and grab a booth before Kika arrives."

"Too noisy. I'd rather stare into the back of my pickup. Be next to the river. Feel the cool breeze. Listen to the wind sway in branches above. This is heaven, Howie. Besides, got something to show you. Better to talk about this stuff outside. Before Miss Windsong arrives." A waft of grease from the café's exhaust fan climbed into his nostrils. His growling stomach competed with the sizzling grill. "I'd like your take on these two articles." The Ranger pulled two folded sections of newspaper from his back pocket. They were flatter than a one dollar bill. "Been stuck in my craw since Monday." He handed his best friend the newspapers. Wheeler resumed his stare into the bed liner. "Most intriguing, they are. A little mystery for you to mull over this afternoon while I ponder my own theory."

"These haven't been stuck in your craw, they been glued to your butt. How long they been there?"

Wheeler grinned and looked down at his imaginary conference table for the answer. "Since Monday, off and on. Do you believe in coincidence? Seems awfully strange these two articles appear in different newspapers the same week. In law enforcement, I don't take anything for granted. There's no such thing as coincidence. Can't quite put my finger on it, but I feel the articles are related. That's the basis of my theory."

"My schedule's clear after lunch," said Parker. "Heading over to Montezuma Creek for a new pipeline right of way. I'll mull it over." He pried apart the first article. It was published by the Daily Times in Farmington, New Mexico. A pause in wind gusts allowed him to unravel the second newspaper. It was reported by the Navajo-Hopi Observer. He held the articles side by side. Before he was able to read the first sentence, tires crunched on gravel next to him. He clutched the newspapers before the wind did. The men glanced left. Kika Edison Windsong had arrived. The young Navajo looked as elegant as her shiny red '69 Plymouth Road Runner. She maneuvered the rebuilt marvel next to Howie's truck. Howie folded the papers into a thick mass and stuffed them into his pocket. Wheeler grimaced.

Kika Windsong floated across the gravel as though Bert Parks had just proclaimed her Miss America. She held one hand in front of her and flared her lips into a moist pucker. A single puff landed on her palm. A second puff launched it into the wind. Seconds later, the imaginary kiss widened Howie's smile. "Let's go inside. I'm starved. Need to get out of this heat. Did you know its 100 degrees?"

"97, to be exact. Please lead the way," said Wheeler, alacrity in his stride. His serenity was incumbent upon food.

Howie looked up at the bridge carrying Highway 163 across the San Juan. It had been put in after the Anasazi Café was built. The bridge spanned a portion of the café's rooftop. On the opposite bank, the highway rose into wide-sweeping switchbacks. It crossed into Arizona before passing the entrance to Monument Valley. Twenty-four miles beyond that lay the dusty, wind-swept town of Kayenta, Arizona. Strong winds were always a factor in Kayenta, marching Arizona's sand into Colorado and New Mexico. It was a satellite hub for Navajo Nation services. Its meager existence also depended upon Black Mesa's coal mines. Moreover, uranium mines abandoned in the 1950s dotted its landscape. Most were no more than shafts poked deep into the earth.

Parker's eyes failed to meet a white van with dark tinted windows parked in a neighboring lot. The lot was connected to an old, rundown trading post. Three small telecommunication dishes and several oddly-shaped antennae protruded from the van's roof. State of the art eavesdropping hardware made for easy pickings. Each word uttered by Parker, Windsong and Wheeler was recorded. Within seconds, their dialogue was downloaded to an innocuous, two-story Brownstone in a Baltimore neighborhood. Remote sensors strategically hidden within the café could be directed to any booth.

The trio stepped inside. Young busgirls cleared tables. Some were Ute, some were Navajo. Silverware, plates and glasses smacked together as they plunged into deep gray trays. The decibel level during the robust lunch trade was staggering. Listeners leaned forward in their seats and pretended to hear. Yet, service was prompt at the Anasazi Café. And the food was exemplary. Customers returned time and time again. Dozens of regulars made it their second dining room.

A turquoise-adorned, elderly Navajo seated them in their favorite booth. She handed them menus which included scrumptious daily specials. Wheeler sat across from the love birds. He stared out of the window. A beverage server brought a pitcher of iced tea. She welcomed Kika in Navajo and smiled at the men. Condensation dribbled like tears. It was real iced tea, unsweetened, tea leaves brewed and steeped. Then, refrigerated overnight. Being adjacent to Four Corners, patrons flocked from four states to drink it. Their server said she'd return in a minute. Kika scooped three mounds of sugar into her glass. Glasses were raised to toast. A glassy spank rang out.

Parker studied the menu like a ransom note. Kika's cell phone rang. The tone announced it was her cousin, Luciana Jim. "Hi, couz. Uh-huh, I'll be there at 1:30. Right, our house. Yeah, no kidding it's hot. Let's take your car. Better air conditioning. What? Really? Is he…" She ambled to the entranceway engrossed in girl talk.

"Time to read," said Howie, pulling the crumpled wad of newspapers from his pocket. Semlow was fixated on the grill. A befuddled look smeared his face. He looked woefully deprived. "What's up, Wheeler?"

"What's up is I'm famished." Visions of a tiger pacing in its cage filled Parker's head. "We finally get inside to do what we're supposed to do. Instead of ordering, Kika up and disappears and you burrow into the newspapers. Thought we'd order first."

"Flag her down and order chips and salsa. That'll tide you over. You're the one who wanted me to read these articles."

Parker unfolded the Farmington newspaper dated three days earlier:

> "SHIPROCK- A joint statement issued by the Bureau of Indian Affairs and the U S Department of Energy declared that federal officials have closed a 52 year investigation into the disappearance of a scientist in April, 1953. The victim, a German immigrant, employed by the US Geological Survey, was conducting topographic mapping surveys for the Southwest office of the USGS. A spokesperson indicated that the surveyor, Dietrich Schisslenberg, was working in extreme northeastern Arizona when he went missing more than a half century ago. He was survived by his wife, Maxine Schisslenberg, and a three-year-old daughter, Della. Maxine Schisslenberg passed away in Frankfurt, Germany in 2000. Details regarding Della Schisslenberg were not disclosed.
>
> In officially closing the case, the spokesperson said there was no reason to suspect foul play. He was quoted as saying: `Schisslenberg had been working in extremely remote desert country. Field employees were not equipped with two-way radios in those days. There are hundreds of places a person could have become disoriented and ended up lost. Varmints such as poisonous snakes or coyotes could have played a role. The victim could have been dragged off by a

coyote to its den or a deep arroyo. His loss was an unfortunate and rare occurrence. There's hope someday his skeletal remains will be found.' He declined further comment."

"Why'd they wait 50 years to close an investigation?" asked Howie.

"52 years and one month to be exact," Wheeler said. "How long do you think the Bureau of Land Management would search for *me* if I disappeared, huh? I'm just a little piss ant law enforcement ranger for a federal land manager. Bet your sweet ass it wouldn't even be 52 days!" A cynical frown appeared. "Heck, that German scientist must have been one important *hombre*, huh? That's damn near a lifetime for some folks. Extreme northeast Arizona, huh? That'd put him just west of Shiprock, huh? There's all sorts of old mine shafts in those parts. Uranium mostly. USGS, huh? Sounds fishy to me."

"Wheeler, you're the most suspicious guy I know. Hasn't anyone ever told you that you don't need to end all your questions with a 'huh?' Just raise your voice an octave or two. Or your eyebrows."

He acknowledged Parker's advice with a frown. "Fifty two years, Parker. Do the math. Doesn't matter what branch of government it is. That's way too long for a missing person's case. Hell's bells, they wouldn't have looked for Oppenheimer that long. Read on." A second later he bombarded Howie. "That Schisslenberg guy was onto something. Mark my words. That's desolate territory west of Shiprock. It's a no man's land. I'll bet you right here and now my butt falls off straight onto this floor if he was doing routine survey work. I don't buy it." Wheeler rocked from one buttock to the other. "And, speaking of my butt falling off, I'll be right back. Salsa on an empty stomach's done me in." He rose at an angle. "Where's Miss Windsong anyway? Where's our waitress? Damn!" Parker fixed a wide grin. His best friend's antics were hilarious. And his puns. "Just read on. But don't order for me. I'll be right out." He set a bull-legged gait to the restroom.

Kika returned. "Where'd he go, running off like a sacked quarterback? Had a weird look about him. Thought he was anxious to order?"

"It's a long story. Short version? Chips and salsa took a nose dive to his bowels."

At 25, Kika Windsong looked 18. An ageless mix of genes blended from her Pima Indian father and her Navajo mother. Mixed gene pools were common in northern Arizona as Natives sought lifestyles outside bordered traditions. She squeezed her shapely figure into a turquoise silk blouse and tight, faded jeans. Tony Lamas peeked out beneath the cuffs. A cluster of thin bracelets dangled from her right wrist. Navajo silversmithing at its finest. Her watchband was old pawn. It clutched the face of a handed-down Timex. Jet black hair nestled softly on her shoulders. Coal-black pupils peered from eyes reserved for a goddess. Her skin tone was mocha. If her complexion were any smoother, it would have slid off of her face. She smiled and placed her palm inside Howie's thigh. It stirred juices. A highly charged current raced through his groin. He nudged her hip and looked into her eyes. The coals were hot. They could have melted Greenland.

"Hey, you two, this is a café, not a cheap motel," Wheeler said, sliding into the booth. "Our gal been here yet?"

"You look like a new man, Wheeler. You and Kika carry on for a minute while I read the second article. You know what to order for me." The second article was reported the same day as the first, May 16, by the Navajo-Hopi Observer; headlined: "Three Trespassers Arrested":

> "WINDOW ROCK- Navajo Nation Police arrested three men Friday, May 13 and charged them with trespassing on tribal land. They were apprehended in a zone restricted under the Navajo Natural Resources Protection Act as a uranium cleanup site. The arrests took place one mile from their vehicle, parked along Navajo Road 33. Road 33 traverses the Kah Bihghi Valley approximately 35 miles west of Shiprock, New Mexico. Two of the men reside in an unspecified eastern state. The third is a resident of Santa Fe, New Mexico. The suspects pleaded innocent, alleging they were touring the greater Southwest to photograph unique landscapes. They were apprehended less than 100 feet from a sandstone arch. The arch is located at the southwestern tip of the Carrizo Mountains where they unfold into the Kah Bihghi Valley. The region is off-limits to unauthorized individuals. Signs are posted to prevent trespassing, particularly by non-Navajo

16

subjects. Sacred Navajo shrines are located nearby. A tribal spokesperson for the Dine Division of Natural Resources reported the trespassers were caught peering into an abandoned uranium mine near the natural arch. She asserted that recent geologic activity caused minor uplifts along the Comb Ridge fault line, situated 30 miles west. Navajo Nation investigators from Shiprock confirmed that a deep vent in the earth was recently exposed. The spokeswoman added that tremors of sufficient force dislodged surface boulders from the Carrizo Mountains to reveal previously undisclosed mine shafts. Tribal authorities added that the U S Department of Energy and the Bureau of Indian Affairs would assist in the investigation. A hearing was set for June 9."

Parker lowered the newspapers, speechless. Wheeler stared across the table, beyond Howie and Kika, watching wind sculpt sand into a corner of the parking lot. "Like I said, in my business I don't take anything for granted. See the connection?"

"The only connection I see, Officer, is that both events took place in the same vicinity. Fifty two years apart. What's the link you see that I don't?"

Lunch arrived. Steam rose from green chili smothering Wheeler's fries. Kika poured a side of salsa onto her Navajo taco. A mound of sour cream disappeared. Howie unscrewed the pepper shaker lid and blackened his patty melt. Then, he deposited a lake of A-1 sauce onto his plate. The sandwich became an island. Semlow watched with fascination. His fries swam in a pool of green chili. He was in no position to criticize.

"As you know," Wheeler began, "I'm on my way to Moab for an archaeology conference. I won't have time to snoop around the canyons first. Archaeological looters are a constant nuisance. Shards disappear, petroglyphs get defaced, and Anasazi dwellings get sat on and crumble." The BLM archaeologist-turned law enforcement officer knew the term "Anasazi" had returned to the fold of acceptable terminology in most circles, although the term "pre-puebloan ancestors" was still used by many. "We can't possibly monitor our vast resources without people like you two volunteer site stewards. That's why I'm going to Moab. To shore-up Utah's statewide SiteWatch Program; to expand it beyond the southeastern part of our state. Our bordering states, Colorado, Arizona and New Mexico recently jumped on the bandwagon. Even Texas has a program."

Howie mentally reviewed what their duties consisted of as site stewards. They'd been trained in the field, and then accredited one year ago. Besides overall monitoring of specific archaeological sites, they had a twenty-point job description and code of conduct to adhere to. Their geographic assignment consisted of two archaeologically-rich Cedar Mesa canyons, including Snow Flat Canyon. The region belonged to a geologic province known as the Monument Upwarp. Arterial-like, verdant-bottomed canyons creased the high plateau of Cedar Mesa. Early settlers nicknamed one such fissure Snow Flat Canyon.

Wheeler suddenly sought relief. The green chili had scorched his throat. He clutched it as though being garroted. His milkshake was too thick to drink with a straw. He excavated huge mounds with a long spoon. His mouth held as much as a dump truck. Seconds later, his intestines resembled a smoldering landfill. Like a brisk squall, the discomfort passed. He continued devouring the green French fried inferno as though nothing had happened.

Parker loved watching his best friend eat. It reminded him of a hippo widening its jaws. "You haven't answered my question. What links the two articles?"

"Hunches, nothing conclusive," Wheeler said. "Call it intuition. The public is led to believe that a German immigrant scientist worked in the early fifties on a USGS mapping project. Mind you, that was during the heyday of uranium mining. Perhaps surveying was a cover for a more secretive government project. No, I don't buy into the articles. He must have been on special assignment. Fifty two years, Parker. Go figure. Looking for a surveyor? No way *Jose*! He was a scientist, not a mapmaker. And, don't forget, no one saw any hide or hair of him ever again, including his wife and three-year-old daughter. But, here's the real corker. Who in Farmington New Mexico gives a rat's ass that a 52-year-old investigation involving a surveyor is being shut down? Why would they bother reporting it? And, the same day an Indian newspaper reports that three Anglo sightseers trespassed in that very region. Peering into mine shafts recently exposed by seismic activity. Granted, that article bears far more relevance to public interest. Is it coincidence? Heck no, it sounds fishy to me. I'll have to do a little mining of my own; dig deeper into Schisslenberg's work back then."

"And, I'll cover the bases on my end; ask if anyone working Navajo pipelines has a relative who remembers Schisslenberg." As he spoke, something clicked in Parker's right brain. He couldn't put his finger on it. An idea. A plausible plot. A crime. A tentative grin cracked his good looks. "Wheeler, what if---."

Semlow's cell phone chimed. It was Chief Ranger Audrey Quirk, his superior. A minute later he clicked off and looked up at Howie and Kika. "By the way, Ms. Quirk knows nothing about these articles or my personal inquiry into them. Let's keep it that way. Now, where was I? Oh, yes, come to think of it, I do have a friend in Shiprock who worked for the Highway Department back then. Retired now."

"Didn't think New Mexico had roads in the fifties," Parker chuckled. He repeated his query. "Wheeler, what if---."

Wheeler rudely interrupted a second time. "Got a buddy in Farmington," he blurted. "We're in the Reserves. See each other every month. I'll call him when I'm in cell range on my way to Moab. He's a spook, plain and simple. Super top secret stuff." He looked at his watch. "1:00. If I hit the road soon, I'll arrive for freebies at the hospitality suite. Great appetizers, cold beer and wine."

"Christ almighty, Semlow. You haven't even finished lunch and you're worried about free food and drinks? You're pathetic."

Their server arrived. She'd overheard Howie's remark. "How's everything over here? He giving you a hard time, Mr. Wheeler?" she asked, topping off their iced teas, smiling wide.

"Know what?" Wheeler replied, looking up at his favorite server. "Before we leave, bring me a side of three chicken tacos. Just to spite that smart aleck sitting across from me. Hard shell, extra salsa. I'll munch them as I drive."

"They'll be ready when you are."

"Back to business, Howie. Got one more theory to run by you."

"Shoot."

19

TWO

"The first article said Interior and Energy closed their cases on the missing scientist, correct?" It wasn't a question. Howie and Kika nodded their heads. Kika scraped guacamole off the rim of her plate. "Then, why'd the second article report both agencies would assist Navajo investigators? It's contradictory. If a case is closed, it's closed, right? Besides, the FBI has jurisdiction on reservation land."

"Semlow, the case against the alleged trespassers is a *new* case," said Howie, tightening the cap on the A-I sauce. "That's why those agencies stepped up to the plate again. You're the only person trying to link the two cases." Remote sensors aimed directly at their booth. Agents inside the surveillance van watched monitors as syllables graphically transcribed into words on their screens. Transmissions to the Brownstone occurred simultaneously. "And another thing, don't underestimate the US Department of Energy. DOE is omnipresent! They practically run the labs at Los Alamos. Besides, sounds to me like maybe that Shiselberg - what's his name again?"

"Schisslenberg, Dietrich Schisslenberg."

"Right. Could be the perfect crime. I'll bet some bureaucrat fed with a hard-on tenaciously held onto the case. A personal vendetta, one which never got freed until now. Kind of like that TV series "The Fugitive." Lieutenant Gerard never let go of hounding Dr. Kimble. Think of it, Schisslenberg comes over to the Land of the Free shortly after World War II. A prestigious government agency brings him under its wings. Sends him on his way to poke around rich uranium country. No one around to check up on him. Then he disappears without a trace. Perhaps he found Utopia. Or, ended up in South America like dozens of Nazi war criminals. What type of scientist was he before he emigrated from Germany? Perhaps you could start digging there. Maybe that's why the US Government kept its case open half a century. You know? Perhaps you are on to something. You bet I'll mull it over."

Wheeler paid close attention without sacrificing a single bite. Parker watched his friend's cavernous mouth inhale a sopapilla. Two-thirds vanished instantly. A special blend of honey-butter varnished his knuckles. Bad cholesterol raced through thirsty veins. His food disorder never interfered with his rock climbing skills. His muscles were honed like those of a pro. Yet, backcountry outings produced an endless cycle of starvation, followed by dreams of food, followed by small quantities of high energy snacks, followed again by his perception of starvation. Mealtime consisted of bland foods designed for wilderness consumption. He despised them. The cycle repeated itself several times daily. Backcountry trips were soul tonic for most. Not so for Wheeler.

Stays beyond two days were torturous. Mental acuity waned. Parker refused to let him lead climbing routes when so afflicted.

A busgirl cleared four plates from Wheeler's side of the table. It resembled a normal playing field again. His eyes locked with hers above the table. "Ah, think we'll order dessert. Could you kindly inform our waitress?"

"Coconut cream pie is a big hit today. Still have some left." She turned and let her words dangle in front of him.

"Let's talk canyons," Wheeler said. "Backpackers been talking about suspicious looking characters nosing around. Two men who appear out of sync with these parts. You know, city-like attire. Shiny loafers, creased dress pants, dress shirts. Been camping in Snow Flat Canyon near prized archaeological ruins. Notably, Inner Ruin. One report claimed they looked like big city thugs. Scary, kind you'd see in movies. Not your typical archaeological tourists."

"Nothing illegal about that," said Howie. "No one's seen them looting or pillaging, right? You think they're connected to the articles? In cahoots with those three tourists snooping on the rez? Perhaps Tribal Police would cooperate with you. If you're willing to miss the beginning of the Hospitality Hour in Moab, we could hike into Snow Flat Canyon this afternoon. I'll reschedule my appointments."

Wheeler reacted as if Parker had suggested a root canal. Instead of answering, his jaws opened wide. He held the second sopapilla in midair. Slowly, using two fingers, he lowered it. Howie envisioned a crane loading the hold of a ship. His mouth rolled like a cement mixer. He swallowed in the manner of a snake ingesting a gopher. Lumpy dough passed his Adam's apple. Howie felt full from watching. Words slurred when he began to speak. "Not so fast," he began, licking his fingers like a dog licking its wounds. "It's more complicated. That's where you two come in. Perhaps you could perform a weekend gig as site stewards. You two can keep tabs on things. File your report Monday morning with Ranger Quirk. If anything gets out of hand, call her. My advice? Pique your senses. Observe from a safe distance. Stay out of trouble."

"No problem," Kika chimed, "we know the site steward rules." Parker didn't always agree with them. As an accredited site steward, he pledged to obey guidelines by *not* serving, or creating the impression of serving, in any law enforcement capacity whatsoever. That was up to law enforcement officers like Wheeler, or other Feds. As a former marine, he hated to play the role of a patsy. He liked to roll up his sleeves and dive into the action. Confrontation was a genetic trait. "Not everyone hiking on Cedar Mesa has to look like Mr. REI," she continued. "I've seen all sorts of weird clothing in the canyons. Even nakedness. We can be inconspicuous when we want to. We love dropping down to the canyon floor where it's cool and moist. The May runoff is happening as we speak. Water trickles through folds in the sandstone, cradling into deeper folds. It creates an oasis. We can blend into the riparian landscape, see up to the ruins. It's difficult for others to peer down. Did you know there's thousands of teeny tadpoles in those pools?"

"Honey, our purpose is not to study tadpoles."

"But they're fun to play with. It's soothing to dip our sweaty feet into chilly water." Her eyes sparkled like two jewels. She scooped from her Navajo taco. She'd always order the same quantity as hungry men. Yet, tuck it away with the grace of a queen. Not a drop, not a spill anywhere. It left men baffled.

"Let's go back to what you said a minute ago," Howie said. "About the thug-looking men hanging out near Inner Ruin. If that's true, it means they have basic rock climbing skills. It's the only way in or out of that ruin."

Wheeler added that to his mental in-basket. He pictured looters anchoring onto a large boulder and rappelling down. Perhaps skillfully using a seam in the sandstone 100 feet east of the village. Could even be prehistoric Anasazi holds pecked into those seams. He'd seen them elsewhere. Never checked Inner Ruin. He nodded but said nothing to Parker.

"Their shoes," Kika said. "Reports mentioned city loafers. Creased dress pants. Seems contradictory. It doesn't compute."

Another mystery to investigate, thought Wheeler. The list kept growing. He reminded them that if they did agree to spend their weekend as observers, they should record disturbances on proper forms, including sketches and photographs for documentation purposes. He issued a stern reminder - that they were NOT the law. No revenge seeking. No tempers flaring out of control.

Howie bit his tongue at that one. He smiled, glanced at Kika for support, and spoke in a comforting tone. He told the officer what he wanted to hear. "Please, no more reminders. We understand our role as site stewards. We're to *help* the BLM, not interfere."

Wheeler mumbled incoherently, fixing his head like a statue. He swallowed a scoop of icy milkshake the size of an iceberg. "Looters...will face...huge fines...uh...serve time..." Words trailed off like a dying man's. Glacial ice sealed his windpipe. It was a severe case of vanilla flavored "brain freeze." He gagged, cleared his throat repeatedly and swallowed again. Moisture oozed from every pore. He raised the beach towel-sized napkin and unfolded it like a magician hiding the rabbit. Showmanship at its finest. Slow, deliberate wipes to his forehead. Then, he moved to his cheeks, neck and arms. It was as if he was taking a thorough morning shower. He waited for his windpipe to thaw. He felt a burp brew but it submerged. Dumbfounded, he folded his damp towel into a large square. The rabbit never showed. His next words sounded hoarse. "Thought you'd like to know. At the conference, Dr. Brewster will present a paper on prehistoric feather holders." His vocal chords hadn't thawed completely. His voice remained hollow. "I'll be sure to ask for a copy of his talk. I know how special feather holders are to you."

Parker worked closely with Dr. Phillip Brewster, famed archaeologist and museum curator, last summer at Chimney Rock Archaeological Area excavations. Unearthing a prehistoric feather holder was the most exciting discovery of his life. After the artifact was catalogued and photographed, Brewster extemporaneously pontificated about the ceremonial significance of feather holders. Said less than twenty of that type of feather holder had been discovered in the entire world. Most were excavated at Chimney Rock and Chaco Canyon. Brewster was recognized as one of the hottest tickets going in archaeological circles.

Kika looked at her watch. "Better order that pie if we're serious about it."

Their server appeared like a genie. "I heard that. Should I include the officer too?"

"Miss, why tease a hungry lion? Would you poke your head into his cage? Quit playing games and bring us the pie!" He squared off his broad shoulders. Then, displayed wide front teeth as he squirmed uncomfortably in the booth. Howie read him like a book. The spicy green chili took its toll. He knew his best friend's gut would expel toxic gas any second. Wheeler shifted weight between his right and left buttocks for the second time during the same lunch hour. Howie chuckled.

The officer's look turned frantic. It came without warning. A preemptive attack launched from his intestinal tract. The prodigal, gastronomical explosion returned at last. Like a breached whale on a placid ocean, he bellowed a blockbuster belch. It caught nearby patrons off guard. Parker and Windsong weren't embarrassed. The three were family. It happened all the time. Wheeler was a natural actor. Had he been standing, he'd have taken a bow. Embarrassment escaped him. He turned toward the patrons and smiled. Beneath his smile was a cynical thought - "you're lucky as hell it was a burp and not a fart."

"Musta been the fries," Howie snickered.

Wheeler let another moment pass. Silence exonerated him. Abdominal summersaults spewed perspiration like Old Faithful. Out came his damp beach cloth. He wiped himself down like Rocky Balboa between rounds. Then, croaked loudly, "As a backup, I'll give you another phone number."

"My tough guy, my sweetheart here, is always cocked and ready," Kika said with her bedroom voice. "Aren't you, lover boy?" She fastened a tight grip on his inner thigh.

So, here's this other number. A cell phone, I believe. Name is Agent Coldditz. Wendell Coldditz. I'm told he's making the rounds out of our Salt Lake City office. Newcomer to Cedar Mesa. Quirk's briefed him. He'll back you up if you need reinforcements. Happy camping."

Four members of the surveillance team huddled within the van. Each chuckled. Three security agents sat nearby in a custom Land Rover. Small devices nestled in their ear canals. The unique escort vehicle was equipped with enough antiterrorist features to cruise Bagdad. Their arsenal could fend off a battalion. Their commanding officer, Agent Wendell Coldditz, smiled confidently and swiveled from a monitor. His plan had muscle. They'd swallowed the bait. Delilah was primed. He fancied assignments targeting beautiful native women. No matter what country. He was the Agent extraordinaire. A reputation reminiscent of 007. Headquartered at the National Security Agency's super-secret complex at Fort Meade. The global assignments he had handled during his 30 year career made him prolific. His dossier was extensive. He went by several aliases and carried documents to ratify them. He was overqualified to take on the amateur likes of Parker and Windsong. "Easy pickings," he said to his team.

The server brought their ticket. The trio rose and walked to the entrance. Wheeler clutched his carry-out tacos. Men looked up and hurtled eyeballs at Kika. She and Howie were used to it. She truly *was* stunning. The Navajo hostess stood at the cash register, a serene aura radiating from her. Respect came with age on the reservation. Dignity was inbred.

"How is it Navajo grandmothers have such deep wrinkles and still look youthful?" Howie whispered his question into the nape of Kika's neck.

His nose tickled her. She loved it. She turned, and using the café as her audience, gripped his broad shoulders, stretched onto the tip of her toes and smacked his mouth with a wet kiss. "That's what I love about you Howie Parker. *You love my People.*"

Outside, hot air struck like a furnace. Kika ran to the shady riverbank. Howie and Semlow ambled slowly behind. Semlow gripped Howie's arm. "You're a lucky man, Parker. Isn't a man on the face of this earth wouldn't give anything to have her."

"I know. You've told me before. But don't be deluded, my friend, into thinking she's all looks and no guts."

Kika came from hardy genes. Pure as a maiden yet tenacious like her ancestors. She knew how to live amongst sparseness. Underneath a layer of pretty skin were the strength of a wolverine and the speed of a cheetah. Pure stealth. Howie believed she was one of the smartest women he'd ever met, but disjointed teen years dwarfed her "book smarts." She perfected a "street smarts" instead, surviving nearly four years as a runaway. Lived in and out of Indian slums, ran with a wild bunch across three reservations. Lived in the wild with her animal companions. She could blend into any landscape, and out-climb and out-hike both Parker and Wheeler.

They caught up with her. She sat next to the water. Tony Lamas were off. Toes splashed in the current. "Big day for you, huh?" Semlow asked.

"Uh-huh." The men sat down, Howie on a slab of sandstone, Semlow on a cottonwood log. The water ran as smoothly and quietly as velvet. Coldditz's van was hidden from line of sight. Two satellite dishes atop the roof rotated 30 degrees and angled down slightly a moment later. Streamside conversation yielded exceptional resolution.

Kika radiated. She and her cousin were driving to Kayenta to enroll in on-line classes at Dine College. An admissions counselor worked in Kayenta one day per week in an outreach program. She assisted with on-line course selection and operating guidelines. Kika had received her General Equivalency Diploma two years ago. That had been a giant step forward after her wayward teens.

"I found out that running away at age 15 took its toll. Been digging my way out ever since. My cousin, Luciana, studies computers at UNM in Gallup. She plugged me into the cyber world. Now I love it. It's practically all I want to do anymore. After we meet with the counselor, we'll drive to the Navajo Chapter House in Chilchinbito." She swirled her feet in the current. "We're enrolling in a new program to engage Navajo seniors with young Navajos. We'll become computer interns assisting elders. Seniors will be able to reap benefits from information age technology. Pretty neat, huh? Over 110 Navajo Chapter Houses are already linked to the worldwide web." Her feet stopped swirling. She lifted one foot above the water. Drops cascaded off her smooth skin and fell back into the current. "Like me returning this water back to the river. Back to where it belongs. In a similar way, young whizzes like me can teach elders a thing or two. Youth can give back to their elders. For generations it's gone the opposite direction."

Wheeler liked her metaphor. He tossed twigs into the water. They were sucked into the current and tossed like dinghies in a rough sea.

25

"Sounds like generational reciprocity," he said. "Imagine the Navajo Nation bridged in nano-seconds by satellite!"

"Beats smoke signals," she said.

"Uh-huh." Wheeler rose and strode to his BLM truck. It bore large letters: "RANGER."

Howie and Kika arrived at the Plymouth Road Runner. Her cell phone rang. "Be there in ten minutes," she said to Luciana. She turned to Howie. "Did you remember I asked my cousin to stay the night? It'll be too late for her to return to Gallup."

"She's family," said Howie. "Of course I remembered. Dinner will be on the back burner. Good luck this afternoon."

They embraced in a tight farewell hug. In spite of the heat, they held it longer than an afternoon goodbye called for. Howie's palms pressed wide and firm over her butt. He tugged her in. She melted. She felt a strong throb from his groin. "Later," she whispered into his upper lip. Her teeth tugged at it like a playful kitten. "Wait. When we're camping on Cedar Mesa tomorrow night." Inhaling her sweet breath with promising words excited him further. A second throb. Her eyelids fell like a curtain. Gradually, they pulled an inch apart. Their eyes smiled at each other, so close they could *see* each other's thoughts. "You're on," he whispered. "Tomorrow night." Their embrace loosened.

Kika turned and walked to her shiny Road Runner. She cranked the ignition and revved up the racy 335hp engine. Its hum could have tuned the London Philharmonic. Howie had overhauled the muscle car's cool-air induction system, known as the "coyote duster." He was wild over that name – a perfect one for the Southwest. The speedster sported a powerful advantage on wide-open desert highways. They could chase anything. Or anyone. Kika navigated the Road Runner across the San Juan Bridge and ascended the switchbacks.

Parker walked toward his company-owned pickup. He had an excellent job. Good salary and top benefits. One of the perks was a rugged Dodge pickup. His territory was his playground. He could work some, rock climb, and explore archaeological sites all in the same day. After a stint in the Marine Corps, he had landed a job with an interstate pipeline company headquartered in Phoenix. Two years ago he had been promoted to the Native Affairs Office. He became a chief liaison officer, working closely with representatives from several Indian Nations. His job was to ensure pipeline easements didn't interfere with prehistoric cultural sites. He coordinated with Officer Wheeler and other federal agencies.

Wheeler leaned against the tailgate of his truck; a toothpick augured between his exceptionally wide teeth. Suddenly, a strong wind

26

gust blew through the parking lot and kicked up dust. Within seconds, a micro-tornado molded itself into a small whirlwind. It had a lively pulse. His eyes traced the phenomenon's birth. It passed from the embryonic stages to giddy childhood antics. He looked up and watched it gaily twist and churn. Soon, energized particles spiraled two stories high. Next, the whirlwind dropped like an elevator as the energy marvel capered about friskily. It danced away like a jester performing on Main Street. Suddenly, it turned and churned through a field toward the San Juan.

"Frisky little dust devil, wasn't it?" he asked.

"Feisty indeed. But, Kika can't call them that. No word for 'devil' in Navajo. Calls them whirlwinds."

Wheeler's phone chimed. He held it tight against his ear, away from the wind. He paced back and forth along the side of his pickup. "That was my buddy in Farmington." He looked Howie square in the eyes. "He's assigned to the Defense Intelligence Agency."

"Farmington seems like a strange outpost for an arm of the Pentagon."

"I don't ask questions. He's tight-lipped. Tells me only what I need to know. Farmington's at the epicenter of four state boundaries. Rich deposits of weapons-grade uranium are minutes away by chopper." Parker winced. "It's regionally centralized to major defense installations in New Mexico and Colorado. Not to mention the proximity to Los Alamos and Sandia National Labs. Minutes away by air. Spatial significance, Parker, spatial significance. And, I needn't tell you, it's accessible to virtually every Anasazi ruin in the Southwest. My buddy claims he's onto something." He yanked the newspapers from his back pocket and waved them like a magic wand. "He's on the trail of a Department of Energy employee. Has a phantom e-mail account. Transmissions to a second phantom e-mail address have quadrupled recently. The terminus is Santa Fe. Their transmissions are scrambled through new DOE software. Hopes to crack it today."

"How old is your DIA contact?"

"Ten years older than us. Mid-forties."

"Thought all computer geeks were in their teens."

Wheeler smiled and looked at his wrist. "Hum, 1:45. Better leave now so I can scarf some free food and drink. I'll call the second I hear anything."

THREE

Howie and Kika lived in a nicely appointed double-wide purchased two years ago. It was centered on ten acres close to Arizona's border with Utah. Driving time to Mexican Hat was fifteen minutes. To Kayenta, thirty-five minutes. Breathtaking panoramas of Monument Valley stood at their doorstep. Since it was situated on the reservation, the land was entrusted to Kika Windsong through extended matrilineal kinship. By Navajo custom, it was not *her* land per se. And certainly not Howie's, nor hers *and* Howie's.

Luciana waited patiently in her air conditioned Ford Taurus. Kika parked her Road Runner in its usual spot, secure within Howie's spacious workshop. She activated a switch to lock the hood, gas cap and ignition. Then, she set a separate alarm for the doors. It wasn't meant to alert neighbors one mile away. Instead, it engaged a high-pitched shrill capable of damaging the ear drum. After 60 seconds, moderate ear canal damage combined forces with debilitating nausea.

She despised the violent side of her boyfriend. He was maladjusted to dealing with anger. It was the one character flaw she had difficulty coping with. The one impediment to their relationship. Howie shackled his rage demon within a dark cavern. It rarely stayed there. It sprung its shackles the instant he angered. For Howie Parker, that happened frequently. There were days when the demon roamed unfettered. True, he needed to protect his masterpiece rebuilds. Nonetheless, Kika felt the alarm was too harsh. To her, it was combative, not deterrent. It hurt her to watch him explode in rage. She loved Howie. Besides, it carried her back to childhood. Her drunken mom had a mean temper. In all other respects, Howie Parker was quite normal. He was responsible and very affectionate, exceptionally so.

Kika devised a counter measure. She locked away a dark secret of her own. Also shackled in a deep cavern. She would never, ever tell him for fear of his reaction. To Howie, disappointment festered into disagreement. That marinated into a personal offense. That became a grudge. The grudge spewed revenge. Revenge crept down to the cavern and unleashed the shackles. Rage exploded in a tempest at his target, whether justified or not. That cycle worked as a marine under siege along the Iraqi-Kuwait border. It was a detriment among peaceful Navajo. Especially Kika. She sought peaceful solutions to conflict. Although she didn't live a perfect life, native consciousness brought harmony to her existence.

She snapped out of her thoughts and greeted her cousin. "Hey Couz, be out in two minutes. Gotta pee." Before activating the shop-door security alarm, she glanced proudly at another of Howie's prized rebuilds. A modified 1978 Buick LeSabre, strong as a tank and wide as a jumbo jet. Kika loved it. Safe as a fortress, it was the ultimate res car.

Her cousin was dressed more casually than Kika. She wore a loose, scooped-neck rayon top, black with muted appliqué. It neatly concealed twelve pounds of extra weight. Baggy melon-colored shorts sported wrinkled cargo pockets. Nice Chaco sandals. "My car's not the rocket you arrived in, but it'll ride smoother. Gets triple the gas mileage." They raced down the gravel driveway. Luciana was a speedster. A plume of dust hung in the air. Collective Soul competed with the air conditioner.

"Two days ago," Kika said, "I couldn't see any of this landscape. That nasty sandstorm was insane. Sand blew through every crack of our house. Even found a way into our sheets. Felt like camping. A fine layer still covers our countertops. Haven't seen a sandstorm like that in 15 years. Now this heat. Damn this global warming."

Luciana smiled and turned down the volume. "So, how are you and Howie doing? Are you lovebirds inseparable, as always?" The cousins smiled at each other. They were closer than sisters. "You guys are unbelievable. I know how much he loves you. Nice thing is he's not all clingy like some guys I know. And, he's willing to let you out of his sight. That's a biggie. Not like the guys who hit on me."

"Comes with being ten years older, I guess. Don't worry, you'll find a guy like Howie someday. To answer your question, we're doing great. More in love than ever. The best thing we've got going is that neither one tries to change the other one." Kika turned sideways in the seat and studied Luciana's profile. Her cousin looked beautiful in casual clothes. She rubbed her fingertips on the dashboard as though doodling with finger paint. A smiley face emerged in a thin film of sandy dust. She drew a halo above it. "For now, our love halo protects us. We have a pact - to accept each other, faults and all. No matter what we did in our past. He's got only one fault I know of. But, I don't want to talk about *that* today. Let's have fun."

Luciana ignored her cousin. She ripped a scab off an old wound. "So, you've never told him?" Her question stormed the gates of Kika's secret cave. It gripped the bars and shook them wildly.

Kika's reaction was stigmatic. Blood practically dripped from her pores. She bit her cheek, trying to compose herself. Her heart pounded louder than a drum. She inhaled deeply. She finally let it out slowly and turned to her cousin. "No I haven't. Maybe I never will. That's *my* secret, *my* past. It happened in my wild runaway days. Feels like a lifetime ago. I've kept count, Couz. Let's see, it's been eight years, four months...and uh, six days to be exact. That's how old my daughter is now. Wherever she is." Her color was scarlet. Navajo scarlet.

"I...I'm...sorry." They drove in absolute silence for several minutes. "Look, I'm sorry, really sorry," she resounded. I shouldn't have brought it up. It's just that I'm so happy for you two. You've got such a good thing going, I'd hate to see any sudden surprises throw you guys for a loop."

"I'm never going to tell him. I've told you that before, Lu. Never! I wasn't fit to be a mother. My baby girl wasn't even one month old. Adoption was the right thing to do. It was the only choice. – the best I could do for my baby." The car rode like a coffin. The whine of rubber on coarse blacktop seemed to rise from hell.

Luciana tried to imagine Kika's agonizing ordeal. She glanced at her cousin compassionately. Kika was captured in her own sobering gaze. At that very instant, the sun reflected brightly off the windshield, like a sunburst, blinding Luciana. "Wow, that was a trip," she cried out, blinking several times, reducing speed. "You see that flash?" But Kika was startled at another sight. She leaned forward and stretched her neck, emerging from her reticent mood. She pointed out the windshield - to a large whirlwind a half mile into the desert. Luciana let up further on the gas. It resembled a sand colored tornado, swiftly churning up desert grit.

"Messenger people," she whispered softly to her cousin. Faster and faster it swirled, circulating violently in a vertical spiral, increasing in ferocity as it danced along the desert. "Wow, there's another one! Smaller, right behind it. See?"

"Way cool," Luciana said. "We don't see many whirlwinds in Gallup. City's gotten too spread out. Remember Uncle Lenny's story about the Messenger People?"

Kika closed her eyes and nodded her head. "I'm trying to remember his exact words. That was so long ago. We were just little kids. I think about the gist of it often, though, cuz I see millions of whirlwinds where we live. Luciana coasted onto the shoulder. They stepped out and stared at the two whirlwinds.

Most Dine don't want to talk about them," Luciana said. "Believe they're *ch iidii*." The Navajo word represented ghost-spirits of dead Navajos.

Kika struggled to access childhood memory. "Not me, I go with what Uncle Lenny says. If a *ch iidii* spins clockwise, he says, it's a *good* spirit. *Bilagaana* use the words 'dust devil.' Everyone seems to be prompted to think bad thoughts whenever they see a whirlwind. It's gotten blown way out of proportion. I go with what Uncle Lenny told me, that whirlwinds are the Messenger People. Remember the day he told us the story? Let me see if I can recall it." Gradually, his folktale sifted through her memory. Words mirrored upward like coins in a wishing well. They looked to be within easy reach, but clear water distorted the distance. After several attempts, she pretended to reach deeper into the chilly water, deeper into her memory. "There!" she proclaimed, grasping the imaginary coins. "I've got them. I remember Uncle Lenny's words."

She closed her eyes and visualized the serene setting. An afternoon long ago when her maternal uncle, Leonard Atcitty, a Navajo elder, gathered Kika and her cousins to hear the tale of the Messenger People. Atcitty was highly venerated as a storyteller, gifted with colorful verse in all Navajo creation stories. Although he wasn't a *hataalii*, a medicine man in traditional Navajo terms, Atcitty was viewed as a visionary, a dreamer, a crystal gazer, capable of seeing past and future on numerous planes of existence. Some believed he was a "closet shaman," always with his *jish*, or medicine bundle. Others thought him loco. No matter what label people tried to pin on him, he was gifted with shamanistic powers. He could envision and dialogue on matters no one else could see. He never practiced witchcraft by Navajo definition, although he'd chant for days about celestial, extra-spatial dimensions beyond boundaries of Navajo cosmology.

The setting from which Uncle Lenny shared his folktale was as magical as the chronicle spilling from his lips. The youngsters had sat in tall grass beneath shady cottonwood trees. Beside a stream meandering through her mother's land, water tickled over smooth cobblestones. Its cadence metered to the melodic flow of her Uncle's narrative. Gradually, almost trance-like, Uncle Lenny's words flowed from her lips:

> *"The people who lived in this land long, long ago were called the Ancient Ones. Some were our ancestors; some were prehistoric people vastly different than us. Still others were our ancient enemy, called the `Anasazi`. The Ancient Ones lived before any telegraph or telephone, so they had to rely on Messenger People to carry information over great distances. They also called them "wind people", since they traveled as whirlwinds. They were a gift from the grandfathers and grandmothers. A gift to be respected. Wind people gathered up information to communicate and molded it into a whirlwind. Just like today's whirlwinds gather up desert sand and debris. They carried these communications from place to place; this being one of the gifts to Ancient Ones from the grandfathers and grandmothers.*

31

"In time, the Ancient Ones began abusing their gifts by mistreating the wind people. It would be like in today's times illegally wiretapping someone's telephone line. This greatly concerned the grandfathers and grandmothers. So, a council of elders convened to establish codes of conduct for the Ancient Ones. They asked the wind people to travel by whirlwind to circulate these codes. They warned them to stop interfering with their gifts. The Ancient Ones continued to misuse them anyway. They became hostile. They mocked whirlwinds and ignored their messages. The council of elders cautioned them of impending doom if they continued to disrespect wind people.

"Then, a terrible thing happened. The Ancient Ones killed one of the wind people. The grandfathers and grandmothers were enraged. They spoke to the Ancient Ones, telling them: "in three days time the sun will come down from the sky and burn up all the people." And so, in exactly three days, that did happen. The sun came down and scorched the Ancient Ones.

"Today, if you glance quickly up at the sun you will see hundreds of tiny sunspots. These are the charred remains of the Ancient Ones.

They serve as reminders to the Dine of the day the sun came down and destroyed the Ancient Ones. They remind us to respect our grandfathers and grandmothers. The tiny sunspots are not the same as the four sunspots placed by First Man and First Woman, guardians of the four directions. This tale explains why archaeologists, modern ones, find very few burials among scores and scores of Ancient Ones who inhabited villages long ago. Burned vigas, charred dwellings and many graveless ruins are mostly what are found. Some say severe drought and savage warfare brought on their detriment. But my children, I tell you this so you may respect whirlwinds as gifts. Think of them as Wind Messengers. When you marvel at their fury, listen for their message..."

Kika drifted out of her trance. She blinked repeatedly and shielded her eyes from the sun. She looked up quickly at it. She knew better. It blinded her. She shook her head hard and fast. Gradually, she could see again. She shielded her eyes and looked at the whirlwinds.

Luciana stirred her foot aimlessly in the sand. "Did you see tiny sunspots just now?"

"No. It blinded me."

"When Uncle Lenny finished his story," Luciana said, "he chanted and sang long into the night. Remember? We all sat silently, half dazed by his story, watching him. I kept very still and breathed slowly. After he took leave, I strolled back into the tall grass. I rolled around like it was a fluffy bed and listened to the wind blow high above. It was magical. The stars were ablaze. Then, I fell sound asleep. Did you look up at the sun after he told his story?"

Kika chuckled and answered with a sheepish grin. "Yes, just like I did a minute ago. I think I saw tiny spots. The dead people he told us about. But, then again, at that age, I could have imagined it."

"I did too, but I won't look up at it today."

Kika removed a deerskin pouch from her purse. She pinched small amounts of corn pollen, paused at the four cardinal directions and cast small amounts into the wind. "Thank you grandfathers and grandmothers for your gift, the wind people." As though ordained by the Creator, gusty winds fell in repose. Silence brought reverence. Mystical forces created a desert sanctuary for the two Navajo women. Thousand foot spires witnessed what they felt. It was an extraordinary blip of time in their busy afternoon. "I feel very Navajo today, at home on our Dinétah. I'm ready to work with elders."

They were situated eight miles north of Kayenta, near a sandy plateau in front of Nokai Mesa. She touched Luciana's shoulder. "I wonder what they're trying to tell us."

Luciana looked perplexed. "They're wind messengers, aren't they? If we open our senses, we'll hear what they're saying. Uncle Lenny said so."

MAC used two hands to pry open one eye. It contained gritty, gooey matter. It felt like peeling the wrapper off a half-melted chocolate bar; one containing chunky nuts. Strands of gritty mucus clung to his eyelid. The other eye didn't cooperate either. He doused a rag in his canteen. After a thorough soaking, he finagled the lids apart. He looked up to the sky and emptied the canteen to rinse out the scraps. Vision in both eyes remained blurry. He and his partner struggled with the sandstorm's aftermath. It was Thursday morning, two days after the raging storm.

During its fury, Mac and Whitey had huddled into their campsite to ride it out. They were perched at the edge of a sheer cliff named Muley Point on Cedar Mesa. During the storm's early stages, they were entertained by gazing 1100 feet below into walls of sand blowing across Arizona. Sixty mph winds exported it to Colorado and New Mexico. An 80-mile panorama seen on clear days closed like a veil. Vehicles navigated through the sandy blizzard using headlights and flashers. Before nightfall, the storm reached atmospheric proportions. It blanketed their campsite. Drifts buried their gear. Their flimsy tent, no more than a shade structure for an urban park, filled with sand. It was the same sandstorm Kika and Luciana had been complaining about. Even with upturned collars and kerchiefs tied like bandits, it was debilitating.

Mac was a gangster. Sandy-colored hair receded above a heavily creased forehead. Muscles bulged from his six foot frame into his upper back. His biceps nearly tore apart his shirtsleeves. He was extremely fit for 37. His narrow face embodied thick lips; lips which slanted down to the right, lips which partially covered uneven teeth. His skull had been surgically restructured after encountering a wrecking ball head on. A deliberate act ordered by the Mafia. His head was shattered like a Christmas ornament, leaving the left half severely uplifted and the right half hanging down as if a puppeteer let go its strings. His cohort, a killer named Whitey, rescued Mac from complete annihilation. Minutes later, the crane operator received a gruesome stipend from Whitey.

Whitey accompanied Mac to Cedar Mesa. The massif rode out the sandstorm like a giant saguaro in the Arizona desert. After rescuing Mac from the deadly debacle, he felt obliged to protect Mac forever. A hatchet-man surgeon pieced Mac's head back together. It was more an act of recreating Frankenstein. Used only in dire emergencies by the Mob, he'd lost his medical license years earlier. The surgical procedure was no different than sliding puzzle pieces around a game table. The disaster also affected Mac's glandular functions. Saliva and tears either dried up like a desert or flooded unexpectedly. As recompense for his sloppy job, the good doctor endowed Mac with a truly magnificent feature - a saber-like front tooth. It wasn't really a tooth. It was a weapon forged from a broken tooth, capped in titanium, and angled into a short scimitar. Over the years, he'd perfected a lethal bite.

Mac found it physically challenging to smile. Occasionally, his lips punctuated into a sneer. It resembled a primordial mask. His ever-shifting eyes were hypnotic. They snared adversaries like insects to a spider web. He slithered around reptilian style. Yet, he mastered one skill to perfection. To an outsider, it appeared an anomaly. He used it to his advantage. The gangster perfected the skills of rock climbing and mountaineering. When he wasn't courting death with cut-throat scams, he was doing so high above the ground. His other hobby was body-building. He was a daily fanatic.

Two years ago, Mac had orchestrated an illegal investment scheme. He and his consorts conned their way to a retirement community near Phoenix. They bilked millions out of investment accounts from innocent seniors. Federal officials came up empty-handed. Witnesses were unwilling to testify against the outfit. One year later, November 2004, Mac hid out after a second scam turned sour in Tucson. He and three other rock climbers disappeared in southeast Utah's craggy canyons.

They spent time in Snow Flat Canyon. Mac saw numerous archaeological ruins. His devious mind concocted how he could turn prehistoric artifacts into hard, cold cash. While his partners waited on a ledge 125 feet below, Mac anchored a belay line to a large boulder. For over seventeen thousand years, the colossal stone sealed artifacts from a lost civilization. As he "slung the boulder," it dislodged and revealed a T-shaped sandstone plug, seams slightly separated. He muscled it aside and scraped through a low passageway. He donned a headlamp and stared into the musty, dusty atmosphere in disbelief; amazed by the vast array of exquisite artifacts. A long altar consumed the space to his right. Feathers lay atop it, small statues nearby. A fire pit contained ash.

A malodorous, vacuum-like atmosphere was inhaled by his criminal thoughts. His eyes darted wildly. His partners yelled impatiently from the ledge below. He hurried to the altar and picked up an object with a slight curvature. Sized similar to a thin brick, it contained several drilled holes through the top edge. The under-surface felt scratchy. It contained strange symbols. The smart-alecky, tough guy in him viewed it as nothing more than old Indian junk. Then, the scam artist kicked in. A lucrative barter deal hatched. The wrecking ball had jumbled his skull, not his brains. He knew just the place to peddle it. Santa Fe, New Mexico, ripe in black market antiquities. It would be his biggest heist ever. It would set him and Whitey up for the rest of their lives. He gripped the artifact and crawled through the tunneled passageway. His hand pressed too hard and it broke in two. Cursing, he tucked one-half in his pocket and recklessly slid the other half into the chamber. After resealing the secret chamber, he belayed down to his partners and kept silent. He knew which slime bag, back-stabbing Santa Fe dealer he'd contact. Purporting to trade legally in pre-Columbian art, the gallery owner bartered artifacts for illegal arms. Connections to international syndicates rewarded him fortunes. His empire was garrisoned by the best attorneys bad money could buy. It was simply a matter of time before Homeland Security would link him to terrorist cells.

Mac did his homework during winter months. By May 2005, his scheme transformed into a workable blueprint. Monies were fronted, an outfit of thugs assembled. He recruited them on the promise of a fast-cash job. A payload of millions. A three day gig tops. Two professional thugs had arrived in Farmington, New Mexico the day before. It would be their job to rent a box-type truck and have it substantially modified. Engineering specifications were sent to a truck chop-shop in Farmington. The shop owner had a rap sheet as long as an interstate. One of the thugs was a transportation and logistics pro with Pittsburgh Mob connections. He doubled as a hired killer. The second man was a firearms expert who'd hung out in Cleveland. A trigger-happy loser who shot first and never asked questions later, he boasted about his quick draw. He drew another weapon quickly too. From his pants, often against underage prostitutes. He was a hardened pervert nationally registered as a sexual offender.

Whitey rounded out the initial four man troupe. Others would join ranks later. He was the indefatigable brawn, an enormous monstrosity of unfinished creation, resembling more beast than man. His singular skill was killing. His reputation spanned the globe. Mac incorporated him into each deal. Figured he owed him that much for saving his life. "Collateral," he'd say to his clients. "Shake hands with Whitey. Look him straight in the eyes. Whitey will never forget your eyes. If you cheat me, he'll know when he looks in your eyes again. Then he'll kill you. Straightaway. Simple as that. Killing is his one God-given talent. He's the best in the league. Believe me when I tell you, don't ever give Whitey cause to look you in the eyes twice."

Mac's own eyes were still blurred from the gritty residue. He stared at the unconscious carcass laying ten feet away. Fresh claw marks gouged his face. He was sprawled outside their tent on windblown sand. Aptly named because of his blizzard-white hair, he embodied a fairytale giant. Squadrons of ants marched obediently in single file inches from his obtuse skull. Mac wanted to divert the insect army into his nostrils and wide-snoring mouth. Simply as a joke. Instead, he kept his cool, respecting the enormity of his loyal bodyguard. Better to let sleeping dogs lie.

Initially, Mac was concerned Whitey would be a liability for southeast Utah. He thought that maybe he was too much an oaf, too clumsy to handle fragile artifacts and that he belonged in urban slime. That he'd be like an elephant packing Granny's crystal. Staring down at the sleeping giant, Mac laughed at Whitey's distorted head. It was an ironic gesture by someone as disfigured as himself. Beneath the crop of blizzard-white hair, his skull resembled the first pass by a rookie chainsaw sculptor. As though, frustrated on his first stump, he left behind a pathetic attempt at chainsaw art. A thick mass of irregular muscle formed into a skull above his shoulders, leaving no room for a neck. A well hammered anvil formed his chin. His fingers, including both thumbs, had been sawed off tortuously one inch from the knuckles. They became his weapon of choice, forming lethal projectiles shot from spring-loaded arms.

Whitey's voice box was the prodigy of repeated garroting. It sounded like a garbage disposal grinding without water. That didn't matter. Silence reigned supreme in his deadly attacks. He exploded in violence while remaining speechless. Death blows were delivered silently. He longed to hear his opponents' flesh tear; loved the sound of joints rip and bones crack. The flipside of Whitey's killer instinct was that he himself was impossible to kill. Mac liked that.

Mac reminisced over one of Whitey's worst scrapes. It had earned him his nickname "Impossible to Kill." It all began when a Mob leader sent six muscle men to wrangle him to his yacht for execution. In a death-defying struggle, Whitey mauled three of the thugs. By a stroke of luck, the others bound his massive head in a noose employing heavy marine rope; the type used to moor tugboats. They had bound the rest of his carcass like a mummy and tossed him into Lake Erie. Next they had tied the heavy rope to the stern of the Mob leader's yacht. Powerful engines dragged him for six hours through Cleveland's harbor into open water. The boss man and his entourage of eight bikinied bimbos sipped cocktails on the stern deck; chortling at the stumpy snag, toasting victoriously at the waterlogged corpse bobbing in their frothy wake. Three miles from shore, they cut his soggy corpse loose, shouting triumphantly as the current sucked him into a bed of eels.

But he survived. Whitey, Impossible to Kill. A legend in his own lifetime. Three days later, Mac's stevedore cronies tipped Whitey off. He tracked the three goons to a Cleveland shipyard, listening intently to their laughter, their gloating over the yacht-style execution. They busied themselves tuning outboard engines and testing them in a 2,000 gallon tank. Whitey appeared without warning, as quietly as a panther. Mac watched through binoculars from a neighboring shipyard. The giant killer snatched each man by the neck, stubby fingers penetrating flesh like raptor's talons. He raised them three feet off the ground, erect, and carried them to the test tank. Then, he fired up two outboard engines and angled their propellers toward the surface. At 125hp each, they contained enough RPMs to propel a ski boat. Mac could no longer watch. He turned his back as Whitey fed the hungry outboards, one man at a time. Alive. The beast was in his prime. When it was all over, he bellowed only five words: "Me, Whitey, Impossible to Kill."

FOUR

Parker's kitchen clock read 10:30 pm. Kika hadn't called. Driving time from Chilchinbito Chapter House was 90 minutes. She had told him they'd arrive by 8:00 pm. He had turned off his concoction of sloppy Joes two hours ago. It thickened on a back burner.

At 10:45 headlights appeared. He relaxed and stepped out into the warm night air. Two beams of light raced up the driveway. A giant dirt cloud billowed behind. Luciana skidded to a halt. The Taurus rocked in place. Both women ran from the car before the cloud imprisoned them. Kika cleared the four entryway steps in a single leap. She raced past Howie. Indistinguishable words trailed behind.

"Half-dead woman" was all he could decipher. She yanked a blanket off the sofa and turned like a relay racer, yelling hysterically, sprinting past him again, bounding the steps like a cougar. Another round of gibberish hung in the darkness. He netted it with his ears. "Badly beaten. Side of highway," was all he made out.

Luciana climbed into the back seat. Kika threw her the blanket. She wrapped it around a woman. She ran back to the house for washcloths. The lapsed time rivaled that spent by a racecar at a NASCAR pit stop.

Howie threw up his arms. "Would someone mind telling me what's going on?" He reached out, grabbed Kika's arm, and stared into her eyes. Fright greeted him.

She trembled. "We rescued a woman. Stumbling on the side of the highway. Beaten up horribly. Left for dead. Ten miles south of here." She stepped back and sank into the couch. It slid against the wall. "Fire-up the Buick before she dies. Get her to Kayenta."

Confusion spread like a rash across his face. "What in the blazes you talking about? Slow down and tell me. What happened?"

Kika slouched into the soft cushions. Gradually, as if raising an anchor, she lifted her head. "We were almost home. Suddenly, a figure appeared in the headlights. Stumbling along the side of the road. Tripping and staggering. It was pitch dark. At first we thought she was drunk. We slowed way down. When we saw it was a woman, we stopped and backed up. She collapsed before we reached her. Right on the side of the highway.

"And?"

"We jumped from the car. She cried out in agony. That's when we realized she wasn't a derelict drunk. Her speech was garbled. Said something about two men. We saw cuts and bruises. One shoulder sagged way down. Coughed up blood. Howie, go outside and see for yourself. She can't die on us!"

39

Howie reached for a flashlight. He cursed its faint glow. He had meant to change batteries last week. He sprang for the door and ran to the car. Luciana cradled the woman. Two damp washcloths covered her face. He slammed the heel of his hand against the flashlight. The beam flickered. Kika emerged from sullen depths. She raced into the house for a better flashlight. Using the car's dome light, Howie removed the washcloths and unrolled the blanket to inspect her injuries.

Kika hadn't exaggerated. The "Jane Doe" had been severely beaten. She was limp and appeared half dead. Tattered hiking apparel was twisted around an otherwise fit, athletic frame. Late twenties, he guessed. Short auburn hair cropped close to her neck. Familiar objects stared up at him. Carabineers and a rappel device were clipped to a belt loop. Another loop sported several quick-draw carabineers. He knew instantly - a rock climber. His mind searched for answers. Why out in the valley? On the side of a highway? Miles from any canyons or climbing routes...?

Kika returned with a bright headlamp. He examined her more thoroughly. She moaned in semi-consciousness. Bleeding abated, but she'd lost a lot of blood. Her face and neck were bludgeoned. The right shoulder was separated. He touched her ribcage. She screamed. Shock set in. "I'll get the Buick."

Kika grabbed his arm and locked her eyes into his. "Wait." She echoed a nightmarish story he'd heard before. Horrid flashbacks to scenes like the one she witnessed an hour earlier. Back to when her mom made her wait in their car outside a bar near Flagstaff. Hours later, she'd come outside giggling and hanging onto a strange man. They'd climb into his pickup truck. They'd come out all frazzled and go back to party more. At closing time, she'd stagger out alone, trying to act sober, walking stiff and upright. But she was drunk. Kika'd squirm in the back seat; head propped up on the back of the front seat, trying desperately to help her drive. She'd poke her mom to make sure she'd stay awake and remained on the road without passing out. They'd passed other drunks stumbling along the road. Their car swerved all over the highway. It was a miracle they never hit one. "Horrible nights, horrible memories, Howie. Ones I relived tonight when we saw a person stumbling on the side of the road. This time it was a beating, not a drunk."

Howie set sympathetic hands on her shoulders. "I know. I'd have run away from home too if my mom was like that. Now, let's get our butts in gear. Her life's hanging by a thread. Run inside and fetch another blanket. We must keep her warm."

"Hurry and get the jumbo jet," she yelled. "Pull up next to the Taurus."

"Kayenta's not a true hospital," yelled Luciana. "Just a rural emergency room. She needs a trauma center. Should we call 911?"

"We're too remote. I can drive there faster. Kika can call ahead. Tell them what to expect. Order a Flight for Life chopper. Have it standing by. Transfer her to Flagstaff the second she's stabilized." Howie took one last look at the grizzly sight. His eyes were ablaze with rage. Anger rose to explosive proportions. He shot a quick look at Luciana. "Who in God's name would do this? To a woman? This was deliberate damage. Left for dead on the side of the highway. What for? If I catch up with whoever did this, I'll see they end up worse off. Might even kill them."

Kika arrived with two blankets and fresh washcloths. "I heard that Howie Parker. I can't go there now. Neither can you. Hurry up. Speed's the only thing that matters. Sure as heck not revenge!"

"Amen," Luciana piped.

Howie parked the LeSabre next to the Taurus. "Wait!" Luciana whispered, "She's trying to talk. She just came to." Howie leaned into to the mauled woman.

She mumbled incoherently. "Two men." Her lips were nearly swollen shut. They had assumed an oval shape. They opened and closed like a fish out of water. Her nose was broken. Whispers sputtered from uneven exhales. Howie bent down further. He pressed his ear over her mouth. "Backpacking…canyons…sandstorm…two men…stealing." After a minute, more whispers flowed from labored breaths. "Cliff village …digging…said I'd…report …" She was too weak to continue.

They transferred the victim with utmost delicacy. Suddenly, in a reflexive twitch, her head cocked upright. Words sputtered. Howie thought they'd be her last. He lowered his head and placed his ear onto convoluted lips. They were cold as ice. Exhales escaped like air from a freezer. Her last audible syllables sputtered slowly. "…Ugly…monster…wh… hair…kicking …stomach…threw me…van…." She slipped into unconsciousness. Luciana snuggled the blankets around her.

Howie started the powerful engine. He strapped himself in with a crisscross harness used in racecars. He checked the gauges. "Ready? Hold on, we'll reach Kayenta in record time!" They hit pavement with a screech. All eight cylinders maxed out. Speeds exceeded 120 mph. Headlights coursed the night like a flashing relay tower. Kika sat as copilot, keeping vigil for stray deer.

FIVE

"Ain't this a dry, God-forsaken, shit hole of a place? Everything's the same color. Parched and dirty." An ugly thug cast a baneful expression at Farmington's landscape. Except for his color, he could have been describing his own scumbag appearance. He was having a bad face day. It resembled a deluxe pizza. Acute acne and purple birthmarks oozed from the crust.

"Except for one green line running through it. Over there." The driver pointed with his massive forehead. "Trees along the San Juan River." His words coursed the truck's cab like a jackhammer. Thin lips barely parted, as though his jaw was wired. His head remained stationary. He stiffened his arm like a javelin and cast it at the cottonwoods lining the riverbank. "See? Riparian. Green, in case you didn't know. You got riparian growing along the Cuyahoga? You even know where the Cuyahoga River is? We got three rivers running straight through Pittsburgh. Dumped a few bodies in some."

"Uh-huh. Everyone knows trees are green, nickel-dick. But the water's just as brown as the rest of this dumpy pit. Where does their clean water come from? No lakes out here. Everything's dry. Guess they must all crap in an outhouse. When we was flying in, it didn't look like there'd be any plumbing past the downtown strip. Know what? If looks mean anything, you could take this whole place and wipe it off the map. No one would ever miss it. Look, will you? There's not a damn thing out there. How do people live? What do they do? Nothing but a dried up, barren wasteland." His condemnation of the Four Corners landscape meant little to the professional driver. The trigger-happy pervert seated beside him lived in a universe of ghettos and smog. And porno. And underage prostitutes. An urban slug. He eked a sewer-like existence in Cleveland. He only excelled in street warfare and sloppy, b-rated assassinations.

"You never been west of Cleveland, huh? In case you hadn't noticed, this here's the West. And water is king here, brown or clear. You got water you got life. And power. Lots of it."

"Big deal. Don't care one crap about this pit. Where I come from there's lots of water. We got Lake Erie. That'll never dry up. The air's good and thick there. Lots of humidity. I miss dampness. My lungs are killing me in this clean, dry air. Can't breathe very well out West. Hate it. I'll take Cleveland's wet air any day. This job better go fast. I'm here to use my guns. It's why Mac hired me. I'm out West now. Like in the old West days. I'm itching for a gunfight, man. Brought me my best guns." Buzz's trigger finger was prone to unfettered spasms. It twitched as he spoke.

"What? You gone loco? What century you living in? You'll be in for some big surprises, city boy. This ain't the Wild West." Jed looked vexed. He knew what made Buzz tick - pre-teen sluts in it solely for the drugs.

They exited the Four Corners Truck Rental lot and entered eastbound Highway 160. They'd signed a weekly rental contract for an 18 foot box-type truck. The type used for commercial deliveries. Plain white with no lettering. Rivets along each seam of its cargo box. They drove to the fringe of Farmington. "Keep your eyes posted. We're watching for a fabrication shop. Mac arranged for modifications to this rig."

Both men wore dress slacks, ironed shirts and leather Clark's. Jed's hair was combed straight back, held in place with thick gel. It had sheen. Buzz sported a buzz cut, and, in fact, earned him the nickname "Buzz." His swarthy complexion and sordid appearance frightened people. Blotchy, purple birthmarks intensified a menacing persona. He resembled the target of a paintball war. His eyes checked his back often. One holster was a permanent fixture beneath his left armpit. A second hid in the small of his back. Both men were hardened criminals. Occasionally, they were called upon to conduct business with a naive public. They had to dress presentably. Such was the case in renting the white box-truck. They had no intention of returning it. Fistfuls of cash and phony IDs got them on the road.

"Well, slap my face, man. I'm *the* Buzz from Cleveland. I can use my guns like it was the Wild West if I want to. You seen them Hollywood Westerns. Everybody's shooting everybody else dead. Fastest gun always wins." He fidgeted nervously. "I'll be the big hero out here. I'm the fastest gun in Cleveland. I'll make *my* law the law of the West. You wait and see. I'll mow people down if they even look at me wrong. Specially them Indians. And, speaking of Indians, I intend to score me some Indian snatch too. Young ones, specially. Young squaws. So innocent and sweet. Quiet too. Teach them a few tricks, courtesy of my Cleveland whores."

"Are you for real? I'm not letting you close to any broads. You're not lousing up this job. You're way out of line, crazy as hell." Jed was pissed Mac had partnered him with a trigger-happy wacko. He screwed his thin lips tighter, eyes frosting over like a Minnesota lake in December. His icy stare sent chills down the spines of most. However, it was Jed's skull which distinguished him. His physical strength centered in his cranium. Living in "Steel Town USA" was no coincidence. His head was mightier than a solid cube of steel. And as hardened. A lethal weapon, his nickname became "Steel Head Jed."

43

Had a nice ring to it coming from Pittsburgh. One head shot was as terminal as a junkyard compactor.

Both thugs were of the same ilk. If there were a school for thugs, they would have graduated side by side, tops in their class. Buzz had served time in a maximum security prison; convicted as an accessory to murder and sexual assaults of minors. He was registered in the national data bank as a repeat offender. He perpetrated innocent, young women. A pervert. He'd done some sick things to pre-teen girls. He stayed alive because he was slick with a blade and fast with a gun.

Jed penetrated the wacko with his icy stare. He vowed to crush his skull if he jinxed their job. He needed quick cash. Gambling debts in Pittsburgh were beginning to reach the stratosphere. Tens of thousands of dollars. Markers were past due. Goons had warned him he had three days. He'd skipped town to join Mac's team and make the haul of a lifetime. In three days he'd be a wealthy man.

"Hey, you ever worked with Mac and his buddy before?" Buzz asked.

His lips relaxed, but his jaw stayed wired. "Never as a small outfit. Indirectly, through others. That way no one could squeal." .

"Got another question. What do people do with old broken pottery crap anyway? Stuff's nothing but old Indian junk. Who's going to pay a couple million bucks for that? Just give me shiny new jewelry. Like what's on my neck. See?" He showed off a gold medallion dangling from a blazing gold chain.

Jed's icy eyes answered ahead of his lips. "As if I hadn't noticed. It's ugly as hell. In Pittsburgh, only losers wear shiny crap like that. In this desert, people will see you coming for miles. Doesn't blend in with Indian turquoise or silver. It'll glow in the blazing sunlight. Speaking of which, better buy a hat where you'll be posted. Might be your only shade. Sun's like a flamethrower. It'll fry that ugly, buzz-cut head of yours. You'll look like an over-ripe Asian pear. All swelled-up, a perfect target for rattlesnakes."

Buzz snapped to attention. "Well, slap my face, man. You're a real comedy act. Don't forget who's got all the gun power. There's nothing I hate more than snakes. Hate them critters. I'll shoot every snake I see. Don't care where I am or who's around. In town or out in the desert. I'll shoot anything crawling on its belly. I'd shoot you if you crawled on the ground."

"Not if me or the rattler strikes you first. Just watch your step, city boy. And quit talking smack. We each got a vital job. Mac hired us because we're the best. Should only take a couple of days. Then we can clear out and go to Vegas. The job's cake. Millions of bucks coming our way. Yeah, millions! Be set for life. His bodyguard Whitey will…"

"What? Who'd you say? Well, slap my face, man. Say again?" Buzz yelled excitably. His words ricocheted off Jed's steel head. The wacko unclipped his seatbelt. He squirmed and twisted in his seat. He angled his body toward Jed, shocked that his arch-rival could be part of the same outfit. That he'd finally come face-to-face with the legendary, lethal-fingered killer.

"That's him. The ONE and ONLY Whitey." Jed's eyes shone like ice from the land of sky blue waters. Buzz's sewage reflected back at them. Jed's lips parted into a rare smile. "And if he hears you talking like that, it'll be the last words coming out of your blotchy face. Hear me, city boy?"

"Well, slap my face, man. I got me real gun power. Ain't afraid of no one when I got my guns. Not even Whitey."

"Don't matter against him. And, don't forget his nickname. Every man who's tried is dead. Let me give you some advice, pal. Way I see it, I'm pleased to work with Whitey. Honored, you might say. To say I pulled off a job with Mac and Whitey. Might even open doors for me."

"Well, slap my face, man." His eyes glowed like hot coals. He patted his holster. Threats meant nothing to him. He bragged more about the tight young ones he'd porked. Suddenly, he found himself staring into black ice.

"They were all under twelve years old, you pervert. Look, I'm going to tell you this once. ONCE. And just ONCE. Got it? I got me a niece that's 12. You ever come close to her or anyone else that age when I'm around, and your plump Asian pear, fuzzy little head's going to look like it got tossed out of a friggin' airplane. And, let's get another thing straight, city boy. I need this job, hear? Don't go screwing it up." His arm became a javelin. Its point hovered two inches from a seething cauldron of acne. "And don't forget my advice about Whitey. Play him to your advantage. If you don't, you'll end up dead. Might anyway, kind of crap spewing out of them braggart lips." He slowed down and paid closer attention to driving. His eyes darted back and forth to the side mirrors. He hoped his warnings sunk in.

"You ever come to know what happened to Whitey's fingers? Not that I really care one crap for him, but, how'd all ten fingers end up that way? What happened to that deformed moron?" A snicker hatched between blotches.

"Better get another thing straight. Right this second, city boy. Whitey's no moron. *Comprende*? He may be slow catching on, but he's no dummy. For all we know, his brain could be as big as the rest of him. You forget that and you'll be dead the first time you cross him." Buzz glared out the window, the driver continued. "Best I remember, Whitey had an unlucky encounter with a posse of drug thugs. Asians, not the same outfit who dragged him like a dingy around Cleveland's harbor. Ever hear that story?" Buzz's demonic, shit-eating grin answered. The look fit him like a Sunday suit. "The Orientals caught up with him in an alley one night. In the struggle, Whitey maimed the drug lord's kid. His only son. Guess the kid pulled a blade. Whitey grabbed the kid's hand in a death clutch. Squeezed the life right out of it. Kept silent and stared him down until the kid passed out, bent over on his knees. Popped every bone like bursting bubble wrap. Didn't let go for five minutes. Was the grip he's become famous for. Tighter than a vice. Kid's maimed for life. He'll never use that hand again, entire arm's shot. Might as well saw it off."

Buzz chortled in his seat at the gruesome scene. "I brought me my best guns, man. I ain't scared. You still haven't said nothing about his stubs for fingers?"

Jed slowed and pulled into an abandoned strip mall. He held a rumpled map showing directions to the truck shop. "Need to find this joint." His forefinger stabbed an X on the map. "Guy who runs it got out of the pokey a few months back. Got connections with our Mob friends in Cleveland. Keep your eyes peeled. Name of the joint is Gordy's Welding and Undercarriage. Up here on the left someplace."

"Out with it. Did those slant-eyed Chinks catch up with Whitey?"

Icy eyes reflected back at Buzz. "You got ethnic problems? You against other nationalities? First it was Indians, now it's Chinese. Guy who'll be working on this truck is Polish. Name's Krenecke. Got a problem with that?"

"One Polak's just as dumb as the next."

"You're a real loser. You and your loser gold necklace. You ain't going to last long out here." He flexed his head of steel. Like a body builder flexed his biceps. "Yeah, they caught up with him alright. Told him they'd save killing him for another day. Someday when he least expected it. Said they'd rather teach him a lesson about hands. A lesson for the whole world to see. A lesson he'd live with every day of his pitiful life. When they subdued him, he exploded like a raging bull. Killed two in the process. Broke them clear in half. He does that to his vics, but that's another story. Finally, they got him tied up. Then, they took a dull, six inch drywall saw. About the size of a kid's Fisher-Price tool. Very, very dull. Know what I mean? They butchered his fingers one at a time. Way I figure, must have taken pretty near half the night. Each guy took a turn. Gory enough for your wacko mind?"

His acne oozed with joy. A putrid grin slithered from the cauldron. He rocked like a psycho succumbed to a straightjacket. "Three guys, huh? All ten fingers, huh? Wonder what lucky Chink got the fourth finger?" He pounded the dashboard, laughing hysterically.

"Real funny. There it is. Ahead on the left. Metal sign. Cutout letters."

The yard was extremely neat for a metal fabrication business. Rusted metal sat neatly on pallets spaced in even rows. Truck chasses and tractor parts were organized by size. Property lines were garrisoned within seven foot cyclone fencing. Tightly coiled razor wire rose 15 inches higher. Jed make note of the yard's surveillance system. The shop accommodated large, off-highway rigs used in Farmington's oil and gas fields. Eight shop bays, each with an over-sized door faced north. Zero visibility from the highway. Krenecke designed it that way.

Buzz turned to Jed. "Whitey ever catch up with those saw-toting Chinks? Come on, finish the story."

"Sure as hell did. I'll keep this short and sweet. We got business inside. Man's expecting us. Guess who got the last laugh from the stern of a yacht?"

Buzz cackled. "I heard about him pureeing bodies at the shipyard. Like that flick *Fargo*, that dude feeding the chipper machine. I get off on that."

"Well, Whitey had the last laugh this time. One month later, three waterlogged corpses were discovered by an underwater salvage crew. There they were, three thugs, Orientals, twelve feet below the surface of Pier 24 in Cleveland's harbor. Cinched to pylons with aircraft cable. Orange. Each one erect against the pylon. Bound from head to foot, looking like stripes on a barber's pole. Autopsy claimed the vics were alive when they were cinched. Best part was Whitey supervised the execution from the aft deck of a yacht. Idling near the dock. Both hands bandaged like polar bear paws. His raspy chortle filled the air."

The two men jumped to the ground. "Let's do business."

"Well, slap my face, man. Glad I've packed my best guns. In case Whitey steps out of line."

47

SIX

The Chief Ranger sat erect at her desk. Dark wavy hair fell to a straight line at her shoulders. She was notorious for punctuality. Her staff followed suit. Impeccable grooming complimented a crisp Bureau of Land Management uniform. She donned a clean one every day. The Government-issue wardrobe matched her stoic personality. Her day commenced at 4:30 am. She reported for duty at Kane Gulch Ranger Station at 5:00 am. Her commute consisted of a 150 yard walk from staff housing units. Days off were infrequent. They were tightly structured and regimented too. Quirk was a role model bureaucrat - a stickler for procedure. She made her superiors shine. The only male in her life was Spike. The jet-black feline was the antithesis of her highly structured lifestyle. Unkempt and undisciplined, he'd escape for two weeks at a stretch. When he returned, he looked like he'd gone nine rounds with Mike Tyson. It made him humble, a concept foreign to Quirk.

Repulsive thoughts raced through her head. Her remote outpost boasted some of the priciest real estate, archaeologically speaking, in the Four Corners region. The thought that thugs might be looting it turned her life upside down. Devoted bureaucrat that she was, she nonetheless despised what had become of the federal budget. Like other federal land managers, her budget had been slashed. She knew it was impossible to police every square inch. Yet, she and her field staff had made remarkable progress in containing vandalism. Eventually though, programs that had been in place for decades were disemboweled. Some were eliminated. Monies were diverted, as with nearly all public land-use agencies, to Bush's War on Terror. Safeguarding the nation's natural resources and cultural heritage programs hung by a thread. It seemed the only attention paid to land held in public trust was *to open its borders to drill for coal-bed methane gas - the kiss of death to pristine landscapes and cultural resource preservation*. Although a loyal "lifer," she couldn't adjust to downsizing the elephantine bureaucracy.

Department of the Interior and related public land managers began losing jobs through early retirement "buyouts" and outsourcing. She knew many of them. The protection of pristine cliff dwellings and other archaeological treasures lost priority in the government's overall scheme of things. Hundreds upon hundreds of ruins lay ripe for the taking. She truly believed budgetary losses caused irreparable damage. Volunteer, citizen site-steward groups, significant as they were, weren't able to fill the void. Several local protection initiatives gave birth to official, statewide SiteWatch volunteer programs. What Quirk really needed to augment volunteers was a battalion of law enforcement officers like Semlow Wheeler.

She stared into a speakerphone. The tips of her fingers formed a tent beneath her chin. Mountains of reports were stacked with fastidious precision on shelves lining the walls. Save for two writing instruments - one red, one black - and a new writing pad, her desk was bare. A two-way radio clipped to her belt crackled at low decibel. She spoke in animated gestures to the speakerphone as though it was Wheeler's face. Her law enforcement officer grazed on buffet delicacies at the archaeology conference in Moab, Utah. She briefed him with fresh accounts of backpackers who'd filed reports of mysterious goings-on. Their conversation focused on Snow Flat Canyon; Inner Ruin in particular.

"That's why I'm here, Chief. You know my sentiments. I'll alert Parker and Windsong immediately. Make sure they're still on for this weekend."

"Our new man out of Salt Lake wants to investigate the reports firsthand. Call Parker and Windsong off."

"Really? What does Officer Blue Sky have to say about that?"

"We spoke one hour ago. It wasn't pleasant."

Officer Dudley Blue Sky, Navajo Nation police officer, was stationed in Kayenta. He was the officer on duty when Howie and Kika carried the near-dead backpacker into Kayenta's clinic. Although Cedar Mesa was not reservation turf, he took a personal interest in helping federal land managers protect all ancestral sites. In recent years, he had assisted BLM in tracking, apprehending, and bringing to justice dozens of archeological looters. He was considered "on loan" for those thrilling engagements. He and Wheeler teamed up with Parker and Windsong to form a stellar foursome. Orchestrating each episode was Chief Ranger Quirk. They'd earned only six convictions under Chapter 53 of Title 18, Section 1170 of the U S Code: "Illegal Trafficking in Native American Human Remains and Cultural Items." Convictions were hard to come by. They were only four people.

"So, back to Parker and Miss Windsong. What do I tell them?"

"Tell them to stay back. Not to intercede. Not to go near Inner Ruin. Our new man, Coldditz, will validate the backpacker reports. I've strict orders that any suspected looting is subject to his patrol. He's usurped my authority in such matters until further notice."

"But…"

Quirk cut him off. "No buts. If Parker and Miss Windsong see anything suspicious in other canyons, or anywhere on the Mesa, tell them NO INTERVENTION. No bounty hunting, no revenge. Understood? Are we clear on this?"

It wasn't the Audrey Quirk he knew. She'd been his superior for five years. Something very strange was amiss. "Ah, yeah...Audrey...I...know how to follow orders...but it doesn't mean I understand. So, if I read you clearly, Howie and Kika are simply private citizens on a weekend canyon-land vacation. No different than any other happy campers or hikers. Right? Is that the gist of it?" He smiled. Quirk smiled. She hadn't heard him chew crunchy food into the handset for over a minute. This made her very happy.

Wheeler held his phone at arm's length. He refrained from burping. "Er, ah...well, Chief, we may have a problem with the agenda you outlined."

"Let's hear it." She angled toward the speaker phone.

"Officer Blue Sky called me after he spoke to you. Thirty minutes ago. Said he wanted to speak from one law enforcement officer to another. Said he's piecing together a theory about the barbarians who savagely beat a woman and tossed her from their moving vehicle. Said the half-dead woman became more lucid this morning. Before being air lifted to Flagstaff. Provided additional, albeit spotty, information."

Quirk exploded. First a stranger named Coldditz usurped her authority. Then, a long time associate, Dudley Blue Sky, withheld information about a gory crime. She straightened as stiff as an I-beam and bent a pencil to the snapping point. "What are you talking about? What savage beating? What barbarians? What half-dead woman? Where?"

"Until he pieces more together, mum's the word. He's a genius cop, Audrey, he won't keep us guessing very long."

"Genius or not, he should have informed me of the crime first! Where'd this occur? When? The canyons are outside his jurisdiction." Wheeler remained silent. "Speak to me, Officer!"

"It's a complicated mess. You'll have to speak directly to Blue Sky. It's not as simple as it sounds. Worse yet, Parker and his girlfriend are connected to that gruesome bludgeoning."

"What are you talking about?" She bolted out of her chair, standing as straight as the crease in her pants. "How in God's name could they be connected? What's going on here? Why am I the last person to learn of this crime? So help me, Wheeler, someone's going to pay for this."

"Kika and her cousin discovered the beaten woman on the side of the road. On the rez. Loaded her in their car and drove to where she and Howie live. Those three kept her alive, and then raced to Kayenta's Health Center. Doctors said they saved her life. Blue Sky was on duty."

"Good God. Did the vic utter anything to Parker? He might know too much to be traipsing around *any* canyons." Her office was too small to pace in. Using a pencil as baton, she stepped in place like a majorette.

"According to Blue Sky, whatever she said in the ER is privileged information. Yet there's no telling what may have jumbled from her lips before she fell into unconsciousness. When Parker was tending to her medical needs. Still haven't positively ID'd her yet. Crime scene investigators, including the FBI, are on it."

Quirk turned white. "I've heard about Parker's rage. How his temper flares out of control when he's hell-bent on revenge. Call him off, Officer. Tell them to abort the entire weekend! That's an order. Understand?"

"But it gets stickier yet."

"Now what? One more shock and I keel over. Tread lightly."

"Back to the issue of jurisdiction. The Arizona Highway Patrol has asked for a full investigation. Dudley believes the scene of the crime, the precise location where the woman was found, is within Navajo Nation jurisdiction. And then there's us. It's possible she was abducted and brutally beaten on Bureau of Land Management land. Either way, the FBI moves in. Toss Agent Coldditz into this smorgasbord and we've got a classic donnybrook. It'll get real dicey by day's end, Chief. Conflicting egos could run awry. I see multiple collisions."

"Just call off your volunteers, Wheeler, and don't worry about a thing." Her tone shifted noticeably. She calmed slightly. "Agent Coldditz will handle everything. Not you, not me, and certainly not Howie Parker. Coldditz is calling the shots." Wheeler hated her metaphor. "You just enjoy the conference and call me Monday morning." She hung up abruptly.

Wheeler stared angrily at his cell phone. His brain turned to mush. Words wouldn't gel. Sensors operating his tongue shut down. He couldn't even cuss. A severe ache struck his gut. It was worse than hunger pangs. He stared into a void. No one had hung up on him in ages. Nor had the rug been yanked so swiftly from beneath his feet. A kick in the groin better described the ache inside. He all but doubled over. He tried to process his thoughts but he was too confused. Something about Quirk had changed radically before she'd hung up. The tone in her voice had become calmer. Why, he wondered? What wasn't she telling him about the new man, Coldditz? Why the discourteous termination of their call? And, why was he being distanced from his own herd, ensconced at the conference, too far from the action? He needed answers. He decided to call his best friend, Howie Parker. Just the tonic he needed. Howie'd tell him exactly what he needed to hear. He'd clear the fog. Hope brought back his voice. "Damn it," he cursed, "two felonies occurring right under my nose and no one's doing squat."

A rappel line dangled 48 feet from the canyon rim to the amphitheater ledge. Whitey stood within Inner Ruin. The human bulldozer decimated fragile archaeological assets and delicate ecosystems. His gargantuan mass was not intended to occupy small room blocks. He churned like a cyclone everywhere he walked. Truly a holocaust.

Mac was oblivious to the destruction. He and Whitey busied themselves within the secret chamber. Priceless artifacts were wrapped and stowed in plastic crates. They worked at night with the aid of lanterns. They labored through two hour shifts. Then, took ten minute breaks in fresh air at the edge of the amphitheater. They quit before dawn and slept until 11 am. Then, changed wardrobes and tried to imitate what normal hikers did at archaeological ruins. Mac took photographs and stared in awe at the majestic cliff village. Whitey pretended to gaze at unique petroglyphs.

Precautions were taken in the event backpackers or rock climbers were encountered. Between shifts in the secret chamber, they sealed the T-shaped passageway. Tools and crates were hidden beneath tarps. Their acting was exemplary. But, if anyone approached within talking range, they'd be busted instantly. They spoke Thug, the only language they knew. Mac's crooked sneer and titanium tooth made him look anything but touristy. Same with Whitey. He belonged on the midway in a carnival act. Mac's casual loafers boasted a white stripe, like a skunk pelt. Luck prevailed, no one approached.

One striking feature perched on the amphitheater ledge: a gigantic boulder the size of a school bus. Sometime during its 220 million year history, a huge chunk of Cedar Mesa sandstone splintered off Snow Flat Canyon and rolled onto the ledge. It came to a rest upon the very edge, teetering seesaw fashion. Weighing hundreds of tons, it seemed a delicate spider could launch it 125 feet to the ledge below. Perhaps crashing through that precipice and impacting like a meteor on the canyon floor. Then again, it might stay put for another 220 million years.

SEVEN

"Come on, Wheeler, you can't miss the next presentation." The voice hit him from his left. It came from a fellow law enforcement ranger in Moab's District. "Brewster's got the podium. Friday afternoon's keynote speaker. He's just begun."

"I know, been wrapped up in some sticky business. Trying to reach my buddy before he leaves for the weekend. Must be out of cell range by now. I'll be right in, Brewster's the reason I'm here." The auditorium was wall to wall people. He stood at the back until his eyes adjusted to the dim light. An aisle seat two rows forward was empty. He slid in without disturbing anyone.

The presenter was Dr. Philip Brewster, a highly esteemed professional of Southwest archaeology. His current post was that of Principal Curator at a distinguished museum in northern Arizona. He was five minutes into his talk. His intoxicating charisma captivated the audience. Always cheery, always suntanned, always sparkling blue eyes, Brewster sported a healthy crop of brown hair. It faded into a distinguished shade of silver at the temples. Admirers pegged him at ten years younger than his true age.

Stunning power point visuals magnetized the audience's eyes to the screen. The current image projected an extremely rare artifact that had been discovered during last summer's excavation at Chimney Rock Archaeological Area in southwest Colorado. A ceremonial feather holder, complete with exotic feathers, filled the screen. "Fewer than two dozen artifacts bearing these specific characteristics have been excavated in the Southwest," Brewster stated. "They were used during sacred ceremonies of prehistoric cultures living on the Colorado Plateau." Using his electronic pointer, he highlighted specific features of the feather holder. Semlow scribbled notes. He admired his scholarly mentor; in fact, he idolized him. Had he pursued an advanced degree in anthropology, he would have asked Brewster to be his advisor. Like Howie, Semlow had earned a Bachelor's of Science degree in anthropology. His interest in law enforcement came later.

Brewster held the audience at the edge of their seats. His exuberance was contagious. His career spanned decades, his handsomely weathered face proved he spent most of it performing fieldwork. He was not a desk-bound archaeologist. He described the ceremonial artifact as a small clay slab, shaped and sized like a thin brick. A slight curvature formed its concave, primary surface. The back surface was polished smooth. An awl shaped from bone was used to drill quill-sized holes. He advanced to the next image. It portrayed a brilliant array of exotic feathers. He spoke conversationally, rarely referring to his notes. The feather holder had been buried with Macaw and Parrot feathers. Hence, it had probably been imported through Mesoamerican trade routes.

The next image reflected his adaptation of ceremony. Digitally-enhanced images created his concept of a ceremonial kiva. Circular in shape and beneath ground level, a stone altar stood close to the east edge. Torchlight illuminated the feathers' dazzling plumes. For effect, the lighting in the auditorium was dimmed further. He posited that feather holders played an even greater role than what archaeologists could possibly grasp. He encouraged increased archaeological survey work among Cedar Mesa's canyons. He paused to let the professional archaeologists absorb his mandate. "Research designs directed to intensify fieldwork should be aimed at discovering that greater role. Discovery of additional feather holders may lead to a broader understanding of prehistoric ceremonial rituals. New excavations should be conducted at ruins linked to the Chaco network." The audience stood, rewarding the speaker with thunderous applause.

Several dozen people rushed forward and surrounded him, scribbling notes like reporters. Semlow sat in awe. He knew what he'd seen were photos from the same excavation Howie volunteered at last summer. His urge to call Howie took a quantum leap. He stepped into the crowded aisle and rushed outside. He found a shaded bench and punched redial on his phone. It was 1:30 pm.

HOWIE and Kika left home at 1:00 that afternoon. Their camping destination on Cedar Mesa was two hours away. Magnificent geologic formations circumvented their route. To Howie, the grandeur of all Southwest landscapes appeared as though he had a tiny IMAX lens implanted in each eye. He believed the astonishing fault lines, volcanic uplifts, and erosion-shaped statuettes were acts of Mother Nature. He pointed to a rainbow of colors dotting the limestone hills on the opposite bank of the San Juan River.

Stunning landscapes didn't jar Kika like they did Howie. Instead, she viewed them as natural patterns connecting Navajo's Dinétah ordained in Creation stories. The beauty of Navajoland was just that - their natural and beautiful world contained within four sacred mountains. Navajos called the land upon which they lived Dinétah, representing beauty, harmony and health. "I know it's just a phrase people use, but I have no concept of who your Mother Nature is," she said with a curt smile. "Many rock formations are seen through Navajo eyes as sacred. Some represent ancestors turned to stone during our emergence from lower worlds." She gazed at the primordial landscape with contentment. "The rainbow colors you refer to are a ric-rac pattern hemmed into the hillsides. Like the hem sewn on my mom's ceremonial regalia - a wavy, chevron design. Various shades seen in the San Juan Canyon are known as *The Navajo Tapestry*. The exact shades depend on the position of the sun. Or passing clouds. When our Sun Bearer is brightly shining, I see rusty red and purple. If it's shady, I see olive drab and tans, like nature's camouflage. So, if there is a Mother Nature, as you say there is, she can alter colors by forming clouds."

Four miles northeast of Mexican Hat, they turned onto Highway 261, the only road leading to Cedar Mesa from the south. They approached the 1100 foot sheer cliff which led to the Mesa. A large sign warned motorists of approaching hazards. Clear as day, it read: "10% Grades, 5 mph, Narrow Gravel Road. Oversize or Overweight Vehicles Prohibited." They angled upward on the first of eleven switchbacks. His cell phone rang. Wheeler's voice burst with excitement.

"Where are you guys?"

"Just starting up the Moki Dugway." The name referred to "*Moqui,*" which is what some Spanish settlers called prehistoric Natives.

"Not a great place to drive and talk. Should I call back?"

"No, I'll be fine. Driven this a thousand times. How's the conference?"

"I've got good news and bad news."

"Forget the bad news after last night's nightmare. Hit us with the good stuff."

"I just came from Brewster's presentation. He described the Chimney Rock excavation you worked on last year. Terrific, audience loved him."

"Semlow, what're you doing?"

Silence filled the space between them. "Ah... what do you mean Howie? I'm talking to you."

"No, Semlow. I mean what else are you doing? Right this very second?" He spit his words tersely while negotiating an imposing hairpin. Oh, uh-huh, I see where this is going. Keeping tabs on me, huh? Well, I'm busted. Munching cold leftovers I snatched from the buffet."

"Ah, that's better. Of course you are. That's what I was hoping you'd say. Admission of your food disorder is step one in recovery. Just wanted to hear *you* say it."

"Food disorder? No way, *I'm a connoisseur.*"

Howie maneuvered another switchback. He sipped from his coffee and clutched his phone while turning.

"Let me cut to the chase. I heard all about your rough ordeal last night. Who would commit such a barbaric act?"

"There'd be no reason for us to know. It's a Navajo Police matter. But the SOB had better hope I never catch up with him." Kika skewered him with both eyeballs.

"The authorities will figure it out. They're trying to ID her this very moment. She's been transferred to Flagstaff. But here's the main reason I'm calling. Stay out of Snow Flat Canyon, Howie. Don't go near Inner Ruin. Watch your backs. Don't trust anyone. Something very strange is going on. Even Quirk doesn't sound her usual self. It's like a bad wind. Can't quite put my finger on it."

"Must be the bad-news part of your call, eh? Well, don't worry. You gave me a backup phone number."

"Therein lies the problem. Listen up as if your life depended on it. Forget that number! That man Coldditz. Screw him. Hard to trust a man I never met. A transplant from D.C. to Salt Lake makes it even worse. What does he know about southeast Utah? Like I said, something's amiss. Don't even think about calling him. Roger that?"

Howie let up on the gas and coasted into a pullout for slow vehicles. "I know how to take care of myself... and Kika."

"Wrong answer. If you want to enjoy your weekend, please stay far away from canyons east of Highway 261. Go into Grand Gulch, come out Bullet Canyon. You haven't done that in a year or two. Quirk insists you steer clear of Snow Flat Canyon. Wherever you end up, exercise extreme caution. Could be killers lurking about."

"Yes, Mother," he said sarcastically. "If you're in the loop, call us the second you hear something on that Jane Doe."

"If you stay west of the highway, toward Todie Springs and Grand Gulch, you'll be in cell range most of the time. Well, I suppose I'd better mosey on back to the auditorium. The next speaker has begun. You guys... Oh, wait, almost forgot! Got an update on those newspaper articles. Hold on a second." Wheeler finished swallowing. Water chestnuts wrapped in bacon. Swore he could make a meal out of those critters. Except for the toothpicks. Vowed to earn his first million making flavored, digestible toothpicks. Would save a lot of trees.

Howie stayed idling in the pullout. Wheeler spilled the latest news from his DIA contact. Claimed the German scientist worked for *more* than the United States Geological Survey. Surveying and mapping was his cover. "So the plot thickens, as they say. Reminds me of the last time I pulled a one-inch thread from my shirt button. Kept pulling and pulling, and the thread kept coming and coming. The button got looser and looser. Until finally, the thread reached its end and off popped the button. All we have to do is unravel the thread, Howie. My associate is tugging harder every minute. 52 years makes for a big spool. Said he'd update me this weekend. Claims his Pentagon contact can hack into the Department of Energy's new software. Should only take him a couple hours."

"Hang onto those flattened newspapers. Let me know when you've unraveled the thread. Gotta go, been idling too long. *Adios.*"

For the past two minutes, Kika had been staring silently out of her window at geologic promontories known as Valley of the Gods. She watched a large whirlwind several miles away. It danced gracefully across the open landscape. A smaller one partnered behind it. The larger one disappeared behind Sitting Hen Butte, a unique rock formation jutting hundreds of feet skyward. Its partner skipped southeastward toward an outcrop named Seven Sailors. Some of the Valley's spires resembled stately deities; others stole the appearance of imaginary animals. Natives had their own names for the stunning features.

Mid-afternoon sleepiness caught up with her. Within seconds, she found herself neither asleep nor fully awake. She envisioned evenings spent at her aunt's home. Luciana's mother would gather kinfolk for a winter's evening of Navajo storytelling. Grownups fed logs into a cast iron stove. Folktale after folktale was told until bedtime. The fond memory gave birth to a question. She wondered why she'd seen more whirlwinds than usual in the past two days. She knew of a second folktale concerning the wind, but the details escaped her. She wondered what the Wind People were trying to tell her.

She opened an eye, achieving a state of "uni-hemispheric sleep," in which it was possible to doze with one eye open, a practice migratory birds found helpful to react quickly to signs of trouble. A legendary practice among villains on the run as well. A coyote crossed in front of them and scurried into thick sagebrush. It was the key that unlocked her memory. The folktale surfaced. It spoke of the origin of Coyote and Badger, formed in the presence of First Woman and First Man. Two columns of whirling dust approached, one from the south and one from the north. The base of each gathered dried brush and tumbleweed. And energy. The whirling columns merged and then, with a loud bang, evaporated into the sky. Two beings remained, dusty in color. One was Badger and the other was Coyote. Prevailing upon their wisdom, First Woman and First Man called the north wind's creation Coyote. He would forever bring trickery and laziness to the universe. Through his cunning and apparent innocence, he'd favor shortcuts and always fool others into doing his chores.

The south wind brought Badger. First Woman declared he would represent perseverance and industriousness. Kika asked more of her memory, trying to recall which direction the whirlwinds had travelled. The two she had just observed in Valley of the Gods traversed northwest to southeast. Yesterday's, the opposite. A true dilemma. As they crested the Moki Dugway, Valley of the Gods fell out of view. Confused, she asked herself if their weekend would bring Coyote's trickery or Badger's perseverance.

During the prolonged silence, Howie processed a wide range of information. Overwhelming events stacked up. An attempted murder, reports of strange men in the canyons and orders to keep out of most canyons on Cedar Mesa. Then a mystery man named Coldditz appeared out of nowhere. Two bizarre newspaper articles printed in the same week. Wheeler had a point, who in Farmington gave a rat's ass if a 52-year-old investigation was closed? How did Wheeler's absence at an archaeological conference fit in? Coincidence? He was too exhausted to process the data. They hadn't slept much last night.

No matter what the outcome, he was obliged to bring the woman he loved into the loop. He turned onto the road leading to Muley Point and turned off the ignition. His expression said it all. He briefed her on *most* of the details of his conversation with Wheeler. She listened quietly and asked few questions. She too was tired. She couldn't process information either. They agreed to wait until they arrived at camp, only 18 miles further. However, Howie withheld the most critical part, that they were instructed, downright ordered by Chief Ranger Quirk, to stay out of Inner Ruin and Snow Flat Canyon.

He returned to the highway, where the road leveled out and became paved. They had arrived. Their odyssey on Cedar Mesa was set to begin. Coyote and Badger would play decisive roles. Their survival would depend on their interpretation of which metaphor held true and when.

EIGHT

Jed flashed a wad of 50 hundred dollar bills inches from Krenecke's face. He clutched his tattooed arm at the wrist and slapped them into his greasy palm. Neither man smiled. It was strictly business. The truck modifications had to match blueprints furnished by Mac. He informed him there'd be 50 more crisp bills with Ben Franklin's mug shot when the job was completed. His thin lips stretched tight when he barked the words, eyes colder than a frozen lake. He gave him until the next day, Saturday, at 6 pm. If he wasn't done, or it failed inspection, Buzz would deal with him. All the while, the trigger-happy lunatic protected Jed's flank. He stood fifteen feet behind him and to the side, right arm poised at his hip holster. His preparedness was unwarranted. Circumstances weren't hostile. The gun-slinging pervert from the shores of Lake Erie was a showoff. Besides, Jed could take care of himself. He hadn't found a match yet for the steel cube he called his head.

"Let me get this straight," said Krenecke. He realized that his business, and perhaps his life, was on the line. His work had to match Mac's specifications, it had to be flawless. He knew he'd only get to keep a fraction of the money. The rest would be laundered back East. "Your boss man wants us to weld three new suspension leafs to the frame, right? Then machine new U-bolts and springs. That'll raise the whole rig up by about 12 inches. That's how I read it."

"That's right."

"Way I figure, it'll boost your payload by about 10,000 pounds."

Jed waved a phony BLM mining permit in the air. Good enough to let them quarry sandstone monuments from Cedar Mesa. Huge slabs lay scattered about for the taking. He said they'd peddle them to a landscape outfit in Sedona, Arizona. That required reinforced capacity and higher clearance to do the job right. It was all a lie.

"Well, slap my face, man," Buzz mumbled beneath his breath. "What a lying sack of shit. You're good, Jed." He continued his tough-guy role. Dark sunglasses and a half-crazed smirk. His stance was upright and firm, but his ridiculous expression, sunglasses and blotched face made him no more a threat than a vaudeville farce.

Krenecke reminded Jed that his modifications would raise the rig's overall clearance to 17 feet, give or take a few inches. They needed to be extremely careful where they drove it. "You should have rented an air suspension model. It'd handle heavy loads better," he said.

"Best we could do. Mac arranged it. Know what, grease head? Ten grand's a lot of dough. So I'm adding to the job. Here's a paint chart. I want the entire cab painted Sand Dune. Color code is 538. It's got to match perfectly." The color matched the tan found on many government vehicles. He stepped inches from the mechanic's face. He spit the words from his mouth in a direct threat. He changed his mind a second time. He instructed Krenecke to paint the entire truck. It'd look more official for the wealthy Sedona crowd.

Gordy's color turned cadaver. He nodded tentatively. His mouth was parched, but his face cold and clammy. His tongue too dry to moisten his lips. His voice was hollow. "Uh-huh. By the way, what kind of license you got to drive this rig? Class B?"

"Know what, Krenecke? Mind your own business. I'll mind mine." His eyes transformed to black ice. "Quit asking so many questions. You already know more than you need to. You clear on all this?" Buzz shifted to a wider stance. Perspiration soaked through Krenecke's work shirt. Wet palms clung to his pant legs. "Another thing, if anyone asks, just say you're doing a favor for an old friend. Now take me around the shop. Got to make sure you're capable of the work."

Buzz shifted his eyes when the two men walked away. He spotted a sour-faced woman mechanic. She was in her late twenties. Her uniform was oil-stained and tattered. Grease smudged her skin like an Army Ranger ready for combat. A cigarette drooped from her lips, perhaps permanently, as blue-gray smoke enveloped her skull. It was no halo. A larger blue haze clung to her work bay. She had scraggly, dirty brown hair growing from a disproportionately tiny skull, no larger than a grapefruit. Her face resembled a wadded-up rag. Wrinkles converged at her mouth, puckered as though she had just bitten into a sour lemon. Buzz gave her the same smile he gave all women, a perverted sneer. His hand moved from his hip to the front of his pants. Grinning, he rubbed his crotch with exaggerated movements, like he was masturbating. She turned away in disgust. Lucky for him, Jed hadn't seen his outrageous act. He'd have cold-cocked Buzz immediately. Steelhead Jed didn't need much of an excuse.

The two men returned from their tour. Jed noticed the unkempt, puckered-face woman too. He remarked to Gordy how messy she looked for such a tidy operation. Only her red tool rack was neatly organized. He stared directly at her, but barked an order to him. "Tell that rag woman to call us a cab. Tell her to hurry it up. Now!"

THEY arrived at their modest, single-story motel on the outskirts of Farmington. It sat next to a heavy-duty truck shop. A salvage yard full of rusted treasures occupied the opposite side. Jed felt at home. He dispatched Buzz to the front desk to pay for another night's lodging.

When he returned, he asked, "So, where're we headed once all this truck work is done?"

"Next, we'll pick up ATVs at a dealer in Bluff, Utah. You'll be stationed between Mac and Whitey's camper van and the big truck. They'll shuttle Indian junk and trinkets past you on ATVs with trailers. I'll stay with our big truck, you'll keep them covered in case of an ambush. But before we head up to the Mesa, we have one last errand. It'll be the last town you'll see for several days. A wind-blown, dusty Indian town. Name's Kay-Enta. Something like that."

"Well, slap my face, man. Indian town, huh? Like them windy towns in old Western flicks? I told you gunslinger Buzz would fit right in. Think I'll walk me down the dusty main street in Kay-Enta and shoot me the first Indian that looks me wrong."

"Like hell you will. You're beyond help. I know all about your trigger-happy past. Surprised no one's killed you yet."

"I'm faster with a trigger than anyone else. I'll show those Western hokies a thing or two about guns. Teach them some big city tricks."

"Just remember, I warned you. You'll meet your match. The West is rugged, tough *hombres*. You won't last five minutes in Kay-Enta. People will laugh at your ghetto gun show. You brought the wrong weapons, nickel-dick. So don't get all trigger-happy."

"Well, slap my face, man. Who're you to give advice?"

"Look, just do your job. I don't care what you do AFTER Mac's job. Remember, it's fast cash. In and out, quick. I need the money bad. You're here to protect the exchange of goods. You're here for gun power. *No other reason.* So lay low and protect the shuttles. If anyone or anything looks like a threat, *then* you can play with your toys. Otherwise, stay out of sight. And watch out for rattlesnakes."

"Well, slap my face, man. Piece of cake. Sounds like easy money. He walked to the door and set the "Do not disturb" sign on the outer handle. Then he latched the deadbolt and placed the secondary door lock over its catch rod. He opened the combination lock on his custom briefcases. They revealed a formidable arsenal of handguns and weaponry. "If it's OK with you, I'm going back through everything I packed. Break it down and clean it again. Then I'll be ready for action. All the dirt blowing around this windy hellhole. Can't keep nothing clean. Even locked up. Not like our clean streets in Cleveland. Cleveland's heaven compared to this dirt dump."

"Christ Almighty, nickel-dick. They've been locked in your suitcases. How dirty could they be? Clean or not, don't forget what I said about useless urban guns."

61

Buzz donned a psycho grin. "Hey, partner, what'd you think of that cute little prissy at Gordy's? Sure jostled the juices in my big *cojones*. Just the way I like them. Tight and dirty."

"She's none of your business until the job's over. Nor any other woman. You hear? She's nothing. Forget her. We stick to Mac's plan. No deviations. You've got a one-track mind, you pervert."

Buzz picked up a .357 Ruger Blackhawk and twirled it in the air. Jed watched without interest. He wasn't sure if the Cleveland lunatic was trying to warn him or impress him. He didn't care. He'd play his upper hand. "Let me tell you what'll happen to Gordy if he doesn't do his job right. He and everyone in that fancy joint will end up in pieces floating down the San Juan. Even that rag face who gave you got a hard-on. You may know guns. I know explosives." Jed cocked his steel-hardened head toward Buzz. Frigid eyes fixed like blue LED beams. His head was more of a threat than Buzz's .357.

"Well, slap my face, man. Sounds cool, but I got me a better idea. If that Polak fails, instead of going to all that trouble blowing up his place, I'll take care of it for you. I'll just stroll in there and show them a thing or two about big guns. Loud machinery going and all, no one will ever know when the others get popped. It'll be over in two minutes. I'll save that tight little prissy for last. Give her what she was begging for this afternoon. Maybe I'll pop her the same time I'm popping her pussy real good. Ever seen that done in them snuff flicks? Nice to go out orgasmic."

"That's the dumbest thing I ever heard. You'd probably screw it up. My way's untraceable. Won't be nothing left bigger than a fingernail."

"Got me another idea. Ain't going to let that ugly meat wagon Whitey mess with me. These here bullets will go through his thick rhino hide just as easy as anyone else's. Ain't taking none of his crap."

"Now you look here, you fuzzy little pervert." Jed jumped off the bed, his face red as ingot. Eyes still frozen. "How many times to I have to tell you, retard? We've got an important job to do. Going to make tons of cash. I'll tell you one last time... don't go screwing it up. Don't even think of messing with Whitey."

"Hey, when I'm finished cleaning these, let's order some pizza. Then maybe you and me could walk over to that bar and see about scoring us some Indian snatch."

"You sick sack of fuzzy shit," Jed screamed. Saliva burst like shrapnel. Some of it landed on Buzz's acne. "How many times do I have to tell you? This is my final warning. No women until this is over! That's the last time I'm telling your sleazy gutter mind. When the job's done, you can go to Vegas. You'll have tons of cash. Buy any kind of sick fantasy you want."

Buzz reassembled the Ruger and held it up to the light. "Well, slap my face, man. Don't think I can wait that long."

"Slap your face, my ass, sewer skin, I'm going to splinter your frigging skull!"

FRIDAY'S hospitality hour waned. Wheeler dropped three empty plates into a trash bin. He used two napkins to wipe scraps from his face. He felt a tug at his elbow. He pivoted and found himself staring into the sun-weathered, cheery face of Phillip Brewster.

"Greetings, Semlow. Just the man I'm looking for. Figured I'd find you at the top of the food chain."

"Ah, Dr. Brewster. Thought you'd already left for dinner with your uppity-up colleagues. "How've you been?"

"Very well. You and Ann?"

"Fine. She's looking younger than ever. Younger than I do, in fact. It's not fair."

"A woman's prerogative, I guess."

"Knocked them out with your talk this afternoon. Mind if I take Howie Parker a copy? Remember him from the excavation? Next weekend we'll camp together on Cedar Mesa. Site stewardship duties."

"Of course I remember. Works as liaison with several tribes, right? I'll leave a copy at the front desk. Now, as to why I hunted you down..." His cheery face turned serious. "Have you got a few minutes? There's something I *must* show you. Our timing is perfect, everyone's gone to dinner. Room's empty. I'll ask the server cleaning up to lock the door behind her." One tray of iced beers remained. He grabbed two bottles of Heineken and two Coors Light, opened his billfold and handed her a fifty. "Please fetch me a chilled pilsner glass from your kitchen and lock the door as you leave. I'll phone the front desk when we're ready to be let out. Thank you."

When she returned, she poured his beer half full. Semlow watched. The endless rise of bubbles baffled him. It had since he was a kid. She placed his Coors Light on the table. He preferred drinking straight from the tall neck. She locked the door when she left.

"So why'd you skip dinner and track me down?" Wheeler began.

The archaeologist's face grew as hard as the earth he dug. "Your BLM law enforcement territory extends west from Blanding to Fry Canyon Ruins. Then on to Lake Powell, right?" Wheeler nodded. "Including Cedar Mesa?"

"Yes, even east some. It's a lot of geography. Budget's been shrunk to ridiculous levels."

"Very good. Had to be sure." He unlocked his briefcase and withdrew a zipped plastic bag. He placed it in the center of the table. A label was affixed to the top. A series of numbers and dates filled most of it. Wheeler knew they were his museum's official artifact catalogue numbers. The distinguished curator leaned into the table and glanced once more in each direction. He removed soft cotton gloves from a sealed bag and slipped them over his hands. Carefully, he removed the contents. He held the artifact in one hand.

"Wasn't there a scene just like this in an Indiana Jones movie?" Wheeler asked.

His Santa Claus cheeks glowed. "Ha. Never lose your sense of humor, do you? It'll keep you young forever. If I remember correctly, they were pounding straight shots, weren't they? Or drinking straight from the bottle? And the digs were a lot rowdier than this." Seconds later, humor evaporated. Wheeler only knew the cheerful side of Brewster. Graveness was a new dimension.

He unfolded a black velour cloth and set it in the center of the table. Then tantalizingly placed the artifact on the velour. "Official radio carbon dates aren't in yet. Preliminary thermo-luminescence dating places it in the neighborhood of, say, 18,000 years ago. Give or take a thousand. Long, long before Clovis."

"You did say 18,000 *thousand*, didn't you? Doesn't T-L dating release trapped electrons, which emit photons as a pulse of light, thereby revealing the approximate date of the last kiln firing?"

He nodded. "In addition, there doesn't appear to be any signature in the western United States for the type of clay used in the mold. A colleague, or uppity-up as you call them, who specializes in Mesoamerican prehistory is researching it. An associate at Los Alamos National Laboratory is researching its trace elements, among other things. We believe its mineral inclusions will disclose it came from south of our border. Perhaps way south. We'll find it. That's what experts do, they don't eat or sleep until a mystery's solved. This rare treasure, or at least half of it, was recovered from Cedar Mesa. We think Snow Flat Canyon. According to sources in Santa Fe, the man who placed it in our hands was granted immunity for assisting investigators. Since Cedar Mesa is your playing field, we're asking for your help."

Wheeler knew instantly that it was a feather holder. He suddenly realized Brewster's clandestine behavior was not theatrics. The locked, empty room, sterile white gloves and shroud of secrecy made sense. He studied the broken relic. "What exactly do you mean by 'your help?' You curate the most prestigious museum in the Southwest. Why me?"

"This priceless artifact came to us via remarkable circumstances. We believe it's been cached for tens of centuries. It traveled a circuitous route to end up here in Moab, Utah. An undercover agent in the FBI's Art Theft Division got first wind of it. He intercepted someone's sloppy maneuvering in cyberspace. Happened to be a front for an antiquities dealer with a notoriously sleazy reputation. You know the type, cutthroat jerks who specialize in signed forgeries of famous potters and jewelers. The sleazebag put feelers out through an internet site. That was his first mistake. That and having a nasty reputation for black market bartering. Name's Wainwright, in case you two have ever crossed paths. The FBI believes he's in cahoots with terrorist cells. During questioning, the front man claimed it came to him as a good faith 'show and tell' deposit. He alleges this tiny fragment is one of thousands of artifacts of the same quality. Virgin, so to speak. Never before seen by modern man. From an unexcavated site on Cedar Mesa, perhaps a cliff dwelling." The curator took his eyes off the artifact for long enough to down a long pull from the pilsner. Then he opened a second Heineken. "Dealer said he's willing to pay the looter 15 million dollars for the entire assemblage. The instant the FBI found that out, cloak-and-dagger types from Washington stepped up to the plate." He leaned into the table, close to Wheeler's face, and whispered softly. "You know, spooks. The CIA, I believe, but I'm not certain. They think he'll barter contraband sensitive to national security. That's when things escalated way out of *my* league. And that's where 'your help' comes in, Wheeler."

The Kane Gulch law enforcement man watched bubbles rise inside the green bottle. He stared pensively for a minute. "What exactly would you like me to do?" A strange mixture of trepidation and excitement flickered in his voice.

"Time is of the essence. An exchange is imminent. Not weeks, but days. In spite of what I said in my lecture, we don't have time for full-blown excavations. That can come later. It's imperative that we discover as many feather holders as possible. In very short order." Brewster's eyes danced, a smile cracked his reddened cheeks. "I've got an idea for a starting point. A datum, if you will. I need to identify all unexcavated cliff dwellings on Cedar Mesa as soon as possible. And, since you're Cedar Mesa's law enforcement officer, I have to know if there's been any looting recently in the canyons. During the last six months or so. The other half of that feather holder must be up there. I doubt the scoundrel who put it up for bidding in Santa Fe broke it in half just for show. He lost it or left it behind."

Wheeler pressed a magnifier loupe into one eye socket and examined the fracture. Brewster was right. The fracture causing the break was recent, not 18,000 years old. He turned the object over to study its back. His mouth locked open. The loupe remained glued to his eye. "Good God. What do you call these?" His eyes met Brewster's above the table.

"Those may be," he responded slowly, "the most unique hieroglyphs in the world. Undecipherable, as far as I can tell. One of the world's foremost scholars offered his services to try and crack it. He's working around the clock. No blips on his radar screen yet. My theory is that it forms a logogram or an ideogram. Possibly a mysterious blending of each." Question marks formed on Semlow's face "Oh, yes," Brewster explained, "a logogram is a symbol used to represent a specific word, assuming they had a language back then. Ideograms, on the other hand, utilize symbols to represent a thought or an idea. A concept, *but not the particular word for it*. Hence its name, ideogram. *Comprende?*" He picked up his glass and drank. Very few bubbles remained. "In other words, a symbol that represents *not* the object pictured, but rather an idea or object that the picture *suggests*." He grinned triumphantly.

"Clear as mud," Wheeler whispered. "I think I see the difference. But is the cryptic message significant? I mean, it's not like we're trying to decipher enemy codes from the Taliban. Could they be 18,000-year-old art forms? Symbols etched to represent landscape features? Or constellations in the heavens?"

"Fair enough," Brewster said. "But the experts believe they *say* something, that a message is being communicated. A message vitally significant to mankind in the twenty-first century."

"What do the spooks think?"

"They too are experts, at cryptographic analysis. But they don't know history. Or ancient civilizations. Or culture. The man at Los Alamos used to work for the Defense Department. Today, he's a world-renowned leader in solving ideograms. He's our best bet for cracking it. Besides, Washington is extremely hush-hush. They're looking at the big picture, the entire cache of artifacts, the $15 million, and the possibility of a large barter deal with terrorist cells set to go down in the Southwest US. It's their business to keep everyone guessing. You've heard of spy games. It's not just a concept, it's real." He frowned, holding his Heineken, but not taking a swig. "Personally, I believe the spooks are treating this as nothing more than broken pottery. Almost worthless, except to collectors. They're like piranhas. They want the big fish, the dealer and his contacts."

"Have any other feather holders you've excavated contained glyphs?"

"None. This is an entirely new phenomenon. We *must* find the missing half. And we have to be quick to discover other artifacts that contain similar incising, if they exist. That's why the list of unexcavated cliff villages is crucial. The experts require a larger sample to properly decipher its meaning."

"Count me in! I'll call Quirk at 4:30 am tomorrow. That's when her day begins. She'll arrange for you to visit our Monticello office. They'll pull every report regarding Cedar Mesa cliff dwellings, excavated or not. Our records at Kane Gulch are limited. Monticello has it all."

"Great. I'll skip the morning presentations and leave early. Should be an hour's drive, right?"

"54 miles due south. I might be of help from another angle too."

"Oh?"

"It's a sensitive topic. I need your undaunted trust on this."

Brewster let loose with a slap to his thigh and a hearty laugh.

"Oh, and I suppose I haven't done that very thing? Assumed I had your trust? I just showed you an 18,000-year-old artifact containing an undecipherable ideogram. Part of a cache reputedly never before seen by modern man. And you ask about trust? That's precisely why I hunted you down for this secret mission. Seems to me we're both vulnerable here. Extremely so. We're both stretched way out on a limb, aren't we? Meeting like this."

"You're right. Sorry." Wheeler held his bottle near the base and thrust it outward to toast their bond. The curator aimed his pilsner in Semlow's direction. "You know," Wheeler continued, "there have been mysterious goings-on at Cedar Mesa. You asked about the possibility of recent looting. Well, right this very moment, as we speak, certain events don't compute. My intuition smells a rat." He took a pull from his long neck.

"What're you talking about?"

"It could just be dirty laundry. You know, bureaucratic politics. Ranger Quirk sounded very strange today. Not like herself, not like my boss of the past five years. As I said, it could be politics. I suspect it has something to do with a new agent assigned from our Salt Lake office, a certain Agent Coldditz. He's meddling in her rice bowl. She's acquiescing, setting the stage for a classic territorial dispute." His thumbnail created a rift in the beer label. He scratched off the left half. "Also, several backpackers have reported the possibility of looting in Snow Flat Canyon. Isn't that where you said the feather holder was stolen?"

Brewster jumped from his chair. "What? Have you caught them? *We* need to be there excavating. This is no time for plunderers to be stealing our treasures! What if they find it first?"

"The new agent claims he'll take matters into his own hands, that everything will be OK. But if I know Howie Parker, he'll do just the opposite of what I asked. Bet a fortune on it. Bet he marches straight into the canyons east of Highway 261."

"You *must* keep me posted. Up to the minute if you have to. I repeat, *we're* the ones who should be excavating in Snow Flat Canyon, not some greenhorn new to the area. And certainly not looters, for God's sake."

"I'm under orders to chill out, to remain at the conference. Coldditz is the new man in charge." He stood and looked at his watch. "Hum, 8:35. I'm afraid two beers is my limit. Had enough. Think I'll call it a day. Give Ann a call and turn in." No sooner had he spoken than both newspaper articles scrolled before his eyes. And then his analogy of unraveling a thread to solve a mystery. He judiciously suggested to Brewster that all communications be conducted on landlines. Ditto for his scholarly associates. Until the murkiness cleared up. Wheeler's gut feeling.

The esteemed archaeologist concurred. He walked to the courtesy phone and called the front desk. One minute later, the door lock clicked. He handed her a twenty on their way out.

They walked through the lobby and arrived at the elevator. Heavy doors slid open. The elevator rocked to a stop on the second floor. The doors opened noisily. They bid farewell and the doors began to close. Brewster yelled out, "Wait." He inserted his arm between the doors. They rebounded loudly. Wheeler did a 180 and walked back. "Good God, I almost forgot," Brewster exclaimed. He reached into his pocket and withdrew a wad of crumbled business cards. "Ah, here it is. But before I hand this to you, I insist on setting my boundaries. My responsibility ends here. Right this very minute. Let the record show that I'm the dirt digger. That's all I want to be. You're the law enforcement guy. *You* play cops and robbers. Leave me out of those games, those spy games. That's where this is headed, you know. My interest is in hieroglyphs, not black markets. In spite of all appearances, I'm really not the Indiana Jones type. Keep me out of that loop. Just find those suspected looters, Wheeler. And make it fast. Call me the second my people can start digging. Shovels and trowels are standing by." He handed him the crumpled card and removed his arm from the electric eye. "It's the number of a federal agent in Santa Fe. He's willing to assist in any way he can."

Wheeler glanced down at the card. The doors slid closed. It was Semlow's turn to intercept them. He quickly squeezed two fingers into the rubber edge guard and pulled hard. The closing mechanism rebounded. He stared at the wrinkled card with an "I thought so" type of grin. "Phillip," he blurted excitedly, "that unscrupulous black market dealer in Santa Fe... The alleged barter deal wouldn't happen to involve high-grade uranium, would it? Mined on the Navajo Reservation...?" His words trailed off, but visions of the newspaper articles did not.

Wheeler withdrew his hand and the doors closed for good. He listened to the whir as it rose. His eyes fixed again on the card. **"Wendell A. Coldditz, Special Investigator, US Department of Homeland Security**."

He felt a powerful tug on the thread. The button loosened. He smiled.

NINE

Highway 261 rose and fell to the undulating surface of Cedar Mesa. Deep canyons gutted the Mesa like arteries beneath earth's skin. Rutted ribbons of sandy soil directed vehicles to canyon trailheads. Hiking trails descending into the depths were rated moderate to difficult.

The land was dotted with vast quantities of spirit trees. These weathered stumps and ghoulish remnants played a vital role in the Mesa's ecology. A tapestry of colors was arranged as though nature had triumphed in its own making. Afternoon sunlight embellished each shade. At ground level, red-orange soil gave way to green juniper and pinion trees. Their deceased counterparts, spirit trees and spirit stumps, splashed the tapestry with contrasting shades of barn-gray. Nature's palette placed finishing touches of creamy-white limestone, deep red sandstone and blackened volcanic boulders on the canvas. Pale yellow and white pigments filled the voids with flowering desert brush. Approaching the rounded edges of each canyon, slick rock ran like coarse concrete unevenly poured. Laced throughout were water-drenched cupules and patches of black-tipped cryptogamic soil, a carpet-like feature that was by far the Mesa's most fragile component. A lapis sky crowned the mosaic. The masterpiece balanced upon nature's easel with compelling harmony.

Exhaustion prevailed on the intrepid couple. Kika turned away from staring contently out of the window and inched closer to Howie. The horror of last night's rescue molded her vulnerable mind from a pensive state into one of negativity. It sat there and brewed like a cauldron. Morbidity volleyed haunting questions in the recesses of her mind. "What if those suspicious characters have accomplices? What if there's an organized outfit looting in adjacent canyons? What if guards are posted, with orders to shoot without asking questions? Did they maul that innocent woman backpacker for no good reason? Or did she get too close for comfort, threaten their fortunes? Come on, Mr. ex-Marine, connect the dots, would you? Are we walking into a trap?" Grimacing, she lay her head on his thigh, too tired to dialogue with her boyfriend.

Howie, meanwhile, used the silence to manufacture his own plot. Asserting a life-long character defect of *contempt prior to investigation,* he concluded that the thug-looking men seen in the canyons were GUILTY. And should be avenged for savagely beating the woman and tossing her from a moving vehicle. It was then that he made a life-altering decision. He'd ignore Quirk's and Wheeler's orders. After all, he was a trained combatant. He'd packed high-powered, semiautomatic handguns. He could kill in seconds with his two hands. They'd be safe. He and Kika were masters at camouflaging themselves among sandstone cliffs. They'd descend upon those bastard pillagers like ninjas from a temple roof. Then report back to Quirk. That was his plan.

Following the prolonged quiet spell, Kika rose and planted a soft kiss on his cheek. She extended her legs and straightened her body in a much-needed stretch, followed by a sleepy yawn. She fiddled with a string of Navajo protection beads dangling from the rearview mirror. Strung with dried juniper berries and turquoise beads, they afforded safety and protection from evil spirits. In a friendly, non-sensual gesture, she pressed her thigh against his. "Let's talk about having fun this weekend, shall we? You'll never guess where my eyes were when we drove up the Moki Dugway."

Her question shook him from his exciting fantasy of playing canyonland ninja. "Huh? Oh, sorry, my mind was wandering."

"I started to say... I saw two whirlwinds dancing through Valley of the Gods. I sensed majesty and rhythm in their power. You were on the phone so I didn't point them out."

"You'll always call them that, won't you? Whirlwinds, I mean. I know how important the Wind People are to you. But I'll still call them dust devils most of the time. Alright?"

Her expression remained gleeful. "We don't have a word in our language for `devil`. I'm not happy you call them that, but I'll live with it because of our vow. That's our deal, not to change each other. Right? As long as you respect my belief that whirlwinds *are* Wind People, the Messengers. I believe they speak to us, Howie. They tell us what's happening in our world. I haven't had time to tell you this because of last night's horror. But Luciana and I saw two whirlwinds yesterday driving to Kayenta. We parked and jumped out to watch them. Awesome sight." She spread her hands and twirled them like two whirlwinds.

Something clicked in Howie. Certain brain waves bent toward her way of thinking. Perhaps the concept of Messenger People wasn't all hocus-pocus after all, he thought. He reasoned that last night's life-saving recue occurred *after observing two whirlwinds*. That could only mean one thing. "Perhaps the fact that you just saw whirlwinds in Valley of the Gods is a *good* omen," he said. "The Valley is special. It has power."

A smile flickered, even though she couldn't muster enough energy to tell him the story of Coyote and Badger. She needed time to sort out the polarity of trickery versus perseverance, the duality of two spiraling wind forces colliding from opposite directions. A peaceful evening in camp would lay the groundwork. Perhaps later that night, staring into campfire embers or gazing up at billions of stars, perhaps then she could tell him that folk story. If not, then during tomorrow's hike in majestic canyons.

"Let me say it a different way, being as open-minded as I possibly can."

Her reaction was catalytic. She practically jumped onto his lap. "Are you coming around to my way of thinking?"

He smiled. "Don't get too excited. Just an idea. About yesterday's two whirlwinds. It's possible that we're both saying the same thing. Think about it. You two arrived at precisely the right place and time to save that woman's life. Right? At nearly the same location on the highway where you saw the whirlwinds. Am I right? So how could the Messenger People be anything but a positive force? Perhaps their message was one of taking positive action, not doom and gloom." He rested his palm on her thigh. "We'll be fine this weekend, honey. Equate the recent whirlwinds as a *good* omen. They may even bring us luck."

Kika sighed. "I hope you're right. Guess I'm too tired, being too hard on myself.   Negativity is my default mode when I'm not in harmony, not experiencing *hozho*. I learned to be negative from my mom."

Howie suggested camping near the rim of Owl Creek Canyon, the opposite direction Wheeler had suggested. "It'd be close to the trailhead for a bright and early start tomorrow morning. That'd save packing our rig and driving from Todie Springs, west of Highway 261. We'll have a 45-minute advantage." Not suspecting any ulterior motives, she gladly agreed.

"Looks like we're skipping Grand Gulch and Bullet Canyon then, huh? Fine by me, means we'll approach Owl Creek Canyon from the Mormon Trail of 1880."

"Yes, I'm amazed it's still discernable after 125 years." Kika removed the lid from a large bucket of deep-fried chicken and potato wedges. She grabbed a large breast and placed it on a paper plate, then loaded it with a handful of greasy wedges and passed it to Howie. She reached into the glove box and handed him his pepper shaker. He held it between his knees and unscrewed the lid. The other hand gripped the steering wheel. He dumped a mound onto his food, rivaling the eruption of Mt. St. Helens.

Kika munched on a drumstick. Her favorite. Food brought relief. She reflected on Howie's positive outlook. She knew better than to view the Wind People in anything but a positive light.

TWO men drove east on Highway 160 in a Land Rover. It stood out from other SUVs. Anti-terrorist armor and military security devices met NSA standards. Not a fortress like armored personnel carriers, but certainly overkill for any assault encountered in southwestern states. Its driver scored the highest rating in counter-assault driving techniques. Annual tests still ranked him near the top of all certified drivers worldwide. A unique brush guard was attached to the modified front suspension. It could withstand virtually any collision, crash through buildings or mow vehicles in half. Tactical weapons and body armor lay within easy reach. The rig was one of three attached to the roving surveillance van. The driver left the pavement and drove slowly onto the gravel shoulder. He looked left. A sign on the garrisoned building read: Gordy's Welding and Undercarriage.

"That's it," the passenger said. They made a U-turn and parked on the highway in front of the shop. The sun was behind them. If necessary, they could make a quick getaway without squinting into bright sunlight. They were trained to maintain a tactical advantage.

"This'll be short and sweet," the passenger declared. Fifteen minutes later, they emerged from the shop. They scanned both directions and walked to the Land Rover. A look of confidence covered their faces.

"You were right," said the driver. "Just the way I like it. Short and sweet. Simple. But I do have one question."

"And what might that be?"

"That's one hell of an impressive shop. If Krenecke was in the pokey until last fall, how'd he come into those digs so fast?"

"No one's positive where he gets his money. Seems to do a lot of cash business. Our friends in Taxation and Revenue have kept him on their radar for six months. They're sure it's a laundering setup, but can't nail him yet. They don't want us ruffling any feathers either. My department's ignoring several parole violations."

"This much I know," said the driver. "Krenecke's plugged into a huge power grid back East. Nasty people. But I'm not interested in him per se. I'm concerned about the outfit he's doing business with. Been watching them for some time now. They've wrangled a four-man outfit to these parts. Their leader's got undesirables strung out from Pittsburgh to Phoenix. Four of them showed up in the Four Corners area this week. Others are waiting in the wings. Don't like the smell of things. Our information is sketchy, but it'll form a picture soon. Always does."

Minutes earlier, the two men introduced themselves under false pretense - ranking corrections officials from Santa Fe. Claimed they were visiting ex-cons who'd become model businessmen. While one of them kept Krenecke occupied, the clandestine one, the driver, casually lit a cigarette and strolled through the shop. Unnoticed, he disappeared behind Jed and Buzz's rental truck. Within seconds, he secured a sophisticated tracking device beneath the engine mount.

AN hours-old campfire glowed like molten lava. Red-orange embers caused the air above to sway in gentle waves. Gray wisps of smoke rode the waves skyward and disappeared into darkness. Kika threw a pinion log onto the embers. It smoldered, giving birth to thick blue smoke. The night was still. The smoke mushroomed above their heads. Suddenly, the log ignited into a bright torch. Campfire smoke was intoxicating. Howie dreamed of bottling it to savor its aroma at home.

Their camp chairs hugged close to the ground. Kika wore a fleece hoody pulled over her head, hands buried in the pockets. Howie sported a light fleece jacket with two zippered pockets. He loved pockets. They had to be zippered. A Benchmade auto-release combat knife lay in his right pocket. The other contained a super-bright LED headlamp. His Walther PPK 380 semiautomatic lay next to him on a sandstone slab, reachable at the blink of an eye. It was his oldest and favorite firearm.

Kika removed a hand from her pocket and placed it on Howie's arm. She slid it down slowly until it met his hand. Their fingers interlocked. They stared at the dazzling night sky. Faint star clusters within the Milky Way gave it the appearance of half-cloud, half-star. In late May, it bisected the sky spanning southwest to northeast. Kika recalled the Navajo myth of how Coyote's impatience was responsible for casting flecks of stone and star dust skyward, creating what they called *Yikaisdahi*, the Milky Way. Looking to his right, Howie pointed toward red-hued Antares in the constellation Scorpio. The star family hung low in the sky forming a giant sickle.

"You know, sweetheart," he said, straining his neck beyond the back of the chair. "The billions of stars remind me of an artist sitting cross-legged on the ground, dipping his paintbrush into the palette and rocking backwards as he snaps the brush skyward." Kika stirred the embers and listened politely. "Before I was deployed to Kuwait, I learned the name and position of over 40 stars in both hemispheres. It shattered my paintbrush myth. But it made me appreciate how alive the night sky is. Knowing so many stars by name allows me to look up and check in with many of them each night. It's almost like they're as alive as those lights in Blanding 30 miles away." He pointed at the eastern horizon. Lights flickered in the small community of Blanding, Utah. "The universe is alive, Kika. I know there's life up there. We just haven't found it yet."

Kika used a small juniper branch to stir the fire. The sweet-smelling wood burst into flames instantly. She looked at Blanding's lights dancing on the horizon. Their fingers remained interlocked. "Well, my sweetheart, I grasp what you're saying, your artist analogy. It's quite interesting, even though my personal views are somewhat different. You approach the cosmos from the ground up. Navajos do too, that much I can agree on. In fact, Navajo storytellers weave our creation folklore in the same direction, upward. Ancestors moved in a challenging ascent up from lower worlds toward more light, to a higher domain where they could live in comfort and harmony.

"Recently, however, my thoughts have viewed life from beyond the cosmos, beyond the placement of stars in our creation lore, looking back inward to earth through the constellations. And so, to me, the stars resemble tiny pin-pricked holes made by ancestral spirits from the other side, honoring us with a glimpse of the brilliance found beyond our world. I believe life is everywhere too, Howie, including up there. Look how busy the sky is. Of course it's alive. It has to be. We're just one tiny speck here on earth. But, my love, those are my own personal thoughts. In terms of Navajo beliefs, such talk of the afterworld cuts across wide sections of Navajo society. Risky business for me to meddle in."

They sat in silence, staring upward. One "star" moved steadily across the sky in a southwest to northerly direction. It passed directly through the Big Dipper. It was a satellite. He relaxed his grip. It was his turn to stoke the embers. The only noise was that of the sizzling wood. After several minutes, he took his hand and, with an open palm, placed it very softly over her upper thigh. She wore thin flannel sweat pants. He felt through the soft material. It felt like bare skin. It aroused him. He could still taste her breath, still feel her kitty-like teeth tugging at his lips, recalling her enticing invitation yesterday after lunch.

Kika's mind read the same. She recalled melting snugly into him, feeling the force of his throbs. How he cupped her round buttocks with both hands. She loved it when he played around back there. He slid his palm further up her thigh. She responded by slouching lower in her chair, making foreplay more convenient. She was ready. His hand arrived at its destination. Kika's eyes were half open. She gazed dreamily at the red-orange embers, unable to focus. She breathed deeply.

"Hey, my little horsetail," Howie whispered, "perhaps it's time we roll onto the soft sand. He'd given her the nickname "horsetail" when they first met. Kika's jet black hair ran in a ponytail down the length of her back, mid-way down her butt. Early in their relationship, she tied her hair back like a show horse, especially when they were fooling around. Whispering the words "my horsetail" in her ear became a sensuous trigger.

She straightened and leaned into him, tenderly kissing his ear, pressing her moist tongue deep and curling its tip in and out. She panted faintly and nibbled at his earlobe. An electrifying tingle burst inside him. Sense of an outside world was foggy. He became light-headed and vulnerable. He was under her spell.

Butterflies swirled within Kika. She breathed a moist statement into his ear - half tongue, half words. Her mouth felt like a volcano. She continued massaging his ear with wet lips like a doe at a salt lick. She exerted every ounce of sexual energy, every bit of her 25-year-old goddess-like youth into their love acts. She slid her hand slowly down his torso in a teasing, circular motion until she unfastened his belt and unzipped him. It was akin to slow-motion torture. "You've got a horse-like feature of your own to be proud of, my love. Can I let this stallion out of its corral?"

TEN

Quirk's cell phone chimed at 4:35 am. Five minutes into her tightly structured day. She considered Wheeler's request and immediately e-mailed her chief at Monticello's district office. A reply came ten minutes later. Arrangements were set for Phillip Brewster to peruse field notes of Cedar Mesa excavations. Numerous archaeological sites had merely been mapped and surveyed, but never excavated. That would make for practically impossible odds of discovering incised artifacts.

One hour later, Wheeler called Parker. He envisioned them sipping coffee and watching the sunrise at a pristine campsite near Todie Springs. He knew it would be a spectacular sight, rising somewhere between the Abajo Mountains and the outline of Mesa Verde. Howie's voice messaging greeted him. Perturbed, he was certain Todie Springs fell within cell range, even though coverage was spotty on the 420-square-mile Mesa. That was his first trigger that Parker hadn't followed orders. Impetuously, he stabbed redial and barked an urgent message concerning news about Schisslenberg and last night's clandestine meeting with Brewster. About his DIA buddy tugging ferociously on the thread with both hands. Frustrated, Wheeler realized that was his last chance to reach Parker and Windsong until nightfall. Within minutes, conference participants would depart on a field trip to visit iconic North American rock art. Out of respect to the sacred sites, cell phones would remain behind.

HOWIE and Kika lay sprawled in a web of interwoven body parts, crafted into one entity with eight limbs. He opened his eyes and freed an arm to caress her neck. She lay in a dream state. They'd slept soundly after dizzying climaxes. Ecstasies were screamed into the desert night. They lay near the campfire in a dreamy afterglow for an hour, whispering that they actually *needed* that sex. That primordial instincts, hatched from Thursday night's traumatic episode, intensified their orgasms.

Daylight brightened the landscape at 5:20 am. Howie's inner voice sparked an electrifying message; to get an early start, to hike into the canyons as soon as possible. He knew time was of the essence, that they had only two days to cover a lot of ground. Quirk and Wheeler would never have to know where they'd been. He'd lie that the canyons *west* of the highway were as spectacular as ever.

Coffee would jump-start him. He needed a strong mug of Joe. He planted a kiss on Kika's temple and lowered himself from their camper bed. He believed coffee and his peppered food should match - very black. He traveled everywhere with a coffee thermos and a pepper shaker. Kika insisted her coffee be diluted from the robust brew he consumed. She often drank instant, an irrevocable sin in the eyes of coffee connoisseurs. She also insisted on sizeable measures of cream, preferably half-and-half. Howie didn't consider what she drank to be coffee. But he humored her anyway. That was their deal. No forced changes. Next, he poured a tall glass of pineapple juice. She despised orange juice, but loved every form of pineapple, even canned.

He practically inhaled the first mug while loading their backpacks. A refill accompanied him outside into cool morning air. Daybreak was in its infancy. It was 5:45. He figured they'd be on the trail by 6:30. Windless 48-degree air greeted him. Invisible peacemakers of the night brought calmness to the Mesa. They'd disappear by dawn's early light. He inhaled sweet desert perfumes. Pale-white blooms of cliff rose scattered divine aromas. "Truly rivals the nard of Eden," he commented to the still air. He reveled in tranquility at sunrise and sunset. It was his form of meditation. During the transition between day and night and vice versa, he insisted on being outdoors.

But this morning was different. He was anxious to receive an update on the newspaper articles. He knew that'd have to wait. Even if he was within cell range, he couldn't tell Wheeler where they were. He sought to observe firsthand what other hikers had reported. Parker loved contradicting orders. It was the primary reason he hadn't signed up for a second tour with the Corps. Disobedience molded him into the man he was.

The sun raced skyward. Shadows taller than skyscrapers retreated into eastern cliffs. Soon, still morning air would also retreat. May's unmerciful winds would prey upon hikers. Stinging grit and unceasing shrills would torture skin and eardrums. Kika believed all strong winds were the Wind People. A reminder to the Dine of the seriously parched land they inhabited. And to use resources sustainably. He tilted his head and drained the second mug. Then he turned his thoughts toward the day ahead. Kika's loud screams jarred him. He raced to the door in four leaps.

"Howie, Howie," she yelled, panic-stricken. "Help me! Where are you? I can't see you. Howie, I need you. Where are you?" Disoriented, she repeated her plea. Her landscape was blurred. Everything looked hazy and muted. Indistinct images swirled before her. Sand particles pricked her face like needles from a wool carder.

She was trapped in an hourglass-shaped crucible. Being sucked into its narrow neck, slipping slowly into bottomless sand. Wind shrilled in her tiny universe. Low-voltage electrical shocks tortured her. Annoying, but not life threatening. "It *must* be a whirlwind, not a sandstorm," she yelled to anyone who'd hear. She pleaded for Howie, lips quivering hysterically. Another shock. She sank further down. Her mind played games. Perhaps Howie was correct, that twirling columns of wind *were* dust devils. She felt their energy, their electrical pulses. She screamed into her blurred galaxy. It crackled. Blowing sand choked her senses. Still no Howie. She yelled despairingly to Uncle Lenny, accusing him of telling no more than fanciful myths, challenging his Wind Messenger story, doubting if the Sun truly came down from the sky and scorched the Ancient ones. "But you're my oracle," she pleaded. "My source for Navajo teachings. What's happening to me?"

Time passed eternally. Gradually, another blurry form appeared. It was a woman lying beside her. The image materialized. It was a surreal version of the brutally beaten woman. Her lips were puffy. Her cheeks swelled rhythmically. Kika was terrified. The beat of her own heart matched that of her billowing breaths. She turned. Standing behind them was a man in police uniform. It was Dudley Blue Sky, erect and expressionless, leaning nonchalantly against his tribal police car. He looked like Smokey the Bear in a billboard ad. Semlow Wheeler loomed on the horizon. Her eyes zoomed in. He stood amongst thousands of glass shards. They glittered against shiny new blacktop.

Thinly veiled dancers took form. They fluttered as if floating in the wind. Desperate, she yelled, "Are you the Wind People? Are the shocks I feel you reaching out and touching me? Is that how you communicate? *What are you trying to tell me?*" She shivered in awe. The images danced around her like a circular sand painting. "It must be the Messenger People, that's who is inside all whirlwinds." She turned and emptied her lungs: "Howie!" The shrill grew louder. "I've gone insane."

Her skin was clammy. Sand clung to her. At last, Howie came into view. He held a rattlesnake high overhead. "That's a morbid message, Howie. You're supposed to rescue me. What are you doing? Snakes are taboo. We're to avoid them. If you're playing games, it's not funny." She'd watched a Hopi snake dance when she was a child. Dancers held poisonous snakes in their *mouths*, not over their heads. The snake above him rattled loudly. He kept it at a safe height. His other hand clutched a pistol. "Now what? Certainly you're not going to use that on the snake. Howie, it's taboo to kill a snake. Release it. Come over and save me before I slip through the neck." He released the snake and took several steps back. The whirlwind raged on.

Minutes later, her sandy hell began to dissipate, one veil at a time, until stillness prevailed. She rocked from side to side like a cradled newborn. Her life passed before her eyes. Suddenly, a bright white light filled her view. Howie called *her* name. "Kika, Kika. Come on sweetheart. Time to wake up," His voice was a long way off. "Wow, what a dream you must've had! You're drenched." He placed his hand on her forehead. "Are you waking up? Coffee and juice are waiting." He reached behind him and turned off the kettle. The high-pitched shrill ceased at once.

Her T-shirt looked like she'd been swimming. Her neck was loamy. Perspiration pooled on her forehead. Her black hair was matted against her head. She blinked drowsily. Still groggy, she lifted a hand to wipe her face. She inspected it for evidence. No sand. She rubbed her neck and looked closely again. Still no sand. She blinked repeatedly and rubbed each eye inward toward the nose. No grit, no matter. Howie watched her with curiosity. "Guess I really was dreaming," she breathed sleepily.

"Its 6:00 o'clock, honey. I'd hoped we'd be hiking by 6:30. Will you be awake? I've begun loading our backpacks for a long day. Scrambled eggs will be ready in five minutes, OK?" She remained groggy and half-asleep. "Hey, love, you alright?"

"Yeah, sure. I'll be fine in a few minutes. Toss me my shorts, please." Her hand covered a long yawn. Then she rolled onto her side and propped up on an elbow. Her drowsy eyes needed more rubbing. She did so for a full minute and examined each finger carefully. "I'll be damned. No sand." She felt inside her sleeping bag, slid her hand all around the mattress and looked at Howie, befuddled. "Do you feel any sand in here? Did you sweep it up already? That dream was so real. I was petrified, trapped in a whirlwind, walls of sand spun around me. I screamed your name at the top of my lungs. I saw blurry faces. People's lips moved, but no sound came out. Hope it all makes sense someday." She yawned again and sipped her creamy coffee. "Um, yum. I really need this. Know what? I have to write what I remember in my journal right this second. Do you mind? Please? Can we leave just a few minutes later?" He agreed. He knew she had an extraordinary sixth sense. It was, in fact, an amazingly powerful gift of intuition.

"I'll get it all down in my little dream book and then we can leave. I can't forget this one. I know it carried a message. Want to hear something really crazy?" He turned and faced her, holding a thermos of coffee for later that day. "I think I saw the Wind People, Howie. They resembled eerie pictographs painted on the cliffs behind my mom's house. And here's the weirdest part. I felt mild electrical shocks. I heard crackling electrical sounds. I was ready to give you credit for your dust devils. Do you think I'm crazy? Have I lost my mind?"

He studied her and smiled. "You have a gift, Kika. You're not crazy. But I wouldn't chalk it off as *just* a dream. We'll be extra vigilant in the canyons today."

She sat up and beckoned her lover. The elevated bed placed her love nest mere inches from his face. She hooked both arms around his neck and interlocked her fingers. She stared with dreamy, bedroom eyes into blue irises. Time stood still, neither one flinched. It could have gone either way. Odds were high for another orgasm. Morning sex was like candy to them. Instead, she stretched forward and kissed the tip of his nose. "I love you."

Kika stepped down from the camper at 6:45 and adjusted her backpack. Howie read from a checklist, a practice ingrained from backcountry rescues in Utah's rugged canyons. Whenever Kika thought checking and double-checking was heinous, she'd adopt a bratty air and mimic Q debriefing James Bond. Donning a British accent with Navajo flair, she'd outline the features of their state–of-the-art gear. They both loved it. It was a playful interlude. And few told better stories or mimicked humorous lines better than a Navajo.

They agreed to split up and hike in separate canyons after lunch, then rendezvous at the mouth of Owl Creek and Snow Flat Canyons. Targeted arrival time back at camp was six o'clock. They set a barbeque and star gazing date. Howie's primary survival tool was natural instinct, not gadgetry. His greatest asset, "Situational Intelligence," saved his hide many times. No high-tech instrument could replace his innate sense of stealth and survival. He cocked his wrist and looked at a Chase-Durer Special Forces watch. It featured a superb illumination system. He needn't have looked. His internal clock told him it was within seconds of 6:50. He was sixty-four seconds off. It was 6:51:04.

They hiked east. Slickrock made for easy hiking. He looked over his shoulder and took a bearing based on the most distinguishable landmark for 75 miles: Bears Ears. The promontory consisted of two massive, flat-top buttes rising 2,100 feet above their surroundings. Heavily forested, they resembled the ears of a grizzly bear whose head was hidden in tall grass. Bears Ears had been used for centuries as a sure-fire way of "dead reckoning." It was nearly as good as a compass. Motorists approaching Cedar Mesa from great distances felt secure in their directions.

Kika advanced in front of Howie. She moved gingerly, joy filled her momentum. They were two miles from camp and had descended into the first of several deep canyons. 350-foot walls towered above. Partial shade along the canyon floor brought coolness to their fast-paced hike. Howie admired her gait, derived from a gene pool that

81

typified inborn agility. A blending of her Pima father and her Navajo mother. Natural instincts yielded added dividends. She graced slickrock like an aquatic insect skimming a pond's surface. As a climber, she scaled up and down like a lizard. Strong forearms, focused attention and willingness to trust someone with her life. All packed into an extremely fit 5'4", 115-pound frame. She was in her zone. She bounded over folds in the slickrock and patches of cryptogamic soil. She baffled Howie with her capacity to conserve water in stifling temperatures. An ancestral gift. She pivoted suddenly, smiled straight into his eyes and continued a brisk pace backwards. "Don't forget, lover boy, Navajos can out-camp and out-backcountry you Anglos any day. Think you can keep up?" She turned and sprinted ahead.

He rose to the occasion and raced forward, reaching out and grabbing her elbow. "You must have read my mind. I was just admiring your gait."

"Like hell, you were. You were staring at my butt. Don't tempt yourself like that, Howie. This'll be a very long day. Tonight's a long way off so why torture yourself?" She smirked, then stopped, stood on her tiptoes and gazed into his eyes. "That was wonderful last night. Her lips gently touched his. "Can't wait until tonight!"

Like silencing a handgun, Howie contained the tingling in his groin. They hiked side by side. The only human encounters were experienced backpackers. None of them commented on suspicious, out-of-their element men. No alarms were tripped. No thugs or killers lurked about. No ambushes. Remnants of two abandoned camps were visible. Each one had been vacated several days earlier. Everything appeared normal.

Kika selected an idyllic spot for lunch. It surrounded a glimmering, aqua-colored pool of fresh water. She'd spotted it descending into an adjacent canyon two hundred feet above. A dreamy oasis hidden in a world of red sandstone. The pool was carved out of a natural cavity in the ancient streambed. A nearby spring seeped purified water from bottom folds of the canyon. Seeps became drops. Drops became trickles. Gravity transformed them into a gentle flow that meandered along the eons-old riverbed. Gradually, it joined other seepages until it became a crystal-clear stream. Along the way, it collected into slight depressions to form pools. Truly an Eden. A soft breeze swept lazily along the canyon floor. It rippled the surface, forming opaque reflections of the cobalt sky. They enjoyed lunch on the shady shoreline.

After their meal, she removed her hiking boots, then her sweaty socks, and waded into shallow water. Howie joined her a minute later. The sandy bottom massaged their feet. Chilly water refreshed their spirit. Tadpoles materialized. Kika was fixated on the tiny black swimmers darting along the bottom. Each step produced a flurry of escapees. Howie snapped two dozen digital photos. He framed Kika in her state of bliss. She reveled in the simplest of delights. They waded to a natural bench on the opposite shore. Tadpoles approached their toes. The young creatures grew slightly larger each day. When pools vanished in years of drought, dried corpses became crispy critters for those next in the food chain. Likely a leopard lizard or a gopher snake.

Howie stared into macabre reflections rippling the surface. He pondered the use of still water as a mirror. "How do you think the Ancient Ones reacted to seeing their reflection? Was it a mystical experience? When did they begin using mica, or schist, as a mirror?" Kika hunched her shoulders. She savored her rapture and remained quiet. Her eyes floated over the oasis and peered at a sandstone outcrop. Fractures revealed numerous cracks. Like a womb, one crack delivered forth the twisted trunk of a dwarf cottonwood. Exposed roots clung for dear life like multiple umbilical cords. The trunk knotted and twisted around itself so many times that it dipped into the pooled water. Battered by ageless winds and torrents of flash floods, it grew in scarred and irregular spurts. It distinguished itself, misshapen and imperfect as it was, as a timeless beauty. Remarkably, it gave birth each spring to bright green leaves. The color brought balance to the red landscape and blue sky. Kika recognized that. She herself felt in harmony, in *hozho*.

They emerged from the water and stood on the bank. Then Howie filtered water from the pool to replenish their hydration bladders. "Since we'll hike separately this afternoon, we need to be very precise with our orientation," he said, unfolding the USGS topographic map for Cedar Mesa. "Just in case. We have no cell phone service down here. It'll be us against the elements." He placed both hands on her shoulders and gave her a serious look. "Are you still up for going it alone?"

She nodded. "Only if you promise me one thing. You stick to observing. No Marine war games, Mr. Parker. Promise?"

"Yes, dear." He fought the urge to grin. "Now, we'd better get started. If you see those suspicious-looking men, stay hidden from view. If your paths actually cross, nod politely, keep your eyes peeled, and keep walking fast. You've got your new little Guardian, right?" She nodded. He referred to her birthday gift of a NAA .32 ACP Guardian. A small handgun designed for up close and personal protection. The small weapon packed a lot of power.

"It's in my little holster. Top compartment of my backpack. I can reach it in seconds." She grinned at her own version of a Navajo-British dialect, pantomiming it during her response. "Only to defend myself, of course."

He removed his sunglasses and pointed to the map with the temple piece. "Now, back to the map. We're right here at this bend. You should hike southeast toward its mouth. I'll hike in the opposite direction toward the head. Then I'll scale up and cross over to Snow Flat Canyon, where the action is. You stick to Owl Creek. We'll do our job for the BLM," he lied, "we'll observe like mad all afternoon." He patted his high-powered 10x40 monocular. It was secure in its own sheath. His shirt pocket held a special "doubler" magnifier lens. It attached to the nitrogen-filled monocular in seconds, thus eliminating the need to schlep a bulky spotting scope. Kika was less high-tech. She complemented their backcountry needs with basic necessities. She unzipped the top of her backpack and displayed compact 8x35 powered binoculars. They nestled next to her Guardian.

His tone rang like a commando. "Alright, then, it's 1:00. We'll meet up at 4:30. No later, no exceptions." They embraced and kissed. A minute later, they set off in opposite directions, turning around only once until they were out of each other's sight.

ELEVEN

The canyon narrowed and closed in on Howie. Kika's journey saw the canyon widen as she approached its mouth. Howie's terrain was extreme, spiked with dense foliage and huge boulders. He contended with dozens of cascading ledges formed by ancient waterfalls. They were spaced every 100 feet or so. Most of them formed layered steps, some formed neck-high walls. He scaled both with ease. Such hazards sabotaged a steady hiking cadence.

The further he hiked, the worse it became. He bushwhacked through prickly underbrush and dense tamarisk with a short machete. He watched closely for snakes. Once their metabolism balanced in morning sunlight, some retreated to the kind of moist, dense foliage to which he was headed. Others slithered beneath ledges or into crags in the canyon's sunnier mouth. He looked before each step. Although venomous snakes were not a major threat on the Mesa, they made an occasional appearance. He knew that if he didn't step on one, he'd probably avoid being fanged.

Kika hiked two miles down the canyon. Preceding its mouth, narrow slot canyons formed a series of labyrinths. An eerie feeling seized her. Thursday night's trauma left lesions of fear as she trudged past the dark sandstone passages. They bred opportunities for ambush. Instead of feeling wholesome and exuberant in the environment she loved, she succumbed to anxiety. Images of the savagely beaten backpacker haunted her. So did stories of the disappearance of Dietrich Schisslenberg fifty-plus years ago. "His body could be stashed anywhere in here," she mumbled. "I wish Howie hadn't told me about those articles."

Her mind played tricks. High cliffs closed in like a vise. She felt stifled, even claustrophobic. A seldom-opened memory vault sprung its hinges. Out jumped images of her horrifying ride on I-40 to the adoption center. New demons arrived every second. They swept out of subsidiary canyons like apparitions. "I'm a failure. As a woman and as a mother," she declared. "It's been years   and I've never really processed my feelings. I can't bear the guilt any longer. It's like self-flagellation. I've never even opened up to a counselor or a close friend. Heck, Luciana's my best friend and I slammed the door on her during our drive to Kayenta."

She descended into gloom's abyss. Her shoulders drooped. "Back then, I toughed it out as a teen runaway. I bragged about being the last bastion of self-reliance. I was resilient. Now I'm twenty-five. It's time to take out the scalpel and dissect my feelings. Ugh! Introspection."

The concept stung like a scorpion. "Why am I talking out loud? And to whom? These canyon walls? Are they listening?" She studied the smooth, rich sandstone cliffs. "Good God, what if *this* is the very canyon where that woman was beaten? How could she be so stupid as to befriend strangers out in the wild? Oh, walls, do *you* hold the secret? Can you tell me what happened? If only you could speak to me!" She ranted like a beggar pleading for scraps.

She advanced her pace, kicking stones in her path like a pouting child. They shot like bullets. Each kick released pent-up anger. Mid-afternoon shadows darkened the cliffs. Mineral-based leeching, called desert varnish, ran down like dark tears. Begrudgingly, the porous sandstone *did* inhale her pain. Seconds later, it expunged her guilt back in the form of haunting echoes, making her angrier. "Quit talking that way to me. I've carried this crap long enough!"

After another loud outcry, her guilt burst like a ruptured appendix. She trembled before shame's curtain. It was a scary place, a barren battlefield littered with skeletons from her past. Scattered about was a broken heart and a tiny wrapped bundle portraying her baby. They were suspended in a hologram before her eyes. Suddenly, the screech of a playful killdeer shattered her, sending chills down her spine. "That's my baby girl screaming for me."

She broke, dropping to her knees, trembling and crying uncontrollably. After several minutes, a dim ray of light shone from afar. Afternoon sunrays streamed down the canyon and filled her space. She stepped into the sunlight. A mood-altering enzyme, better than any drug, boosted her outlook. "I won't be haunted by guilt any longer." Triumph rang through the air. "*I* chose to flee my drunken mom. *I* chose not to abort my baby. *I* chose not to face teen motherhood. *I* chose to go it alone and not accept help. No one did it to me. *I chose my own path.* I must accept the consequences."

A tear formed in each eye. At age twenty-five, Kika Edison Windsong finally forgave herself. She claimed her past. "I must move on with my life, become a wholesome and enduring partner to Howie Parker." A lump swelled in her throat. Tears of joy became rivulets. They streamed down her cheeks like desert varnish on the cliffs. It felt good. Serenity swept in on a gentle breeze. Old wounds opened wide and expelled the past. Cells began to heal.

Alacrity returned to her gait. She shouted gleefully. A melodious tempo echoed in the canyon. Forgiving Cedar Mesa sandstone welcomed her back. She sang joyously. "Tsailie, my little girl, please forgive me. I love you and I pray that you are well. I release you to live a free and happy life. I know there's more work to do, more healing ahead. But for now, we can both be free. My next step is to confess to another person. A Navajo. Uncle Lenny? And then to my love, to Howie. Ugh, I dread the thought."

Her watch read 3:12 pm. She felt courageous and adventurous. She studied the map and devised a quick side trip to peek at Inner Ruin. She was compelled to observe *someone,* to confirm or disconfirm the hubbub over suspicious looking men. "Heck, a whole day has gone by. All we have left is tomorrow. We can't go home empty-handed. What a drag that'd be." She reached the summit and checked her bearings. Bears Ears stood to her northwest. Snow Flat Canyon lay a quarter mile away. Cliff rose sweetened the atmosphere. It matched her gaiety.

After ten steps, a flashy color caught her eye. It extended from an outcrop of sagebrush. Not sagebrush growing naturally, but dead branches piled high to conceal something. Or someone. She dropped to all fours and inched closer. It was a rope, a standard, multicolored 10.4mm climbing rope. A camouflaged object lay beyond the end of the rope. It was deep purple, like a giant eggplant. She slipped her Guardian from its holster and crawled forward, poking at it with a stick. Then she grabbed hold of it and dragged the heavy mass toward her. It was a large backpack, big enough for a week's gear. The colorful rope was looped to a carabiner.

She slid the pack within reach and scanned the horizon. "Maybe your owner ventured off to explore. Left you behind to lighten the load. I've done that plenty of times. But I've always left a subtle mark in the landscape so I could find it easily later, not covered it haphazardly. Something's not right, someone went to great lengths to hide this. If a rodent hadn't dragged out the rope, I'd have never seen it."

Fidgety, she knelt down to inspect it, grateful it was a backpack and not another body. The thought of who it might belong to made her nauseous. She unzipped the main compartment and the scent of a woman wafted out. She dug deeper and pulled out two pairs of women's underwear. A minute later, she found what she was looking for. The woman's I.D. The name read Marianne Lofty. She tucked the I.D. into her shorts, returned the backpack to where she'd found it and covered it hastily. She marked a cross on her map, formulating plans for her and Howie to scramble to cell phone range the second she returned. Blue Sky and Quirk *had* to know. She gained momentum. "If I rush, I'll have just enough time to observe Inner Ruin and meet Howie on time."

HOWIE arrived at their rendezvous early. Reconnaissance during his afternoon hike produced no signs of looters, thugs, or horror-film-looking characters. He pledged to make tomorrow different. He'd set his alarm for 3:00 am. No idyllic lunch at an oasis, no lollygagging. They had to get to the bottom of the reports filed by other hikers. Were scary-looking men pillaging Inner Ruin?

50 yards to his left stood a knoll. It rose 100 feet above the surroundings. He climbed to the top to gain cell coverage and watch for Kika. He aimed his device toward Blanding. Luckily, there was a moderate signal. First he listened to three voice messages. All three left by Wheeler. He called him immediately. Wheeler was still on his petroglyphs outing. He avoided calling Quirk. They were, after all, not to set foot in canyons east of Highway 261.

He phoned Officer Blue Sky, the officer who'd taken their statements at the Kayenta Health Center early Friday morning. He figured he had every right to check up on the beaten woman. The phone rang five times and then shifted to a different pitch. Two rings later, a very pleasant voice greeted him, a woman's voice whose English toted a strong Navajo accent. Sentences formed a melodic ring.

"Is this an emergency?" Sweet Voice asked.

"No, ma'am, this is *not* an emergency. I'm calling to check on something." He looked up to see if Kika had approached. "Or some*one*, I mean. My name is Howie Parker. We brought that Jane Doe into the Kayenta emergency room late Thursday night. The woman was severely beaten."

"Yes," her pleasant Navajo voice rang.

"Do you have news of her condition? Was she transferred to Flagstaff? Is she OK?"

A long pause. "Could you state your name again, please?" Politeness harmonized with a vocal dance. Howie was certain she doubled as a telemarketer.

He tugged four syllables from his mouth. "Howie Parker. I brought the victim in with my girlfriend, Kika Windsong, and her cousin, Luciana Jim." A lip-reader could have translated.

"Yes, I got that. Please hold. I'll have someone else speak to you. Officer Blue Sky is not available." A lifetime passed. Still no Kika. Finally, Sweet Voice returned. Her prose rang poetically. But not her message.

"Mr. Parker? Where are you now? Can you come into Kayenta headquarters? We'd like to speak to you in person."

"Madam," he said as politely as impatience allowed, "I'm deep in the canyons of Cedar Mesa. I climbed onto a knoll. I'm lucky to have cell service. I won't return to Kayenta until Monday morning. I can come in then. Please just tell me what condition that woman is in."

"She's dead."

Her words dropped like a guillotine. His day came to an abrupt end. His neck twitched. Wind whistled through the phone cupped against his ear. "Please hold, I have another call."

Howie froze to the knoll like a deep-rooted oak. The once-hardened Marine and Operation Desert Storm veteran felt his rage overshadowed by empathy, even a tinge of compassion toward the victim and her family. "She died early this morning," she continued. "Severe head trauma and internal bleeding." Despite her melodic cadence, the words tore through him like a barrage of verbal bullets fired in slow motion, single-action to intensify the pain. A second round came sooner than expected. "For all intents and purposes, I'm told, she was kicked to death."

After several hoarse attempts, words finally scraped out. "Then… it's murder, right?"

"I can't answer that. But Officer Blue Sky left the name and number of someone to call. He has all the details. Perhaps he could help you." He felt the blow coming. This time, they wouldn't be small bullets. It would be huge cannon shot propelled into his gut. "It's a contact number of a federal agent in charge of the case. Navajo Nation Police are cooperating to the fullest extent, *but he's the man in charge.*"

"I'll bet he is," Howie ridiculed. He held his phone at arm's length and sneered into the canyon. Kika was still nowhere in sight. Howie Parker, adventurer extraordinaire, ex-Marine gifted with brilliant "Situational Intelligence," had been duped again.

Her Navajo accent continued. "Are you ready to write this down? His name is W. Coldditz, and his number is…"

"I know his number," he yelled angrily. "You're the second person in as many days to give it to me. Forget it. No one even knows who he is! No one besides Quirk has even met him, for Christ's sake. He's Mr. Mystery Man. Yet, somehow, he's the bozo in charge. Doesn't make sense. I'll call Dudley later when I'm back in cell range. Thank you for your time." His thumb reached the end call button. "Oh, wait, wait," he blurted. He listened closely. They were still connected. He felt slightly ashamed. "Ah, look, I'm sorry I'm so bitter. You've done no harm, you're just doing your job. I'm awfully confused right now. And very angry. Can I ask one more question? Could you tell me the victim's name?"

"I'm still here," she said in her mild-mannered Navajo ring. Despite his pepper-hot assault, her voice disarmed further confrontation. "Name's Lofty, Marianne Lofty. Poor thing. Only 31. Her mother and fiancé arrive in Flagstaff tonight. Blue Sky's there to

89

get their statement. Anything else I can do for you?" But Howie had already flattened the lid with his thumb.

"Well, I'll be damned," he shouted into the wind. "I'll show that mystery dick a thing or two. I'll call everyone's fat-assed bluff and phone that SOB right now." He stared through his monocular up Snow Flat Canyon. No sight of Kika. His watch read 4:35. "Damn! She's late again. She's got no sense of real time. Only Indian time."

He punched in Agent Coldditz's number with angry force. The signal transmitted to a ground station compatible with Parker's cell service. Because the call was directed to the super-secret National Security Agency, satellite telephony took over and facilitated the switching function instead of a ground station. An encrypted frequency reached into outer space and found a low, earth-orbiting satellite. It processed the signal and then transmitted it to a secret communications satellite circling the globe 700 miles above earth. That orbiting spy in the sky relayed it via extra-high frequency to a top-secret ground station facility, which, in turn, transmitted it to a microwave antenna located atop a two-story brownstone in a respectable neighborhood of Baltimore, Maryland. The antenna handed it over to nanotech software inside. The facility was known to a select few as "The Annex." An elite corps called it "Brownie."

An array of data instantly identified Parker's global positioning coordinates. They were relayed to nano "chipboards." The ultra-sensitive device listened intently to Parker's angered breathing at the convergence of Owl Creek and Snow Flat Canyons. It also recorded wind gusts on Cedar Mesa and displayed vital atmospheric conditions. Each sound wave was digitally updated in real time. If the call represented a national security threat, it would be targeted for an initiative. Deployment would occur in less than eight minutes.

Then the "chipboards" routed his call to complex software within a Cray supercomputer. There, it diverged in circuitous routes through a digital voice analyzer. Total lapsed time between Parker's thumb depressions and the mainframe's software was 7.2 seconds. If instructed, a National Security Space Office satellite could have positioned itself to relay life-sized images of Howie Parker's angry antics. Because he was a veteran, voice recognition software identified his "vocal signature" immediately.

Howie chalked off the minor delay to calling via cell from remote Cedar Mesa. Wendell Coldditz's phone rang. After four short rings, Parker was greeted by an automated voice. It sounded more authentic than most humans did. "You have reached Mr. Wendell Coldditz, agent for the US Department of Homeland Security. Please state your full name and the purpose of your call. Mr. Coldditz, or a senior assistant, will return your call within five minutes." Howie had no clue of Coldditz's true employer or rank. Wheeler had told him Coldditz was a transferee from BLM's Salt Lake City office. But Homeland Security?

"My name is…" He dictated a short message. "That's it? That's all it takes to contact the mystery man? What kind of garbage is Quirk feeding us about a BLM affiliation? Whoever he is, he has no idea how frustrated I am. No idea I'm out here in the boonies waiting five minutes for him to return my call!" He clamored down the knoll. Agents viewing satellite imagery inside The Annex enjoyed a good laugh.

KIKA reached the rim of Snow Flat Canyon. She stared across at Inner Ruin. A large overhang protected ancient villagers from summer's heat and trapped winter's solar gain. She squatted low and inched along the slickrock. Then she slid over the rounded edge and carefully landed on a ledge eight feet below. She crawled behind a centuries-old juniper tree. Next to it grew a large pinion, a pillar of its species. It was over 400 years old, but its bark looked even more ancient. A reflection startled her. She squinted. "There, again, shining straight toward me." Her heart pounded. "A rifle? Crap!" She slithered behind the giant pinion. "There it is again. Holy godfather, it's a man." She raised her binoculars.

Her watch read 3:55. She realized that if there was anything to observe, it had better happen fast. She'd be late no matter how fast she high-tailed it back. Peering through her binoculars, she scanned the cliff village. "Ah ha, there you are. Who are you?" A man stood next to a crumbled masonry wall, one of few in that state. Dark dress pants, muscular build and a head of light, sandy-colored hair. She dialed the focus. "What's with your bizarre face? And that thing in your mouth. A tooth?" She panned sideways to the school bus-sized boulder. It rested precariously close to the edge. "Wow, what the heck's keeping that from toppling over?"

The next sight left her breathless. A figure emerged from behind the boulder and strode to Inner Ruin. She studied him until he disappeared. A distance of two football fields separated them. Plus a 300-foot chasm to the canyon floor. Still, Kika was petrified. The man's shoulders widened like the deck of an aircraft carrier. His head was grotesquely misshapen, like the stump Howie used to split firewood. He wore khaki slacks and a knit shirt. Granite-like muscles bulged from the soft material. But one feature stood out more than a nun in a whorehouse - a crop of snowy-white hair as unkempt and shaggy as a bleached mop head. Her lips pursed in a show of

91

recognition. Her head nodded. "Uh-huh, got ya dialed in, know who you are!"

She surveyed the cliffs surrounding the ruin. "Bingo, there you are too. Just what I'd hoped to find." She stared at a series of natural hand and foot holds running up a seam in the sandstone. They led to the ledge above. They were followed by another set leading up the fractured cliff to the canyon rim. Rounded depressions, pecked by the Ancient Ones, enabled villagers to scale the sheer cliff. They were sometimes referred to as "Anasazi holds." She was ecstatic.

She tucked the binoculars next to her Guardian and made a crucial getaway before being spotted. It was 4:10. She'd be late for sure. Howie hated that. Always blamed it on Indian time. She raced along the canyon floor, jubilant, having observed what she came for. The first day of observations wasn't wasted after all. But Kika Windsong knew something was out of place with what she'd seen. The scene was too good, almost staged. Freaky as they looked, they acted too normal. Like tourists, or pretending to be. And she knew there was no mistaking a man with snowy white hair.

She raced ahead like a horse to stable, chuckling at Howie's reference to "horsetail" last night. He hadn't called her that for a long time. But it worked, oh how it worked! So did her reference to *his* horse-like feature. She licked her lips and picked up her pace.

TWELVE

"But I'm telling you, it *was* them." The gavel fell hard. Her voice rose loud. Kika Windsong, judge presiding over Cedar Mesa's outdoor court, sternly handed down a verdict of GUILTY. Howie's face was positioned only two feet away. It was a blip on their relationship radar. She rarely raised her voice at him. "Remember the near-dead woman's icy lips billowing in your ear?"

Howie stepped back and asserted himself. He stood his ground. He insisted that since the two men weren't excavating or pillaging, they weren't doing anything illegal. At most, nosing around Inner Ruin without a permit. But lots of tourists did that, unfortunately. He remained non-argumentative while attempting to paint in his mind the scene she had viewed through her binoculars. He couldn't tell her. Not yet. Couldn't admit they were acting against strict orders.

Kika stood her ground too. She repeated her plea, scraping her foot in the sand in frustration. "Who else could it be? There's no mistaking a monster man with blizzard-white hair!"

He finally got it, snapping out of the stupor induced by Sweet Voice's morbid news; and Coldditz not returning his call. "OK, OK, I get it, I see what you're saying. It's just that we have to be absolutely certain before calling in a response team. We can't just call because you saw two men, respectably dressed, one with white hair. We have to catch them red-handed, digging stuff up, stealing and destroying archaeological materials. Then we'll call for help." A second later, he delivered the blow, reiterating what the dispatcher had told him. He looked her square in the eyes. "For all intents and purposes, the woman was kicked to death. Dispatcher's words exactly."

The news hit Kika like a freight train. She gasped in horror. "Good God, now it's murder!" Tears formed. Neither one spoke. She bent down and plucked a sprig of sagebrush. Howie caught a whiff of its pungent aroma. She held it in front of her and slowly turned clockwise, pausing at the four cardinal directions. She spoke softly in her native tongue, casting smaller sprigs to the wind. Strong gusts carried them aloft. She looked beyond the canyon to the dusty mesa. It was a land that spawned many whirlwinds. The jagged spine of Comb Ridge filled her view. It matched her mood. The transition from verdant canyon flora to barren badlands was as shocking as the news. "She never had a chance, did she? I mean, what we did just prolonged her agony, didn't it? Damn, those creeps kicked the life right out of her." Her tears streamed through the canyon dirt on her face. It resembled "war paint." She was prepped for battle. She turned to face Howie. "Did the dispatcher tell you her name?" He nodded. "Could it be Marianne Lofty? Is that right?"

Howie's jaw dropped. "What the heck? How'd you know?" She told him about discovering the woman's backpack. Fury pierced his fiery eyes. His demeanor was hotter than a foundry furnace.

"What?" she yelled. "What's that look in your eyes?" She stepped back, arms akimbo. "You'd better not be, Howie Parker. You better not be planning revenge before we call the authorities. I'll hike straight out of here if you are. Immediately. I'll leave. I mean it! It's not your job. Let Quirk and the Feds handle it. The only involvement I want from you is this, promise me you'll protect me no matter what. That you'll keep that scary giant far away. I don't want him within a thousand feet of me. I'm serious, Howie. Promise?"

"Yes, dear," he said, rather patronizingly. "Come on, now. Let's clear out and work our way over to Snow Flat Canyon. I remember an observation point where we can remain hidden, double-check what you observed earlier." They secured their backpacks and hiked up the canyon, searching for a route to the rim. A fierce wind raced toward them and thundered past like a fast moving train, eerily screeching as it sped away. Kika listened to its moan, the sound of a spirit crying out in despair. The wind calmed. She felt a vacuum. Shuddering, she whispered, *"The Wind People."*

The sun slipped below the rim. Shadows sprang like bandits poised to ambush them. The temperature dropped ten degrees. Canyon colors changed quickly from rich sandstone to blood red as though an artist had suddenly switched palettes. It cast a haunting mood. She hooked her arm through Howie's and told him about the prehistoric climbing holds she'd observed.

"They'll come in handy. I believe there's an amphitheater ledge above and slightly east of Inner Ruin. It'll make an ideal observation post. Huge boulders calved off the cliff eons ago. We'll use them as cover. Our line of sight will be awesome. We'll spy on them without them seeing up to us. Acoustics are superb in amphitheaters. Bet we'll hear every word. We'll approach before dawn."

"Were here to observe," she said, not realizing it was *Howie's* mandate, *not* Quirk's or Wheeler's. "So, by God, observe is what we'll do. From as close as we can safely approach. We'll have something with real muscle when we call the authorities."

"3:00 am it is, then. I'll set the alarm. We'll cover the two-mile hike by moonlight and stars. There'll be enough natural light that we won't need headlamps. The moon's full in three nights and won't set until 4:15 am. We'll arrive at the north rim and descend to our perch like master ninjas."

Their stride was fearless and determined. They were an eighth of a mile from the rim. A compass was unnecessary. Bears Ears was in sight. Howie's S. I. quotient gifted him with remarkable sight fidelity. Indispensable in the backcountry. He could return like a migratory species to previously visited locations. The Corps loved him. Sight fidelity sensors directed him accurately every time, without radar or GPS devices. They had observed Inner Ruin twice during the past three years. In minutes, they'd arrive within ten feet of his destination.

A nonpoisonous bull snake slithered across their trail. It sought a hideout for its crepuscular activities as daylight dimmed. Soon it would secure a guarded post to preserve its cold-blooded metabolism. Then the nocturnal hunt would begin. He held up a hand for Kika to stop. She slowed to a tiptoe and stood next to him. She saw the snake. It saw them. She looked away.

"It's a beauty," said Howie. He watched the pale mustard and black reptile disappear into the brush. "I wish everyone would respect snakes. They're not aggressive unless they feel threatened, you know. Whenever I hike in snake habitat, I begin with a short affirmation. It acts as my passport. It's like asking permission to enter their range. It goes like this: *This is your territory, not mine. I'm the guest here, not you. Your space is blessed. I respect you and all your poisonous cousins in this, your soil. I ask your permission to safely share your space. I mean you no harm. I will try not to offend you. You are a precious being."*

They stood in silence. Before Howie moved to the Southwest, there was a time when he would have drawn his pistol and shot that, or any snake, dead on the spot. Not so after working closely with Natives out in their rugged terrain. After a moment, Kika stepped closer and touched his arm. She reached up and kissed him. Her lips were chapped and salty from the outdoors. "Honey, did you know I dreamt about a snake last night?"

"It's time you told me more about your dream."

"Yes, I know. I wrote it in my journal. We haven't had time to talk. Our lunch at the oasis was too idyllic to talk about it. Tonight by the campfire, OK? But I will say this. I dreamt you held a large rattlesnake high above your head. Your other hand gripped your gun. After a while, you set the snake on the ground and vaulted back ten feet. End of scene. Weird, huh? And Wheeler, that was also strange. He was in the middle of nowhere standing in piles of shattered glass. On a highway with shiny blacktop." She looked down at the ground and stirred her foot. "I don't like those images, Howie. And I didn't like the tone of that wind roaring through the canyon several minutes ago. The Wind People, I swear."

95

He started to speak, but his phone rang. It shocked him. He slung his backpack to the ground. "What the heck? Had no idea we were in range. I'd packed it away. Might be Coldditz." The display said otherwise. It was Quirk. He let it go to voicemail, knowing he couldn't fake their exact whereabouts with Kika standing next to him. It pained him. He wanted answers. Who was Coldditz anyway? Why were they ordered to stay out of Snow Flat Canyon? He lied to Kika. "It was Quirk. I'm not speaking to her until we reach the rim and confirm or disconfirm what you observed an hour ago. I'll call her from camp tonight."

What greeted them at canyon's edge was cataclysmic. 150 yards across from where they crouched, Mac's unscrupulous enterprise was in full swing. Shovels, picks and dozens of lidded crates lined the plaza close to the room blocks.

"I'll set the alarm for 3:00 am."

THIRTEEN

"Well, slap my face, man. It's hotter than hell itself. And this frigging sun, I'd just as soon shoot it out of the sky." Buzz's eyes were ablaze. They were puffy and watered profusely. The "whites" were beet-red. He'd been squinting all day. The flaming hot sun had gotten to him, just as Jed had warned. All because he wore cheap sunglasses. He had picked them off a stiff in Cleveland.

At 5:00 pm Saturday, Jed decided they'd waited long enough. They stood outside the motel in 100-degree heat. Buzz paced back and forth, cursing the West and its dry, dusty air. The taxi arrived. Buzz's irritableness grew hostile. Then lethal. Preconditioned to terminal judgment, his trigger finger twitched. He climbed in and sat behind the driver. Before he reset the meter, Buzz accosted him, swearing and yelling loudly, accusing him of being an illegal alien. He went ballistic, shouting more profanities and threatening to kill him. He called him every sick, ethnic slur imaginable. Jed restrained his lunatic partner from firing through the backseat into the driver's back. The taxi had no air-conditioning. Its fan motor burned up during the last fare. Buzz blamed the driver. He swore he'd waste him one way or the other. A pistol pummeling or outright execution when they arrived at Gordy's shop. He tunneled the barrel of his semiautomatic into the driver's neck. Jed seized the moment before blood splattered the windshield. He handed the driver a wad of cash and forced him to pull over immediately. The man sped off before the doors were shut.

They walked the last quarter mile to Gordy's. "I told you the other day, man, you could take all of dirty Farmington and wipe it right off the map. No one would ever miss it. I'll take clean Cleveland any day. Hate it here. Place is good for nothing. Junk heaps for cars, rundown pickup trucks, ugly trailers for houses. Why do people live like this? Everything's the same damned dirty brown color. Pisses me off. I'm itching to pull the trigger. Shoulda wasted that wetback driver. Now I'll pop the first Western dude that looks me sideways." He fingered a passing motorist. "Dude's lucky I didn't shoot him. New slant on drive-by shootings. Like that?"

"Drop it, you wacko. You forget to take your meds or something? Why are you crazier than usual?" He noticed a bulge above Buzz's ankle. He reckoned it was a .32 caliber. "Why are you toting a third piece? We're in the city for Christ's sake. If Krenecke didn't do the truck right, *I'll* take care of him, not you. That's the way Mac wants it. Save your guns for the desert, got it?"

"Well, slap my face, man. Who put you in charge of my guns? Told you all along I'd handle that Polak if I felt like it. You're just a driver, that's all. I'm the hired gun. Beats your silly-ass rank. None of your business how much heat I pack."

"Your job starts in the desert, not in the city. This is my turf. The truck's my job. Settle down before you louse things up. Another thing, if you think Farmington's an inferno, wait until you're posted in the desert. Most hellish place you ever been. No real shade out there either. Sagebrush mostly, a few scrubby trees... and rattlesnakes. Lots of them. Upwards of 105 degrees. It'll kill a man if he ain't prepared. Told you already, you need a hat over that fuzzy pear head of yours. Sun'll bake your retarded brains like stew." He sneered in Buzz's face.

Buzz turned to face him. "Shut up, you Pittsburgh flunky. You talk about my head like that once more and I'm taking you out. Don't care who you are. He slid his hand to his holster. "You know how much I hate this dirty hellhole. Never figured it'd be like this."

"Listen to me, you nut job. You'll regret you ever threatened me. `Take me out`, huh?" He stabbed his fingers into Buzz's chest. His sternum thudded. They stood 200 feet east of Krenecke's. "Forget Vegas. When this is over, you and I are going to settle this score." His lips stretched razor thin. His words cut just as deeply. "You'll never make it back to Cleveland alive."

"Well, slap my face, man. I ain't scared of you. I warned you the other day. Don't care who I kill or what I kill. I'll shoot at anything that moves weird. Don't care if it's you, Whitey, coyotes or snakes. Got that?" He spit through a slit separating his two front teeth.

A five-pound hocker landed on Jed's boot. They could have had it out right then and there, but Jed was used to Mob infighting. He insulated himself from petty bullshit. He was a team player. He committed himself to Mac's scheme. He'd never let him down. Mostly, he needed fast money to stay alive. He let it ride, vowing, however, to kill the sleazebag later. "Come on, we're early, let's catch Gordy off guard."

But Krenecke was ready. He led Jed to a glass-enclosed cubicle. Buzz stood guard 20 feet away. They scoured Mac's modification blueprints, comparing them with "as-built" drawings prepared by Krenecke's engineer. They emerged from their meeting and circled the truck. Jed was alarmed at its overall height. It was overkill, far too extreme. Next, he crawled beneath it and inspected the rebuilt suspension. A minute later, they took it for a test drive.

Buzz turned to the rag-faced mechanic. His eyes invaded her work bay. She was as unkempt as on Friday. The work day was over. Other mechanics lined up at the time clock. A pink ribbon was pinned to her grease-stained calendar. Pink magnets clung to her tool chest. Her mother had died four weeks earlier from breast cancer. He donned a cocky grin and stalked the woman the way a hyena would an injured wildebeest. "How's it going there, my little prissy?" You got a name or should I call you 'my little prissy'?"

She thought if she kept it brief, the conversation would end. "Name's Trixie. I'm not your little prissy!"

"Ooh, a feisty one, eh? Bet you'll be a bundle of fun when I squeeze you in my arms, little prissy. I got wild fantasies about you and me." Her sourpuss face closed like a sea anemone. She turned her back. "Go ahead and turn your back. I like the tender backside of my little prissy. You did say Trixie, didn't you? As in tricks?" He slithered to within inches of her. "I'm good at pulling tricks. Do it all the time, especially when I'm ready to blow someone away." He sneered. It was his best attempt at a smile.

Trixie murmured beneath her breath, wrinkles converging into lugubrious creases.

"See you got pink ribbons all around," he added with as much couth as the steel I-beams above. "Pink's my favorite color. Cleveland's lap-dancing bimbettes wear pink thongs. All young teens where I hang out. The younger they are, the pinker they are." His words slurred through drool pooled in the corners of his mouth. He grinned, then snaked a massive tongue out of its cave and lapped up the sickening excretion.

Trixie gagged. "You pig, that's the ugliest tongue I've ever seen." She turned away in disgust.

He got off on her tone. "And I use pink condoms too. Got one right here. Wanna see?" She gagged as if to vomit. "Got a better idea. How'd you like to take a little road trip? Come along with me and my flunky driver. Get to know each other real cozy-like." He humped the air with thrusting hips.

"Not interested, mister. I'd never go anywhere with a jerk like you. My uncle wouldn't let me."

"Oh?" His lips bent into a twisted smirk. "Bet I could convince him otherwise." Predator Buzz was in his zone. He loved it when women first said "no." He was a pro at preying on vulnerable women. Trixie fit that profile. She'd be an easy trophy.

"By the way, name's Buzz. I hate 'mister.' Don't rush off there, my little prissy, not just yet. Need you around until your uncle and my partner return. You're collateral."

He patted the inside of his thigh with his left hand, below the crotch, and then slid it up until he gripped his penis through his pants. His right hand gripped his holster. His eyes were crazed. He tried a smile on for size. It didn't fit. Trixie was totally invaded. She prayed for the madman's charade to end. She prayed harder for the return of her uncle. Two minutes passed. Buzz's hand still covered his crotch.

The truck arrived. The men jumped from the cab and circled the truck. Inspection passed. The tracking device went undetected.

"It'll work for Mac, so it'll work for me," he told Gordy. "I'm the one driving this rig. Color matches perfect too. Here's your five grand." They shook hands and walked toward Buzz. Jed sensed trouble. The air was tense, like he'd stepped on a landmine and could step no further.

"Plans have changed, boys," Buzz said, withdrawing a Walther 9mm. The model was a double automatic packing 24 rounds. The lunatic placed his arm around Trixie's waist. "This here's Trixie, Jed, and she's decided to join us. Wants to be my companion, take a road trip through the desert. See the sights, you know. Get real close to me. *Real close.* Catch my drift? The kind I've been hankering after for days." A sick grin smeared his face. The barrel of his Walther penetrated her side, below the rib cage. It was a superb weapon. He never messed around with lesser guns.

Jed's lips quivered in anger. His neck burst from its collar, the veins resembling rope. His face was a shade of lava. "Shut up, Buzz. Quit talking smack. What're you talking about? You crazy? I'm running this show, not you."

"Well, slap my face, man. You're right, I'm not running the show. *But this is.*" He brandished the 9mm in full view. "You seem to forget, I'm the one with gun power here." All life drained from his hostage's face. "She's coming along, whether you want her to or not. Maybe we should call it like it is, Krenecke's performance bond, his personal guarantee that all his fancy shop work holds up after we drive out of here. You know, protect Mac's 10K investment. If things go well, we'll drop her on the side of the highway. Next week." He thrust his hand over her pubic area. "Like I said, been itching for some nice, soft companionship. Haven't had me a woman since I arrived in this dusty hellhole." He twisted like a snake and pressed his body against hers. His crotch bonded to her hip. Their hips moved to the rhythm of a hula dancer. "I need me a woman. She'll do just fine. Bet she hasn't had a *real* man like me in a long, long time. Maybe never."

"For Christ's sake, you moron, come to your senses. What the hell's gotten into you today? I'll take you out tonight and buy you a whore. A dozen of them if you want. Any kind of sick fantasies you want. But you're not taking her!"

"Oh, yeah? Well, slap my face, man. I'm doing it." He pressed the Walther into her skull behind the ear.

Jed sprang like a tiger. He stopped one foot short of them. Buzz squeezed Trixie tighter, turned and aimed the gun at Jed's forehead. His expression turned glacial. "Listen here, you demented little prick. Listen to me real good cuz I'm only going to say this once." His words exploded like a cannon. "You're making a big, big mistake. You're a lot dumber than you look. You're downright crazy." Buzz stretched his arm until the gun pressed against Jed's nose. Jed kept right on shouting, nose buried in the barrel. "This isn't going to work, you idiot. You've crossed the line. *Now you're the enemy. You're off the team. I'll kill you.*"

Buzz lurched backward. "Well, slap my face, you flunky driver. You're blind as a bat. Maybe my gun was too close. See it now?"

Jed's face hardened. He hissed like a cobra, head swaying side to side. "I'll give you one last chance. We're part of an outfit. Mac's got big plans. I won't let you louse them up because of your sick dick. If I don't kill you first, I can guarantee that Whitey will. He'll break you in two. Seriously, he'll pick you up, lay you horizontal, raise his knee and slam you down. It'll literally crack you in half. I've watched him do it. I was there, wacko. It was gruesome." Saliva spewed from his mouth. He paused and caught his breath. "Whitey broke the poor bastard in two. Another minute of this craziness and you'll be reckoning with him. That'll be your *dead reckoning*. Don't get croaked over this ugly, rag-faced woman. I've warned you over and over, no snatch until this gig's done!"

"Well, slap my face, man. She's so ugly I find her sexy. I've had enough of your bullshit threats. Now get in the truck and drive us out of here. Hey, Rag Face, get your sweet prissy ass up there too. Krenecke, you stay quiet. You'll get her back someday. If you're lucky."

Gordy sucked in a breath so deep he nearly fainted. He waved the wad of hundreds at Buzz. He dropped to his knees, begging frantically. "Here, take your money back. I don't want it. You can have the first $5,000 too. I still got it, it's in my safe. The job's free. Here, take it, just give me my niece." Perspiration poured out of him. Saliva hardened into goopy mounds on his lips. The gun pressed deeper into Trixie's neck. "Please don't kill her. She's my only niece. She's all I got since I been out of the joint. I promised my sister on her deathbed that I'd always protect her Trixie. Please..."

Buzz's eyes riveted Krenecke's. His snicker had the warmth of a cadaver. "Guess this ain't your lucky day, Pollack. Or your ugly Pollack niece's."

Reality struck Jed. The possibility of a botched job with no cash payoff was beyond comprehension. The Mob'd kill him for sure. Before lowering the tuck's cargo door, he spotted a spool of cable and a twenty-pound winch bar misplaced by a trucker. He tossed them into the cargo box and slammed the door shut. "Might come in handy," he mumbled to himself. As he approached the driver's door, he was seized with a rage so powerful it caught Buzz off guard. Jed used the side of

101

the cargo box as a punching bag and soccer-kicked empty lubricant cans into the walls. Then he saw his prize target. The Pittsburgh Steelhead raced forward at a full sprint into a row of empty 55-gallon drums stacked in a pyramid. He lunged forward and cocked his head back. In midair, his head snapped forward. He hit the drums like a minuteman warhead. The result was a head shot drilled into the top drum. The impact was so harsh it bent the jagged edges inside. He removed his head without a scratch, grinned victoriously and raced toward the truck. Buzz stared in awe through the windshield. Jed raised his arm and brought it forward. The same gesture a ref used to signal first downs in football. He repeated the arm movement and stared Buzz down, leaving no doubt about who his next target would be.

Buzz's head protruded from the window. He sneered. The Walther remained buried in Trixie's neck. "Well, slap my face, man. Quit acting so weird and start the truck. Let's hit the road so me and my little prissy can make up for lost time. She's just itching for me, ain't you, my sweetness?" His left hand snaked onto her thigh. She shrieked. It slithered into her pubic area, moving in slow, circular patterns. His eyes shone crazed and glossy, his finger throbbing one millimeter from the trigger.

Jed climbed aboard and gripped the dashboard with both hands. He turned toward the lunatic gunman, eyes shooting ice daggers. "You and I are done. The second this is over, and I mean the *second* we're done with this job, I'm going to kill you. MAYBE BEFORE." It was a solemn oath. "You're a dead man, Buzz Lane. Heed that oil drum. Hope you watched closely. Next head shot's for you."

"Talk's cheap," Buzz declared. But his tone didn't ring as confidently it had two minutes earlier. Jed's Panzer-tank frame and pile driver head ramming a steel drum affected him. The rumors were true. He saw it with his own eyes. Steelhead Jed was no myth.

Jed started the truck. He had a plan. He rolled down his window. "Hey, Gordy, I promise to keep this horny goon off your niece. I'll bring her back safe and sound. The desert will teach this trigger-happy pervert a thing or two. Once the blazing sun's ripened him good, you'll see pieces fly all the way back to Farmington."

He put it in gear and entered westbound Highway 160. The truck rocked severely from side to side. It was unstably high. Their first stop was Bluff, Utah, below the escarpment of Cedar Mesa.

FOURTEEN

Their alarm shrieked like a dentist's drill, piercing the camper at 3:00 am. They slipped quietly outside into the shadows. Mild 50-degree air welcomed them. A puff of wind swirled powdery grit into their path. Howie held up his hand. She paused. He disappeared and circled camp. Stars twinkled against an ink-colored sky. They were lucky. Earth's celestial clock was in their favor. The moon was nearly full and would shine brightly until ten minutes before the break of dawn, sometime after 4:00 am. Reflections off slickrock appeared like stage lights. Howie counted on enough natural light to arrive unnoticed before scaling down to the observation ledge. They would use headlamps only as a last resort. Operation Desert Storm trained him right. "I think the coast is clear," he said, slithering into view.

She nodded and followed. "The moon looks like half a cantaloupe," she whispered. "It's so close." Tiny ice crystals formed cirrus clouds that stretched across the sky. Winds scattered them into patterns resembling vertebrae. "You're right about no headlamps. This is incredible. The landscape is translucent." The Big Dipper hung overhead in the northwest at a slight angle, pouring its contents into the Little Dipper. The constellation Scorpio, sporting its giant sickle, huddled close to the opposite horizon. Castor and Pollux faded into the northwest. The Milky Way scattered creamy stardust across the heavens, as if waved by a magical wand.

Kika paused and stretched her head back at an impossible angle. She stared at the celestial drama above. Embraced by the cosmos, she felt the totality of things, an order to the universe. She pictured her life span as a split-second blip in space and time. Tiny, but not insignificant. Navajo creation stories filled her imagination. It was a magical time to be outdoors. The connection between earth and its galaxy became transparent. "Our origin myths weave tales about this," she said. "How earth and sky were positioned in an orderly fashion, not thrown together randomly." Howie gave her space. They had a few minutes to spare. It wasn't often she shared Navajo creation stories. He listened closely.

"How First Woman and First Man, with help from Fire Man and impatient Coyote, purposefully placed stars in the sky. How star alignments bearing the names of constellations in this, our fifth world, represent all the laws our people need in order to exist. They are printed in the sky as constellations," she declared, "where everyone can see them. First Woman also said that one man from each generation must learn the laws so he may interpret them for others. And, as he grows old, pass this knowledge on to a younger man. That younger man will then become a teacher of Navajo ways." Howie stared at the heavens above.

"Then one day I heard something I've clung to. I'm not positive if it's truly accepted as Navajo teaching or not. Someone told me that the order of the Dinétah was an interstellar, celestial phenomenon. That it was aligned during creation as a result of peering *through* the universe, *through space and time*, toward earth and not the other way around. That our people are connected to this orderliness. That the Ancient Ones aligned their communities using the wisdom of the Elders. That they considered *terrestrial-scapes*, not just obvious landscapes. Here's the part I really love; *that their perspective, their wisdom, looked inward through the universe toward earth.*" She lowered her head and faced Howie. "I've decided to visit Uncle Lenny as soon as we return. He and I need to talk. I want to learn more, Howie. And I need to ask him the meaning behind all the whirlwinds I've seen lately. How they're connected to recent, rather bizarre events. Everything's connected, you know; there *is* an order to things. He might help me better understand what that order is."

They remained silent. Still night air set an excellent backdrop for their celestial interlude. A minute later, Howie brought her back to reality, reminding her that their feet were still planted firmly on earth. That they had a job ahead of them. "I'm ready when you are." He stepped forward at a comfortable pace. "So, by my estimate, we should arrive at the rim above Inner Ruin at 4:15 am. About the same time the moon sets. The sun won't rise until almost 6:00. As daybreak unfolds, our sight will improve with each minute. We can also use my night scope, of course. I packed infrared goggles too. They might come in handy."

"Sounds fine, Mr. Bond," she said in jest. "But what if those men worked through the night? Or have a guard posted?"

"You're asking a pro. Trust me, we'll be extremely careful. By the way, you meant Q, didn't you?" "He's the one who dispensed newfangled gadgets."

"Just testing."

A southwest bearing was set toward the head of Owl Creek Canyon. Jupiter was ablaze all night, so large that it seemed like another of earth's moons. Once at the canyon's head, they traversed craggy folds and scrambled up to a finger-thin mesa. They reversed direction and hiked toward the mouth of Snow Flat Canyon. "The point above the ancient footholds will become ground zero," he said. "Just in case anything goes wrong, that'll be our benchmark. There's a thick cluster of junipers 50 yards away, toward the limestone ridge. There's a shallow cave there too. If we get separated, hide in it. OK?"

"I don't plan on getting separated."

Howie's sight fidelity negated the use of a GPS device. He was a natural, as if a compass chip was programmed into his DNA. He only used a GPS device at work and nowhere else. It was packed away with his backcountry briefcase. "I studied the cliff above Inner Ruin very closely yesterday. "I've got a pretty reliable means of computing vertical distance through my monocular. I'd say the distance from the rim to the lookout ledge is 21 feet. Then another 27 feet to the cliff dwelling ledge, give or take a foot. Of course, we won't descend to that ledge unless we're required to take matters into our own hands. You still alright without a headlamp?" She nodded.

"My optometrist in Flagstaff has a technical, mumbo-jumbo name for how our eyes automatically adjust to natural light. She's an anthropology nut too. She explained it like this. 'Howie, how many times have you used the phrase "I could do it with my eyes closed?"' She said the phrase isn't used only because people perform repetitive tasks. She claims that, linguistically, it can be traced back thousands of centuries when there was *no* artificial light, that it's in our genes. The human eye adjusts to the available light no matter what, whether it's day or night. Given enough time, our eyes even adjust to pitch darkness. When only *natural* light is available, three-dimensional images are best received by the retina. This hike, Kika, what we're doing right here and now, this unique combination of moonlight and starlight is the zenith of that phenomenon. When a flashlight is turned on, it screws everything up. That's when two-dimensional views come into play. No doubt it's necessary in modern society, but it also changes the nature of the human eye." He wore a proud smile.

"The point I'm trying to make is that the human eye has become less of the organ it used to be, less than it's capable of. Burgeoning urbanism, radical light pollution, excessive exposure to TVs and computer monitors are a few of the culprits. Not to mention depletion of the ozone. The human eye has changed, Kika, with dire consequences for those in the backcountry."

"Quite interesting, Howie. But you want to know something? We're carrying on as though we were dining at the Anasazi Café. I thought this was a clandestine patrol, not lunchtime talk." Howie grinned sheepishly. They hiked in silence. To Kika, the predawn hike was a spiritual experience. She found it awe-inspiring. To Howie, it was just another morning hike, growing brighter by the second, not darker. Reminiscent of the Gulf War. Ten minutes passed. Acquiescing, Kika broke the silence. She slowed her pace. "I can't help saying that hiking by starlight stirs me profoundly. So let's talk more about your beliefs. And light. Your creation story teaches that your God made two great lights, right?" Her tone stimulated Howie's memories of Sunday school.

"Uh...yeah...," he replied. "I'm not sure where this is going, but you're right so far." The words dragged slowly from his mouth. They walked carefully through the sagebrush, close to the edge of Snow Flat Canyon. A rattler would strike if stepped on. "The greater light to rule the day and the lesser light to rule the night. It's somewhere in Genesis, I think. Is this about the rest of your dream?" No response. "Is it about church stuff? Did you become Christian? You're Navajo."

"It was hard being raised by a drunken mom. Sometimes she'd drag me to Catholic mass. Around the usual holidays. Or out of guilt after a rowdy bender. Or after a strange man slept over. Home was a staging ground for abuse. A battlefield. Fortunately, my aunt and her family took me to church. I felt safe being out of the house for the day. After church, Luciana and I would play all day. I'd go to school Monday morning with her."

"And you never wanted to move in with them? I still don't know everything about your past, Kika. Especially the years you ran away from home."

"Someday I'll tell you all about it. Now's not the right time."

"I respect that. So did you ever become Catholic?"

"No. Well, I actually did both. A little church and a little Navajo. Then one day, my mom found out she couldn't drink anymore. The doctor told her she'd drunk her liver away. My Uncle Lenny is a respected elder. Even though he's my mom's brother, he never tried very hard to stop her from drinking. Said he saw it too often in their family. That she would quit when she had to. Or die first. Like so many other relatives." Kika stopped and raised one foot onto a boulder, preparing for her next statement.

"Then one day, Uncle Lenny could see she was really serious about giving up the booze. Once he saw she was willing, he became willing to help. He came to our property and arranged for ceremony. It lasted several days. It was during my runaway years so I wasn't there. Too bad for me. It may have been right for me too. It is said that Navajos living far from the rez need to return home to become renewed. To be in ceremony. To chant and to sing. Anyway, Mom didn't tell me about that experience until three years ago. Other family members were there to support her. The ceremony may have been a Blessing Way. I don't know for sure. But she hasn't had a drink since, and now she's trying hard to follow Navajo tradition. She spends more time with her brother Lenny too. And other kinfolk."

Howie didn't say anything. Her story touched him. Silence helped process her feelings. Her foot remained on the boulder. He respected her mother's new life. He'd seen the effects of drug and alcohol abuse during Desert Storm. "So you and your mom have made up, grown closer?"

"Ah, not totally. We've become good talking buddies. We're still setting boundaries, not bonded yet. Someday, we may actually become friends. I'm sure it was her drinking that caused me to run away. I had just turned fifteen. I figured that was old enough to be on my own. I was furious over her nasty habits, the creeps she slept with. I had to escape. Living with Luciana and my aunt wasn't the answer. I was restless. I never wanted to come back. I wanted to leave my whole family behind. I never believed she would quit drinking for good. I mean, you wouldn't believe how many times she made that promise. You wouldn't believe how many Mondays she called in sick."

They resumed a normal pace along the rim. Idle chatter drifted between them. Twenty-five minutes passed. They were still one mile from ground zero. Howie looked for a protected position to review their strategy. A quick coffee and granola bar would hit the spot. They'd made excellent time. He selected an enormous sandstone slab behind fallen boulders, sat down and poured hot coffee into the lid of his thermos. Kika was good for only two swigs without cream. Howie finished off the lid and refilled it. "So," he began, "what do *you* think about that talk in Genesis concerning Creation? Do you think it's all a bunch of hocus-pocus?" Kika held up her hand. She'd had enough coffee.

"You mean how God made the heavens and earth, like in six days and then set aside the seventh day to rest? You're asking *me* if I believe in the Biblical creation story? Like a single god created everything? Absolutely everything? Even the things we can't see? In just six days? Huh, that takes a lot of faith."

"Seems to me like it's either all or nothing," Howie proffered with a grin.

"Right, like your Biblical God made everything, huh? Including every animal, man and woman: the air we breathe, all the water, all the planets, and all those zillions of stars up there? Versus evolution? Or some other deity, some other supreme creator?" She cocked her head back and looked straight up, stroking the sky as though waiving a magic wand.

"Uh-huh," said Howie, still smiling. "Of course, science tells us that a planet congeals out of debris from dust and gas floating around in interstellar space, usually as a remnant disc from supernova explosions. The process is a natural one. It invites order out of chaos and disorder."

"I can't honestly say right now, Howie." She lowered her head and rubbed her eyes. "This topic is way too deep. It's too early in the morning to philosophize about astronomy. I should have never brought it up. I've had my coffee and all, but this just isn't morning conversation material. We need to have this discourse sitting around the campfire gazing up at the sky. You know, looking for UFOs, watching for shooting stars, talking about life on other planets, aliens, and all that good stuff. *That's* the time to talk about evolution versus creationism. Besides, we're here on a mission. We've got a job to do." She stood and slung her backpack over her shoulders. "I'll leave you with one last thought, though."

"I can walk and listen at the same time."

She scraped her hand across the boulder next to her and stomped her foot on the sandstone. "We believe that the landscape surrounding us is an important part of our creation story. See?" Observing an ancient custom of pointing with her chin rather than her hand, she swept her eyes over large silhouettes gracing the horizon. "These mesas, buttes and mountains are sacred to us. They define our boundaries, our *Dinétah*, how the Holy Ones set the cosmos in an orderly way." She gesticulated as she spoke each word. "You have your own Christian version of 'first man and first woman', right? How God formed Eve by plucking her from Adam's rib. In our creation story we believe our ancestors ascended from several underworlds up into today's world. Some stories relate to this being the Fourth World, others to it being the Fifth World. Either way, in this present world, Changing Woman made her own people. She made four clans out of flakes peeled from her own skin. These flakes were human forms."

Howie thought for a long, long while. "Sounds about the same to me. Is there really a difference between God plucking woman from Adam's rib and First Woman removing flakes of her own skin? Is it possible the same deity could have done both?"

"Well..."

"My point is this," he said. "We all had to come from somewhere. Some power greater than us, some*thing*, no matter how big or how small, no matter when it first started a long, long time ago, had to create us. We didn't just come from nothing."

"*My* point exactly, Howie Parker. If you've ever seen a newborn baby come out of its mother's womb, all wet and purple-red, and watched it spanked to life, and observed how it opened its mouth...and hear its first gurgling scream...well, it's rather hard to imagine there isn't a master creator in charge of it all, is it?"

Howie nodded silently. All of a sudden, he nudged closer and said. "Good point. I can't argue that. Kika, have you ever see that?" His question hung in the air. She failed to grasp it. "I mean, have you ever been right there when a new baby was born?"

A conspicuous silence intervened. The air felt like lead. Kika jumped unstably over loose rocks. It was strange for her to lose footing. Howie saw it. She looked down into the path before her, speaking directly to the rocks instead of to him. "Yes, Howie. Yes I have. I've seen that once. It was many years ago. But that's another long story. *A very long one.*"

"You mean it's another campfire and star gazing kind of story? We're up to two so far. Both dealing with creationism and evolution. We're going to need a huge campfire. An all-nighter."

Years of guilt hung in the balance. One side of the scale told Kika to abort the conversation immediately. Not to tell Howie. The counter scale was overjoyed. It told her to charge forward full steam ahead. That her dark secret stood outside its cave, *anxious to be revealed*, anxious to break through into the sunlight. She'd confessed to the canyon walls yesterday. Why couldn't she do so to the man she loved? For a moment, the scales were evenly balanced. Then, one lost ground; it teetered and dropped, all because of her hesitation. It was baffling. What was stopping her? Why weren't her words pouring out in joy? What was Howie to do if he became angry? Leave her stranded in the middle of the night? However, those thoughts never registered. The scale tipped more heavily in one direction. She opted for the easier, softer way. The joyous scale never had a chance to rebut. The result was devastating. Kika Windsong's silence clipped the wings of her soul. It kept her from soaring to freedom. It would also eclipse a fulfilling relationship with Howie Parker. Deadened with defeat, badly bruised and heavily scarred, her dark secret dragged itself, inch by inch, back into its cave.

Words finally escaped. "Yes, that's right. We'll definitely need an all night campfire. We'll look up to the heavens and poke at the embers. We'll talk about *everything*. Until daybreak." She regained her footing and stepped ahead with a determined stride. "Now, come on. We're losing time."

He grabbed her arm. "But, you *will* include that part of the story, won't you? About seeing a newborn baby?"

"Promise. Once this canyon business is over."

Their movements were stealth. The starlight began to vanish. Howie's watch read 4:12. The half of a cantaloupe, which is what Kika called the moon, reached the horizon. It cast shadows resembling scary giants. Suddenly, it dropped below the dark line separating night from day, missing Bears Ears by the width of a fist. Starlight guided them before the first light of dawn.

They'd reached Ground Zero. Slowly, he guided her to the edge. She tiptoed softly, staring at the ledge below.

FIFTEEN

Forty eight vertical feet separated them from the looters. Silence prevailed. Like ninjas, they descended the Anasazi holds precisely when moonlight faded into predawn light. It took thirty seconds. Perfect timing. They completed their approach without headlamps.

Marine Corps discipline imbedded itself in Parker. Other tactical skills, such as his S. I. quotient, were bedrock DNA traits. "Be at your absolute peak when sniping the enemy," his CO had instructed time and again. "It'll make *them* the dead guys, not you." It worked. When his senses were piqued, he was as concealed as a chameleon; his strike as deadly as a Gabon viper.

Their ledge perched twenty-seven feet above the amphitheater ledge, home to Inner Ruin. Howie leaned their backpacks against the cliff to facilitate a rapid escape. They scrambled close to the edge and crouched behind a boulder larger than most cars. His Chase-Durer read 4:19 am. The two observers had one hundred minutes before daylight. His night vision scope would prove indispensible.

He scurried back and forth to find the best lookout; an optimum angle yielding the best line of sight. He was in his zone. His heart pounded. Three minutes later, he scrambled back to Kika. The boulder she waited behind was perfect. She'd picked it. He raised his scope and scanned the magnificent cliff dwellings. Inner Ruin was constructed on a ledge which arced 300 feet across. He estimated its depth at seventy feet. The village, abandoned sometime late in the thirteenth century by cliff dwellers believed to be peoples of the Anasazi tradition, encompassed 56 room blocks, a plaza area in front of the village, and two storage granaries adjacent to the rear wall. There were three circular-shaped two story tower structures. It was obvious that Inner Ruin had been constructed over ancient, crumbled ruins of indeterminable age and origin, abandoned by a civilization unidentified by anthropologists as late as 2004. Howie and Kika's ledge was also an arced amphitheater. Dimensionally smaller, it spanned slightly east of the cliff dwellings, placing the pillagers in direct sight.

"If they've posted guards," Howie whispered, "we could already be locked in a sniper's crosshairs."

"Perhaps we're the *observed*, not the observers. This looks like grand scale looting. If it were me, I'd post guards."

Howie peered below to inventory their gear and tools. He noted technical climbing hardware, three climbing ropes and harnesses, several shovels, picks, trowels and related hand tools. Lining the rear cliff wall were dozens of empty plastic crates with open lids. Three large tarps covered what he figured were filled crates.

110

"Wow, Kika, I had to see it to believe it. This isn't a quick pot hunting spree by a passing backpacker. More like open pit mining."

He focused on two men asleep inside a room block. Anxiety skyrocketed. He broke into the widest grin Kika had ever seen. The scope ringed his eye socket. He resembled a submariner gripping the periscope and commanding his gunner to fire away. It was a look seething with devious confidence, knowing the torpedoes would strike. All that he and Kika had to do was wait and observe the men in action. Then, climb up and race like mad into cell range.

Although he'd seen, even surveyed, many cliff dwellings as an amateur archaeologist, he was always struck by one phenomenon - it seemed as though the villagers had packed up most of their belongings in the middle of an ordinary day and left for good. He handed the scope to Kika. She refused. She knew what she'd see. Uncle Lenny's whirlwind chronicle explained it all. Instead, she envisioned living there when Inner Ruin stood at its zenith eight centuries earlier. It was one of a handful of large Southwest cliff villages accessible *only* by climbing in or out. She tried to imagine hauling wood, water, food and game, plus tons of other necessities up and down to their village. Did they live on a cliff ledge for defensive purposes? She pondered.

He nudged her again with the luminescent scope, egging her on. She raised the scope and pretended to peer through it. But she couldn't. Her eye remained shut. Instead, she pictured two powerful whirlwinds near Monument Valley. To the day she had recited Uncle Lenny's story, almost trance-like, about the burning of the Ancient Ones when the sun descended from the sky. And about the charred ruins and the sunspots. About the mysterious lack of what logically should have been thousands upon thousands of burial remains in the greater Southwest.

Kika knew it was taboo for Navajos to dwell on the deceased. Yet, she realized they were on a vital mission. She *had* to look at what lay beneath her. She'd looked at other ruins before. She'd even stepped through them once or twice. She could do it again. Yet something stopped her. She continued her pretense of looking through Howie's scope. She even swiveled her head from side to side. "Uncle Lenny knows the ways of the Ancient Ones," she told herself. "He's a visionary, a crystal gazer, he sees things no one else can see. His whirlwind folktale must be correct.

She opened her eyes and handed him the scope, remaining silent. Howie respected that. Without saying a word, he raised the scope a third time and studied the ruins. He shuddered at the destruction caused by the looters. The plaza was decimated. Once a harmonious space where children played, communal chores were performed, and turkeys were penned, two ludicrous thugs had now set up shop and were rapidly decimating it. "Criminal," he declared in a breathy whisper. "I hope these scoundrels are put away for the rest of their lives."

"Shameful," she said. "I can almost hear the ancient spirits crying out in despair."

"We'll put a stop to this as soon as possible. Illegal as hell!"

"Just leave that stumpy creep to the authorities. He's not our concern. We're just observers."

At 5:53 two men began moving about camp. Howie looked up at the pale blue sky. Sunlight wouldn't strike canyon depths for another 45 minutes. He got his first glimpse of the white-haired freak. He nicknamed him "Blizzardhead." Kika thought it was too kind for a monster. Within minutes, they disappeared from view. Their voices faded. Howie and Kika turned to each other, bewildered, each racing to ask the same question. Each wondering how they could simply disappear. Their voices echoed from a distance.

The idea of a kiva or even a storage granary at the rear of the village made sense, Howie thought. Then his mind created a brilliant scenario. A hidden room located behind the village. Possibly carved into the cliff itself. Kika liked his theory. They were on the same page. They crawled out to the extreme edge, careful not to cause any pebbles to fall. "Know what? This is a horrible idea if a watchman is posted."

"If they'd have wanted to, they'd have picked us off by now." She shot him a dirty look. They leaned over the edge. He raised his monocular. Still, the men were nowhere in sight. He weighed in on his thoughts. Excitement danced in his eyes. He proposed a risky idea. Dropping down to their level. Down to the ruins. He asked if she was up for it, then studied her reaction closely.

They had veered from the same page. Involuntary reflexes caused a deep gasp. Her abdomen constricted. Air escaped her lungs. She paused for an eternity. She was indeed in a pickle. Minutes earlier she had faked looking through Howie's night scope. Out of the blue, he asked her to descend into a village swarming with uprooted, ancestral spirits. Occupied by men she was certain had savagely kicked to death an innocent backcountry climber. *Reconciliation had to occur.*

She stirred her forefinger in the sand and held a pensive look. Gradually, an idea took hold. It matured slowly. She nodded her head affirmatively. Its rationale snapped her to attention. She articulated to herself. "Got it. The dust there, the dirt down there, is ancestral matter. Just like particles within a whirlwind is ancestral matter. So are my people's ancient artifacts, timeless weavings and other ancestral objects. They're all particles of ancestral matter. They've all been held by ancient spirits. If I'm allowed to touch and feel my culture's ceremonial objects, I ought to be able to walk purposefully among their ancient village." Her rationale seemed solid. She also based it upon motive. "If my *motive* is to abort illegal activities, then it must be acceptable to enter Inner Ruin. I'll be protected from *chindi*."

She stopped doodling in the dirt and looked up at the man she loved. "Give time time is one of my favorite slogans. Thanks for letting me think things through. I'm game. But, Mr. Ex-Marine, I'm not cracked up to engage in any do or die battles. My little gun would act like a peashooter against Blizzardhead." She planted her face two inches from his. "After all, there's no escaping once we're down there! We'd be trapped. On their level! Have you considered that? What happens then?"

"I'm pretty well armed, babe. You've got to trust me." He looked at his backpack and nodded his chin. "I've got my Kimber and my Sig in there. My Walther is locked in the truck. Sig's got better hand dextenty. " The Kimber was a new stainless TLE II version. Definitely overkill as a backup weapon. The 45 caliber packed a powerful shot. "Speaking of which, I'll grab our backpacks."

Prior to scaling down from their observation ledge, they agreed upon simple hand and facial signals enabling silent communication. Carefully, they inched over the edge and lowered themselves down another set of Anasazi holds. A two foot drop landed them on the eastern boundary of the village. A furtive landing ignited Howie's S. I. quotient. He thrived on life-threatening risks. Living on the edge had also been a factor during Kika's runaway years. The feeling returned forcefully when her feet hit the ground.

The air felt different at village level. Acoustics within the amphitheater caused a variance in atmospheric pressure. Her ear canals "popped." Past centuries fast-forwarded in her mind. She realized they stood within what had once been the Ancient One's entire universe. Some had lived their whole lives within that one grand, communal living space. It had shaped their world view. They had experienced a profound spiritual life from where she stood. They had practiced ritual and ceremony. *And dance.* It had been a village of harmonious living. They had based their life on the seasons, the positions of the sun and the moon. In time, agriculture had blended with hunting and gathering seasons. One look at their stunning architecture spoke for itself. They had been master architects, village planners, and stone masons with the societal infrastructure to support this advanced lifestyle.

The intrepid couple crouched low behind room walls and inched across the village. Only a few walls had deteriorated into piles of rubble. Otherwise, Inner Ruin was preserved incredibly well. Temptingly close enough to reach out and touch, the gargantuan

113

boulder balanced at the edge of the amphitheater. It was nearly as large as their house.

A guttural, raspy voice echoed from the rear of the village. It was neither a yell nor a whisper, simply muffled as though it came from a long tunnel. Dull pinging sounds of a shovel impacted rock. Seconds later, they heard sharp blows of a pick-axe, followed by smooth scrapes from a trowel. Parker glanced at Kika with dagger eyes. His lips pursed tight and he slammed his fist to the ground. She watched anger brew beneath his skin as though a kettle had boiled over. They crept closer. Dim light fanned out from a tiny opening. Parker's theory was correct. There was a hidden room. Kika smiled approvingly. She'd seen doorways patterned in a T-shape at other archaeological sites. Its corresponding T-shaped, sandstone plug leaned against the cliff next to the opening. The passageway was very narrow and low to the ground, well hidden.

"Must have been a tight squeeze for Blizzardhead." Kika mused. They remained squatting. His mind raced. He had to see for himself what they were excavating. Kika had other thoughts - shouldn't they bolt and summon Quirk? Crawling ahead and peering into the cavern was fraught with danger. She feared they were already too close. They had no business trying to snake forward and squint through the opening. She wanted to clear out while the getting was good. That additional evidence was unnecessary. The sounds generated by their tools was enough evidence - these two men were guilty as hell. She tugged hard at Howie's sleeve, jerking her head toward the plaza, silently forming the words "let's go" on her lips. She pulled harder, trying to drag him away.

Howie shook his head forcefully from side to side, jerking his thumb in the direction of the opening. "Damn, we've come this far, just one quick look," he pleaded to himself, unwilling to break their code of silence. He dropped to his belly and began to crawl. Armed with an automatic combat knife and his Sig, he crawled to the cavern's opening. Reluctantly, she followed thirty seconds later, squatting and advancing "goose-like" instead of crawling. Her movements were silky smooth; her impact as soft as that of a flower petal. They listened to a new voice, cutting and mean. The pair inched closer and peered through the passageway. Shadows danced hauntingly off chamber walls. Howie got his first look at the man with the crooked face and titanium tooth. The ceiling, blackened with a thick buildup of soot, sloped down to the rear wall. It met the floor sixty feet from the entryway. He shaped the size of the chamber with his hands.

Kika crept closer. The hissing sound generated by three gas lanterns hanging from the ceiling seemed deafening to her. She broke their code of silence: "That's the other scary-looking guy. Do you think that's really a tooth?" Her whisper was barely discernable.

Howie realized the noisy lanterns eclipsed her whispering. He held two fingers to his lips and separated them, then leaned into her ear. "He *is* a freaky-looking dude. It *is* a tooth, a damn weapon-tooth." He peered deep into the chamber a second time.

He was alarmed at the sight of three interior room blocks. Further shocked that the stone masonry differed vastly from the village rooms behind them. He shrugged, squinting through irregular shadows formed by lantern light. The unique stone masonry reminded him of archaeological sites in South America. Perhaps pre-Inca design, bearing the world's most precisely carved and fitted stones. Where the prehistoric builders used no mud mortar, each stone was instead mortised and tenanted, one into another, with exquisite, artistic skill, yielding joints closer than a beautiful set of teeth, joints virtually impenetrable, even with a needle. However, that was just the beginning. The shock of his life struck him when he stretched forward. His eyes bulged far from their sockets. A blender churned within his gut. His heart skipped a beat. Two. He gasped. Quietly, he panted breathy words. They came in soft exhales. "Oh, my God, those artifacts. I never, ever imagined anything like this!"

Kika stretched her neck like a whooping crane. Her chest pressed firmly against his back. He felt her heartbeat, felt her upper body tremble. He knew the throbs were not of romantic origin. He understood why. The looters were also murderers. It was no spurious conclusion. He would never forget the beaten woman's icy lips pressed against his ear, gasping: "Wh...hair." They remained statuesque outside the passageway. Howie recalled what his optometrist said about two-dimensional retinal sight when unnatural light was used. He felt safe. Chances were the two men couldn't see out.

Raspy words exploded into the chamber. Blizzardhead claimed he'd had enough of the sooty air, of his partner's stinking body odor, of the sickening lantern fumes. He pleaded for fresh air. A plethora of profanities spat from his hoarse throat. Kika wondered if he had an artificial larynx. One with a microphone pressed too tight against the throat. Or a cheap model lacking volume control. Ignorance was bliss at that moment. She had no clue its source was hundreds of attempted strangulations and foiled garroting. Plus an all-afternoon body cruise through Cleveland's harbor sporting a noose. Otherwise she'd have bolted immediately. With or without Howie. He rose from his belly and squatted. They inched backward. Suddenly, shouting erupted from the chamber. They stopped in their tracks.

"Careful, you imbecile." Words rifled from Mac's slanted jaw. He threw his shovel hard to the ground, saber tooth shining in Whitey's face. "Whitey, you retard, what you're calling 'a piece of junk' is worth a quarter mil. Or more, you lamebrain. Careful with it. Roll it in bubble wrap, and then roll it again in burlap. Place it gently into a crate over there." He spread his crooked lips and pointed with his titanium weapon-tooth. "It may not look it to you, but *all* of this old Indian junk is priceless. We're going to make millions. Millions. If you don't break it all first. Now, is that too complicated for your worthless brain?" He had always pictured Whitey's head as a massive chunk of soggy nothingness, like green Styrofoam used in floral arrangements.

"So," Howie breathed, "Whitey's his name. How fitting."

Seconds later, Whitey bellowed a raspy question: "Hey Mac, what's this junk?"

"Aha, Mac and Whitey. Now we've got names to put with these bozos. And, enough evidence to lock them away."

"So, let's GO. I want OUT," Kika pleaded quietly. She began her retreat, having passed the point of no return. Howie reluctantly inched backward. Shouting stopped their retreat a second time. Whitey yelled at Mac. He tossed an object into the air. Then, caught it in midair like a showoff juggler, carelessly fumbling it with stubby fingers, yelling again: "What's this thing?"

The curiosity was far too strong. The observers scrambled back to the T-shaped opening. Howie's eyes strained through dust-particle light. Awestruck, staring in total disbelief, he withdrew from the opening and stared at Kika without speaking. He didn't have to. His face said it all.

SIXTEEN

"Coldditz in camo, Coldditz in camo." The veteran recon specialist spoke directly to the Roundleaf Buffaloberry engulfing him. The Agent extraordinaire frequently referred to himself by nickname, "Coldditz in camo," acquired during his 30-year career in covert field ops. He was tops in his field, an icon, at remaining undetected. Intertwined in thick clumps of desert brush, beside the precipice of Snow Flat Canyon, and exposed to creepy-crawly menaces of Cedar Mesa, he lay flat on his stomach. His hands gripped an infrared thermal imaging camera.

Roundleaf Buffaloberry, one of the densest brush-forms found on Cedar Mesa, grew adjacent to clusters of Gambel Oak and Cliff Fendlerbush. Coldditz was invisible to the naked eye. In fact, his natural canopy was too perfect for reconnaissance. It was better suited for a sniper. It was also ironic he'd chosen Roundleaf Buffaloberry for "eyeing" his subjects. The shrub was directly related to vision. Navajos prepared a salve from its fruit to treat irritations to sheep's eyes. Later that morning, as sunlight intensified, it would facilitate squint-free "eyeing" upon Inner Ruin.

The agent was semi-retired. Occasionally, the Agency reactivated him when sensitive assignments required a veteran. One *condition precedent* of reactivation was his insistence upon calling all the shots. Cedar Mesa was such a mission. The Delilah Project, as it became known, was Coldditz's brainchild. That morning, he focused upon all four subjects at Inner Ruin. He was entertained by the antics of Howie Parker and Kika Windsong. He chalked them off as amateurs, despite Howie's stint as a marine in the Gulf War. The same went for Jed and Buzz. They were easily disposable accessories to Mac's feeble arsenal.

All four being small fish, his main prey was higher up in the criminal food chain. Horace Wainwright, illicit antiquities dealer, who owned a gallery in Santa Fe, New Mexico. He had first appeared as a blip on Coldditz's radar in 2002. Illegal arms bartering. The FBI had requested quasi-illegal electronic surveillance by the NSA to determine the extent of Wainwright's links to foreign terrorist cells. Coldditz conducted his own "deep-clean" investigation. He waded through several layers of bureaucratic muck. Next, he'd scoured the careers of a dozen mid-range bureaucrats. They all had ONE thing in common - the commodity terrorist cells demanded most - URANIUM, depleted or otherwise, integral to the manufacturing of dirty bombs and related holocaustic devices against the infidels. Quite by accident, he tripped over what he believed to be a mole buried within the US Department of Energy. Coldditz code-named the mole Delilah. Intuition, coupled with prodigious field experience, told him the gender was correct. She'd become his *guerre a outrance*, his *war to the utmost*. If he played his spy game skillfully, McAllister and Wainwright would perform all his dirty work. All he had to do was untangle an intricately spun web connecting Utah's canyons, northeast Arizona and the Department of Energy.

Prior to the formation of the U S Department of Homeland Security, the Agent's normal cover was that of sensitive assignments envoy, US State Department, attached to diplomatic delegations dispatched throughout the globe. He would typically "feather" into his cover, disappear, complete a vital assignment, and resurface when the delegation's efforts became part of the evening news. Or, as they boarded military aircraft to return to Washington.

His mission in southeastern Utah was related to national security. Since Coldditz loved working in dry, desert environs, he had volunteered for the project. Otherwise, he lived a comfortable, if not somewhat opulent, lifestyle in a custom-built chateau nestled in the Maryland countryside. His estate was within easy reach of the NSA's headquarters at Fort Meade. There, he occupied an office shared with other "retirees". It was situated in the fourth subterranean level of the top secret complex. Serving as the nerve center for all communications transmitted throughout the globe, as well as outer space, he was proud to be entombed beneath ground level. He boasted that success in the D.C. area was based upon how far *beneath* street level an office was located, not on the number of floors above ground level.

There was a tone of arrogance, even narcissism, when he spoke through the dense brush. He was positioned six feet from the south rim of Snow Flat Canyon. He'd watched the amateurs descend the Anasazi holds through his high-definition, multisensory infrared thermal imager. He admired their graceful moves in the waning moonlight. He'd made arrangements with Quirk, an offer the officious bureaucrat couldn't refuse, ordering the pair to remain *out of* the eastern canyons, knowing full-well Parker would disobey. He'd memorized Parker's military dossier like his own palm, thus gambling a vital leg of the Delilah Project on the NSA's Predictability Index published on him. Through that morning's early hours, Parker's behavioral traits played out like a blueprint - sleuth-like maneuvering within the ruins, securing themselves beside the T-shaped passageway, and persevering at close range to their adversaries. The Predictability Index was square on its mark. Kika's native intuitive powers were also right about one thing - they *were* positioned in someone's crosshairs - she just had the wrong spotter, although his mission was *not* to assassinate the couple.

Coldditz also kept tabs on Jed Trepke and Buzz Lane. Satellite imagery relayed the modified truck teetering out of Krenecke's shop.

The tracking device he'd mounted kept the pair under his thumb 24/7. Yet, he was confused at what appeared to be a third image generated by the satellite's long range, target detection infrared sensors. Two days ago, his "spy van" had intercepted a cell conversation between Jed and an ATV dealership in Bluff, Utah. Arrangements were made to rent off road vehicles and support equipment. Parker's conversation with the Navajo dispatcher informed him that he and Windsong decided to stay through Monday. That provided superb intelligence. His plan needed more time to gel. "Yes," he declared to the camo netting encircling his head. "I've got each of you puppets in the palm of my hands. Soon, I'll tug on your strings and bring Delilah down like a sinking ship."

The agent spoke literally. He glanced at a new instrument developed by the NSA for urban warfare - a palm-held quasar, digitally-enhanced infrared imager and global positioning device. Scientists entombed in the NSA's research and development "playpen" nicknamed it DIC. They joked about field agents holding their dick in the palm of their hands. Sick jokes were common among geniuses sequestered to the NSA's playpen. Inner Ruin was displayed as a color icon. Coordinates of other significant locations were locked into memory and could be displayed in real-time; thus, instantly accessing Howie and Kika's camper, an abandoned uranium mine northeast of Lukachukai Arizona, Quirk's office at Kane Gulch, and other coordinates critical to the Delilah Project. His surveillance van circled Cedar Mesa's perimeter continuously. Directional-parabolic microphones and digital cameras aided the Project. Dish apparatus and swaying antennae caused the slow-moving Ford E350 to resemble an alien insect.

Coldditz had also spied upon their campsite two nights ago. He was entertained by explosive campfire sex. The sleuth was a loner. A prime character asset for his profession. One of his glaring defects was a taste for perverse sexual fantasies. He acted them out during overseas missions. They were exorbitantly expensive. Yet, he was subject to an undaunted, never audited, expense account. His forays were buried in a heap of dirty money associated with dirty ops. Superiors at Fort Meade had bailed him out of compromising situations dozens of times. His escapades had precipitated in a divorce 25 years ago. There were no offspring and he never remarried. Neither had she.

"Parker's S.I. quotient must be drained," Coldditz snickered to his thicket. "Bet you never guessed Uncle Sam would be *observing* you observe, did you? Well, Mr. ex-marine, I've got news for you. There are deep layers of illegal enterprise occurring in the canyons. You and your sexy Indian are simply one thin veneer." He poked his pinky finger through the camo netting and scratched a nagging bite. "One more night, two at the outside, before Delilah is all mine."

He lowered his continuous zoom infrared scope and uttered what sounded like instructions. He tucked the unit in a compact case next to him. All images of nighttime action at Inner Ruin were recorded in real time. A transmitter relayed the images to his surveillance van. Uplink capabilities transmitted them to Project headquarters at the Brownstone.

A thin, coiled wire ran from his ear below his collar. It attached to an encrypted transmitting devise. He repeated his command into the facial netting. Agents in the roving spy van received instructions. His self-engineered spy game, the Delilah Project, gained momentum. He never once talked to himself. Or to the Roundleaf Buffaloberry.

SEVENTEEN

"I'll crack his Neanderthal skull in two if he drops that," Howie whispered in near silence. His lips remained stationary, jaw locked in shock. "If that's what I think it is, I'll tear that freak apart limb by limb." He excelled in hand to hand combat. His limbs struck decisively, like a blacksmith hammering an anvil.

Kika shook her head vehemently, eyes piercing like lasers. She gripped his forearm tightly and whispered: "NO. We're too vulnerable. No backup. No place to run." She jerked her thumb and yanked her head back, hoping he'd obey her signal. He didn't budge. Inquisitively, she peered around his shoulder, aghast at the source of his rage.

Whitey held a slightly curved, rectangular object the size of a thin brick. He tossed it in the air like a juggling pin. A massive paw scooped it up before it hit the ground. He tumbled it teasingly in his palm, never noticing glyphs incised on its back. He boasted to Mac that his finger stubs weren't as clumsy as people thought.

Howie turned. Their faces touched. "God help him if he drops that..."

Blizzardhead haphazardly tossed his new toy onto a stack of burlap bags. He disappeared for thirty seconds. When he returned, Kika's heart stopped. Her hand clutched her mouth. Festooned in the back of Whitey's coarse white hair was a colorful Macaw feather. A second feather pierced the top of his hair, horizontally, forming a cross. She drilled her forefinger into Howie's ribcage. Finally, she adjusted her stance and crouched behind him toboggan-style, drilling a second finger into his kidney. He turned and glanced at her. "Let's go," she uttered, louder than she would have liked. She jerked her head and cut her throat with her hand.

The lantern closest to Mac faded and hissed. He threaded a new LP canister into its base. Fully charged, it was louder than the others. He ordered Whitey to wrap things up in five minutes. They'd take a break, get some much needed fresh air. Whitey exhaled a raspy gurgle. Mac assumed that meant agreement. Even with his titanium saber tooth, he'd never penetrate the massif's stegosaurus hide.

Mac repositioned the refueled lantern. It exposed a sight Howie would never forget for the rest of his life. An array of stone figures stood erect on an altar built into the east wall of the cavern. He was spellbound. The stone work of the altar and its surrounding bench seat was identical to the three small rooms, artistically interlocked in a mortise and tenon design. He raised his monocular and studied the artifacts. Intricately carved figurines perched majestically. He wondered why they hadn't been removed yet. Fashioned out of shiny obsidian, one appeared slightly larger than the others. He adjusted the focus. Its eye sockets were white as snow. Red pupils. Somber, regal, standing upright on the altar.

Suddenly it struck. His head bobbed for a full minute. He accessed a deep memory vault, retrieving images one by one, in stop-motion frames, advancing like a slide show. *One he'd seen years before.* At university - a presentation during Latin American anthropology studies which featured lost civilizations. The statuettes before him were small replicas of the enigmatic statues situated on Easter Island. The isolated, tiny spec of volcanic rock in the Pacific Ocean. So named when a Dutch oceanic explorer first sighted it on Easter Sunday, 1722. He recorded the miniscule dot on his expansive sea-voyaging charts as the most isolated island in the world. The University slideshow depicted one substantially larger than the others. No student in class would forget the white coral eye sockets and red pupils polished from rare Redstone. Like the miniature one centered in his monocular. He knew it had a strange name beginning with "M." He remembered it represented the civilization's creator.

For some unexplained reason, all three lanterns hissed louder than earlier. He broke his decree of absolute silence and filled his lungs to whisper, realizing it took more trapped air to whisper than to speak in a normal voice. "How could these little statues, replicas of the behemoth ones 10,000 miles away, end up in a hidden chamber on Cedar Mesa? Huh? Answer me that one!" They were connected by their faces again. He suddenly realized the immensity of what lay in the secret chamber. A new dimension, one of quantum proportion, had entered the picture. The discovery would have worldwide ramifications. But, was it a chance, virgin discovery by thug-looters, criminals he suspected of murdering an innocent backpacker? "Is this why mystery man Coldditz is calling the shots? How could he possibly know? Is Homeland Security that pervasive? Did Marianne Lofty know?" Kika bit her tongue. He was beginning to see why Quirk insisted Snow Flat Canyon and its contiguous canyons remain OFF LIMITS to him and Kika. His questions begged an answer.

Kika read him like a book. She pressed against him and nudged her lips into his ear. "It's got to be something else, Howie. Coldditz couldn't possibly know about this secret chamber, could he? We're missing something...something much bigger. Something *we* haven't discovered yet. *But Coldditz has."* She sucked air into her lungs. "And, here's the real bomb..." Words vaporized at 98.6 degrees. "I'll bet Ms Lofty *did* know about this chamber! Maybe she snuck up on them like we're doing. After all, she too, was a rock climber. Maybe she had threatened to turn them in. Or had wanted some of the goodies for herself." Silence filled their space. Two minutes passed. Her hypotheses had the effect of a 9.5-scale earthquake. Transfixed in ear-to-lip closeness, she let the aftershocks rumble into the distance. Howie stroked his stubby chin. Stooped in the shadows of a secret passageway belonging to a lost civilization, they realized simultaneously there could be more than met their eyes. Effortlessly, their minds united as one. Her next mind-boggling reality check pierced Howie like a knife. She tapped the face of her watch and pantomimed lips and hand signals. "Time's up, they'll take a break any second now." She scraped backward on her butt.

Howie held her arm. He didn't share the same urgency. He wore the look of a prizefighter in top form - one whose opponent had sagged into the ropes in a senseless stupor, awaiting the final punch so he could drop with dignity instead of collapsing. He shook his head and held both hands in a "time-out" display. His eyes danced with victory, whispering into her ear, a full dose of cockiness, even humor, in his tone. "Don't you get it?"

She tugged hard at his shirt, her eyes filling with venom. "This is no time for games, Howie. Get what? How we'll be killed? Very funny. You *promised* to keep Blizzardhead far away."

He still didn't budge. She saw that look again, the one of the submarine commander gripping the periscope, torpedoes streaming toward their mark. "No, look around you. We're on the *outside* looking in. They're trapped. We have nothing to fear. We've the upper hand here. They're trapped inside the sooty chamber choking on fumes. I could keep them at bay with both hands tied behind my back!" He grinned.

He made sense; the kind of sense that kept her from bolting. It took her a minute to craft a reply. "It's no longer about evidence, is it?" She read the answer in his eyes. "It's about broadcasting this discovery to the outside world, isn't it? Getting a conviction is secondary. Huh, am I right?"

"They must be apprehended, Kika, that's true. But, let's face it, this is a colossal find. Imagine it. Feather holders, obsidian figurines, pre-Inca stone masonry. Oh, my God, Easter Island!"

"We'll wait until dark. Then, ascend and make the call of a lifetime. Until then, let's scale up to our ledge and wait it out." She crawled backward on all fours. He did the same. They hid in rubble behind collapsed room walls. Neither one moved a muscle, neither one spoke. Kika raised her binoculars and scanned the canyon. Howie listened for the slightest sound, eying village room blocks. She nudged him. "Don't see any snipers. I think the coast is clear. Come on."

123

"You're not supposed to see snipers, Kika. Ever. When we get to our ledge, I'll post first watch while you rest. We'll switch every two hours. If we're lucky, maybe we'll even overhear their plans when they're resting on the plaza." Yet, his mind plucked at three thorns stuck in his craw. The first was whether the dead backpacker, Marianne Lofty, *had* seen the astonishing artifacts - and whether or not her dying words disclosed that in Flagstaff. The second dealt with how Coldditz *truly* fit into recent events. And the third, the proverbial question of the day, how could artifacts coincident with Easter Island end up in southeast Utah?

Kika snapped her fingers in his face. He emerged from deep thought. They crouched low and scurried in a zigzag pattern to the edge of the village.

Mac's voice thundered behind them. Whitey gasped as he squeezed through the narrow, T-shaped tunnel.

"Must be like fishing the cork from an expensive bottle of wine," she said, gleeful to approach freedom.

"Break time," Whitey bellowed. "I'm out of here! That ain't no ceremony chamber, it's a torture chamber."

Exercising extreme caution, they located the pecked climbing holds. The voices behind them grew louder. Whitey was ten feet from the plaza. Mac two seconds behind him, head swaying side to side, disdain blanketing his slanted face.

"Hurry, you lead," Howie exclaimed. She lifted one knee to her chest and placed her toes in the first hold. Next, she placed both hands in the seam overhead, and exerted finger strength to pull herself up. He trailed inches behind her, both gliding as gracefully as ancient Lizard People. Exposed to a sniper like flies on a wall, Howie threw her a question near the top - "why were there *three* climbing ropes and *three* harnesses when we only saw two men?" Its impact would have wrenched the average climber from the wall. Not Kika Windsong. She was in the zone, intensely focused upon each move. Her Navajo heritage kept her focused. Colorful images filled her mind, those of her ancestor's upward movement and emergence from the underworlds. How they had ascended higher and higher until they were just beneath a blue dome representing sky; seeking a crack, an opening, to emerge to a new and brighter world above. The sky above Kika was bird-egg blue. Contrary to their perch near the hidden chamber, their world grew brighter.

ACROSS the canyon, an observer moved his lips as though talking to the brush. Camo netting covered his face. A high-powered scope was glued to one eye socket. A thin wire dangled from one ear. He smiled proudly.

EIGHTEEN

Mac's sixth sense engaged the second he reached the plaza. Parker's right foot disappeared just as Mac's eyes angled upward. They swept like a searchlight. He tasted the scent of another human. It infiltrated the ruins. Yet, he saw nothing. Before ascending, Parker had scraped away the footprints from the liftoff point. He dribbled pebbles to restore a natural setting. It prevented an ugly confrontation, possibly saved their lives. The dagger-toothed killer gripped his handgun. His frenzied, back and forth pace resembled a hyena that had lost its scent. He was onto them. He just couldn't see them. Pivoting 360 degrees, he stared up at the ledge again.

Kika yanked Howie from the edge. They rolled as one for twenty feet. Her panicked eyes locked with his. He cocked his head signaling further retreat. Crouched low, they scurried like hunchbacks to the cliff. He lowered their backpacks and propped himself against the wall. Kika joined him, breathing harder than ever, both sliding down on their butts. They were sweaty and clammy. Grit clung to exposed skin. They crawled behind the largest boulder and lay flat on their backs. Safe for the time being, exhaustion set in.

"Too close for comfort," she panted in whispers, heart pounding against her chest. Howie actually heard it. "Think they're onto us?"

"I covered our tracks when we lifted off." He laid his hand over hers, apologizing for placing her in harms' way.

She glared a "we should have bolted earlier" look, a mild condemnation. He was lucky she could only whisper.

"How about a power nap? I've got first watch. I'll wake you in an hour. Here, some protein before you nod off." Dried fruit and almonds complemented hard salami and cheese. She barely swallowed her last bite when her head bobbed. A second later she was fast asleep.

MAC stopped short nailing-down the trail of their scent. Instead, he ranted and raved during their ten minute break, kicking fragile masonry walls, swearing he'd gone mad at being cooped up too long in the sooty chamber, thinking his imagination got the best of him. Greed drove him. The lure of millions outweighed another human's scent. That, and the incessant schedule dictated by their buyer, Horace Wainwright. The thieves reentered the ceremonial chamber and continued slaving away.

Thirty minutes passed. The village below was quiet. Howie's mind raced at the speed of light. So much of what they'd observed didn't make sense. It contradicted the Southwest's archaeological record. A connection between Easter Island, ancient Peru and Inner Ruin? Unconscionable, he thought. Theories floated in a bottomless cell deep in his brain. It was an intellectual playing field he often visited whenever sleep escaped him. Deep-cell thinking yielded prodigious results. Postulates appeared before him on a continuum. They ranged from challenges to the Bering Strait land bridge theory to famed anthropologist Thor Heyerdahl's reed boat voyage. He toyed with the notion of extensive coastal migration routes into the Americas. He'd always been a skeptic of the Bering Strait theory, never buying into *one* migratory window into the Americas from the north. Practically daily, he'd spot an Internet announcement which contradicted those in the Bering Strait camp.

His eyelids fluttered. Embryonic hypotheses circulated deep. Some took shape. "Could twenty-first century dating techniques and nano-technology turn earlier migration models upside down? Can DNA samples be derived from the artifacts? Can anthro-geneological specialists be consulted? Did the Ancients leave traces of mitochondrial cells in the ceremonial chamber? If even some of this is true, the discovery will transect several scientific disciplines. Legions of archaeologists will spend decades bridging the gap between southeast Utah and the southern hemisphere. Which institute, or museum, will land the excavation and research contracts?" He was suspended in a deep-cell zone, yet, sufficiently consciousness in case Mac climbed up and snooped around.

"Where did we come from? How did we get here? Natives have their own emergence stories. What about the rest of us? Didn't people want to know?" Hypotheses clustered in his brain. Most led to further challenges. His mind loved a good puzzle. Nevertheless, the conundrum at hand seemed to defy solution; offering only clues, which took him down an endless path stretching to infinity. Thinking merely spawned more questions. "Ultimately, the quintessential question, the hurdle scientists with even a dozen PhDs need to answer, is this: How reluctant will academia be to rewrite history? Will they readily reconfigure the Holy Grail of human migration into the Americas? How does Clovis Man fit into this picture? Will migratory patterns be traceable *northward* from the southern hemisphere instead of vice-versa? The secret ceremonial chamber *must* contain the answers. It must! We must recover every imaginable bit of physical evidence. It has to withstand bombardment by the scientific community. Skeptics will be in their zenith. They'll trumpet a shrilling voice. And, if what we've seen is even remotely plausible, a new history will be chiseled into granite. What's more, ill-fated, north-to-south migration routes will be sealed as having told only part of the story." His body remained list, his cerebral vortex achieved near-nirvana. Suddenly, it all came crashing in. Theories retreated. Reality struck when Kika elbowed him.

"What's happening?" she begged, echoes thundering nearby. "Where are they?" She rose to her knees and melted into the boulder protecting them.

Howie pursed his lips. "Shush. They must be arguing again." He crawled from their safe haven and approached the edge.

Kika was energized by her power nap. She clutched Howie. Howie clutched his Sig. They listened intently.

The shouting below them reached explosive proportions. Howie leaned forward and quickly withdrew. They crouched exactly where they had been twelve hours earlier. Upwards of fifty crates were stacked on the plaza. Howie spotted a second set of Anasazi holds pecked into the cliff in a deep seam on the west side of the village. They bypassed their observation ledge and led straight up to the rim. The seam was so deep, and the holds likewise, that it allowed for even oaf-Blizzardhead to climb or descend. They might have been used by ancient villagers to haul heavy loads or by physically-challenged occupants. Mac and Whitey had used them for sure. Kika saw what he was staring at. She knew that the goings-on at Inner Ruin would cause archaeologists to revisit other cliff villages, if for no other reason than to re-examine their rear cliff walls.

Howie's watch read 5:55. The sun's rays sank below the rim. The temperature dropped just as quickly. Bronze shadows filled Inner Ruin. A reflection startled Howie. He spun around and squinted across the canyon. His falcon-like vision did not see a single thing worth worrying about. He raised his monocular. Still nothing. He studied a ledge ten feet below the rim. Thick brush grew against a wall crowned with Roundleaf Buffaloberry.

Mac's voice echoed like ammo. The team of two was breaking down. Whitey's huge paws dropped an artifact. It shattered like a Christmas ornament. "You idiot, damn you," Mac screamed. "That could have been a hundred grand in our pockets. Listen, retard, from now on only carry loaded crates to the clearing. That's all! I'll do all the wrapping and crating."

"Oh, yeah? I quit. I'm taking a long break. Maybe for good. Tired of this crap. Been hunchbacked too long in that piss-hole cave. No air. I'm outta here." His words struck like a sledgehammer.

"Get back in there you raw sewage. It's you that smells up that rat hole, you fat, stunted slug." He placed a hand on his holster. Howie watched in awe. Mac's lips labored as though a dentist shot them with Novocain. Finally, at gunpoint, he coerced Whitey into continuing. Reluctantly, the titan carried more crates to the plaza. He was a hired killer, not a manual laborer. His productivity slowed to a crawl as meager as the slug he'd been called. The air was battlefield tense.

128

Another scuffle was set to detonate. Seconds passed into minutes. Eighty crates lined the amphitheater. Whitey covered them with large tarpaulins.

A late-day cobalt sky hung overhead. It was 7:04 pm. "Go back inside for one more haul. We've got to finish by tomorrow - our last day in this lousy Indian hellhole. Tomorrow night is payday. It's why we're here." Mac attempted a smile. Greed slobbered out. "We'll turn this junk into hard cold cash."

Howie plunged his eyes into Kika's. A broad grin smeared his face. "You're brilliant. Glad we waited before climbing up to the rim."

His smile evaporated. Trouble erupted again. "Let's inspect your pockets, numb nuts," Mac commanded. "You stashing any trinkets for yourself? If you steal anything, I'll pick up where those Asians left off, hatchet your entire hands at the wrist. Then see how good you climb out of here." Whitey sputtered a litany of hoarse, indistinguishable grunts. Then, ambled bull-legged to the T-shaped opening. His stiff gait matched that of a giraffe, as though on stilts.

Howie focused his monocular on Blizzardhead's face. "Any idea how he got those horrible scratches? Looks like he tangled with a tiger. And, he's walking oddly. I never noticed when he was angled over in the ceremonial chamber. He's stiff and bull-legged, like he's favoring his groin."

Kika stared through her binoculars. A minute later she released them and bore into Howie's eyes. Rage spit from her lips, greatly challenged to whisper. "I think I know what happened! My guess is that Ms. Lofty was mangled more by *him* than by Slantface. But, not before she doled out her own punishment. Think of it, if I was her, I'd fight back like a tiger. Like my life depended on it, which hers obviously did. I'd kick, squeeze, and bite anything I could sink my teeth into. And, you can be damn well sure I'd grab onto his groin so hard I'd damn near castrate him." She caught her breath. "With me so far?" His eyes narrowed to slits. His lips tightened. He nodded. "And, I wouldn't let go until the absolute end."

"Or, got tossed out of a vehicle."

"Uh-huh." Her breathing was labored. Beads of perspiration formed a mustache. *"That's* why his face is all clawed. *That's* why he walks like the Dallas Cowboys stomped on his nuts. I'd bet anything. Let's hope forensics wiped her clean as a whistle. Got every bit of evidence."

"Let's hope so. Kind of tough to get prints when he's got no fingertips. Convenient for a killer." Whitey dawdled out with the last load. The men sat on separate crates.

129

Evening air struck like an icy waterfall. Howie checked his watch. 7:50. "Before we climb to the rim, keep one eye posted across the canyon. Thought I saw something move two hours ago. Could be nothing." But he knew better. Another axiom taught by his CO tapped his memory. "If you think your eye has spotted something, it probably has. Run with it as though your life depends on it. Like I've said, that'll make *them* the dead guys, not you." Common sense, thought Howie, recalling those tense days involving Iraq-Kuwait border skirmishes. Then he remembered something else - under the stress of battle, common sense and rules of engagement often competed. For the first time that day, as he and Kika waited to escape by moonlight, he felt an ache in his gut. The flicker he'd seen aggravated him. *Had they become the observed?* Had roles been reversed? And, if so, by whom? Kika raised her binoculars and studied the opposite canyon walls.

Without warning, Whitey's throat regurgitated a vile message. How he'd roughed her up so brutally. The two observers bolted upright, staring angrily at each other. Whitey bragged about the gory scene and how he had tossed the limp woman from their moving van. "Kicked her silly, didn't I? She finally stopped moaning. Ain't going to squeal to no one now."

THE call came over secure satellite transmission at his mobile command post. It was routed differently than Parker's earlier cell phone call. The caller from Kayenta, Arizona used a satellite phone compatible with the Agent's. His voice reached into space and hooked onto a low earth orbiting satellite. From there, it dropped down to a ground station, which transmitted it back up to the satellite, then down again to Coldditz's receiving instrument. Ultimate security. Encryption was handled at the ground station. It never passed through a land-line or public-switch network. Since the agent was next to his high-tech, mobile surveillance van, a nano-chip passed the call to the NSA's super computers for analysis.

The voice on the other end reached him Sunday evening at 8:03 pm. He sat peacefully beneath shady cottonwood trees, a brief respite from his lengthy recon stint. Sunset was minutes away. The van was situated near a gigantic slice of earth's geologic timeline, Comb Ridge. The gigantic hogback ridge was a major fault stratum piercing the Colorado Plateau. It had been appropriately named because it bore hundreds of pointed, spiny-sloped ridges along its 75 mile stretch.

Officer Dudley Blue Sky's voice sounded too clear for the great journey through outer space. The relay took five seconds and covered a scant 60 ground miles to Cottonwood Wash. Blue Sky sat calmly at his desk. He looked calm and serene. Before him was an incident report faxed over from the Utah State Police.

"Got something you should know about," he began with an inviting tone. "Found a corpse in short proximity to Snow Flat Canyon. A vacationing family with two young kids discovered it wedged beneath a cattle guard. The guard itself was lying cockeyed. They couldn't cross it. You know; the loop which drops below Salvation Hill. Not a pretty sight for happy vacationers. Kind of negates millions of dollars spent on advertising by Utah's tourist bureau. Some outdoor playground, huh?" The policeman grunted.

After pulverizing the end of a toothpick, he flipped it around and speared its sharp end between two front teeth. "Its north of our jurisdiction. Utah State Police thought we should know since it was discovered on Cedar Mesa. Thought it might be related to the dead backpacker. I'm calling Quirk next. She'll be pissed. A second corpse associated with her turf, and on her watch, in as many days. Guess she'll need Wheeler back from that feeding frenzy in Moab, huh?"

"Negative, Wheeler stays put." Coldditz glossed over Dudley's cynicism. His mind was far away, orchestrating his next move in Snow Flat Canyon. He planned to return the instant his call was finished. The incident report was old news to the sleuth. Forty eight minutes earlier, an agent had walked from the van and handed Coldditz a printout. It was the same report that Dudley was looking at. The NSA's dragnet missed nothing. "How was the vic killed?" the Agent faked. "How long's he been dead?"

"Tests haven't come back yet. Coroner gave his best guess at two days, three max. He'll know by morning. That puts this murder in the same timeframe as the woman's. Here's the strange part. There weren't any backhoe or tire tracks. Nothing. I ran up there and scoped it out for myself. I don't believe in coincidence, you know. There's a cause and effect to everything. All events are connected somehow. Guy who lifted that cattle guard and tossed in the corpse must have been the Incredible Hulk. Ever try lifting one?"

Evening breezes swayed branches thirty feet above Coldditz. Blue Sky heard them rustle. The agent's phone was ultra sensitive. "Never intend to." His reply rang through outer space, then into Blue Sky's ear.

"Vic's head looks like it was put through a drill press. Bore straight through the vic's eye sockets, through to his brain. Mind you, I'm speaking in layman's terms. I still find it impossible to comprehend terminology in a medical examiner's report. Gotta' be a bloody surgeon to read one. ME states the vic died elsewhere. Cattle guard was just his final dumping ground. Not your typical disposal MO, I might add." He inserted a fresh toothpick. "Says what killed him was not the bored-out eye sockets. Or the brain tunnel. More like the one inch hole bore through his windpipe. And as if that wasn't enough, he was also crushed from a fall. I suspect he got too close to the canyon where our suspects were last seen. Perhaps he was thrown in."

"Wouldn't have mattered, guy couldn't see anyway." Branches swayed rhythmically above.

"Good one. Could use some humor before calling Quirk. Somehow the killer, or killers, carted him off and stuffed him beneath the cattle guard. Like I said, it wasn't a pretty sight for a vacationing family to stumble upon. First day in Utah's canyon country, and all."

"I agree," Collditz replied. "Anything else found at the scene?"

Blue Sky sat upright in his chair and cleared his throat. "Almost as strange as the death itself. There was a very, very old map, tattered edges, print nearly worn off. A bunch of faded scribbles and circles were inscribed. Near some place marked 'vortex' a large `X` was colored in red, near the Navajo town of Cove. I know the place well. On the opposite side of Lukachukai Pass. Breathtaking beauty. Tucked into the convergence of three mountain ranges. Part of the reason it's named Cove. Many abandoned uranium mines in those parts. Several deep mine shafts still exist. Had an uncle contract cancer after mining in the area. Damned U S Government, never admitted the leeched poisons killed him. Never paid a cent toward medical bills. Bastards. Oops. Sorry, agent."

Collditz hit mute on his handset. He knew precisely where the "X" had been marked. He'd already locked Cove's coordinates into his GPS. "Aspects of Delilah are converging nicely," he uttered. Then, he clicked off mute.

"Collditz," Blue Sky continued, "We want to help. I know we're on the periphery of jurisdiction here, no doubt. But, no one wants a killer roaming our region boring through windpipes and mangling innocent backpackers. You've got our total support. Some of my men are getting antsy. We'd like to assemble a posse and help. I can assure you ranger Quirk will demand immediate action."

Collditz got up and strolled toward the stream. It flowed gently over cobbles the size of Navajo round bread. He crafted his answer skillfully. "Officer, you've never met me. But, you've read the transcript summarizing my credentials. I've made a career out of this sort of thing. You've got to trust me on this one. I'm here on a mission relative to national security. Most players are lined up and in place. But, first, I need to meet Parker and his girlfriend. I need them. I've got logistics covered. The net will come down on this whole operation tomorrow night. You've got my word on that. *Trust me.* You tell Quirk she can go to the bank on that. Good as gold in Fort Knox, my word is.

Tell her to assemble her BLM team and standby until I give word late tomorrow."

Dudley, a loyal Navajo Nation police officer, was also a Navajo traditionalist. It raised the hairs on the back of his neck whenever Whites used the term "national security." "OK," he said, cutting him some slack. "Tomorrow night it is. Or, *we* start to move in. Keep me posted. I'll call Quirk now. I'm not looking forward to it. Won't be pleasant." He opened a drawer and removed several toothpicks.

An agent in charge of encrypted communications removed his headphones and looked outside at his superior. He nodded and gave him a thumbs-up sign. Coldditz smiled. He watched the stream cascade peacefully over the cobbles. It trickled with no more than a faint gurgle. But, his mind was a great distance off. At a skyscraper construction site in lower Manhattan. He entered the van and sat at his monitor, swiftly punching the keyboard. Eight seconds later he found it. He stared at the screen and grinned. The report cited two distorted bodies which had mysteriously fallen from the twenty-seventh floor of a construction project. Construction had been suspended until progress payments were paid to the Mob. Iron girders reached forever skyward, temporary floor planks and a sea of scaffolds loomed like a giant skeleton. Thugs recruited from Cleveland paid a visit to enforce delinquent payments. Things didn't go well for two superintendents who wisecracked to the collectors. Afterwards, rumors circulated that a squared-off, stumpy-looking guy with blizzard white hair pushed them from the planks. The more likely version, based on Coldditz witnessing the corpses firsthand, was that "the stump," as he was known, drilled his fingers straight through their eye sockets. A third hole pierced their windpipes. The superintendents veered blindly along narrow planks until they stumbled, plunging 300 feet to their death. The Stump crossed his arms, chortled hoarsely, and watched them drop into a maze of rebar and I-beams.

The Agent mused on that scene as the sweet-sounding stream filled the evening air. "Blue Sky is a wise officer of the law," he declared. "Events *are* connected. This is no exception. Strange, how the dots are connecting in remote southeast Utah. A few short miles from extreme northeastern Arizona. Where it all began with a German immigrant scientist. Almost as long ago as I am old." He flicked a small stone into the stream. "There *are* no coincidences. And a word for the wise to you too, Howie Parker - you and your Navajo sweetie are way out of your league."

NINETEEN

Quirk had a pact with the Assistant Ranger never to be interrupted on Sundays. The ring of her cell phone startled and aggravated her. Admonishments spilled into her modest living room. On the third ring her eyes caught the display: 8:17 pm. Officer Blue Sky's numbers stared at her. She cupped the tiny instrument and sat erect. "This better be good."

Three splintered toothpicks lay orphaned on the officer's desk. From the tone of her voice, he'd need rawhide strips, not skinny toothpicks. The State Police report extended from his right arm. He stayed mute for twenty seconds. Quirk sat quietly, perplexed at the delay, reminiscing on a series of prank calls last year. When he spoke, she stiffened further, her face turning radish red.

"Tourists found a corpse? Say again? Where? Oh, my God! What do you mean *eyes bored out, hole through his throat?* Are you serious? Hold on a minute." She banged her cell phone on the desk and picked up a satellite phone reserved for backcountry emergencies. She was nearly catatonic when she drummed Agent Coldditz's digits into the keypad. Seven seconds later, a voice message rang in her ears. She jerked the phone away, terminated the call and repossessed her cell phone. The next minute of conversation went exactly as Blue Sky had predicted. She went ballistic, ranting and raving why others had been notified ahead of her. Cedar Mesa was *her* turf. *She* should have been first in the loop. The Mesa was her home field. She was particularly pissed at Coldditz. He should have called her. *He* was the Agent in charge, not the Navajo policeman. After she had lectured Blue Sky long enough, she vowed to destroy the career of the Utah State Police Officer who had failed to fax her the report first. She paused and attempted a deep breath. It was as distant as Pluto. Then, she announced a plan. A strategic one. One that would integrate with Coldditz's twenty-four hour deadline.

After she hung up, she paced the floor. "How could this be? How could my calm and peaceful Cedar Mesa become a slaughterhouse?" She sat down and pondered her own rhetoric. Next, she tried Coldditz's number again - without drilling the keypad. The agent didn't answer. She left a detailed message. Darkness came upon her staff housing at Kane Gulch. She rose and switched on a lamp, turning and staring at her locked file cabinet. Her decision was made. The heavy drawer slid open quietly. She retrieved a semiautomatic handgun and held it firmly. Her strategic plan took a giant leap forward. She placed it and four extra clips in her backpack.

EVENTS in Snow Flat Canyon had reached a critical mass. The *esprit de corps* required for Mac's heist began to crumble. "My ass, roughed her up. What are you talking about? You pretty much killed her. Why? What for? She may already be dead. Why'd you go on kicking her like that? You barbaric jerk. You may have jeopardized our operation. What if she *does* squeal on us?" His face turned to molten lava, steam practically vented through jagged surgical scars. It formed an ugly death mask, titanium tooth poised to strike. He lunged at the stumpy freak.

Whitey hyper-extended lethal finger stubs to shield the attack. It was an anomaly, he rarely played defense. Tooth drawn, Mac stopped one foot short of his mark. The white-haired titan stood his ground and grinned. He wasn't frightened of the man whose life he'd saved. In a swift movement, Mac brandished a Beretta 92. Top in its class. The team of two faced off. The scene looked terminal, like tectonic plates smashing together.

Howie and Kika had a balcony seat. "Maybe they'll kill each other," she whispered.

Whitey pressed his face against the gun barrel. His carnivorous grin resembled a whale shark's. Mac was entombed in a vaporous miasma of the foulest breath imaginable. The heavy exhalation polluted his thinking. Unprepared for a noxious assault, his reaction time slowed. "I'll give you a tracheotomy right here, buster. Make Swiss cheese out of your eyes too. You seen what I do to people, slant face." Mac jumped back from the giant's toxic emanations.

He filled his lungs with fresh air to avoid vomiting. Suddenly he leveled the 9mm at Whitey's groin. "Yeah? I ought to unload a full clip straight into your crotch. Finish off what that woman started when she began shredding your nuts. It's one thing you mangled her like chopped liver. But, it's another to gloat over it while we're working our asses off on this once in a lifetime heist. A prize worth fifteen million bucks."

"I done worse things to women," growled Whitey. "Maybe the coyotes or snakes already got to her. Lucky I didn't kill her outright, that's what I do best. Kill. In case you forgot. Especially to snitches. She ain't going to snitch anymore!" Kika's stomach turned sour. Bile formed in her throat. "She's lucky I didn't drill my fingers straight through her head. Like I did that other jerk snooping too close. You like his cattle guard grave? Bet he looks proper under them bars. Got his own private jail cell."

Howie's rage exploded like pyroclastic bombs, bursting into every cell of his being, secreting from his pores like stigmatic lava. Kika quivered with fright. She bent over and rocked back and forth, like a child in a crying jag. Bile coagulated so thick she couldn't swallow.

135

They retreated from the edge and ran to the cliff. She cupped her hands at her mouth. Spasms produced dry heaves. Seconds later, curdled bile regurgitated. It filled her hands, reeking of a foul stench. Each heave matched an erratic heartbeat.

Howie ran bent-over like an angered gorilla. He reached the Anasazi holds and scaled the cliff faster than Kika ever dreamed. She pursued at half his pace, hoping the looters wouldn't overhear them once they receded from the upper rim. Twenty-one feet above their observation ledge and forty-eight feet above Inner Ruin. He clenched his fists into steel balls, ready to propel at cannon force, receding further from the edge. Then, vaulted three feet above the ground and launched his fists into the air. "Kill, kill, kill," he yelled in an angered whisper. "I'll jump off this ledge and kill them both. Even the score for that defenseless backpacker. Maybe that's what Blizzardhead does best - kill - well, here's what I do best - AVENGE and REVENGE!"

He raced toward the edge and pretended to leap off the rim. Feigning invincibility, he repeated the maneuver several times, each one landing him closer to the edge. "Forget the damned holds. I'll launch off and pounce on them." A minute passed. Angrily, he retreated into a small grove of juniper trees and repeated his airy boxing match. He spun around and around, kicking and punching the air. Fists worked like shrapnel. A flood of obscenities echoed in low decibels.

Kika spat more bile. Her breaths turned into pants. She tried to speak. Staccato exhalations formed a hoarse, primordial voice, one that reached back a million years, long before her Athapaskan ancestors. She withdrew from his space. His stammering slowed. She stared in bewilderment at the man she loved. Watching him act out his rage was as beguiling as Whitey's confession. She wondered if her own safety was compromised. At least they were in open space. She could keep a safe distance from his violent force field. She reflected on their vastly different reactions. Hers was visceral, instinctive in nature, an involuntary release of the senses. Muscles quivered, organs became spasmodic, and constrictions in her esophagus caused dry heaves. She viewed those as normal neurological and physiological reactions, given the morbidity of what she'd overheard. Howie's reaction, on the other hand, was neurotic. A neurochemical lever tripped deep inside him. Outbursts of toxicity and rage spewed like a geyser, as though the spirit of Beelzebub had seized him. She knew they were monumentally different people. She wondered if rage was configured into a person's genetic code, or how culturally-based their different reactions were? And, whether or not the torn fabric of their varying cultures could ever be seamed together.

136

She kept her distance. What she'd just witnessed was Howie at his worst. A nasty taste of Rage with a capital R. His unshackled demon had crossed the line. A significant line, one difficult for her to tolerate. Fury and anger was one thing. But violence was yet another. There was no room for violence in her life, a life beginning to align with Navajo tradition. She had to intervene, right then and there, on the rim of Snow Flat canyon, before darkness set in, before they were discovered by the looters or an accomplice. Otherwise, the "Mr. Hyde" within him would continue unbound. That could spell disaster, including exposure to the killers and certain death. Confrontation was her only option. She had to do it, or she and Howie might end up dead.

Two minutes passed. She moved closer, slowly reentering his space. Remaining silent, she reached out and touched him softly. Gradually, she inched up to him, reaching out with a hug that was tentative at best, remembering what her native ways taught - anger dispersed a person's guides, their helpful spirits. It caused them to flee in bewilderment. It kept them from coming to a person's aid when they needed help most. That so long as a person remained angry, they'd be on their own. She didn't want Howie to be alone. She loved him. She looked up into his eyes. They were still aglow. She knew then that if eyes had bullets, Mac and Whitey would have been shot.

"Damn them!" he growled. Rage dripped from his skin like sweat. It *was* stigmatic. He inhaled deeply. "I can't believe what that stumpy, murdering slime bag did to that woman." He shook his head fiercely. "But, then again I *can* believe it. Hell, Kika, you saw her, you were there, right after she was beaten and tossed onto the highway. Damned! We knew they were guilty of this all along. As soon as we saw his white hair. As soon as we nicknamed him. Neither one of us was willing to admit it. I was too preoccupied with the incredulous artifacts. Well, screw that. From now on I'm taking matters into my own hands. Damn my own stupidity." He kicked the ground. Stones cracked against trees.

"Shush. Don't even think of blaming yourself for her death."

"All I can say is this. Quirk, or whomever we reach, better give us the thumbs up to return here immediately." His fists formed grenades. "I'll initiate a preemptive strike on those crooks before the Response Team arrives. I'll rearrange that jerk's slanted face. Then, I'll have fun with Blizzardhead. I'll beat his stumpy head until he begs me to stop."

"Oh, no you won't, Howie Parker. Only over my dead body." The metaphor was a blip. She immediately regretted it. She retreated four steps, arms akimbo. "Look, how many times do I have to tell you this? It's always about your despicable rage. Earlier, you made a solemn oath. You promised you'd protect me, that you'd let the authorities handle everything, that you'd keep those killers far away from me. If you break your promise, I'm running out of here right now. This isn't about our pact to not change each other's traits. This is about life and death. *Our* life and death." Her scorn was anchored deep. She wasn't joking. "I'm scared shitless of that beast. Both of them, really. You can't fight them and protect me too. It's impossible. You can't do two things at once. No matter how great a marine you were." She tugged on his shirt. His muscles bulged. "Please, Howie, I love you, I need you, and you promised you wouldn't take revenge. You promised, Howie. You have to do this. *For me!*"

His face hardened like granite. Kika's eyes kept chiseling away. "No, I take that back. *For you*, Howie, you need to do this for *you*. That's why we're calling the authorities. This is their turf, their jurisdiction. We're not even official Site Stewards this weekend, much less vigilantes. We were sent here only to observe. Weren't we? Or, did you make that up?" He turned meek and fixed a blank stare. Horror seized her again, her lips quivered. "Oh, crap, you mean this whole life-threatening weekend was never sanctioned? Quirk never gave you the thumbs up on our being here? Are we playing another one of your silly war games? How could you, Howie Parker? Speak to me, damn you!" He kept silent. "If that's true, I'm just wasting my breath, aren't I? I'm outta' here!"

"No, Kika, wait. You're not wasting your breath. *Someone* has to do what we're doing. It might as well be us. I felt it in my bones. My gut told me that looting on a grand scale was occurring. *I knew it.* We're the best volunteers the government has in these canyons. And, look at the archaeological discovery. What if we'd left things as Quirk and Wheeler said - that Coldditz would call the shots? Would he have told anyone? Who else would have seen all this? Or - ," His words trailed off. Kika shuddered. She completed the ominous scenario about Coldditz in her mind. "I thought we'd be safe, Kika. I'd never march us into a death trap. Please, cut me some slack here. I do love you!"

A cool breeze swept over them. A part of her wanted to accept him unconditionally, take his word as gospel. Yet, she refrained, holding a small measure of judgment in reserve. His expression told her the score wasn't settled. Words crawled from his throat at a snail's pace: "Yeah, alright for now, no revenge." Instead of kicking the air wildly, he rutted his foot deep in the dirt. "But, I'll tell you this, Miss Windsong, I swear on a stack of Bibles I'll do everything in my power to become the bane of their existence. *I will go after them someday.*"

It was Kika's turn to stomp in a circle, eyes fixed to the ground. It wasn't over. The standoff had just begun. She squared off six inches from his face, black eyes glaring. Howie's face still wore a veneer of granite. She withdrew a sharp chisel and heavy hammer and began pecking away at his moral fiber. Hard. Each blow struck with a loud ping. "I can't live with that, Howie. That's not good enough. You've got to come clean on this or our lives together are done. You have to let go of this revenge crap. For good. I can't let you promise me one thing, while you've tucked away some hidden agenda. One that may spring up later and get me killed. I can't have that. How do I know when you're going to call up your revenge? How do I know when *'someday'* is? If it gets you killed, that's one thing...but I'm not going to let you get me killed because of some stupid need to take revenge. No. Not on my life. I need your word for good. FOREVER! It's not just this incident. It's your constant rage. I've seen how you react. I can't live with it any longer. You will NOT attack those killers. Never. *Not now, not someday.* You'll keep us at a safe distance *and* help ensure that the artifacts get out of here in one piece. It's all or nothing, Howie. That's my final say." Her eyes pooled into an inky substance. They were teary, but glowed with conviction. She wrapped chisel and hammer in a soft bag and retreated. "Or else, I'm out of here. Right now, and you and I are done for good."

Howie stood tall like the proud marine he was. He hadn't been backed up against a wall in a very, very long time. Deep within he liked it. He turned away and paced back and forth, hoping desperately Mac and Whitey hadn't overheard their ruckus. He paused and stood still. A tingling sensation came over him. A force inside was released. The skin on his face softened from drum-tight to natural tissue. He hadn't a clue what was happening, but, he was on the threshold of breaking into a new paradigm. Chakras were awakened. They awakened his senses, offering up courage to lay down his raging demon for good. He began to see that he *could* change from within. Clarity struck. An inner voice whispered that if he continued a life of rage and revenge, he'd forever be on equal footing with his adversaries. He'd be no different than the looters, the murderers or any other menace to society. He hated that proposition. He'd never quite looked at it like that before.

It was as though his genetic code was swiftly reconfigured. Cells invaded tissue to take up battle stations against old behavior patterns. Healthier mutations arose victoriously. They stomped out his stinking thinking, his old ways. He suddenly realized that Kika Edison Windsong had placed him in a "winner takes all" face off with his demon. The one he'd conveniently checked into the penalty box until they were needed.

Howie Parker realized that the scene before him in Snow Flat Canyon was not an abstract, random event. A new message spoke to him in a voice he hadn't heard before, one from his heart.

139

Resoundingly, it said: Your life isn't about your relationship, isn't about bringing murderous vandals to justice, and isn't even about the miraculous archaeological discovery...*it is about you* - Howie Parker, age 35, taking a giant leap of faith. It is about standing at a crossroads in life: about fleeing the dungeon that is shackling you and your pet demon in hell's depths; about purging yourself from equal footing with sordid adversaries.

Last, but not least, it was about realizing that a new outlook on life, coupled with Kika's support, could conquer his rage. It would take work and extreme commitment. Kika's commitment to him was contingent upon it. He would then be able to form a true relationship with another person for the first time in his life - perhaps forever. *That's* why he stood there with his back against the trees. *That's* what being in Snow Flat Canyon at that very moment was all about. Now he finally understood.

Released from his heavy shackles, he walked straight over to Kika, both arms outstretched and placed his hands on her shoulders. He spoke from a new perspective. He was ready for the journey, ready to emerge victoriously from the dungeon, ready to become a free man at last. He cast away his insensitive "tough guy" approach. His words were compassionate, yet direct. Not weak, not apologetic. His attitude was positive, not avenging. Kika melted. "Alright," he said. "You've got my word. No revenge, not now, not ever. *I promise.* I don't want to be like them, Kika, which is exactly what I've done all my life. There'll be no more retaliation, no more descending to the playing field of those who anger me. I can't live like that any longer. All I've ever done is recycle the same behavior over and over. I can't leave us vulnerable, wide open, to be killed. And I can't face the thought of losing you. Ever! Our relationship - you - mean everything to me." He embraced her warmly. She felt courage in his grip. It felt new and exhilarating. Something had definitely changed this very instant.

"Now," he stated gallantly, "let's get this show on the road. Back to our duties. Get this nasty business behind us. Our backpacks and firearms are still on our observation ledge. One last crawl out to the edge behind our favorite boulder. You game? Perhaps we'll overhear their timetable, or find out when their backup help arrives, or how they plan to remove these crates without anyone noticing. The moon will rise in thirty minutes. We'll take advantage of its light again. No headlamps."

The looters emerged from the cavern and entered the plaza. The quantity of lidded crates was beyond an easy tally. Mac and Whitey were still at each other's throats. A yawn filled Kika's face. "I'm drained, emotionally and physically. Need another power nap. You listen for both of us. Wake me in thirty minutes." His Chase-Durer read 8:19.

TWENTY

A postcard-perfect sunset framed vistas between Farmington and Shiprock. The plump, burnt-orange sphere floated over the horizon. It made driving difficult, if not dangerous. Jed had experience with driving into sunsets. Buzz, however, had broken his sunglasses during his scrape with the taxi driver. Squinting into glaring sunlight intensified his orneriness. The Walther's barrel remained imbedded in Trixie's neck. Attempts to shield his eyes from the glare were futile. If he held up his forearm, his arms crisscrossed. When that proved too awkward, he fiddled with the visor and shielded with the palm of his hand. He cursed the West louder than ever before. He yearned for cloudy Cleveland.

Driving through Navajo-populated Shiprock, the trigger-happy wacko reached down to the bulge in his sock. He removed a .32 caliber pistol. Leisurely, he placed the Walther in his *left* hand at the base of Trixie's skull. He dropped his window. Gripping the small handgun, he leaned from the opening and pantomimed shooting Natives walking beside the highway. Each time, he pointed the barrel upward, leveled it slowly and took aim. His lips formed the sound of a spent bullet. "Just like shooting red skins from a stagecoach in the Old West days," he said, with a slobbering grin. "Them Indians is lucky I'm not pulling the trigger, man. They can have this dirty West, every last inch of it. Course, if you was to ask *me*, we should never have given them back *our land*. We fought hard for the West. After we snatched it from them, it belonged to us. We should never have given it back. They don't need no Reservations. What dumb President did that anyway?" He itched one his oozing blotches. "Know what? Wish I was alive back in them Old West days. I'd have fought them injuns tooth and nail every hour. I'd have kept me a gun in each hand. I'd have shown them a thing or two about shooting. About how to use real gun power, man." He leaned out the window and took aim, pretending to shoot school-age kids leaving a bus stop.

"You're the dumbest prick I've ever met. You don't know nothing about nothing."

"Well, slap my face, man. I don't need no lectures from you. You're from that piss-smelter town Pittsburgh. You listen to me, man, about this Indian crap. This here is *our* country, *our* land. Not theirs. It's all I got to say about Indian rights. Subject's closed."

"You got a date with death, fuzz head. Sooner not later. Feel it in my bones. Hope I'm the lucky guy who beats Whitey to it. Course, if Whitey did steal the honors, I'd pay top dollar for a front row seat to watch him bust you in two pieces." Jed's urge to cold-cock Buzz was so powerful he could barely stay on the road. "I'll let the blazing sun reckon with you tomorrow. It'll ripen that skull until it swells up and becomes a perfect target." The maniacal gunslinger ignored Jed. He continued playing his shooting gallery game.   "One last thing, loser. We never gave Indians any land. It was all their land to begin with. It never was ours and still isn't so far as I'm concerned. We stole it from them in the first place. East, West, North or South, doesn't matter. It's all the same. Whole United States was theirs. Stole damn near all of it by force. Slaughtered most of them. Or took it with treaties and the like they couldn't understand. They barely seen White men before, much less seen his language scribbled on funny paper. How'd you feel if someone toting a uniform and huge Colt on their hip shoved a piece of paper with strange scribbles under your nose and said: ` sign this`. All the while a cavalry stood ten feet away with rifles pointed at your heart. Huh? And I'll tell you another thing. Gave them all sorts of diseases too. And killed all their buffalo. Yes we did. Even in Pittsburgh there's Indian names and reminders all over the place. I happen to like Indians. My old lady's got Susquehanna blood. And, one more thing pizza face, quit pointing that gun out the window at those Navajo. Like I said, you got a date with death. Don't care who does it or when, just quit screwing around with Mac's quick money scheme. You get us pulled over because of your silly stagecoach games, I'll kill you myself right in front of the friggin' cop."

"Well, slap my face, man. Talk's cheap. I got me a gun in each hand and you're talking smack. You got balls." He spit through a narrow slit between his upper front teeth. The stream splattered off the floor like he was peeing.

Ten miles northwest of Shiprock, Jed steered into a wide pullout. Russian olive trees lined its perimeter. Buzz ordered Trixie to stay put with her hands on the dashboard. Both men jumped to the ground and walked to the front of the truck. Jed toted a duffle bag. Buzz kept the 9mm pointed in his direction. Jed wiped clean both side doors. A lone car passed on the highway. It appeared he was innocently wiping grit from the truck. Then, he moved swiftly. He had removed the rental truck's New Mexico license plates. Pale white plates reading "U S Government" across the top and "For Official Use Only" across the bottom were mounted. If traced, they would direct the inquirer to a truck of the exact color and style registered in the federal inter-agency pool. He reached in his duffle and held up two saucer-sized decals. They read: "United States Geologic Survey." Pretending to clean off the side mirrors, he let another passing car disappear from sight. Then, he affixed one decal to each door. Beneath that, he attached a rectangular emblem. "Survey Crew."

143

He stood back and admired his work. He was a detail oriented man. He proudly displayed two government I.D. tags. They hung on lanyards. The official USGS holographic seal and employee photo made them look legitimate. Mac hadn't planned on a third passenger, especially a female hostage held at gunpoint. They'd have to wing it if anything went wrong. From an envelope, he withdrew a phony Bureau of Land Management manifest authorizing survey work on Cedar Mesa. It included a permit to operate ATVs across wilderness canyon country.

The makeover was completed in six minutes. Buzz never lowered his guard on Jed or Trixie. Waiving his handgun, he commanded Jed to place both hands on the hood, execution style. Then, he stepped back and relieved himself. While his stream of urine ran strong, the registered sex offender pivoted and aimed it in Trixie's direction. He stared at her with a sickening grin. When the urine stopped, he fondled himself for a full minute.

"If it weren't for that gun in your friggin' hand," Jed screamed," I'd kick your nuts so hard you'd pee through a catheter the rest of your life. Which ain't going to be long, fuzz head."

"Well, slap my face, man. Ain't you the gun-less wonder bragging again? Ridiculing ain't healthy when I'm toting a big gun." His blotches swelled like blood-laden leeches. "Now get back in the truck and haul ass. I'm itching to bunk down for the night with my sweet little prissy here."

Jed started toward the driver's door. He stopped mid-stride and removed an electronic sensing device from his duffle. Then, raised the hood, explaining to Buzz he had one last checkup to perform.

"You're stalling. Don't try pulling a fast one. You inspected this rig before you paid that dumb Polak."

"Just making sure no one's playing with us." He crawled under the rear axle and swept the device forward toward the engine mounts. He held it along the frame and new suspension rigging. He found what he suspected. State of the art tracking device. Outraged, he cursed beneath his breath: "Krenecke, you just signed your death warrant." He remained under the truck and shouted out a pretend check list. He couldn't let wacko Buzz know about his discovery. Otherwise he'd force them back to Farmington and gun Krenecke down before his niece's eyes. Perhaps everyone in the shop. He couldn't let that happen. They'd lose too much time. Mac established a timetable with no margin of error. He'd deal with Krenecke and his shop later. After their gig, after they were paid, after he first killed Buzz. He crawled out from under the truck, slapping dirt from his shirt and trousers. "Clean as a whistle. Pardon the delay. Never can be too careful. Roads on that mesa we're heading to are vile."

The tiny hamlet of Bluff, Utah was dark at 8:55 pm. They drove directly to the ATV dealership. Jed dimmed his headlights and drove to the rear of the building. A row of dirt bikes and ATVs were chained together. He backed into the loading dock and flashed his headlights twice. Loading dock and yard lights were activated. The sellers were ready. A ramp was attached to the truck's tailgate. Within minutes, four all-terrain vehicles were loaded.

Each was equipped with a heavy duty winch. Twelve heavy-duty batteries were loaded to provide standby power. The ATVs would also regenerate a second on-board battery during running. The four wheel drive featured "on demand" control. Noise suppression mufflers and independent rear suspension were crucial for their mission. Four ultra bright headlights were mounted to the steering bar. A dimmer switch could be activated. The last items loaded were trailers measuring 4 feet by 7 feet. Jed carefully inspected the batteries, winches and headlights. He started one of the ATVs. The muffler did its job. The rig was as quiet as an electric golf cart. He unzipped his duffle bag. Four sets of night vision goggles stared back at him. And six grenades, just in case. Jed handed their leader 75 hundred dollar bills.

On the outskirts of Bluff, Jed discovered a golden opportunity. He slowed to a stop and told Buzz he was stepping out to urinate. Actually, he slithered in the shadows and affixed the tracking device beneath a snack delivery truck. He chuckled at throwing off the person tracking them. Buzz was impatient but never detected his move.

They drove north to Blanding. Once there, they steered west on Highway 95 toward Bears Ears. They turned south on Highway 261 to access Cedar Mesa from the north. Trixie remained mum, her gaze fixed straight ahead. She avoided eye contact with her captor. Buzz spat like a spitting cobra a second stream of saliva. It splattered off Trixie's work boots. "Let's do the math, my little prissy," he said. "So far Mac's got over eighteen grand stuck in this desert gig. Plus travel expenses and provisions. Not including a front-end bonus to lure me and Trepke here to sign up for his outfit. All that dough and we haven't even begun hauling old Indian junk away. With me little lady?" He swiveled the gun to her face and pressed it against her nose. "You worth eighteen grand?"

"Ease off," Jed said. "She's not hurting anyone." Pale eyes iced over. They stared at the stupor-faced jackass holding a high-powered weapon to a tiny nose. "Keep her out of Mac's operation. She's got nothing to do with it."

145

"Well, slap my face, man. There you go again, the gun-less wonder ordering me around." He opened the glove box. Dim light shined on his ugly face. Blotches darkened in direct proportion to his agitation. What began as blood-laden leeches spread like tentacles on a periwinkle. "So, genius driver from Pittsburgh, you born yesterday? You *are* dumber than steel. She's got *everything* to do with it. *Like I said, collateral.*"

Jed's head hardened by a factor of ten. He couldn't wait much longer. He visualized the best head shots he'd ever delivered. The ones which caused a victim's eyes to float in nothingness. Then, collapse to the ground, dead on impact. He reviewed optimum speed, correct trajectory, and point of impact. He locked it into memory.

They were four miles north of Kane Gulch Ranger Station. Howie and Kika had entered the Mesa from the south, from Mexican Hat up the Moki Dugway switchbacks. It upset Jed that there were only two routes to access Snow Flat Canyon. He normally plotted several escape routes. That night, they were required to approach from the north. Large trucks were prohibited from negotiating the switchback's eleven tight, hairpin turns. And, they couldn't risk drawing attention.

Darkness blanketed Cedar Mesa. The highway sloped downhill. Seconds later, the southeastern sky glowed, revealing a huge pale-yellow ball. Slowly it emerged, like a newborn's head stretching from the womb. It was a surreal invasion. Earth's moon was the only object before them, disproportionately huge, nearly full. Like the newborn, it took to life quickly, climbing into the starry sky and illuminating the landscape. Trixie studied it closely. It was the same moon soon to guide Parker and Windsong to safety. They were nearby, a scant five miles east resting on their observation ledge.

Trixie embraced the image like a lifeline. It was all she had. A 9mm was pressed deep into her neck. An outlaw drove a truck never to be returned. All three were poised to commit a major crime. The moon's glow was her only salvation. It brightened as it climbed higher. Trixie's hope brightened too. She focused on it as a source of power. Its warmth mitigated the cold gun barrel bruising her flesh. She prayed silently to it. She petitioned it to release her from what seemed like sure death.

The professional driver had memorized road maps in Farmington. As though he'd found the proverbial needle in a haystack, he turned left onto a dirt road. Fifty yards in, a BLM sign read: "Brushy Mesa and Snow Flat." A second sign warned: "Road Impassible When Wet," Portions of it overlay the historic Mormon Trail of 1880. It led east toward several canyons, including Snow Flat Canyon.

Jed crept slowly as the over-height truck rocked sideways in deep ruts. Four miles in, the road forked. He veered left and crept carefully for a quarter mile, and then eased into a swale. A deep arroyo lay 50 feet to the right. Large Ponderosa pines and two groves of pinion trees provided cover. It was the perfect hideaway. Mac and Whitey's camper van was hidden one mile northeast.

They'd arrived, one step closer to pay dirt. "Job's cake," Jed assured his passengers. "A quick in and out job. Easy money. All cash, we'll be instant millionaires. Then, it's *my* turn to shine. Fast getaways are my specialty. Plan's flawless." He drilled Buzz with icy lasers. "And you, you perverted fuzz head? You'll be standing guard in the scorching sun. Baking to death while we sit in the shade."

"Oh, yeah? I'm fixing to rope you off and dig into my little prissy's honey-pot. Nice and sweet, I'll bet. She's been itching for it, haven't you, little prissy. When I'm satisfied, I'll make my way over to Mac's van. Long before sunrise. Find me a shady outpost."

TWENTY-ONE

Brewster reached for his cell phone without lifting his head. Fingers sprinted across the desk like a spider. Lively blue eyes scoured a report stamped: "Confidential." Fluorescent tubes brightly lit the laboratory. "A magnanimous find," he declared, "certain to alter present theories by quantum proportions." His voice was cheerful. It echoed off metal surfaces and shiny tile. Like a gull winging its catch, he scooped up the small phone.

He was the only occupant in the museum's research lab. It was as clean as a hospital's operating room. After all, to an archaeologist it was what the surgery suite was to a surgeon. Six deep wash basins and multiple rows of pale green cabinets, some with glass doors, sectioned it into roomy work stations. Recessed shelving lined all four walls. Fluorescent lights added a diagnostic touch. An array of microscopes, digital scales and computer monitors gave it a scientific flavor. Other high-tech instruments were scattered throughout. Some were covered beneath thick gray hoods. The back corner held a square metal table surrounded by four chairs. It was the "think tank." Researchers used it to brainstorm hypotheses.

The museum's visiting hours ended two hours earlier. The facility was a pillar of Southwest archaeological collections. Visitors were led through magnificent exhibits on self-guided tours. However, access to certain areas was akin to a secure military installation. The laboratory was one of them. Brewster stayed late to examine the confidential report before him. It was rushed by courier from Los Alamos National Laboratory in New Mexico. Significant, considering it was Sunday evening. Two security guards posted on upper levels were the only other occupants of the structure. A third guard roved through the ponderosa forest surrounding the complex. The lab occupied the bottom level of the sprawling facility, grading into a heavily-treed hillside and repository of more than two million prehistoric artifacts.

The famed archaeologist was electrified. The discovery would become the juggernaut of human migration sagas. Tsunami-like forces would flood every nook and cranny of academia's dusty libraries. Research would abound for decades. It would become the single-most significant event of Brewster's career. And, it promised to unravel thorny paradoxes associated with the peopling of the Americas. He looked up long enough to scroll to Wheeler's number. He pushed the green button and continued reading. Wheeler's voice messaging resounded in his palm.

"Semlow, it's Phillip. 7:15 Sunday evening. Please call me as soon as you get this. Extremely urgent. I'm reading the analysis from Los

Alamos. They ran X-ray diffraction and X-ray fluorescence spectroscopy on that rare artifact I showed you in the cocktail lounge. They've identified its trace minerals and chemical composition, but have been unable to pinpoint their precise geographic sourcing. Our little puzzle intensifies. *We simply must find the other half of the feather holder.*" After terminating the call, he realized he'd used his cell phone instead of a land-line as suggested by Wheeler.

He double-checked the lab's security. An LED light next to the heavy steel door blinked reassuringly. The door was connected to a timed locking mechanism. The alarm was set properly. He called the guard station. An officer faced seven security monitors. After radioing his partners, he assured Brewster the facility was secure. Feeling safe, he removed the feather holder half from his behemoth file safe. He stared at the object through its sealed bag. A label indicated that it had been removed by pot hunters from a cliff dwelling in Snow Flat Canyon, presumably Inner Ruin. That was the extent of its provenience. The informant who snitched on the Santa Fe art dealer had said no more. The Santa Fe office of the FBI granted special dispensation to Los Alamos Labs and to Dr. Brewster. They could retain the artifact for a maximum of five days. Thereafter, it would be returned to the FBI's evidence vault. Once apprehended, the looters faced several federal charges under a number of statutes, not the least of which was the Migratory Bird Act, since the artifact was identified by experts as being part of a ceremonial feather holder.

He held the sacred object in his palm. It measured three inches in length, was slightly concave and as thick as a slice of Texas toast. It varied in several respects from others he'd excavated. Besides its incised symbols, the solid ceramic bore a different color. The Los Alamos report identified a high percentage of crystalline minerals, stating: "The archaeological record for ceramic assemblages in the southwestern United States contains no 'signature,' or blueprint, for this pattern of clays. Trace minerals are clearly not sourced in North America." He stared down at the object, eyes squinting, and asked: "*What* do we have here? *Where* did you come from?" He turned the artifact over and inspected the unfamiliar symbols. Then he walked over to a microscope, dialed to a power of thirty and placed it beneath the lenses. An addendum was attached to Los Alamos's mineralogical report.

The statement was issued by Dr. Lin Chao, renowned scholar of Chinese linguistic tradition. Dr. Chao underscored that his comments were strictly off the record. In no way did they represent official views of the National Laboratory. His work at Los Alamos centered upon the peaceful use of nuclear byproducts. He'd opted for an early buyout

149

following his twenty-year career in cryptographic analysis for the Department of Defense, including the Defense Intelligence Agency, before being recruited to Los Alamos National Labs. Virtually 100 percent of his private life was dedicated to the study of ancient script - communication symbols attributed to lost civilizations.

An "old-schooler," Chao ascertained that ancient script communicated wisdom, as thought, through ideographic symbols, without the direct use of language or phonetics. Thus, when deciphering strange glyphs, his key to reading them centered on the ability to grasp conceptual thought patterns. Chao advised against trying to identify a language root, or logograph, of such script. His life goal was to trace the origin of mankind's ability to communicate - and what he'd discovered thus far was that the genesis of mankind's communication centered upon the transference of wisdom - and, furthermore, that mankind had *always* communicated through abstract symbols. "I believe that's what we have here," he wrote, "symbols incised in the form of an ideogram. Much like laughter is the universal language of joy, these symbols speak to us of the civilization's cosmological wisdom.

"Allow me an over-simplified example of thought-transference through symbols. In a manner of speaking, you can liken ideograms to the modern use of way-finding pictograms used in international signage. Obvious examples include symbols depicting restrooms, no parking, handicapped accessible facilities, lodging, food service and the like. Hence, the symbol of a bed, observed by travelers worldwide, is used to transmit the concept of lodging. The scribe never intended the reader to blurt the word 'bed.' Likewise symbols displaying silverware and a plate do not relay the words knife, fork, spoon or plate. They're used pictographically to communicate a thought concept…that dining service is available. Put several symbols together ideographically and the "writer" communicates thought, abstract thought. Concomitantly, through the symbols I randomly selected as my example, the thought of a *traveler* may be inferred. I realize such analogies border on being blunt. However, as you know, I have devoted my life to deciphering cryptic thought patterns. It has not been as complex as you might think. Most were established upon foundations of *simple symbology*. My work at the Department of Defense was no exception.

"Thus, abstract thought is the root of ideographic symbols. Each civilization constructs building blocks of wisdom to communicate with intelligent species. These incised glyphs, however, are truly a mystery. I've subjected them to every means of digital enhancement in our labs. I've also enlarged their images on full-sized, holographic "screens" used in presentations to congressional delegations. Then I set my experienced "mind's eye, intuitive overlay" on them. My intuition tells me that their arrangement may symbolize large monuments, or stelae. Furthermore, after subjecting them to software which integrates abstract symbols to celestial orientations, including interstellar, exoplanet searches, the symbols seem to align with coordinates found on our own planet, namely in the southern hemisphere. My linguistic discipline confirmed that. Prehistoric societies extending from the Tierra del Fuego archipelago to the Patagonian pampas utilized correlative, though not identical, art forms to convey wisdom. That could prove significant since the fragment's mineral composition is not of North American origin.

"Such are my preliminary conclusions. Hopefully, they'll provide us with a basis for additional analysis. Irrespective of technological advancements made at the Labs, *human minds* must ultimately interpret the symbols. And that takes me back to my starting point, and to my dictum: ideograms convey abstract thought; they require abstract human thought to decipher them. As such, these symbols do not represent the object pictured, but rather a particular idea suggested by them. A celestial one. And here's my blockbuster final remark - I am willing to render a broader interpretation, or one possibly sanctioned by the Labs if, and only if, *the entire feather holder becomes available.*" The report ended there.

Brewster's scholarly mind reacted in a nanosecond. He had to test Chao's working hypothesis. He pictured monuments, or stelae. His mind flashed to Mayan stelae seated at world-renowned ruins stretching from Mexico through Honduras. Many were inscribed with glyphs. He'd studied the Mayan code. He'd participated in numerous research projects at Mayan ruins. He could buy into a Mesoamerican connection, but one of South American context was unfathomable. "Extreme southern tip? How? The only monuments I know of in that area are situated 2,500 miles offshore on Easter Island."

He opened his laptop and composed an e-mail to one of his closest colleagues, Raul Jorge Javier Fernandez, PhD, Chair of the Department of Anthropology at the Universidad de Chile. They'd bonded instantly a decade earlier when Brewster was chief advisor to archaeological teams excavating at Mayan sites. Dr. Fernandez was the principal investigator. Following that, Fernandez's career was devoted to excavations at Monte Verde Archaeological Site in southern Chile. His papers published in 2003 postulated migration patterns of prehistoric cultures from extreme southern latitudes in South America. His recent book cited evidence of coastal migrations along the South American coast north to the Chicama Valley of northern Peru. From there, hundreds of centuries later, he plotted human migration *north* into what became Central and North American Pacific regions. Some in academia viewed his theories as too controversial. Due in part to their mutual respect and friendship, in recent years Brewster had joined Fernandez's camp in gathering evidence which weakened the Bering Strait theory.

Early in his career, Brewster endorsed the hypothesis that New World humans crossed a land bridge of exposed Bering Strait sea floor during optimal climatic conditions 12,000 to 14,000 years ago, then survived a trek via interglacial regions forming a corridor southward through the Yukon into northwest regions of the United States. The discovery of the Clovis culture in southeast New Mexico in the 1930's led to the theory that the Clovis people were likely the first human inhabitants of the New World, including South America. And that those peoples had migrated along the Bering Strait corridor and continued southward. Later in his career, however, those theories proved less tenable. He began to acknowledge that *other* significant archaeological discoveries advanced alternate global migration routes, including those into the Americas. Radio carbon dates at those sites suggested human occupation predating the 11,200 BP Clovis culture. Like other scholars of his era, he found it difficult at first to let go of long-established indoctrinations. Beringia and Clovis Man were stalwarts to his early academic discipline, but his scientific and intellectual curiosity demanded a strong consideration of evidence to the contrary.

He spoke excitedly in composing his message to Dr. Fernandez, as though his laptop transmitted voice text. He'd spent much of his career excavating on the basis of *hunches*. He knew that if anyone could shed light on Chao's statements, it was Dr. Fernandez. After scanning the report into his computer, he attached it to his e-mail. Then he clicked the send icon.

The transmission was intercepted by a geosynchronous observation and communications satellite "parked" over the Pacific. It performed dragnet eavesdropping maneuvers for the National Security Agency. It scanned telecommunications and e-mails for "target" words, but was also capable of canvassing 100 percent of designated transmissions. The satellite was positioned properly when Brewster's e-mail launched from his outbox in northern Arizona. It was netted by the NSA at 19:32:41, when it was relayed to southern Pacific communication facilities. Nanoseconds before Dr. Fernandez's server received it, the encrypted text arrived at NSA headquarters in Fort Meade, Maryland. Four minutes later, Colonel Holmes captured it at Brownstone. So did Agent Coldditz in his mobile surveillance van.

Unbeknownst to the NSA, the Department of Energy's Office of Counterintelligence in Los Alamos also downloaded the encrypted e-mail. Cyber warfare didn't stop there. A mole imbedded deep within the DOE's office in Washington D.C. had its own counterintel cyber program. The mole was a master at protecting its electronic assets. Its copy downloaded at the same instant as the DOE's copy at Los Alamos. Cyber spy games didn't stop there either. DIA's satellite nabbed it. An alarm beeped on the monitor of Wheeler's DIA contact. He'd inform Wheeler at the conference. The BLM Officer could yank harder on his metaphorical thread.

HE hadn't killed anyone in 15 years. Since Iraq. Killing. The concept lost its appeal after his epiphany with Kika earlier that evening. His motives had transformed, aligned more with keeping the two of them alive as opposed to militarily anchored in seeking revenge. Their goals had changed also - to protect the astonishing artifacts and report their discovery to authorities. Had Parker not changed, the cost would have been extreme. Kika expressed that in no uncertain terms. Unless he changed, her affection and their three-year relationship would go down the drain.

Their systems had completely shut down. They'd slept like hibernating bears. She had bargained for a short power nap. He had planned to keep watch, rest and regroup. What they got was four hours of sound sleep. Shocked, he read 12:48 am on his watch. He crawled to the edge of their lookout and glanced below. Mac and Whitey slept next to a smoldering campfire. Fortunately, old thinking didn't surface. Otherwise, he would've slipped over the edge and slit their carotid arteries. Sound asleep, Kika would never have known.

He took a bearing. Canyon walls exposed only half the night sky. The arced handle of the Big Dipper was visible in Ursa Major, the Great Bear constellation. His eyes extended in a straight line from the handle. Arcturus shone brightly. His orientation was confirmed, he had his bearings. Senses honed, S.I. quotient piqued, he leaned over to awaken Kika. He stopped suddenly. An idea struck him broadside. It illuminated artifacts he and Kika had glimpsed through a narrow passageway hours earlier.

A plan hatched. More than that; it solidified before his very eyes. Everyone slept soundly. It would be a quick, sneak-peek recon mission. It required twenty-five minutes, tops. He *had* to touch the feather holder held by Whitey. Plus the obsidian figurines. He packed latex gloves. Then he leaned over Kika without making contact, silently whispering that she'd be safe until he returned. "Great Bear's stars will watch over you."

He donned a nylon waist holster for his Sig, one that kept the weapon close to his lumbar. He adjusted the strap of his super-bright, 3 watt LED headlamp. It could direct light nearly 200 feet. He strapped a

Ka-Bar combat knife above his ankle. Before descending, he reminded himself: "Careful, now, Parker, don't overdo the Indiana Jones routine. Nor 007's. Mac's got real bullets in that Beretta, and Whitey...well, this isn't a Hollywood set. This is the real thing." Mentally fortified, he scaled down the Anasazi holds and slithered through the ruins like a cat.

THE loud ring of a land-based phone startled Brewster. He sprung from the microscope and darted across the room. He picked up before the third ring, eye sockets bearing indentations where they'd pressed against the microscope. Wheeler sensed tension in Brewster's otherwise jovial voice. He informed him he'd return from the conference Thursday. And that he and Ann intended to camp with Parker and his girlfriend at Todie Springs.

"Can you possibly make it Wednesday?" Brewster pleaded. "I'll meet you in Kayenta. Say, noonish at the Wetherill Inn for lunch. There's something you *must* see. In person, as soon as possible. It concerns the artifact I showed you."

"I see. Well, I'll do my best. Perhaps I can skip the last day of meetings. I'll call you from Moab Wednesday morning. Let you know for sure. I take it you're referring to the Los Alamos report?"

"I'll give you one hint. The mineral sourcing is *not* of North American origin. Its temper composition is igneous. Dr. Chao believes it could stem from volcanic activity at the extreme tip of South America. I think he's really onto something. Something he believes will shock the world." He paused and swept sparkling eyes over the empty lab, reflecting on his last statement. Solitude pervaded. "Need a favor. An urgent one. Can you contact your two friends, the BLM volunteers you'll be camping with? Have them begin searching for the other half of that feather holder. Also, please call Quirk this evening. Grease the skids for me. I must lead a survey team into Snow Flat Canyon. I must be on-site; my team will assist others in finding the missing half. We'll commence excavations Thursday at dawn if the paperwork is approved. Try to get a verbal from her. Just a simple yes or no. Instill in her that my mission has earth-shattering ramifications. Call me in exactly thirty minutes."

"No way to reach Parker and Windsong tonight. They've been out of cell range since late yesterday. But I'll be e-mailing them in a few minutes. I've got breaking news on another front. News Parker must read the second they arrive home. I've been using him as a sounding board on a few of my own theories. Let's see," he continued, burping a mild tremor after consuming vast quantities of spicy chicken wings, "it's Sunday evening. I'll call Quirk, but she won't like it one bit. No one messes with her on Sunday evenings." He burped again and raised a can of Dr. Pepper high above his cavernous mouth. The stream resembled water pouring into a steaming radiator. He even gurgled. It sounded like he was drowning, but Brewster knew Wheeler all too well. Like capping the radiator, he pressed his hand to his lips to squelch a loud belch.

"Thirty minutes, Semlow. After you've spoken to Quirk." He returned to the microscope.

HOWIE maneuvered along the eastern edge of Inner Ruin. Moonlight turned from friend to foe. It illuminated two thirds of the village. He wove through it like a thief through a laser security grid. Bent low to the ground, he maximized what little shadows there were. He stepped lightly over loose stone and debris. In two minutes he crawled through the passageway and rose up in total darkness. He stepped silently, afraid to turn on his headlamp. It'd been several hours since he and Kika had stared into the chamber. Anything could have happened. The thought that a guard could be posted *inside* freaked him out. "Might be why no one's shot us yet," he said to himself. He inched to the extreme right, to the mortised ledge where he'd seen carved figurines.

Lapsed time thus far was seven minutes. It'd take him seven minutes to return. That left eleven minutes to drool over the artifacts. To touch treasures sealed for centuries. He flashed his headlamp for three seconds and took a bearing. Darkness returned. He looked at his watch again. The second hand advanced like the timer on a bomb. He felt pressured. His photo-telegraphic mind recorded the placement of each artifact cluster. He listened to absolute silence, then filled his lungs with centuries-old air. He was overwhelmed, like he'd stepped through a time window instead of into a sandstone chamber.

"This is my chance. I'd have been shot by now," he said internally. He flicked on his headlamp.

He approached the altar in awe. His foot grazed a small object and sent it sliding across the well trodden floor. Wearing latex gloves, he picked up a carved statue. It *did* replicate a towering *moai* on Easter Island. Pivoting, he gazed at similar statues carved from shiny obsidian. On the mortised bench lay two stacks of feather holders. Tingling as though he'd touched the Holy Grail, he ran his fingers down the edge of one stack. He counted eleven feather holders.

The one Whitey had juggled lay crossways atop both stacks. He picked it up and held it. Three holes for inserting quills were meticulously drilled across the top. He'd seen thousands of rare artifacts in field excavations and in museums. He recognized intricate craftsmanship when he saw it. The eleven before him were superior to

155

anything he'd ever seen. He flipped it over. A pattern of tiny symbols was etched with precision. Carefully, his gloved hands lifted all eleven feather holders. The bottom of each was intricately incised.

He stepped back and swept his eyes over the altar. One discovery after another was illuminated before him. An array of exotic feathers lay flat on the altar. A woven quiver and various tapestries surrounded them. Nearby, a sandstone shelf held several ring baskets and a large carrying basket. Twelve double-mug vessels took his thoughts back to South America as the obsidian statuettes had . He studied the woven basket more closely. It also carried an identifier of South American origin - *totora* reeds, grown in only one location on the planet - what had became known as Lake Titicaca, high in the Peruvian Andes. He recalled that one human migration theory posited that *pre-Incan societies* migrated to Easter Island before a wave of Polynesians arrived.

A glance at his wrist showed that two minutes remained. He switched off his headlamp. Images of the astonishing artifacts danced in his mind. He felt as though he'd dreamt the entire scene. The same question phrased itself mentally as it had earlier: "How did ancient South American civilizations travel here? When? How long did it take them?"

Time was up. He oriented himself to leave. The sound of a cracking joint froze his every muscle. It came from the tunneled passageway. It was followed by a quiet scraping sound. He tiptoed quietly backwards and flattened against the wall. Suddenly a beam of light shone into the room at floor level. It captured millions of dust particles, suspending them without gravity. Howie matched his breathing to the suspended particles. The intruder's light darted to the opposite wall. A hand appeared. Advancing at a glacial pace, a second hand emerged. It clutched a shiny Berretta. Howie was strategically positioned to the right-hand side of the opening. He had reason for doing so. Combat training taught him that the human eye, in search of objects, focused first on objects slightly left of center, nearest ten o'clock.

He knew exactly who it was. He felt confident. He still maintained the upper hand, literally, over the intruder crawling pitifully on his belly. He was no more a threat than a snake at thirty degree temperatures. He knew that Crawling Man would be incapable of launching an offensive. Part of him still loved that. He slid the Sig quietly from its holster. He picked up a small stone. The instant a head emerged, he tossed the stone far to the left, deep within the chamber. The beam followed the noise. "Oldest trick in the book," he rejoiced silently. Suddenly, the light shone upon an object lying on the ground.

The same object his foot had kicked and sent sailing across the hardened floor. Words exploded in his brain. *"That's one half of a feather holder!* That means there's more than eleven. And that another half must be lying around somewhere." A body fully emerged in the chamber, still scraping on its belly.

TWENTY-TWO

"When in blazes you guys coming home? Been calling since five o'clock. Why've you been out of cell range so long?" His tone was curt. Words ricocheted off walls like bullets in an alley. A sixty-second timer counted down on Parker and Windsong's answering machine. "Call me at the hotel no matter when you get in. Check your inbox too. I'll dump as much as I can in an e-mail."

Wheeler guzzled from his third Dr. Pepper. For all the sugar and caffeine he consumed, he never had a sleepless night. He walked to the sliding glass door which led to the balcony. His second-story room looked beyond Arches National Park. A blend of indigo and crimson illuminated the western sky. The sun had dropped out of sight six minutes earlier, streaking to the International Date Line. The same sun, the same evening, and nearly the same minute that it blinded Buzz Lane.

He turned his attention to a bag of chips sitting atop the TV. It was wide open, tempting him to resume an earlier frenzy. He sat at his laptop instead, wearing a proud smile, anxious to spill the beans, to tug relentlessly on his proverbial mystery thread. For the past two days, he had avoided "networking" with associates between meetings. Instead, he spent every minute trying to uncover the untold story, the one he was certain was masqueraded by both newspaper articles. If there truly was a connection, Wheeler would find it. His fingers floated one inch above the keyboard. They fluttered. His mind raced. Fingers fluttered again. His mind followed. Like two hummingbirds fighting at the feeder. A giddy smile appeared. He pulled hard on his thread. There was so much to say. Touchdown, two fingers landed, one on the shift key, the other on "H."

"Had a breakfast meeting this morning. With myself. Skipped the morning conference. Sat at the table three hours. Coffee was great. Server left me alone. No interruptions. Didn't overeat. Mulled things over. After the second hour, several puzzle pieces actually faced picture-side up. Others I couldn't quite figure out. Gradually, a pattern took shape. My Defense Intelligence Agency contact in Farmington has been indispensable. I'm convinced. When the Feds closed their case on Schisslenberg, it was truly a diversionary tactic. Pretty much all the Farmington paper had to say about him was that he disappeared while employed by the United States Geologic Survey. The Indian paper reported that Navajo Nation Police took three men into custody. Claiming to be innocent tourists, they were caught snooping around an abandoned uranium mine. One recently exposed by seismic activity. They were also photographing a prominent sandstone arch. Both mine and arch are within shouting distance of sacred Navajo shrines. Bottom line - no place for three *bilagaana* to idly mill about.

"More tidbits. A sleuth from D.C. is stirring up dust in the Southwest. No pun intended. The DIA's guessing it's their archrival the NSA. A dealer in pre-Columbian art located in Santa Fe recently popped up on the DIA's radar. The DIA does *its* share of eavesdropping on the American populace too. It's also the clearing house for all military intelligence. Last month, it intercepted transmissions emitted from a benign "dead drop" in Washington DC. Source: The Department of Energy. Identification of a specific office is difficult, but he's working on it. He dug deeper. Turns out our buddies at Homeland Security traced similar intercepts two years ago. Although they never identified the source, the e-mails terminated at the same Santa Fe antiquities dealer. He's a sleazy one, that dealer, with connections to illegal arms traders and terrorist cells. The whole lot of them is on Homeland Security's terrorist watch list. HS turned their electronic files over to the FBI's counterterrorist division instead of archiving them. My buddy extracted them from right under their nose. The FBI slept soundly. A miraculous feat. He's the best!

"Then, four months ago, a new transmission popped up. Sourced in Santa Fe. My DIA genius traced its terminus to a residential neighborhood in Baltimore, Maryland. A Brownstone. Nice digs. Those transmissions carry a sophisticated security scramble. Smart money says the Brownstone belongs to the NSA. Look for yourself, Fort Meade and the Brownstone are on the same map. If it was simply the FBI's Art Theft Division software, he'd have cracked it. This one's a lot tougher, impenetrable. Another tidbit. Last week, several transmissions originating from Brownstone terminated at Cortez, Colorado. They carry the same signature code as the NSA. Bottom line - *The NSA seems to be closing in on our turf.* Look again, Cortez, Mesa Verde and Cedar Mesa are all on the same map. Why would the NSA be snooping around the Four Corners area?

"Hark! Enter the newspaper articles. And enter a previous unknown, one Wendell Coldditz. That's the real clincher. Out of the clear blue sky, smack-dab into the entrenched careers of two BLM staffers, enters a stranger. From...guess where? Quirk initially said the BLM's office in Salt Lake City. Brewster handed me Coldditz's card reading Homeland Security, Santa Fe office. How convenient. What's even more mystifying is that *he's the one calling all the shots.* Instead of Quirk, a career bureaucrat, or me, who live, work and breathe Cedar Mesa. Suddenly we have no say in looting and murders. It doesn't compute, Howie. I'm telling you, something really huge is about to go down. Right under our noses. I smell a rat. I say we're being set up.

Well, I'm not going to sit around idly at some conference and get left out in the cold. I'll dig deeper tonight and shoot you another e-mail in the morning. Then I'll return to Cedar Mesa whether Quirk wants me to or not.

"Ready for the next shocker, the real thread-tugger? In the early fifties, the government began testing super-secret prototypes of what later became GPRs - Ground-Penetrating Radar devices. A host of gizmos were delivered to an elite corps of field operatives. Top-secret exploratory field tests were conducted wherever uranium and vanadium deposits were thought to exist. The devices were light years ahead of other technology.

"Must have been quite a scene, huh? Picture a government techno-geek disbursing those contraptions to operatives like Q to a group of James Bonds. The field operatives were actually government scientists. Their cover, sensibly so, was the United States Geologic Survey. The Cold War was in full bloom. And Dwight D. Eisenhower, being a decorated general and all, was hell-bent for election...literally...to abstract any and all weapons-grade uranium as quickly as possible. Eisenhower dispatched scientists all over the West. They showed up like ants at a church picnic. The race toward atomic domination was on. The stakes were high. Global holocaust loomed as a realistic threat. And our famous general-turned-president was determined to win.

"Just so happens the Navajo Reservation sits on the largest deposit of uranium in North America. Been called the Saudi Arabia of the West. A major deposit lies southeast of our sacred convergence, across the Chuska Mountains, north of Crownpoint, New Mexico. Reprehensible actions were delivered by our own government in remote areas of the uranium-rich West. Atrocities were inflicted upon peace-loving Natives, details of which will never become public. Sad to say, but horrific health issues and gory deaths among Navajo, Hopi and other Natives are just the tip of the iceberg. Government-sanctioned mining poisoned their aquifer. What wasn't poisoned was depleted. *Billions and billions of gallons!* Either way, we siphoned their lifeblood. Good old rapacious Uncle Sam, huh? I say it all started at Plymouth Rock.

"So we stole their land through bloodshed and exploited their natural resources, then gave some of it back through treaties they barely understood. Last but not least, due to complicated, reciprocal Bureau of Indian Affairs agreements, our benevolent government hardly paid them a dime. It may look like they did, through royalty payments for oil, gas, timber and grazing rights. But the Natives were swindled. Reservations may look like Indian land, but if you follow the money trail, there's a very, very fine line between the Bureau of Indian

160

Affairs and sovereign Indian Nations. Minerals, water and even the damned bedrock itself are largely still under the "care, custody and control" of Uncle Sam! Second greatest travesty we ever forced upon our Natives.

"Want to know the first? *The greatest travesty of all?* Documents relating to land leases, water rights transfers, property sales and countless other transactions favoring the exploitation of weapons-grade uranium on native land were sealed for eternity. Reputedly, it happened in a secret pact between the Department of Defense and the Department of the Interior in 1954. Not long after Eisenhower settled into office. Unfortunately, and as we've heard in recent rhetoric, such actions were taken for the benefit of 'national security.'

"Here I am, a government employee regurgitating this. I've been dying to dump this on someone for a long, long time. I realize, "old boy," that if this e-mail falls into the wrong hands, I'm in a heap of shit. A gag order would be mild, an official reprimand a soothing antiseptic. Most people delving into these issues have a short life span. Some disappear for good.

"Which brings me to the missing scientist. Ah, yes, one Dietrich Schisslenberg. Once again, my DIA contact proved indispensable. Turns out Schisslenberg's paycheck *was* issued by the USGS. Although his true employer may never be known. Perhaps even a foreign government. Like where he emigrated from. Germany. Maybe our spooks even gave him some running room to see if he was connected to the Eastern Bloc. Most of our guys playing spy games back then were old SOS boys from Eisenhower's European theater anyway. Who knows? Complex spy and counter spy games were part and parcel of the Cold War. But I'm convinced that Schisslenberg's real mission was *not* mapping. He was clearly playing around with prototype GPR gadgets in remote crags of Navajo country. Mapping caches of the highest-grade uranium in the West. *Then he up and disappears.* How convenient. The Farmington article says he was survived by a wife, Maxine Schisslenberg, and a three-year-old daughter, Della. We dug deeper. Guess what? In 1956, three years after Schisslenberg vanished, widow Maxine changed her name and that of her daughter. She shortened it to a less German-sounding one. Anything to disassociate from Hitler's Fascist Germany. Her new name became..."

A loud ring jarred him. His head jerked. He was accustomed to the gentler tone of his cell phone. He saved his e-mail as a draft and raced to the nightstand. The news wasn't good. He listened intently to Officer Blue Sky. When he learned that Parker and Windsong would remain in the canyons until tomorrow, his mind played tricks, creating worse-case scenarios. He paced aimlessly as far as the phone cord allowed. He stared at a chocolate bar atop the fridge, pissed that he was tethered to the cord. He feared for the pair's safety; he'd have ordered them home if he'd spoken directly to them. When he hung up, he returned to his laptop and stared at the screen. "Heck, they're not home to read this anyway. I'll finish it tomorrow. More research will really spice it up."

PARKER was ready. McAllister should have been tipped off by moving particles in the beam of light. Stirred up when Parker's arm tossed the pebble. Mac's right-slanting skull zoomed left when he heard the object hit. Parker was in Mac's blind spot. The intruder scraped further into the chamber, head cocked left of center. Howie weighed his options. His old self wanted to crush the opposite side of the skull so Mac's ugly deformations would balance out. He dismissed that at once. A non-lethal solution appeared, one which would buy him and Kika time. He deployed his "upper-hand" advantage. The base of the crook's skull thudded. His world turned black.

Parker holstered his Sig and dragged Mac into the chamber. Mac would be out for about 25 minutes, ample time to flee to the rim. So long as it wasn't a trick, so long as Whitey wasn't waiting outside the T-shaped opening. He removed the Beretta from Mac's limp grip, checked the safety and tucked it and Mac's flashlight into his backpack. Silence returned. His light shone on the feather holder half. Holding it carefully on its edges, he flipped it over. There they were. Incised glyphs. Secure in the pocket of his pullover, he raced to show Kika and tell the world. He advanced chameleon-like, slinking through the shadows of Inner Ruin, stopping and listening every thirty feet. Still no Whitey. At the plaza, he peered between room blocks and saw the sleeping giant. He lay like a fallen tree. Yesterday, before his epiphany, he'd have cut him into pieces like a human sawmill.

Kika was still asleep. "Shush, shush," he said, rocking her and placing his hand over her mouth. "Come on, stand up, we've got to disappear." She sensed trouble and sprang to her feet, ready to interrogate him. Howie sprinted to her backpack and cinched it tight. He made sure her Guardian was easy to reach. He shoved the pack into outstretched arms. "Quick," he panted, "we've only got a minute before the fireworks begin."

"What? What fireworks?" Eyeballs skewered him. "What do you mean? What have you done? Have you broken your promise?"

"No, nothing vengeful. Bought us time, that's all. I've got the treasure of a lifetime in my pocket. I'll show you later. Let's skedaddle before we get shot."

"And Blizzardhead? Where's he? You promised, Howie."

"He was asleep a minute ago." He sprang to the base of the cliff.

Kika raced after him. "Hold on a minute, Mr. Parker. "What *exactly* is going on? What have you done?" She looked up and squared her stance. "You gave your word. Last night, you turned over a new leaf. I decided to stay with you. Ring any bells? Mean anything to you?" She anchored her feet firmly. "I won't budge until you tell me!"

Howie bent forward and highlighted his adventures of the past thirty minutes. Kika's backbone relaxed. A smile was unlocked. "OK, but did you have to clobber him? Couldn't you have just held him at gunpoint? Made him surrender?"

"What? Are you nuts? He'd have yelled for Whitey. Then what? I'd have been trapped in that chamber. *Their hostage.* And you? Sooner or later, they'd have gotten to you. Worst-case scenario? I'd be dead and you'd be scrambling for your life. Or their hostage too. I knocked him out so we could escape. I know my new role in life, Miss Windsong. To keep us alive and the artifacts in one piece."

Her lips touched his prickly chin. "Let's move." They scaled the holds like pros and moved swiftly over slickrock. The moon snoozed ten degrees above the horizon. Long shadows raced close at their heels. It felt like Mac and Whitey were chasing them. Howie flashed his headlamp sporadically to avoid deep holes in the ground or stepping on a snake. They ran in sprints, speed-walked for two minutes, then caught their breath while walking at a brisk pace. They repeated that pattern every five minutes. It was a comfortable cycle. Cliffs widened into mesas. It was incredibly windy. Gusts sandblasted them.

"We're almost in cell range," he said, clutching the left pocket of his pullover. He felt a smooth surface and sighed relief. His right hand reached its pocket. EMPTY. Panic struck. His gut tightened. Profanity challenged the howling wind. "It's gone." He stumbled backward in shock. "Holy shit, I can't believe it!" He spun around and dropped his eyes to the ground, practically tilling the soil with his headlamp, circling slowly in a ten-foot radius, scraping his foot and peering beneath sagebrush. He turned his pocket inside out. Still empty. So was his world. He looked back toward the canyon in disbelief.

"What's wrong?"

"I found one half of a feather holder inside the ceremonial chamber. Zipped it in my pocket. Or so I thought. Must have slipped out when I scrambled up the cliff. I need to show it to Brewster or Quirk immediately. It was incredible!"

"You sure it's not in a different pocket? Or your backpack? Could it have bounced out when we ran?" Wind gusts filled the silence. A jackrabbit sprang nearby.

Howie explained how the piece slid across the floor after he kicked it. And how Mac's flashlight illuminated it. "It was incredibly artistic. Had the strangest glyphs incised on the bottom. A language of sorts."

She stood directly before her man. "I'm sure finding it is crucial to you right now. But, sorry as I am, you're *not* going back for it until later. When we return with the Response Team. You can give it to Quirk then."

He shook his head and began circling in a larger radius. It was futile. Anger welled, but he never cursed again. Nor did he stomp the ground or start a boxing match with the empty space around him. He just shook his head in disgust. He looked like he'd just lost a loved one. Kika watched. A bittersweet smile tugged at her lips. Ecstatic he hadn't acted in rage or vowed revenge. She'd take wholesome regret over his old behavior any day.

"Crap, I swear I zipped it tight. How lame. Daylight's just begun. Guess I'll look when we hike back into the canyon to arrest them. Our phone call's more urgent. He removed his cell phone and stared in disbelief. The display was blank. He stiffened like a statue. "Now we're really screwed. I'm out of juice. What the heck do we do now?"

"I thought you tried using it earlier."

"That was six hours ago. Come on, let's move, we've got to keep ahead of them. I'll make something up as we go."

She held him back. "Got an idea," she said, trying to brighten his world. "Let's split up. You try to find their vehicle. I'll return to camp. I hid my cell in the camper as a backup. It's fully charged. Our phones work from the knoll behind camp. I know exactly what to tell Quirk. Or Semlow, or whoever I reach first. You disable their vehicle. We'll meet back in camp in sixty minutes. OK?" She looked at her watch. "6:30 am. At the latest."

He frowned. "Splitting up in a crisis violates all rules."

"There are no rules anymore. Not out here. Our lives are at stake. If you've got a better idea, you'd better spit it out quick." She cocked her head and listened. Only the wind spoke. "I know exactly where we are right now. We passed through here two days ago on our way back to camp. By the time you jinx their vehicle, reinforcements will be on the way. It's a slam dunk."

The wind played referee. He mulled it over as though he had tons of time. Or options. He looked up at the horizon. The sun was poised to launch like it had for billions of years. "Damn," he mumbled, "your logic's bulletproof again. I suppose you're right. The alternatives are ugly. We can't let them escape in their vehicle while we're still on foot. Remember our signal system?" She nodded. "Good. After you make your calls, come down from that rise and hide in the arroyo 50 yards north of camp."

"Aye, aye, sir," she blurted with a grin. "But, so help me, if those two freaks come within range, I'll unload every bullet I have." Her immutable death sentence challenged the wind.

"Whoa there, little lady," he said, donning his John Wayne accent. "That's disgusting. Now you're sounding like me yesterday. What's with your double standard? I reform - and you get a license to kill?" He smirked.

Kika stood up for herself. "No double standard. It'd be to save my life!" Her gaze was steadfast. She stood erect. For an instant, Howie pictured a strong-willed heroine riding side-saddle in a Western film. It spiked his testosterone. Self-defense was license enough, he figured.

They stepped closer and touched each other's hands. It became a hug. "Watch your tail. Keep to tall sagebrush and tree clusters. I'll take care of my business and race back to camp. 6:30, not a second later."

"You watch yours too. Someone's bound to be guarding their camp. A lot's hinging on their ride out of here." She turned away. Tempests pushed her light frame like tumbleweed.

She turned around, raised her palm to her mouth and blew him a kiss. It was a nice farewell gesture, albeit handicapped by gale-force winds. Its effect was identical to four days ago in the parking lot of the Anasazi Café. He licked his lips. They raced off in opposite directions.

TWENTY-THREE

Kika hiked northwest. Their camp lay two miles away. Although confident of her plan in front of Howie, trepidation now set in. Ferocious winds forced her to move awkwardly instead of stealthily. She knew their signal system would never work under such conditions. She'd have to fend for herself.

Gradually, earth's primal elements oozed into her. Open space and release from confining canyons lifted her spirits. She felt close to creation again. A restoration of harmony and balance was underway. Interconnectedness returned. *Hozho.* She embraced the feeling. There was no need for an exact compass bearing. She hiked slightly left of Bears Ears.

Thud! Without warning. She was thrust forward with such impetus that it left her nose and cheeks flattened against the ground. Razor-like stones scraped her flesh. Dirt bulldozed into her mouth and nostrils. The waist strap of her backpack snapped open. It slid up over her head. The attack was so sudden and delivered with so much force that she had no time to signal. Her upper lip cracked open. A stream of blood, unmistakably warm and salty, filled her mouth.

The assailant ripped off her backpack and threw it in the distance. He fisted a clump of jet black hair and jerked her head straight back. He buried his knee into sensitive spinal nerves. He kept it there, unmercifully, plunging it deeper, pulling harder on her hair. Head stretched back, windpipe flattened, she was unable to swallow. She began choking on blood building in her throat. She couldn't even spit. It was unmitigated torture. Like non-immersion water-boarding, she was on the verge of drowning in her own fluids. Suddenly, he repositioned his other knee into the nape of her neck and trenched her face back into the ground. She heard the brash sound of duct tape. She tried screaming. Futile. He forced tape over her mouth. It flattened blood-soaked lips. Her world tasted like tape. Horrified, laying powerless, her fears turned to rape. The capture took less than a minute.

HOWIE chewed an energy bar and a handful of almonds. He hiked north on Brushy Mesa. A strong crosswind pushed him along in a "crabbing" fashion from left to right. He was upwind from his search area. That troubled him. He reasoned he'd give it the full hour if necessary. Kika would understand if he arrived a few minutes late. She'd be safely tucked away in the deep arroyo. He enjoyed carrying on a robust, albeit one-sided, dialogue whenever he hiked alone. He pretended to speak to a fellow soldier during routine patrol. He spoke conversationally and with dramatic gestures. Normally, his invisible comrade kept pace beside him.

He stopped to inspect Mac's prized semiautomatic. He liked the natural, balanced feel of the Beretta. He tucked it into his belt. Next, the ex-Marine surveyed the landscape to establish imaginary search grids. He selected prominent trees, boulders and knolls from which to traverse eighth-mile sections. It was standard procedure in rescue operations; also in excavating archaeological sites, where one-meter grids were normally established. He struck out in the first grid. Then he turned west and commenced a new transect. Walking upright was tonic after crouching, kneeling or crawling for the past twelve hours. Had it not been for losing the feather holder half, their fifteen-hour recon mission had been highly successful. He knew Kika would soon reach camp and sound the alarm to authorities.

A reflection appeared at two o'clock less than one hundred yards away. He blinked reflexively and raised his monocular. A triumphant smile spread across his face. It was a van modified into a camper. Small trees shaded it. A spring seeped nearby. He scanned the footage surrounding it and notched up his defenses. Expecting an ambush, he spurted ahead, traversing landscape features, pausing between advances. Ahead lay a cluster of juniper trees and thick brush. He'd screen himself in it and scour the final stretch before approaching.

THE assailant's knees pressed deeper. A tsunami of pain surged up her spine. Her lungs expunged their last molecules of air. Deprived of oxygen, her life passed before her eyes. She figured she had another minute. Whoever he was, he wasn't playing games. He employed deadly force. She tried kicking again. His hand seized her ankles. Time became meaningless. There was none. Her systems shut down. She passed into the black zone. After what seemed like hours, he loosened his grip. Gradually, she regained consciousness. Wind howled through her ears. That was a good sign. She knew she was still alive. Incrementally, other senses returned. Sand whirled around her neck. She knew that was a good sign too. She had feeling above her spine.

He lifted her upright. Her knees collapsed. A vice-like grip clutched her upper arm. He dragged her like a rag doll. Her world was still black. A dark hoody was tied firmly around her neck. A pungent mixture of tape, dirt and blood made her nauseous. She did everything to keep from vomiting. If she did, the vile liquid had few exit options. Hands tied behind her back, ankles hobbled and mouth taped shut, she was virtually immobilized. "If only Howie would come along," she thought, "I'd beg him to kill this maniac. I could pardon him for taking vengeance *one last time*." As though he read her mind, he tightened the

167

hood cord. Garroting seemed inevitable. "Maybe he hates Indians," she sputtered into the tape. "Maybe his ancestors battled my people." When he loosened his grip, she collapsed again. She lay on her stomach. She was sure she'd be raped. She rose to her knees. Defenseless, she couldn't even communicate, couldn't bargain her way out of her dire circumstances. Couldn't even surrender if she wanted to.

At last he spoke. It came out as ridicule. He called her a dumb Indian. "Well, slap my face, little Indian prissy. You made it too easy." He sneered between ruddy blotches. He was seized by a state of psycho-sexual frenzy, prancing around her victoriously, cackling like a hyena. "Been out scouting for a van since before sunup. Never knew I'd find me a cute little prissy of a squaw in this filthy desert. Like striking gold, makes it all worthwhile." His eyes were on fire. Kika was fortunate she couldn't see him. Saliva puddled in the corners of his mouth. Eyes fixed in a rabid stare, he gloated over his trophy. "After I have a nice piece of you, my little prissy, I'll toss you in our big truck. That loser driver from Pittsburgh can have leftovers. If there are any."

HOWIE felt a powerful force. Swirling air created a vacuum. His eardrums popped. He stopped and turned. A dust devil churned violently, hop-scotching its way across the desert. He stood directly in its path, a mere 200 feet from it. He retreated at an angle. It measured twenty feet at its base and rose more than one hundred feet. He knew that large whirlwinds zigzagged at speeds up to 30 miles per hour. And that the mightiest ones contained strong electrical fields. He and his mate watched the dusty tornado twist counterclockwise. A smaller one churned a hundred yards behind it. "Charged particles can create an electrical field up to 4,000 volts per meter," he told his companion.

He considered what he'd learned about dust devils, comparing scientific fact to Kika's rendition of Uncle Lenny's Navajo lore. He placed the former as an overlay onto the latter. If he stretched it a bit, they had one thing in common. Fire. Whirlwinds strong enough to glow could zap an object with an electrical charge. And that could possibly produce fire. "Perhaps whirlwinds burned the Ancient Ones," he thought, "and not the sun plunging from the sky. At least I could wring out some semblance of truth from Uncle Lenny's story. Could you picture a colossal army of whirlwinds marching upon their villages and scorching everything?" he asked his companion. "Kika speaks of whirlwinds as the Messenger People, the Wind People. She believes they're ancestral in nature, ancestral messengers. *If that's true, my friend, then they're really electric ancestors*. That's how I'll view whirlwinds from now on, as electric ancestors."

His invisible partner was compelled to speak. He owned a voice deep within Howie, a subconscious voice Howie listened to, even though it usually rebutted him. "Permission to speak, sir." Parker nodded. "Sir, your logic is spurious. You have no right whatsoever to bend, twist or interpret Navajo stories.

Whether they're folktales, creation myths or other lore. Their mythology, their cosmology, should be of passing interest to you. Drop it. Leave it to Miss Windsong. Don't try to read into their folk tales. Kika is Native. You're not. You'll never fully understand. You're Anglo, *bilagaana*. Nothing else matters. That's reality. The rest is smoke."

A long, soul-searching moment filled their space. Howie seemed to digest what he'd heard without much exterior effect. The powerful maelstrom stirred beside them. After another minute of contemplation, he nodded and led the way for his partner to follow. "Come on. Let's move out. Find the van."

Two minutes passed. "Stop," he commanded. "That's strange. Hear that? That buzzing? Sounds like a small electric motor." It grew louder. Then, suddenly, it rattled loudly. It was unmistakable, he should have known better. He looked down to his right. A deadly rattlesnake was coiled within striking range. He froze, hoping his invisible mate would follow cue.

Howie knew rattlers' eyes were rarely used to navigate, that pit vipers had an organ located between their nostrils and eyes. The organ was used to register temperature differences between themselves and their surroundings. Prey was located by "seeing" the temperature difference. He'd also heard pit vipers hated the smell of humans. Occasionally, they retreated from their foul odor. The wind caused urine to spray on his boots the last time he peed. He hoped it reeked.

The rattler remained in pre-strike pose. Its broad, triangular head raised four inches above the ground. The rattles quaked eerily and were slightly raised. No matter how they "saw," he decided not to flinch, only to stare back at the diamondback, known as *Crotalus atrox.* He admired its beauty, in spite of potentially deadly venom. Its color was pinkish-gray. Namesake diamond patterns adorned its back. But it was the reptile's head which set it apart. It was disproportionately broad and triangular for its body size. He'd heard they normally drained their venom-filled fangs entirely - often leaving them within their prey.

He continued his stare down. For some unknown reason, the coiled creature lowered its head and receded two feet. Its rattles stayed upright and trembled quietly, but greater separation gave him a safety zone. He'd heard they couldn't out-jump their body length. The snake measured six feet. A jet contrail split the sky, due east to due west. At

35,000 feet overhead, it made him feel like an insignificant speck. Frozen in place, going nowhere, trapped by a creature whose body length nearly equaled his own. Equality he hadn't thought of before. He watched the contrail, his fate measured by its distance to the horizon. Each breath measured one increment in his life. He needed a miracle. Its chief prey, for example, a hawk or an eagle, to swoop down and save the day.

His options were few. He carried three pistols, but couldn't safely reach for them. Besides, he resolved not to kill it unless he absolutely had to. That resolve brought with it an idea, an ingenious one. He wanted to laugh out loud and raise his hands high overhead. Even jump and click his heels. That's when he got it. He praised Kika for saving the day. "Thank you, Kika. Thank you! I love you. You...are...a...saint! *Thanks for your powerful dream.*"

"SAW you coming from hundreds of feet off," the pervert from Cleveland said. "Thought you Indians were better at sneaking around without getting caught." He swished a puddle of saliva like a flushing toilet. He spat the glob through a slit separating two front teeth. It splattered off her hiking boots, leaving them stained for life. "Might have to tear out more hair as my reward. A prized Injun scalp to show off when I get home. Hang it as a trophy from my neck, show my buddies I fought real Indians in the Wild West." Blinded by the hood, she assumed her torturer was Mac. The voice didn't match Whitey's garbage grinder.

"Well, slap my face, little squaw." He spun her around like a top. "Just lookie here." He pretended to see through the material. "You been out here long? Bet you're nice and ripe after a sweaty hike. I like that in my prissies, all funky and sweaty. Bet you're dirtier than my little prissy stashed back in the truck. She was good and funky too. If you're lucky, you two might meet. Might even pop you both. What more could a man ask for? Well, slap my face, little Pocahontas, I've gotten real lucky out West. Better than some days in Cleveland."

Kika pondered his words. "Cleveland? Back in the truck? Woman stashed in the truck?" Confusion added to her misery. If it wasn't Mac or Whitey, she wondered, then who? A rogue lunatic drifting through the desert? An escaped con?

"Go ahead, my luscious little squaw. Move as much as you want. It won't get you nowhere. You'll just get more worked up and sweaty. Got you all to myself now. Little squaw. Ooh, I like the sound of that. A pretty one too. At least you looked pretty before I smashed you into the dirt." He lifted her hood far enough to see blood-smeared tape. He

170

tightened his grip on her hair and pressed his lips over her taped mouth. "Ooh, you been bleeding good. Don't mind that in my prissies either." He released his grip and brandished a Walther double action. He poked the barrel into her chest. "Feel that? Best handgun ever made, so don't try nothing stupid." He spat another stream of saliva upwind. It sprayed her like a fire hose. "Now let's get moving. Find whoever's with you." He cut her ankles free. "Bet you weren't out on a morning stroll all by yourself, huh? Just for your health and all. Who's waiting for you? A boyfriend? Where? Got me lots of bullets. I'll make him drop dead. Even lift your hood so you can watch me croak him." He poked her spine with the barrel. The pain exceeded her threshold. "Ever see a man get shot? Body jerks, blood and guts goes flying out. And there's one thing for certain - they get the most surprised look on their face. Even if they're expecting it. Even if they been battling it out for an hour. Never could figure out why a man who gets shot looks so damned surprised. As if that's the last thing in the world they expected. Amazes me every time I shoot someone. I even look for it."

Kika stumbled ahead and ignored him.

"Hurry up. This way. Got to find that camper." Kika lagged, increasing the space between them. "Don't mess with me, don't try running off. I'll fill you with lead. Hear me, little squaw? Don't bother me none if I kill you first. I'm going to get a good piece of you either way. Dead or alive. Done it the dead way many times. Felt good, her all quiet and such. Still warm and all. Got a life sentence for it. But them smart Cleveland lawyers got me off. I walked a free man. Mistrial, they called it. Off on a technicality. My boss pays them lawyers a whole lot of money. Course, they're all crooked…judges, lawyers, cops. All of them. Just as crooked as the crooks themselves. Amazing anyone ends up behind bars.

"Then they registered me in some big computer. Said I fit a certain profile. That was all, little prissy squaw. No more than a slap on my wrist. Now they got my number. Got me registered. Call me a purp-trator. A threat to young prissies. A predator. Got a nice ring to it, huh? Makes me proud. Predator, kind of smacks of pedigree, don't it? Makes me feel special. I'm a real pedigree, alright." He swirled a lake of saliva with his tongue for a full minute. Then he spat it into the wind. The spray doused them both. He wiped his blotches.

"Getting close to the camper. Bet we find your man here. Maybe I'll injure him good without killing him. Let him suffer while he watches us getting it on. Bet he'd love watching his woman get corked dizzy by Buzz Lane. It'd be his last image. Good thing to carry to his grave, huh? So don't try running off, you got lots to look forward to, my ripe little squaw."

171

Kika lost her footing and tripped over a stone. She fell on her injured back. Buzz watched with a pathetic stare. He offered no help. She rose to her knees and collapsed again. He cackled and sneered. "Ha, just like watching any drunk Indian stumbling from a saloon. You clumsy Injun, get up, quit faking it. You're stalling."

That was the last straw. She'd exceeded her breaking point. She decided to escape at any cost, even if it cost her life. Before it was too late. She faced certain rape and a horrifying death as long as he was calling the shots. She focused on positive thinking. It awakened her will to live. Dormant native genes finally kicked in. She felt warm sunlight. Its glow brought light within her hood. She was a survivor possessing a resilient will. Her mind raced. It sprang ideas by the dozens. One took hold, a good one. "Oh, Howie, you'll be so proud of me. *Thank you for your zany stories*. I love you for them. Even if I say they're crazy at the time. This one will save my life!"

THE contrail evaporated like a forgotten dream. It was Kika's dream that would save his life. "Of all the bizarre things she told him of her dream," he said to his partner, "the one I remember most was the part about holding a snake high overhead: '*At last Howie came into view. He was holding a rattlesnake high over his head.*' That's it!" He cracked a smile. They continued their stare down, rattles upright, growing louder. He reasoned his plan into reality, then rehearsed it mentally several times. "There'll be no trial run, no second chance," he said to himself. "We can't stand here like this forever."

After carefully visualizing free-flowing, gymnastic movements, he began his countdown. Five…four…three…and in one powerful movement, he exploded up and back high in the air. He executed a standing broad jump, in reverse, utilizing every ounce of energy. It deserved a gold medal. In one fell swoop, he increased his distance from the diamondback by twelve feet. After a safe yet wobbly landing, he backpedaled as fast as he could. His companion applauded. Stage one was successful.

The rattler was also on the move. In Howie's direction. Although *Crotalus atrox* wasn't prone to attacking, it defended its ground aggressively if provoked. It was visibly offended by what Howie had done. He walked quickly backward and connected sections of his trekking pole. The diamondback twisted its way directly toward him. Pole assembled, he rigged a snake lasso by looping utility line clipped to his backpack.

He measured the rate of its gregarious approach. He'd observed a snake loop in action only once. On television. The diamondback stopped six feet shy of him. That gave him precious seconds to remove his hiking shirt. He stepped carefully backward and tied off both sleeves and neck. He reckoned if he could loop it, he could bag it.

His silent companion nodded approvingly. The reptile slithered closer, head raised off the ground, rattling loudly, body slightly stiffened, sensors locked in like a missile guidance system. Five feet, four…Howie jerked to the left, and with his right arm fully extended, slung the loop in an upward arc over the triangular head. His arm extended in a smooth upward motion, causing the reptile to twist violently, curling and turning to fight off captivity. He kept the twisting rattler high overhead at a safe distance. It knotted itself like a pretzel.

One tricky maneuver remained. He raised his tied-off shirt and dropped the venomous beast inside. Gravity lowered it. He knotted one sleeve over his hiking stick and marched off humming merrily, carrying the pole hobo-style over his shoulder. He looked like Huck Finn eyeing his favorite fishing hole. "Without your dream, Kika, I'd have never conceived such a plan."

The next step unfolded naturally. He approached the camper. A unique plan to disarm the vehicle materialized. It was mischievous and potentially deadly. A small toolkit gained him immediate access. He opened the sliding door and extended the snake bag inside. Then he untied one of the sleeves and loosened the lasso. Quickly, he leaned into the door and stepped forward, using his body weight to slide it closed. The transfer was smooth and professional. Mac had left two windows open one inch and the screened roof vent raised fully. Coupled with shade trees, *Crotalus atrox* would stay healthy long enough. Howie wiped sweat from his brow and hid in a nearby clump of trees. His imaginary partner did likewise.

KIKA was primed. On some level she knew that she and Howie had communicated. It tripped a switch in her memory - the story about Howie's optometrist friend. His words rang in her mind, about the cliché: "*I could do it with my eyes closed.*" And: "*It's in our genes - the human eye adjusts to the available light no matter if it's daytime or nighttime.*" That's all she needed. It was like handing her the keys to her cell. Her eye muscles relaxed, allowing her retina to form blurry, faint images through her hooded existence. And then another miracle occurred. Images of Navajo folktales appeared. She envisioned scenes of her ancestors' earliest emergence from the underworld. How her people began their journey out of darkness from the First World, the Black World. A place so dark it was called the Place of Running Pitch. Their emergence upward led to light and to brighter worlds, to worlds with color, to Blue Light shining from Second World through a crack in the domed sky. Her ancestors twisted and turned and eventually

173

squeezed through the narrow opening into Second World. "I can be like my ancestors," she told herself. "I can find my way out of this darkness."

Soon, her eyes discerned patterns in the landscape. She used the sun to her advantage. Her captor came into view, blurry. She flexed her muscular calves and thighs. She had a wide range of leg movement, like a ballerina, to reach challenging rock-climbing holds. She'd catch the maniac off guard, find his groin or his windpipe, and with a powerful kickboxing move, disable him. "Oh, Howie, thanks for telling that story," she muttered beneath the tape.

Buzz relaxed his grip on her bicep. His other hand fell from her hair. Mac's camper was fifty feet ahead. No one was in sight. Kika sprang into the air and unlocked a powerful kick into Buzz's midsection. She missed her mark. It was a sharp blow, but not a paralyzing one. He reeled backward without going down. She bolted, hooded and hand-tied, tripping over dead sagebrush. It broke her gait. Her escape was foiled. She swayed awkwardly thirty feet away, upright and vulnerable. Buzz leveled the Walther. An easy shot. She'd be dead before the gun fully recoiled. Suddenly, a movement caught his eye.

Off to his right, a man crouched low and glided from sagebrush to sagebrush. Buzz saw that it wasn't Jed. It had to be her boyfriend. He overran Kika and shoved her to the ground. He removed an urban assault rifle from his shoulder bag and placed a foot on Kika's back to steady his aim. Her lungs emptied, her spine cracked. He raised his other foot and used her as a shooting platform. His target crouched low in the brush. He centered the man's head in the crosshairs and activated a red laser light. Spine-tingling shots rang out. Cordite gripped the air.

TWENTY-FOUR

A red dot glowed on his temple. He saw the beam. "What the f - ?" He lunged to his right. Two 9mm bullets grazed the flesh where his arm joined the shoulder. "Where'd *he* come from? How'd I not see him?" He glanced at his imaginary companion. He'd transformed from hiking mate to lieutenant.

Parker flattened in the dirt, gripping his Sig with both hands, slowing his breathing, listening. Wind reigned. In spite of his flesh wound, he remained confident. His aim was deadly. At the range, he scored a half-inch off-center at 50 feet. Crawling to another shrub, he whispered to his lieutenant. "Shots came from ten o'clock. Range: 100 feet."

Elbows became short legs. He dug them in and crawled ten feet to denser foliage. "Glad they ambushed me instead of Kika." A second round rang out one foot overhead. Seconds dragged like hours. A third round exploded. Then boisterous outcries competed with the wind. He heard a blend of laughter and boasts.

"Well, slap my face, man," Buzz shouted. "Got you pinned down, dummy. Got something else of yours too." He popped off shots like a teen at a two-bit arcade. Bullets sprayed overhead.

"What?" He asked his phantom lieutenant. "'Something else of yours too?' Is it the feather holder I dropped? What else could it be? *Or who*? Oh, no, not Kika! She's reached our camper by now. He can't have her. Must be the feather holder."

His lieutenant knew him all too well. "Look again."

He spread branches and rose up on his knees. The shooter was seventy feet to his left. "What? It's not Mac, nor Whitey. Who's that guy? And why's he using an urban assault rifle? Where's he from? Lousy choice for the desert."

"Couldn't have been too lousy," his lieutenant whispered, sneering. "Managed to hit your shoulder."

Howie shrugged off the sarcasm and raised his monocular. He stared in disbelief. "Gun's a Hi-Point 9mm Carbine tactical rifle. You know, a "ghetto buster." A very short-range weapon. Used by tactical squads, SWAT teams and the like. My Sig's way better. That Hi-Point's city trash." The lieutenant smiled and nodded. "We're trapped in his line of fire. So we'd better stick to the basics and remain flexible. Keep our options open. Avoid crossfire in case there's an accomplice." Dozens more shots scattered above. Much closer. Their shrub could be next.

"Well, slap my face, man. I know you're out there. Me and my sexy little squaw will nail the right bush sooner or later. Course, she's

175

having a little trouble seeing now. But she's bringing me luck." He spat a stream of putrid saliva. It doused her shoulder. "Course, it's really *her* lucky day, not mine. As soon as I pump you full of lead, I'll pump her full of something I been saving up. Just for my little Indian maiden. Yes, sir, cowboy, she'll get satisfied real good by Buzz Lane from Cleveland. Her lucky day, alright."

"You SOB!" Howie screamed. He tightened his dual-handed grip, sprang to his feet and unloaded a full round. Twelve shots. And missed. Left of the mark by five feet. Across the battering wind, he yelled: "Know where you are. Next time, you'll drop."

He lay on his belly and squinted through branches. Shots scattered wildly above. Howie studied his enemy. Buzz stood at an angle, left foot propped up on something disheveled. He loaded another clip and then abandoned his foot perch, advancing parallel to Howie, squatting low. Howie jumped up, both arms fully extended, and took aim. He emptied the round. That time, he connected. The attacker took three hits to his right leg. Two mutilated his thigh. The third shattered his kneecap. The impact was severe. Buzz reeled backward. Reflexively, he pulled the trigger. Shots launched feebly skyward. Blood poured from his wounds. Howie took aim and fired again. The rifle jerked from his grip and flew through the air. He nailed him square in the right arm, above the elbow, spinning him around.

Buzz writhed in pain, gripping his thigh with both hands. He hopped back to where Kika lay. She became another footrest. He stared at Howie. Their eyes locked. Air crackled like live wires. It was just as Buzz had told Kika earlier. Surprise and disbelief spread across Buzz's face. Howie asked himself the same questions Buzz had. Why does a man who's been shot in battle always look so surprised? Like it was the last thing he ever expected.

Shock set in. He moaned in agony. Breathing came in heavy gasps. Howie eyed his blotch-riddled complexion, wondering how blood could have splattered to his face. And why he had drawn such a stupid rifle. Strange things happened to greenhorns in the desert, he concluded.

Beneath his feet, something moved. It was a heaped mess. It moved again. Legs kicked. A body rocked sideways, back and forth several times, and soon rolled downhill. "What the hell? Kika? Kika! Kika!" He bound ahead and leveled his gun at the mortally wounded Buzz. Kika lay sprawled twenty feet away, still hooded. "Kika, stay down, lay flat. He's drawn his other gun."

She disobeyed him and crawled into a clump of mountain mahogany, intentionally snagging the hood on a sharp branch. She jerked her head repeatedly. It worked. The hood ripped apart and clung to the branch. Daylight filled her world. One eye was swollen shut. Her hands remained tied. Then the excruciating part. Akin to crude surgery. She used a sharp, broken-off branch and worked it beneath a fold in the duct tape. It adhered to the branch and peeled off. Her lips looked like raw meat. Although badly bruised and cut, she regained mobility. Her good eye stared into Buzz's crazed eyes. The two glared at each other like two flamethrowers in the wind. "So you're...the perverted jerk...wanted...rape and murder me." Puffy lips exhaled her words in a debilitating lisp. They were cracked and bloody. "Where's...backpack? I'll...shoot your balls off! I swear it!"

"Back off, Kika," Howie warned, taking his eyes off Buzz for a split second.

It was just the time Buzz needed. In a flash, he aimed his Walther at Kika's head with his left hand, arm swaying from weakness, blood spilling from his wounds. His shirt and pant leg were drenched. A rivulet of dark blood seeped from the corner of his mouth. He bled internally. "Stay where you are, Pocahontas. This ain't over yet." He spoke as though his tongue no longer functioned. Even though he was in a state of shock and firing left-handed, he couldn't miss Kika's temple from that range. "Well, slap my face, bitch. It's all your fault, little squaw. I should have corked you good when I first laid you on the ground. Had the chance, you being all ripe and sweaty. Could have kept your head bagged and your hands tied, could have turned you around like a dog."

"Don't waste your breath on sick fantasies," shouted Howie. "Dumbest thing I ever heard. A dying man talking smack. Wasted breath. Take your stupid fantasies to the grave, you pervert." He raised his gun and took careful aim. At thirty feet, he could have shred the heart valve of his choice.

"Howie...no...don't!" she slurred. "Don't kill...him...please." Body language said it all. She twisted furiously and shook her head. No, no...aim for...groin. Shoot his...nuts off...don't kill him."

Howie restrained long enough to get a grasp of the showdown. "OK, maniac, drop the gun or I'll drop you for the last time." His Sig dialed in to Buzz's head. The wounded pervert inched his way closer to Kika. She staggered away in agony, increasing her pace slightly, zigzagging through sagebrush, limping severely, weakened from second degree shock. Buzz slowed, too weak to stumble ahead and keep his gun level.

Kika turned and faced both men. "Howie...beg you...if you shoot...now...it's not...self defense...it's murder...beg you..." She was right. The scenario was simple to assess. It *would* be murder. Gun or no gun, he was so weak that his threats were practically senseless.

Buzz leaned into the wind and scraped along at a snail's pace, following Kika's trail. She sought refuge in their camper van. "Woman's right, don't shoot," he exhaled dryly. "Not as dumb an Indian as I figured her for." He weakened; she strengthened, progressing at double his rate. Odds were virtually nil that any shots would strike her. He began hopping on his good leg, gripping the blood-drenched one with both hands as a makeshift tourniquet, dragging it next to him like a corpse. Kika's spread from his Walther increased to eighty feet as she closed in on the camper. Howie panicked. He realized her destination, a mere twenty feet from camper van-turned-snake pit. "Oh, my God," he screamed into the raging wind. But his attention was divided. He needed a third eye. One eye was on Buzz. The other marked her progress.

Without warning, Buzz turned and aimed at Howie's chest. From a distance of twenty-five feet, he couldn't miss. He grinned through a rivulet of blood, still looking trigger-happy and cocky, acne oozing horribly from his state of shock. "You're a dead man, cowboy, let your squaw bitch watch *this*." The showdown had finally come down to exactly what he'd wished for since his plane touched down in Farmington - an old-fashioned Western shootout. As though fate had planned it all along, Buzz Lane's Wild West fantasy became reality.

Howie had ten seconds to yell a coded message. A cipher Kika would get, but Buzz wouldn't. He had plans for the gunslinger, so he couldn't use the word "snake." She reached the van's sliding door. The wind howled fiercely. Louder than the human voice. It would take a miracle for his message to reach her. She bent forward and raised her hands to the handle. Howie took his eyes off her for a split second. Long enough to fire at Buzz's gun hand. He hit the gun instead of the hand. The Walther flew far away. Buzz shook his tingling hand until it nearly fell off, then collapsed. "Well, slap my face but good, man. Lost me my gun. Never been without one before."

"Your lucky day, bastard. My revenge demon's dead, or I'd have shot *you* dead." Howie turned back to Kika and screamed as though she were on Mars. "Kika, remember that bull-thing which crossed our path yesterday? The blessing I said? '*This is your territory, not mine...I'm the guest here...I mean you no harm...*' Kika, his cousin is in the van!"

One eye darted to Buzz. Delirious, he was oblivious to Howie's cloaked message. Slowly, he resumed crawling. Blood pooled in his wake. Dark, arterial blood. It matched his blotches. After thirty agonizing feet, he steadied himself on quaking legs. Shirtsleeve and pant leg drenched, massive blood loss had taken its toll. Another bullet was unwarranted. Howie holstered his gun and stood idly. He restrained himself for a second time that morning. He adopted neutrality, neither aiding nor apprehending the enemy.

Kika released her grip from the door handle in the nick of time. A series of head nods told Howie she "got it." She peered into the van and then backed away carefully, eyes fixed upon its interior. Her good eye opened wide. It stared into a distinct diamond pattern and enormously wide head. The creature lay coiled on the floor. She continued her retreat, trembling violently. She had to get out of the wind and lie down. Third degree shock was about to set in. She ambled up the arroyo. An Eden greeted her beneath a cluster of shade trees. She collapsed into damp foliage next to a bubbling spring. The ground was refreshing and cool, the wind less annoying. Peace embraced her. She lapsed into unconsciousness.

Buzz scraped his way through the dirt, making slow but steady progress. He arrived at his destination, his final one, and slumped against the van. Howie's restraint was steadfast. "Last night I adopted a new constitution," he declared proudly to his phantom lieutenant. "No more killing just for the sake of revenge. In fact, no more revenge at all. Not sure what to call this, but I'm not going to take *any* action. I'll let events unfold naturally over yonder." He cocked his head at the camper. "Call it restraint."

His conscience, personified as invisible lieutenant, knew him better. "Sir, permission to speak." Howie kept his eyes on the van. "Sir, with all due respect, please cut yourself some slack. The nice part about the epiphany you reached last night is that you haven't scrapped your previous life. It met you right where you were. It didn't erase your past. It *healed* the wounds inflicted by your old rage demon. Look for yourself, sir. That maniac was going to rape and kill Miss Windsong. You restrained from killing him. *That's huge progress.* You had motive. You had opportunity. But you restrained. It's OK to leave well enough alone over yonder." He cocked his head at Mac's camper van. "I trust your judgment. I stand by your side, sir! Now move on and go help Miss Windsong."

Howie Parker stood silent. The moment froze in time. Peace fell over him. The voice inside had told him that restraint was acceptable. That he should remove himself from battle and move on to help the woman he loved. That he could have easily killed Buzz Lane, but didn't. A tried-and-true test, proof positive that his epiphany was genuine. Revenge with a capital R was dead.

Buzz slid along the van until he reached the sliding door. Numbed and weakened, he managed to slide it open just wide enough to gain entry. "Well, slap my face, will you?" Each word echoed hollowly from hell. "Maybe none of this…would have happened…if I hadn't gone off half-cocked...after that Indian squaw." Delirious, vision blurred, he never saw what waited on the floor. Howie watched as the ghostly man lifted himself inside and plopped down on a camping mattress, right side blood-soaked from shoulder to foot. He slid the door shut with his left leg and clicked the locking mechanism.

The click numbed Howie. No matter what, he'd carry that sound to his grave. He turned and ran for Kika. In a matter of seconds, he knelt by her side. Kika's right eye opened, left eye glued shut with grit and teary matter. Speechless, he bent over and kissed her forehead. He stayed in that position a full minute. His touch initiated healing. He dipped his bandana in clear spring water and draped it gently over her forehead and grazed cheekbone. He removed his shirt-snake bag and draped it over her for warmth. She grimaced as salty tears reached her wounds. She wanted to smile, but couldn't. Or speak. Her upper lip was split open. A butterfly bandage was Howie's first task. Stitches were hours away. Skin had been scraped from her chin and ear. Her nose was swollen, but not broken. She would be black and blue for days, perhaps a few weeks. "Hope you're OK with one-sided conversations for a while."

Kika was no fool. She was defiant. Her eyes danced precociously. Finding reserve strength, she propped up on an elbow. Howie was astonished.   "Then...don't   expect...kissy-sucky   ear   jobs either...Parker!" Humor bubbled through a debilitating lisp. Words were costly. Blood seeped through the freshly adhered bandage.

"The gall, Miss Windsong. You got moxie. Where'd that come from? You *must* be half out of it!" He helped her up. They limped along, Howie guiding her by the elbow. "Maybe this is a dumb question, but I don't suppose you reached our camper and called Quirk, did you?"

She stopped in her tracks and turned toward him, eyes dancing, head bobbing, unable to smile. A second and final outburst stunned him.   "Of   course...my   spare   time...uh...before   I   fixed me...breakfast...read my romance novel...or after...sunbathing..." A body giggle followed.

"Yeeee...aah," Howie yelled. "You *are* in shock, Miss Windsong. But your humor's great tonic. You'll heal fast." They continued toward camp. The wind was their ally, blowing them like leaves on a fall day. He never looked back.

180

TWENTY-FIVE

He swiveled his chair and faced the blockbuster file vault. The inscription on a brass plate read: "Y." Brewster asserted that the nameplate itself represented an ideogram. The symbol triggered scientific minds to ask the question: "Why?" After turning two keys, he spun the dial a total of sixteen turns, stopping four times to reverse direction at designated numbers. The locking mechanism delivered a distinct click. He swung open the heavy doors and slid out the bottom drawer. The feather holder fragment lay within soft material and a sealed case.

He slipped white gloves over his hands and removed the ceremonial object, cradling it in both palms with his eyes closed. Then he placed it on a black cloth and laid it atop his enormous desk. More than a desk, it was a hand-hewn rosewood table imported from east India by his grandfather. It measured ten by four feet and served admirably for impromptu conferences. He lowered a high intensity lamp directly over the artifact, raised a loupe magnifier to his right eye socket and leaned in. Nearly one hundred symbols were incised on the bottom. He related to those resembling a serpent, a fish, an elongated head and strange looking shapes forming two crosses, side by side, connected by what appeared to be a line arcing over their top. Dozens of other symbols and shapes were foreign to his eyes. Many looked to be either sideways or upside down. Others faced toward the double cross and arc feature.

The window through which Brewster perceived such images was that of a twenty-first century male, reared in Midwestern Christian cultures, and holding several degrees from Western-tradition academic institutions. His career achievements and publication royalties placed him in an upper socio-economic stratum. His "mind's eye" was also influenced by three decades of field work in diverse cultural settings. Those experiences blended into his professional persona - the person he'd become in life. That "mind's eye" formed the "set of lenses" with which he perceived glyphs belonging to extinct civilizations. It was likely to form a different perception than one viewed by professionals reared and educated in other cultures around the globe.

He set pencil to sketching pad, spending an inordinate amount of time drawing the peculiar side-by-side crosses. The arced line above them extended over the top of each cross to its exterior sidearm. He envisioned a celestial body, perhaps a comet streaking above a constellation. He recalled that Dr. Chao had also envisioned southern hemispheric celestial bodies playing a role in the symbols. Yet he kept an open mind, theorizing that the crosses were probably not truly crosses. Dozens of other cross-like images were used by prehistoric cultures long before the birth of the religious cross. Until the artifact's age was determined, he vowed to stop speculating and concentrate on other matters. He also needed time to consult with colleagues other than Chao. Linguistics, ethno-historians, biogeneticists and other scholars he could trust.

He sat back in his chair and enjoyed the muse. The feather holder fragment atop its black cloth was the only item on his enormous, polished desk. It gave perspective to his thinking. It was the most peculiar and extraordinary artifact ever bestowed upon his humble career. He knew the symbols manifest *thought* in symbolic form. Thus, the saying went: "A picture is worth a thousand words." He and Chao both theorized that the symbols represented an ideogram. By definition, the major challenge facing the decipherment of ideographic expression was that *only* the recipient was cued into its specific thought pattern or wisdom. That's what set it apart from other ciphers and codified expressions. By comparison, communication through formal language was developed slower and over very long time periods, and generally for the benefit of a broader populace.

Suddenly, the new mail icon beeped on his monitor. He swiveled to an adjacent credenza and stared at the monitor. The e-mail was sent by his close friend and colleague, Dr. Raul Jorge Fernandez in Santiago, Chile. In spite of Brewster's accolades, *the message would forever change his picture of the past.*

"Greetings, Phillip: I am in awe, dear friend of ancient cultures, over your query last night. Permit me to share your information with my closest and deeply trusted associate here at university, Alonzo Milad de Mendoza, PhD. He is Senior Fellow at the Institute for Advanced Cultural Studies at the Universidad de Chile. He and Dr. Chao co-facilitated a symposium held in Palo Alto last spring. The retreat sought to establish benchmarks for the decipherment of hieroglyphs which thus far have escaped mankind's solution. The Institute's current focus is cataloging peculiar characteristics contained in each secret language. His research is a macro-synthesis of the big picture. A regional assessment of the pivotal window in time extending from 14,000 to 30,000 years before present. A period in southern hemispheric cultural history which witnessed migrations northward toward the equator and beyond.

"Dr. Mendoza posits that migrations of shamans embarked on journeys across the globe as early as 30,000 years ago, depending on glacial and interglacial ice shields. His team is gathering hard evidence to suggest that migration routes between the two Americas *spread first from south to north.* That "shamanistic ambassadors," if you will, traveled several corridors to spread their teachings.

"Our research is predicated upon one intrinsic axiom - that all prehistoric images, whether found on ceramics, masks, totems, murals, sand paintings, pictographs, petroglyphs, ad infinitum, are a visual language. A metamorphic expression of knowledge. Each symbol, no matter how it is applied and no matter what medium it is applied to, is a 'vision byte,' or 'information byte' capable of communicating a thought, perhaps even an entire story bearing a theme. All symbology conveys wisdom to other intelligent beings.

"Your message electrified Mendoza. Let me see, as you would say, it 'knocked his socks off'. If the feather holder in your possession contains ideographic symbols which correlate with his research, then the publication of these findings could allow you and me to witness a rewriting of the historical record in our lifetime. Origins of mankind in the Americas and emigrational flows of its new peoples could be viewed differently forever.

"I assure you that his research will establish a new paradigm, a new excellence in archaeological evidence and resolve enigmas concerning ancient migration routes. Vague legends will become profound truths. The Institute deals in hard evidence, my dear colleague, not in mysteries. His evidence will vitrify knowledge of life on earth.

"His staff traveled the globe to research thousands of artifacts whose origins relate to Easter Island. Isotopic signatures matched volcanic eruptions from the womb of Easter Island. Small obsidian figurines were scientifically examined. The results were astonishing.

"Initially, the archaeological community assumed the small statuettes were replicas of the colossal *moai* flanking the Island's rugged terrain. However, using optically stimulated luminescence dating techniques, we were astounded to discover that the figurines bore an age of 19,500 before present, plus or minus 550 years. It appears, therefore, that the gigantic *moai* carved and erected on the Island during the fourth and fifth centuries A.D. are *replicas* of the 18-inch carved figurines. NOT VICE VERSA. Publication of such findings will send shock waves throughout the world. Scientists may find it incomprehensible that those stelae were erected in honor of 19,500-year-old sacred statuettes. *But they were,* my devout friend of antiquity, they were! The Institute can and will authenticate that.

"Mendoza's staff is also conducting systematic oral histories. Respondents are reciting oral legends passed down through generations before them. Since they're working with non-written, verbal accounts taught through their ancestors, the process, as you have experienced, is lengthy. It requires exacting different dialects among elders, many of which have never seen written word or traveled far from their tiny hamlets. In order for these oral histories to be published as hard evidence, the transcriptions must be witnessed and certified. Assigning a timeline to them is extremely challenging. Intervals expressed in increments of grandfathers, great-grandfathers, hundreds, perhaps thousands of times over, lead us to establish dates ranging between 14,000 to 20,000 years before present. That time frame coincides with laboratory-certified dates of our obsidian statuettes.

"Hold on, my dear fellow, before you stop reading and unplug your computer. Please hear me out. This is not pseudoscientific babbling. I am not here to say the Island was visited by extraterrestrial aliens. Not by any accounts. However, equally incredulous events occurred during that 14,000 to 20,000 BP period. Shaman pilgrimages transported the most sacred artifact attributable to their civilization - *ceramic receptacles to hold plumes of feathers.* We believe such artifacts were the civilization's essence of ritual.

"According to the consensus of non-certified oral histories, one of the pilgrimages carried twelve *incised* plume holders to an unknown energy vortex. Other pilgrimages may have conveyed feather holders (the preferred terminology), *but only twelve were incised during the span of their civilization.* We are told they convey a message of great import. That all twelve are interconnected, that symbols inscribed in code must be deciphered in precise configuration. Mendoza and I postulate that they form an ideographic message. Elders tell us the message *must* be deciphered in our lifetime. No, not because it warns of Armageddon or false doomsday prophecies, but because it will enable mankind to live simultaneously within this and parallel universes; thus utilizing earth's limited resources in ways never before imagined.

"Concurrently, a statistically relevant percentage of oral histories were conducted with centenarians. They issued a striking prophecy - to decipher the coded inscriptions, mankind must gain access to the Island's largest, most sacred *moai*, the creator statue, known as *Make-make.* Conundrums concerning interstellar relationships which have vexed astrophysicists, mathematicians and philosophers since time immemorial will be solved. A universal 'theory of everything' will be unlocked, revealing *why* statues seen today were erected on that tiny Pacific island, *why* they were constructed to mimic the 18-inch-tall figurines, and *why* each one faces the direction it does. And, most significantly, *what lies ahead as their intended purpose for mankind.*

"If, in fact, what you hold in your possession is a fragment of the twelve incised feather holders, you may be the only person in the world to help Mendoza connect the dots. As I stated earlier, it could force the rewrite of history in our lifetime. It may greatly weaken the Bering Strait Land Bridge theory. That is a salient point, my colleague. For that long-held theory will again be put to its test. New theories will serve as a transparency, an overlay, for academia to place over the Bering model to reexamine human migration patterns across the globe.

"Mendoza and I will attend a conference next month in Mexico City to continue the Palo Alto examination of undecipherable glyphs. Could you arrange your busy schedule to meet us? Dr. Chao intends to clear his calendar and join us. The dates of the conference are 24-28 June, 2005. Please, fellow scholar, in order to help document history in the rewriting, I beseech you to attend. Lastly, I needn't remind you to guard the artifact in your possession as you would your own life. And to use every conceivable means to find the missing half. For the sake of history, for the benefit of mankind, time is of the essence.

"Sincerest personal regards, Raul"

BREWSTER, in spite of his distinguished 35-year career, felt like a neophyte. "Reminds me of Michelangelo's motto," he declared, "*'I am still learning.'*" He leaned back in his chair and stared out the window, in awe over his colleague's electrifying e-mail. The concept that he may hold one half of twelve of the most coveted artifacts in the world left him breathless. That his white-gloved hands cradled what was once sanctified in the palms of shamans was staggering. Shamans who migrated halfway across the globe in primitive times to transmit universal ceremonial wisdom. A pilgrimage whose terminus may have coincided with an energy vortex in the proximity of Snow Flat Canyon. He saw where the clues were headed. Fernandez and Chao were correct. He *must* locate the missing half. That was the long and the short of it. It was truly a race against time. He stood up and circled his desk in deep thought, head pointed down, forefinger tapping pursed lips. He'd shove all other matters aside. Excavation and discovery became his top priority. Followed by meeting Fernandez and Mendoza in Mexico City. Brimming with enthusiasm, he darted to his keyboard and pounded out a reply.

"Dear Raul: Indeed I will meet you in Mexico City. In two days time, I will lead an archaeological research team into ruins where we believe the missing feather holder fragment could be. My team will begin at Inner Ruin, a twelfth-century Mesa Verde-type cliff village. We're not certain it's sequestered there, but if it is, we'll have the means to retrieve it. Additional archaeological investigators will search nearby cliff villages. We have the unmitigated support of government entities with limitless funding. In spite of primitive working conditions, we'll work around the clock. 'Dig 'til we drop' will be our motto.

You're absolutely correct. Mankind *must* unlock secrets contained in *Make-make's* energy field. "Best, Phillip"

The geosynchronous satellite parked above the South Atlantic scooped up both e-mails. They were routed to computer apparatus at Fort Meade and disseminated to the Brownstone. To Colonel Holmes, Counterterrorist Chief and Control Agent overseeing the Delilah Project. Also overseeing agent Wendell Coldditz and his field operatives in southeast Utah. Their state-of-the-art surveillance van received the encrypted transmissions four minutes later.

HOWIE and Kika stopped to rest. Post-traumatic ailments intensified. He eased her back injury through deep-tissue massage. Then he treated her wrists and neck with a salve where garrote burns creased the skin. The same gel was applied to bruised cheekbones and spine. He made her swallow two strong pain pills. A new butterfly bandage was adhered. She'd displaced the first one with smart-alecky outbursts and, in so doing, exhausted her ability to speak. Howie knew it'd be several hours before she'd speak again. So did she. He tried not to gloat over it, even though he'd likely never have that opportunity again in his lifetime.

Guilt and depression replaced giddiness. "If only I'd been watching closer," she told herself. "None of this ever would have happened." Defiantly, she attempted a garbled message. All that spewed out was a weak gurgle. Howie raised his index finger. They made steady progress toward camp, ever vigilant of a second ambush, sticking to higher ground. Swales and arroyos didn't work earlier. "Can't afford to be bushwhacked," he said.

"Whar'e er een?" she slurred.

"You just won't stop, will you! Ambushed. Same as bushwhacked. Hundreds of shots were fired back there. His accomplices must have heard them. Probably be a welcoming party waiting for us."

She stopped and formed a time-out with her hands. Her eyes begged. She held out her palm and pretended to write.

"Ah, hold on a second." He reached in his backpack and handed her a spiral pad and pen. She scribbled. He watched over her shoulder.

"Another man. And woman. Waiting at big truck." Her writing sucked, but he got the message. She scribbled again. "Am I a liability? Hold us back? Get us killed?"

"Quit asking such dumb questions. You're wasting ink. I'd rescue you from the flames of hell. We've survived so far. We'll get through this in one piece. I let my guard down this morning too. Never saw that diamondback. Never saw that lunatic take aim at me. Could've been killed both times. Can't picture what'd happen to *you* if I was dead."

186

Kika scribbled and thrust it in his face like a ransom note. "Quit guilt crap. Saved our lives. You're my hero." It ended with three exclamation marks.

"Seems our troubles began after I crushed the back of Mac's skull. I suppose deadly encounters produce deadly results." They kept a rapid pace until their truck camper came into distant view. Everything appeared quiet and normal, perhaps too quiet. They knelt behind a stout pinion.

Kika raised the pad. "Think Buzz dead?"

She struck a nerve. "I'm trying to erase that scene. Pervert dished out his own fate. Been 15 years since *I've* killed anyone."

"Don't forget," she wrote, "he shot first. Wounded you. Meant to kill. You defended. You could have finished him off. Didn't. Something stopped you. Not my begging." She flipped to a new page. "Your words: '*Deadly encounters produce deadly results.*' He met his reckoning. Let it go."

The huge tree kept them well hidden. "So tell me," he whispered, "when you reached the van's door, what was the one word which got through to you?"

She thought for a minute and then raised her tablet. "Four words: '*I'm the guest here.*' Got it instantly."

They crouched low to the ground and advanced 50 yards. He scoped the surroundings through his monocular. He loaded a new clip into Mac's Beretta. "Your back any better? Need you to crouch real low. When I give the signal, crawl on your belly." She nodded. He handed her Mac's Beretta for their crucial approach. "Got it? It's heavier than your peashooter Guardian."

They half crawled, half crouched the final thirty feet. Howie'd have shot anything that moved. Kika stumbled next to their fire pit and collapsed, out like a light. Howie burst out yelling and stomped the ground. Hopelessness stared him head-on. "Why, that fuzzy little pervert! Hope that diamondback fanged him a hundred times over. Bastard shot out all four tires before he went stalking you. Plus the spare. Shot to shreds. How could our fate still be slipping when we're already down?"

He raced inside the camper. It was a disemboweled mess. Fortunately, Kika had hidden her cell phone exceptionally well. He gripped it tight. It still had juice. He punched in Quirk's number, anxious to get immediate help, anxious to double back and search for the lost feather holder. An answering machine greeted him after the fifth ring. Actually, it was a VARS-linked interceptor which handled Parker's call. It was activated the instant the ground relay station received it. The Variable Analogue Recognition System then activated a simulated version of Quirk's voice. The phone in her office never rang. The Brownstone netted another crucial cell phone call. A re-route maneuver without the intended receiver ever knowing the call had transpired. It was routed to Coldditz's surveillance van within seconds.

ALL artifacts were crated and neatly lined up against the cliff wall behind Inner Ruin. McAllister decided to accelerate his timetable. He informed Whitey that he'd hike out to their camper van and alert Buzz, then locate the big truck and order Jed to get the shuttles rolling. His plan called for two people to hoist crates from the plaza up to ATV trailers, while the other two ran shuttle. He acknowledged there'd be great risks associated with the load-bearing capacities of the winches and cables. Forty-eight vertical feet would place great stress on the system, including the batteries.

However, Mac's main concern was not potential system failure. He knew their operation had been seriously breeched. Flawed. They'd been compromised. An intruder had gained access to the hidden ceremonial chamber and waited for Mac to enter. Worse yet, that intruder was capable of executing a quick getaway without leaving a trace. Perhaps that someone was also waiting to Shanghai the loot once it was completely loaded. He couldn't take any chances. He *had* to accelerate the timetable and call upon reinforcements from Cleveland, those waiting to mobilize at a moment's notice. Fear spread like a rash. He weakened, casting him in a vile mood. He and Whitey argued again.

The titan swayed like a skyscraper after a quake. His voice bellowed in the canyons like a Jake brake in a quiet suburb. "We're done with this Indian junk, boss. I'll find him. Get rid of him for you. I'll bring cable. Orange." But Mac hadn't heard a word. He was in another world. One dominated by demons and flames. A hell within his mind. For deep down, what troubled him even more than their compromised status was the crew he'd recruited. "I musta assembled the most incompetent crew of thugs ever," he lamented to himself. "This job's tougher than I thought. They won't be able to handle this monumental heist. Shit! I better make the call." Mac knew about teamwork. It'd kept him alive as a kingpin warlord in Cleveland's worst thug wars. Without it, his dream "job of a lifetime" would crumble.

TWENTY-SIX

"Don't be alarmed," a voice shouted from thick brush. Howie raised his gun. "Don't shoot! I'm here to help you." A man entered their camp. The intruder was clad in desert camouflage. Military issue. Howie recognized it immediately and relaxed the trigger tension. The man's arms were akimbo, close to a holstered .45. Howie calculated how long it would take a professional to draw. His own finger would win. He relaxed the tension further. "Allow me to introduce myself. I'm Wendell Coldditz." Each word was chiseled out of granite. A lanyard hung from his neck showing photo ID. He held it away from his chest in plain sight.

Howie was stupefied. It was like seeing a burning bush. He locked eyes on the man whose name was synonymous with mystery. Coldditz had become part of his and Kika's daily vocabulary. They stared at each other.

"I've observed your exploits, Parker. Some were quite ballsy. You've earned my respect." Kika stirred in the sand. Too groggy to meet Mystery Man. The flesh-and-bones version stepped forward and held out his hand. Howie holstered his gun.

"And *who* are you?" Howie demanded, engaging in a firm handshake.

"Let's just say for sake of argument that I'm with the Feds. Your tax dollars hard at work." His voice turned warm and welcoming. A likeable smile wore well upon his mid-fifties face.

"I've got one friend, my best friend, who works for the Feds," said Howie. His tone broadcast that he didn't need another one. "I used to work for the Feds too. In uniform. In the Persian Gulf."

"Know all about that. Exemplary service, I might add."

"Whr, yo," Kika exhaled from her sandy wallow.

Howie looked at her, then Coldditz. "She means 'Who're you?' Her face took some nasty blows this morning."

"So I observed." He stirred his foot in the sand, bowing his head slightly. "All's well that ends well, right, Miss Windsong?" His tone held a strange mixture of sternness and wholesomeness.

Kika sat up. Her speech had degenerated further so she kept silent. Howie helped her to her feet. Introductions were unnecessary. She figured it out. They stood twenty feet apart. All three searched for an icebreaker, the right phrase to set them on common ground. Howie volleyed first.

"Hell, Coldditz, you might as well be dressed in a dark suit and a double-breasted trench coat. Felt hat with brim turned down. You reek of cloak and dagger. Tell us, what agency are you with?" Kika studied

189

his camo helmet, replete with netting and transmitter. A coiled line ran from his ear to the collar of his Kevlar vest.

Coldditz returned the volley. He was quick. A pro with a repertoire for all seasons. "Trench coat's being retrofitted by Q. Old chap's adding a new version of heat shields. Makes reentry much easier when I hitch a ride on the space shuttle."

Howie grinned wide. "Good answer. So tell us, what's going on here? On peaceful Cedar Mesa. Who are you, *really*? Looks like you're leading a Special Ops team."

The agent was skilled in avoiding direct answers. He stirred his foot again, doodling idly in the sand. "I've observed you two for the past three days. And those thugs from Cleveland too. The leader, Mac, aka Terry McAllister, he's dumb like a fox. The man's no fool. We're missing a few details, but he's got something up his sleeve. Something big. We've got his buyer in our scopes. He's our big catch. Barters antiquities for illegal arms."

"What do you mean you're not sure?" Howie asked. "Aren't we getting our tax dollars' worth? You'd have to be blind not to know what they're up to. Looting, vandalizing and pillaging, for starters. Throw in murder for good measure. Other offenses a mile long. Hell, a first-year law student could get a conviction. Hands down. So what's your excuse? What kind of spy games are you playing?"

"Good question," the man in camo said. "Sounds like you'll come around. Cooperate with us wholeheartedly, no doubt. Get your tax dollars' worth." He grinned. Howie held a straight face. He'd kept score. Although the agent's personality was captivating, he hadn't answered the last two questions. "McAllister doesn't have a grasp of the entire picture," Coldditz continued. "Thinks he's simply looting archaeological treasures. You know the type. Like thousands of pot hunters in recent years. Thinks all he has to do is show up at the buyer's rendezvous and walk away with fifteen million bucks. Knows only a little about his buyer's real motives. However, he and his stooges are accessories to aiding and abetting a dangerous terrorist plot. Cut-throat dealings in commodities Mac's unaccustomed to. Two separate terrorist cells are involved. We're talking military arsenals, missile launchers, elite weaponry, that sort of thing. And now, we believe, enriched and depleted uranium to spice things up. Up the ante. Adds a whole new dimension to Uncle Sam's view on the matter. That's where I come in. Places Mac in a different league. He's moved up to the majors, so to speak. Trouble is, our assessment is that he can't cut it. Won't make the grade. His four-man outfit is nothing more than a rinky-dink gang from back East. Sandlot league."

"Three-man outfit now," Howie offered enthusiastically. "Unless a man 98 percent dead can wrangle a diamondback with bare hands."

"You mean like *you* did? Very resourceful, Parker. I commend you. Haven't seen a free-standing back flip measure twelve feet in years, much less someone lasso a pissed-off rattlesnake. Could've partnered with you in North Africa."

"You *were* watching everything, weren't you?" He held Kika's elbow and guided her to the camper. "Let's get you fixed up, sweetheart." After quickly straightening the mess left by Buzz, he raised her up into bed. She fell sound asleep without so much as a whimper. He heated water in the kettle. Ice remained in their cooler. He hacked off a chunk, filled a plastic bag and propped it against her face. He massaged her neck for several minutes, then applied another round of salve to her wrists and neck. He stepped to the doorway and faced Coldditz. "I'm ready to feed my addiction - a pot of coffee. Strong, black as pitch. Up for some?"

The agent's face lit up. Friendship was in the making. "*Real*, honest to goodness coffee? Here in Utah? You're joking. Haven't had a real cup of Joe since I set foot in this state. A waitress in Blanding actually spelled it 'kofi' on my bill. Thought I was paying for something I hadn't ordered." He looked at his watch, stood and turned away from the camper. "Got to check in with command. Brew our Joe. Treat Miss Windsong. Get her to heal. Got a job for you two. We'll indulge shortly." The operative strode to a knoll 50 yards away. He cupped the side of his face from the wind and spoke into thin air. The coiled transmitter picked up his voice and launched it into space. His command van, parked in a shaded area eight miles away, received it almost instantly.

Howie removed Kika's ice pack and rinsed her facial injuries with warm water. From what he could tell, the eye itself wasn't damaged. He left the butterfly bandage intact. Her lip would heal fine. Then he took a clean washcloth and drenched it in witch hazel. He added a mixture of aloe and rose water. Kika's favorite soothing concoction. The poultice remedied deep bruises and improved blood circulation. He rested it on her face. Later, he'd begin alternating between an ice pack to reduce swelling and a witch hazel poultice. He rubbed a generous dose of arnica gel to other afflicted areas. In the absence of her Navajo remedies, he trusted homeopathy more than pharmaceuticals.

Coffee was ready. The moment he'd daydreamt about. He poured two generous mugs and motioned Coldditz to sit opposite him at their compact table. Kika slept soundly. Parker didn't mince words. "News travels fast in the canyons. What can you tell me about the dead woman backpacker?" He paused long enough for a hit of black gold. "If you're on our side, agent extraordinaire, where were you when all that was going down? Were you going to let us be killed just like she was? Lot of good *that* tax money would have done us." Lack of sleep combined with a hit of caffeine ignited him. "I demand concrete answers."

The man in khaki was unfeigned. "Come on, Parker, you were in combat. We've studied your record. You killed an enemy combatant. You're not lily-white. What do you call your actions this morning? *Or should I say inactions.* We both know you could have stopped that maniac from entering the van's viperous trap. I'd call it a maudlin form of murder. You're damn lucky Miss Windsong caught your message above that howling wind. Or the diamondback would have fanged her first." His tone was corrosive.

"You watched all that? Damn you."

"Christ, Parker, this isn't a military debriefing. It's a coffee conference. Hear me out." Besides avoiding direct answers, he was skilled in neutralizing conflict. "I had that perverted twerp in my sights the whole time. Had a clean shot. Could've taken him out if it came down to it. Of course, once you nailed him, I relaxed my grip. He was doomed, Parker. You knew he'd never bounce back. Never leave these canyons alive. Never see Cleveland again. Whether that reptile fanged him or not. He was a goner. If it were me, I'd have finished him off right then and there. After what he did to your woman. Then again, maybe that's how you planned it. Bleeding to death is a horrible way to die. I've witnessed fierce warlords beg for a quick ending. Not to bleed out like an animal at slaughter. Seen them on their knees, despair in their eyes, begging me to finish them off. Easier that way, I guess, when the game's finally over. In the end, mercy and judgment go hand in hand, don't they?"

"In the case of the horrifically beaten backpacker, the dispatcher's exact words were: 'Kicked to death.' Where was mercy when Meat Wagon Whitey handed down his judgment?"

Coldditz shot Howie one of those "I'm a Fed, so I'm above the law" looks. It turned his stomach. "You know, Parker, combat's a funny thing. I've spent most of my life overseas for Uncle Sam. Undercover. Collateral damage is a horrible cost of conflict. But it happens. That woman was a prime example of collateral damage."

Howie shook his head vehemently. "Horseshit, Coldditz, I don't buy into that crap. Since when is southeast Utah, Cedar Mesa especially, a combat war zone? Since when is it an area of undercover sleuths plotting deadly spy games? This land is a respite for ancestral spirits. It has one of the lowest tourist impacts in the Southwest. When did it become a playground for murderers, terrorists and government agents?"

"Since prehistoric artifacts and dirty bombs landed on the same bartering table, Parker. And since feather holders moved into the international spotlight. Artifacts for arms. Has a nice ring to it, doesn't it. Wainwright thinks so."

"WHAT? Did you say feather holders?" His shouting stirred Kika. She lay in a state of semi-sleeplessness, too groggy to hear details. "What do you know about feather holders? Is there anything you *don't* know?"

Coldditz couldn't reveal NSA secrets, particularly cyberspace dragnet coups mandated illegally by the Bush administration. He avoided the issue of the NSA's domestic eavesdropping campaign. How they'd netted e-mails between Brewster and his colleague in Chile. Instead, he smoothed it over with a stroke of deceit. "Alright, it's time I leveled with you. I'm National Security Agency. My cover is Homeland Security. By now you've heard I'm the *charge de affaires* in this case. *It's my job to know*. For 30-plus years, I've operated as the invisible man, so to speak. Helping NSA ops centers foil terrorist plots, saboteurs and assassins." Deep conviction and robust passion in the career agent's voice turned Howie's stomach. The agent's hands extended like swords, fingers squeezed without gaps, karate style, voice exuding steel-hardened discipline. "So, Mr. ex-Marine, let me translate this for you, connect the dots."

"Please do." He stood and filled both mugs.

Coldditz smiled and nodded, sipping it like an elixir. "Operations are ranked by a complicated formula. Job security for our computer wizards. A Success Quotient is derived. It's significant to field agents. The outfit Mac's assembled has a low Success Quotient. Has since the get-go."

"Let me guess. They've never been west of Cleveland?"

"Ha. Not bad, Parker. Mac has. He's the one who discovered the secret chamber and its treasured cache. Completely by accident." Howie held his mug in both hands, savoring its contents slowly, staring over its top, listening intently. "But it's more basic than that. They're killers. Plain and simple. All they do is kill. Blunt, urban killing. Not cunning killing. There's a big difference. The second kind is instinctual, professional. It takes years of disciplined training. Like an assassin, for instance, requiring a dispassionate coolness, always with purpose. A primordial catharsis to take the life of another member of the same species. But blunt, urban killing, well, that's an entirely different act. It's sloppy, thug-like, and passionately skewed to the extreme of being brutal and gory. Mac's outfit is that sloppy, blunt urban killing variety. They're in way over their heads out here but don't know it yet. Sure, their leader is a schemer who's made tons of money.

But deep down, he's a killer. Coded into his DNA bedrock. Just like that perverted, trigger-happy moron who tried to take you two out today. Buzz Lane. Biggest turd Cleveland's ever belched out of its sewer plant."

"Where does that stumpy massif, Blizzardhead, fit in?"

"A real piece of work, isn't he? But he's one piece of work Parker shouldn't mess with."

"Thanks for the tip."

"Every imaginable method of killing, other than atomic weaponry, has been deployed against him. None worked. All who tried met a gruesome death. He's batting one thousand. I've got some real stories for you when we have time. Especially the one about his payback at a Cleveland shipyard. Asians don't think highly of him either."

"Law of averages has a way of catching up with people," said Howie. "Give it time. Always worked for me. Maybe I'll be the one to lower his batting average. Permanently." Kika stirred from her sleep. Her foot slithered over the side and speared Howie. Disdain seeped out from her butterfly bandage. "Ah, what I meant was, if he goes after Kika like Buzz did, purely out of self-defense, of course, I might step up to the plate for some serious batting practice. Lower the beast's batting average. I've vowed never to avenge just for the hell of it. Promised myself and Kika." Howie heard a slurred mumble from the bed. "The other man, Mac, how'd he get that way? What's with that shiny dagger tooth?"

"A crane operator took swings at him with his wrecking ball. Had a score to settle. Missed his bull's-eye, but permanently deformed him." The intelligence pro refrained from laughing.

"A wrecking ball? As in demolition?"

"Uh-huh. Next swing was meant to transform him into an I-beam. Took off only half his head, disfigured him for life." He sipped from his mug. "In his profession, you don't schedule yourself into the Cleveland Clinic for elective surgery. A Mob butcher-turned-doctor patched him back together. Doc wouldn't know what a medical license looked like if it bit him in the ass."

Howie inhaled a long pull from his mug. "And Whitey?"

"He saved Mac's life that day. Saw what the next swing would do. Climbed into the crane's cab. Clutched the operator with one hand and wrapped him around the wrecking ball. Cinched him tight with aircraft cable. Orange, I believe. Uses the stuff like you and I use duct tape. Climbs back into the cab and sits at the controls. Never seen levers like that in his life. I mean, who has? Like a kid with a new toy. Took about ten warm-up swings until the pendulum of death arced halfway to

Toronto. Then he brought it back around and swung squarely into the building. Three floors above Mac.

"Did he wear a hard hat?" Howie asked, stone-faced. Kika heard that. Humor aided healing, but laughter was pure torture. Sounds gurgled from her mouth.

Coldditz wiped a grin from his lips. "They've been thick as mud ever since. Mac owes his life to Whitey. He's vowed to take care of him forever. Whitey feels the same way. He's sworn a life of servitude to Mac. Vowed to protect him forever. They're inseparable. In fact, they'd give their lives for one another."

"That's not what we heard at Inner Ruin yesterday."

"Don't be fooled, Parker. Threats are a dime a dozen. Always sorting out their alpha space. And another thing. Our analysts claim Whitey's I.Q. is inversely proportional to his appearance."

"Perhaps he should hire an image consultant." Howie donned another stone face. Sleeplessness mixed with punchiness. Then he laughed hard at his own joke. Kika giggled in pain.

"You're quite the act," the agent said. "Anyway, he's smarter than he lets on. He's just slow. That's different than stupid. He gets it - just takes him longer."

"Why haven't you sent in your troops and nailed them?"

"Can't yet. Mac's not the real target. We're aware of the laws he's violated in the canyons. He'll pay big time for that, rest assured. Like I said, the big fish in this ugly cauldron is that dirtbag dealer from Santa Fe, Horace Wainwright. He's the one we'll be netting. Him and a mole we believe is burrowed deep in the US Department of Energy." He stopped short of elaborating on the Delilah Project. "I'll come back to the mole in a second. Back to our real catch. According to our legal beagles, anyone else standing around during Wainwright's exchange is - "

"Collateral damage," Howie chimed.
"So, to answer your question, we can't nail Mac for looting until the exchange actually occurs."

Howie sprang up from the table, hitting it with his thigh. Coffee spilled. "Oh? Since when do you spooks care about legality? I thought warrantless wiretaps and eavesdropping were banned by Congress ages ago. Until, that is, that Texan in the White House decreed that the NSA and communication companies were above the law."

"Read the Patriot Act. Or the Protect America Act. Plus a litany of executive orders hot off Bush's Oval Office press since September 11, 2001," Coldditz commanded. "If you do, you might be the only citizen who has! Joe Q. Public relies on private media broadcasts. Thank God for that. We can feed them exactly what we want them to hear. Can't you see it? The NSA steps up to save the day. We *change* laws, Parker. That's what we do. Modify them to fit our agenda. The administration's behind us every step of the way. And in case you didn't know, if we can't change them, we go ahead and do whatever we want anyway. Someday we'll probably pay for it, although Cheney believes that day will never come."

"Rest assured, you government types *will* pay for it someday. The worm turns, as they say. You wait and see. Joe Q. Public will only tolerate so much. In the meantime, innocent citizens pay unmercifully. Ever think of that? Or is that another one of your 'mercy and judgment go hand in hand' rationales?"

Coldditz sat silently. Howie watched. He struck a nerve. He could practically see inside the NSA's thinking. The agent prospected for words. "You know, Parker, I'm going to clue you in on a little secret. 'War on Terror' moved into the number one slot of phrases heard in newscasts. One survey claims the average household hears it twenty-three times each day. It ousted 'in the interest of national security' three years ago. That'd been around for decades. Our eye in the sky can pretty much see and hear everything. Technology changes as fast as that second hand on your combat watch." He nodded approval of Parker's Chase-Durer timepiece. "That's how we learned about feather holders. *We eavesdropped.* Mind you, I'd like to say that's the reason the feather holder half fell right into our laps in Santa Fe. Three months ago, through an FBI informant. The scientific community is itching so hard to know more their skin's coming off. They *must* get their hands on the other half. Those glyphs contain a coded message. No one's cracked it yet, but scholars hint it's a matter of global significance."

Howie's mind raced two miles away to their escape from Snow Flat Canyon. How he reached into his pocket and discovered that half of a feather holder had fallen out. His words cascaded onto the table like the coffee had. "The other half... Oh, my God. Kika, did you hear that? There *is* another half somewhere."

But Kika dozed on in a restless slumber of half dream, half consciousness. It began when she heard the words "wiretap" and "eavesdrop." "All those whirlwinds lately, the Wind People *are* warning us," she whispered groggily. "Warrantless wiretaps. I can hear Uncle Lenny: '*...in time, Ancient Ones began abusing their gifts by mistreating Wind People. It would be like in today's times illegally wiretapping someone's telephone line. So...they warned them to stop interfering with their gifts...cautioned them of impending doom if they continued to disrespect the Wind People.*' I have to wake up and tell Howie. People must be warned!" Howie assumed she was moaning in her sleep and never stood to check her.

196

Meanwhile, he was numbed by Coldditz's statement. Shame engulfed him over losing the feather holder. He informed the operative how he'd held the other half in his hands - *the missing half.* "So," he muttered, as if in a stupor, "there must be twelve feather holders in all. What I counted in the chamber was eleven and a half. Each one incised with strange symbols." He spoke from a faraway place, as though his mind were peeking into the chamber and switching on a headlamp. "I still can't believe I let it slip away." Across the table, an all too familiar stare met his eyes. A one-man tribunal. A military stare pierced him, a stare intended to singe the eyeballs of a soldier who failed his mission. His gut ached. "So," he asked meekly, "does the FBI have the other half?"

"No, a museum curator in northern Arizona. Name's Phillip Brewster, *Dr.* Phillip Brewster."

"Well, I'll be goddamned! Are you kidding? Are you aware that he's the Southwest's leading authority on feather holders?" He shook his head, utterly flabbergasted. "Whoooaaa man. I'll be damned. Hear that Kika? So he's seen the symbols incised on the bottom?"

"Like a mother studies her baby's bottom. Explains a lot, doesn't it?" Howie stared into the next universe. "That's the reason international arms dealers have lined up at Wainwright's door. Those artifacts are worth a vastly greater sum than Mac ever conceived. Wainwright knows that, and we're willing to bet the mole at the Department of Energy does too. Face it, Parker, twelve feather holders plus hundreds of ceremonial artifacts. Mac's $15 million selling price is puny by comparison."

"Why the NSA and not the FBI?"

"I believe you know the answer to that. Here's the tricky part. Our analysts believe the source of high-grade uranium is within close proximity to Cedar Mesa. If not these canyons, then others nearby. *That's why I'm here.* To find the uranium and thereby pry the mole out, abort the arms trade." He spoke passionately, teeth shining, eyes dancing.

Howie stared at the man in desert fatigues. He wondered if he was a zealot or a patriotic federal employee. Or a mercenary under the guise of one. Kika began to stir. Howie rose and went to her aid. Coldditz drained the pot into his mug. Howie turned and reached for her remedies. He changed the poultice and turned to Coldditz. The agent's mug was raised, head cocked back, when Howie asked: "So, when do things heat up around here?"

"Tonight. After dark," he said, swallowing hard. "Actual exchange may be close to dawn."

197

"Good," said Howie. "Kika and I will join the sting. I'll see that she's feeling up to it. We're committed to see this thing through. I've vowed to keep the artifacts in one piece. Make sure they end up in the right hands. NO MATTER WHAT."

"And Miss Windsong?"

"Like I said, she'll be fit enough to join in. Bruised and sore, but fine. Another six hours sleep will greatly help. She's a fast healer."

"Brew us a half pot, Parker. Help your woman. I'll check in with command. Then I'll brief you on the details."

TWENTY SEVEN

"Can't wait to winch this junk up and shuttle it out," said Mac. "Bid riddance to this filthy village. How'd anyone live like this?"

"Injuns. Nothing but a stone ghetto," Whitey bellowed.

The two thugs had an industrious afternoon. Inner Ruin resembled a loading dock. "Figure it'll take about 14 shuttles," said Mac. "Then, off to the exchange."

"We'll be filthy rich, right, boss?"

"Yeah, then our buyer trades this Indian crap for important things in life. What the world really wants."

"What's there besides money, boss? And babes. Money and babes go hand in hand."

"What the world wants is weapons, dirty bombs and missiles. Things that really matter. And uranium. So terrorists can be terrorists. Don't worry, we'll get our fifteen mil." He checked his watch. 4:30. "Better hike out to meet Buzz."

"Hear that?"

Mac looked up. "Hurry," he barked. "Behind the boulder." Too late. Whitey reached the boulder, but Mac hid behind crates. The sound grew louder. It was an ATV. He looked again at his watch. "What's going on? Who's that?" The engine stopped directly overhead. Footsteps scraped stones. Several toppled over the rim and bounced off crates.

A shout echoed in the canyon. "Hello? Anybody down there?" Jed peered over the edge and saw row after row of crates. He took an accurate count. He was a trucker, a pro at sizing up a load. Got it down to exact cubic foot and pound every time. He totaled 135 crates plus 28 loose bundles. All neatly wrapped and taped. Dollar signs flashed before his eyes. "Hey, Mac, Whitey. Nice work. It's me, Jed. I'm here with a trailer. Let's move this junk out of here."

Mac bolted upright. He missed his Beretta. He clutched a snub-nose .38 special. Good, but only accurate at short range. Whitey emerged next to the colossal boulder. Boulder and man practically matched. "What's going on, you insubordinate jerk? You're the driver, not the scheduler. Quit playing big shot. Don't forget, I know how much this job means to you. You should be kissing my butt. Better have a damn good reason for not staying at the truck. Where's Buzz?"

"Easy, boss," Whitey growled. "You just said you want to speed things up. Now's your chance."

He turned to Whitey. "What're you, retarded? Am I talking to you? No, so shut up. Let Jed do his own talking. I want some explanations. From him, not you."

"I'm coming down." Jed picked up a remote and attached the winch cable to a large metal cage. He climbed in and lowered himself into the canyon.

"Like a shark cage dropping into the sea," said Whitey, bearing his whale shark teeth.

Jed slowed the cage to a gentle sway for the last two feet. He laid it down gently on the plaza, unlatched the door and stepped out. His hand met Mac's in a firm shake.

"You and Whitey know each other, I presume?"

"We've met," said Jed. Icy blue eyes leveled at the hulk. "Nice working together again."

"Uh," the brute grunted. He protruded a thick limb exactly where a real limb would grow if he were a real Doug fir. His hand was three times larger than Jed's. It caught him off guard. He wasn't sure what to do. His hand took a ride on the limb.

"Let's hear it," Mac demanded.

"I'm worried. Haven't seen Buzz for ten hours." Mac's face ignited. "You know, I hate that perverted prick. Vowed to his sick face that I'd settle my score with him the second this gig was over and we been paid. Thought you should know where he and I stand. You got a problem with that, I need to know now." Mac frowned, Whitey grinned. Mac spit into the dirt and shot a vexing look at Jed. "What do you mean he disappeared? Why isn't he guarding our camper?"

"Maybe we should split up and find the sorry dick. Gotta be on the road by 4 am to make the exchange, don't we?"

"Thereabouts," said Mac. He kicked the dirt and donned his death mask. "Thought I just told you to quit doing my job. I'll decide when we're moving out. Depends. On circumstances. Takes a lot of planning. Logistics is challenging. You should know being a trucker. You just be ready when I give the order. I'll deal with Buzz. How long since you seen him?"

"Took off on a scouting mission before dawn. Said he wanted to find your camper before the sun got too hot. Haven't seen him since."

"Boss, more money for us three if he goes dead." Whitey quarried words from a deep pit. "More millions for Whitey. Suits me fine." He pounded his chest like a primate.

COLDITZ removed his holster and stepped into the camper.

"Can we let our guard down?" Howie asked.

"Got the perimeter sealed."

They sat at the table. "Quite a looter shooter you got there." Howie zoomed in on the desert tan model of a Heckler & Koch USP-45 Tactical.

"You're right. Could be a tad overkill. Especially with hollow points. Hands out a death sentence every time. If I miss the kill zone, it'll annihilate extremities."

"So would you call that blunt, urban killing or cunning killing?

Seriously, Coldditz, for Christ's sake, you're bordering on the fringe. Let's keep Cedar Mesa in one piece. Did three decades of covert ops afford you too much independence?" He swiveled his coffee mug in a circle, as though following an imaginary outline. Coldditz sipped from his. "So where do Kika and I fit into all this?"

He outlined the rendezvous between McAllister and Wainwright as best he understood it. It was a sales job; he downplayed dangers associated with terrorist cells having a stake in contraband. The look of a used car salesman met Parker's eyes. "You're the best. We'll cover you."

Howie broke into a laugh. "That's a joke. I know your track record. Agents covering stooges' backs. What is it? Less than 30 percent live to tell about it? Decoys like me drop like flies. I wasn't born yesterday."

"I have to hand it to you, Parker. In all my years, I've rarely seen anyone materialize a plan out of thin air like you did with that rattler. No time for rehearsal. Rather ingenious for you to have saved him for that lunatic Buzz. He deserved a torturous death." Coldditz smiled to himself that he'd moved the discussion off-topic.

"May the best reptile live on," Howie said. "It was Kika's plan, not mine. She's the one who came up with it." Coldditz looked befuddled. "Came from one of her dreams. I remembered it in the nick of time. Now, back to us. Damn, you're good at skirting questions. What specifically is our role tonight?"

"Can you handle a dose of espionage?"

"Trick question? We'll be back in the game if that's what you want to hear. Why don't we move this outside, this talk of espionage. Kika needs her sleep. Besides, I could use some fresh air." Outside, he set the coffee pot on a stack of sandstone next to the fire pit. They stood in the shade of the camper. Neither one spoke for several minutes. It gave Howie time to think. But he'd already made up his mind. Their discussion felt like a setup. Coldditz had dodged one too many of his questions. The last one put him over the top. He'd asked a simple question to define his and Kika's role in the shakedown. Coldditz evaded the issue. There could be no trust in their newly formed relationship. He decided to play it cool.

"By the way, did you see inside that hidden cavern?" Coldditz asked. Howie was unsure where that was headed. He played his cards close to the vest. He turned away and faced the distant canyons. What followed was a cursory description of certain artifacts, including how meticulously the thugs wrapped and crated them. "Like old aunties packing dainty china," he said. When he reached the part about rearranging the back of Mac's skull, Coldditz's frame jerked. He briefed him on the spirited escapade.

"You're an honorable vet, Parker. We'll need that Frankenstein to reel in the big catch. Your restraint is appreciated, we're glad you didn't finish him off. In appreciation, I might be able to put in a good word for this discovery. How does a federal grant to fund excavation and research sound? Isn't that what first-of-a-kind discoveries are all about?"

"Only in movies and fairytales." Howie studied the career intelligence officer. Maybe he did have an altruistic bone in his body. "So what's the catch? Even philanthropy has a price."

"No catch. Here's my idea. If you handle this properly, that famous archaeologist, the museum curator, Brewster, well...you could notch his fame and fortune up a few levels. His museum could become the principal repository. In the twilight of his career, it'd launch him into the stratosphere."

"Have to admit, no archaeologist deserves it more. But first, let's get our hands on the artifacts. It's all fancy West Point theory until we seize the goods. Still, there's got to be a price. You wouldn't offer that without wanting something in return. What?"

"The mole. We've got the buyer covered. Our trap's set. As soon as Wainwright calls the mole to *confirm* the exchange, we'll have him. So here's the catch, as you say, the only one - don't you and Miss Windsong interfere with Mac and his outfit from arriving at the exchange. That's all we ask." He stirred his foot in a peculiar fashion in the sand. *"Keep a low profile until the net drops.* This is *our* sting, not yours. Blue Sky and Quirk agreed to do likewise."

"And Brewster gets his artifacts? Every last one? No delays? No hang-ups in court as legal evidence? No 'War on Terror' seizing of terrorist's assets? Plus, his museum receives federal grant money? Guaranty all this?" Coldditz nodded. The deal was sealed by a locking of eyes. "When's this huge net of yours set to drop?"

"Don't know exactly. Won't be any earlier than 3:00 am. We believe Todie Springs is the point of exchange. I'll keep an agent posted outside here. Don't worry, he's not a peeping Tom. He'll watch your perimeter. You and Kika get plenty of shuteye."

"That's a crock, Coldditz. Who in your agency *isn't* a peeping Tom?

The agent smirked and walked to the coffee pot and poured its last contents, realizing he needed his sleep as badly as Howie and Kika.

Then the agent did an extraordinary thing. He peered down at his boots and idly planted the toe of his right boot in the sandy soil and began doodling. Two lines appeared. The shape of a cross materialized. "The thing that's frustrating to us is Wainwright's communication hardware. The NSA can't penetrate it. Must have been perfected by the mole in private. We know Mac's phoned from Snow Flat Canyon. And from his camper. But their transmissions are tamperproof." He continued stirring his foot. He formed a second cross. As he spoke, he slipped sideways and joined both crosses with an arc. He never skipped a beat, his speech and gestures were executed nonchalantly.

Howie went ballistic. His shouts awoke Kika. "Holy shit! What are you doing? Step back and look."

"What? Why are you yelling? Look at what?"

"Move back and look, for God's sakes! Do it again. Make another set of those same marks. Just like you did." Coldditz reluctantly complied. "Careful. There, stop. Now connect the two with a line arcing above. Great, that's it! Step back and look."

Coldditz raised his palms. "That's what? What's gotten into you, Parker? Too little sleep? Fraught with PTSD?"

"Yes. Yes. That's it, Mr. NSA. You did it. By God, you drew the exact symbol incised on the bottom of each feather holder. The ones in the secret chamber. Unmistakable, very distinct. The symbol *must* stand for something."

"All I did was doodle like a kid on the beach. What's gotten into you? What's the big deal?"

Howie wasn't fooled. "God, he's good. What an actor," he said to himself. "One minute I consider trusting him, the next minute he betrays me." He turned and faced Coldditz. "I just watched you deliberately draw those symbols with my own two eyes. What kind of games are you playing? Let me tell *you* something. It's about betrayal. Betrayal's one of those things that's hard to detect until it's too late. I should've known better than to talk to a veteran intelligence officer alone. It'd be like a defendant talking to a plaintiff's attorney without his own attorney present. What kind of fool do you take me for? Look me in the eye, Coldditz. You don't go drawing symbols that meticulously and claim it's idle doodling. Unless, unless..." His words blew away with the wind. He studied the agent closely to observe his response to the next statement. He took three steps toward him and lowered the canary into the mine. *"Unless you guys at the NSA really do know everything there is to know."*

Coldditz fielded it superbly. "Come on, Parker, I have no idea what you're talking about." Howie saw right through his lie. "Now I'll let *you* in on a little secret. Our agency is equivalent to the mainframe for all intel. We *are* the big eye in the sky. We're like the eye's pupil. All others playing the intel racket are like tiny specks in the iris. The NSA runs the show from the center. Others look in from the perimeter." He drained his last sip from the mug.

Howie wasn't impressed by his side-stepping dance. The lie was already galvanized, but he volleyed anyway. "Don't get too cocky, Mr. NSA. After all, intel is a two-way street. If you're not careful, the pupil you use to spy on others is the same one they'll use to peer back inside the NSA."

Both men were silent. Ideologically, they'd distanced themselves. The rift widened with each passing minute. One more volley and they'd be at war, although they each knew they needed each other to accomplish their missions. But tolerance only stretched so far. So did betrayal. Howie was glad he'd played his hand close to his vest. "Guess this is a good stopping point," he said, holding out his hand to shake. "It's been a fair introduction. Glad you came into our camp. It's time I redress Kika's wounds and catch some shuteye. We'll be ready at 2:00am."

"I'll dispatch a second agent to pick you up at zero-two hundred hours." He extended his arm. Reflexively it jerked back. He raised it to his ear. His forefinger depressed the coiled wire. He turned and bounded to the nearby knoll. He eased further away. Howie kept his distance, although his eyes never left the agent. Coldditz didn't look well. Stiff as a post, his color was two shades whiter. The wind carried vagaries of his conversation. "Roger that. Yes. I'll return immediately. Fort Meade's in the loop? Brownie? Shit! I'll be there at once. Halt all transmissions." He retreated from the knoll and approached Howie. They finished their handshake. "I have a situation. It's serious. Requires immediate response. My post is on Orange Alert. That's all I can say. See you and Kika at Todie Springs."

The khaki-clad agent faced off with Howie. "By the way, Parker, almost forgot. Draw a sketch of that sand diagram you went ape over. I'll run it through our data base. See if it means anything to Fort Meade." He disappeared into the same trees from which he came.

"Why, you lying sack of shit," Howie uttered quietly against the wind. "You're a likeable chap, but I don't believe a word you say. To heck with your mole business. And Wainwright. And anyone else. Our mission is solely an archaeological matter, not a spy matter. Nothing else computes. And now there's a greater urgency to protect the artifacts from your snares." Howie's gut also cautioned him of one additional fact. That perhaps the government knew *of* the incised symbol drawn by their skilled operative's foot, but he'd bet his life they didn't know *what* it meant. Coldditz was fishing. That's what intelligence agents did best. And good fishermen told tall tales. Sign of a good fisherman. Coldditz was one of the best.

TWENTY-EIGHT

Kika lay in bed, wide-eyed and wide awake. Howie administered a third round of treatment. The swelling in her cheekbone and upper lip had reduced drastically. The bruises weren't quite as dark. Alternating rounds of ice and poultices performed miracles. Another spell of sound sleep and she'd be back in the game, albeit with one very sore spinal column. He affixed a new butterfly bandage and made her swallow three muscle relaxants. His prognostication to Coldditz was correct. She'd be part of the net-dropping team.

As he silently played nursemaid, he reflected on their string of dismal events. Overhearing Whitey's confession, losing the feather holder half, his dead cell phone, Kika's brutal attack, his scrape with a poisonous snake, mortally wounding a fellow human, their vandalized camper, its tires shot out. And having to listen to Coldditz's lies. All on a marathon stretch of time which saw virtually no sleep and no square meals. It was a Monday they'd never forget. What was meant to be a casual hike by normal observers had become a nightmare.

He briefed Kika on his conversations with Coldditz. How they'd been recruited to join Coldditz's team when the NSA dropped its net at the McAllister-Wainwright exchange. That *their* payoff was Coldditz's absolute guaranty that he and Kika would take immediate possession of the artifacts. No hassles or delays, no contingencies or legal snares. They could then deliver the artifacts to Quirk and Brewster. Federal grant monies would follow to support excavation and research at Inner Ruin. "The showdown between Mr. NSA and the crooks should begin between 3:00 am and dawn. At Todie Springs."

"Can he be trusted?" Her improved speech surprised him. She no longer sounded like a bubbling brook, although she paused noticeably between words. His dream of living with a speechless woman was short-lived.

"The short answer is NO. He lied through his teeth. He's a regular Houdini at evading questions. Quite unprofessional of him, even dishonorable, to lie straight to my face. Likeable guy other than that," he added, smiling. Kika tried frowning. It was too painful. Then he described the agent's bizarre foot drawings in the sand. How he'd replicated the double cross-arc motif found on the feather holders. "He flatly denied it, said he was doodling with his foot like a kid on the beach. Bottom line, we can't trust him."

His choice of words struck a nerve. Excitedly, she blurted as loud as her lips afforded, except the cadence was too slow, so it lost its impact. "You just described *him*, Howie, not just the symbol, the double cross-arc motif. That's it, that's the warning we must heed.

'Double-cross,' get it? Our clue. The Wind People warned us. By a stroke of luck you just said the right words. 'Double-cross.' What if your entire meeting was a setup? Why else would he have barged into our camp?"

Howie stroked his stubby chin. He thought for a moment. "You could be onto something. Let me tell you what else happened. When he received a call from command, he turned two shades whiter. I'd pay a small fortune to know what was said that turned him into a cadaver."

Silence filled their space, along with exhaustion. She rolled on her side and looked up in his eyes. "Climb up. Lay next to me. We need to talk." Her tone was melancholy, far from sensual. Although her bodily healing was progressing miraculously, inwardly she was in turmoil. "Tired as I am, I can't rest until I settle some unfinished business." He climbed up and lay on his back, hip nestling against hers. Their thighs seamed. He found her hand. Fingers interlocked. Once horizontal, drowsiness weighed upon his head. Gravity dropped it like an anchor. His chin hit his collarbone. "Hey, stay awake," she ordered, clearing her throat. "I must tell you a story. I'm ready as I'll ever be. Now, before the night goes by."

"Yes, dear," he said patronizingly. "You sure it can't wait until we wake up?

"No, *now*. What if one of is killed later? Showdowns are dangerous."

"What?"

"Deadly encounters produce deadly results. Said it yourself. If something goes wrong tonight, you wouldn't know my darkest secret." She propped herself up and sipped green tea from a straw. "I almost got killed this morning. Before telling you. You'd have never known. No one should go to their grave not knowing who their mate *really* is." He wiped drool from her chin. "I'm ready. I can't run any longer. I'm ready to face the person I've feared most - *the true me*."

"I know you witnessed deadly force in the Gulf War. Torture, dead bodies, you even killed an enemy soldier. You know when life hangs by a thread. Well, that was me this morning. What people say is true. My life *did* flash before my eyes when I thought I was dying. But, this story's about *life*, not death. So let me switch tunes. It's about someone else's life, birth, actually. Remember our predawn conversation while hiking? About a newborn taking its first breath?"

"Uh-huh." He paused, measuring his next words on a scale. It tipped in his favor, so he gambled. "Should I go outside and light a campfire? Will this be the all-nighter you talked about?"

"You're funny," she chuckled, with great difficulty. Speaking came easier than smiling. "Eight and one half years ago, I did

207

experience a newborn taking its first breaths. I *have* heard a baby crying for the first time. I *have* seen its color change from wet, reddish-purple to healthy flesh. It was *my* baby, Howie. I gave birth to a beautiful baby girl. A healthy one. Imagine that! She was all mine for a short while. A cuddly baby girl." Howie was stunned but remained silent. She let out a deep breath. Pressure dammed up within siphoned out, her body softened. Drum-tight muscles relaxed. Teary eyes stared up into his.

"She was adopted. I mean, I put her up for adoption before she was one month old. The biggest mistake I ever made. I've regretted it every day of my life. I should *never* have given her away. She would be eight and a half now." A tear slid down her smooth Navajo cheek. They lay quietly. Repressed guilt from nearly a decade of secrecy eased out. Healthy energy rushed in and cleansed cells, her blood seemed to flow easily now. Her heart drummed a softer beat.

She confessed how a friend, not even a close friend, had come to her rescue when she needed her most. She had driven Kika and her newborn from Gallup to Albuquerque. It was a horrifying nightmare. Kika had sat in the backseat cradling her baby and sobbed the entire trip. They had driven almost two hours in the middle of the night. She had wanted to avoid people who might stare through the windows. Or who might have spotted her at a gas station, likely thinking how happy that mother must be with her new baby. It had been a black and bleak night; moonless and starless, just clouds, and Kika had been staring into the empty desert for the duration of the ride. That typified her life back then. Bleak and empty.

"I was sixteen, a runaway, and didn't know what else to do. Tragically, I couldn't turn to my family for help. I wasn't ready to be a mother. I wanted my baby to have a better chance in life than I did. Didn't want her to have a nomadic mom and no father. I partied heavily in those days. Hung out with a bad crowd. I saw adoption as her only salvation. But I was wrong. Very wrong!" Their thighs stayed seamed together, both lying on their backs. Closeness worked like osmosis. Howie absorbed her grief as it left her pores. Her lisp and pauses between words exacerbated the drama.

"Couldn't the father have taken her?"

Wrong question. She stiffened slightly. "No! He was worse off than me. Besides, he wasn't full-blooded Indian, much less Navajo. Would have gone against custom. You know, Navajo being matrilineal and all. My baby girl couldn't have gone with him. Not that it's never been done on the res, but, not in my family." Tears spilled out upon her cheeks like a breached dam, one after the other, full-bodied, shaped like an artist would shape a tear, born in the corner of each eye, until gravity dragged them down.

"But, the real reason I put her up for adoption is not about me being fit or not. That's just a smokescreen, a copout I've been telling myself all these years. Deep down, I did it to break a despicable family cycle, to jump out of the rut my family's been stuck in for generations. Heavy drinking and partying has always preceded marrying at a young age. Separation and divorce came next, followed by kids ending up scattered across the reservation living with other relatives. Or worse, foster homes. *Their* kids followed in the same rut, as though that lifestyle was normal, as though doing the same thing over and over again was acceptable. I took it upon myself to break that pattern. I did it the only way I knew how. By letting my baby have a fresh start in life, up-front and early. Cuz, if I'd kept her and failed as a mom, someone would have taken her away anyway. That's why I was so scared of dying this morning. I've kept this a secret from you. You have to know, Howie. What if she ever came knocking on our door?" He gently massaged her temples. Her neck relaxed and her head cradled against his. She went limp. He watched her lips stop moving. She fell into a sound sleep.

Howie Parker's eyes were also moist, his nostrils clogged. He sniffled. Her story was leveling. He admired her more than before. It took courage to try and break the Edison-Windsong cycle of family dynamics. Even though in the eyes of some, adoption was viewed as failure. As for Kika Edison Windsong, a young twenty-first century Navajo woman, she'd finally forgiven herself. But as a mother, she'd never let go absolutely.

TWENTY-NINE

Mac ordered Whitey and Jed to load the trailer and begin shuttling. "Still can't believe Buzz went missing. Was he haggard? Maybe found a shady spot to sleep?

"Doubt it," Jed's icy eyes shot back. "Guy always had that bug-eyed, Charles Mansion stare."

Whitey grinned his whale shark grin. "If he's croaked, three way split's better."

"Hold your horses you two. I'm running this show. We need him. We need four people to make the shuttles run smooth. Especially now. Schedule's moved up."

"Bet his sweet little chick of a hostage could help. If the man himself is dead." His statement had the effect of a cluster bomb landing on Mac.

"What? What're you talking about *hostage*?" Nerves suddenly caused tear ducts and saliva glands to secrete profusely. His words shot through a spray of saliva, like a water gun aimed at protestors. "Speak to me driver-man, what did you say?"

Jed wiped his face like he'd just showered. He recapped the horrific hostage-taking scene. How Buzz figured his hostage would be prize collateral to protect Mac's investment in the truck work. How he kept her and him at gunpoint until they reached Cedar Mesa. Mac spun into another galaxy. His dagger tooth shone like a comet, face glowed like the sun. "God damn it Jed," he screamed back to Earth, "I had everything arranged. The deal was all set. All you had to do was make sure Gordy's modifications matched my blueprints. And to test drive it. That's all. What's so tough about that?" He tried spitting but the ducts had dried up. The best he could do was a fizzle. It clung to his chin. Jed burst out laughing. "What's so friggin' funny about this? Huh? Speak to me, man. You were in charge of that Polak's work. Speak to me, for Christ's sake, before I blow your friggin' head off." He flaunted his .38 like Buzz would have.

"Easy boss," Whitey grunted. Mac ignored him.

Steelhead spoke. He didn't mince words. "Nothing I could do except rehearse how and when I'd splinter the prick's skull. Wacko treated her like a mail-order sex doll. But I did my part, Mac. Promise you that. I ain't at fault here. Gordy's work checked out A-OK. Promise. Yes, indeed, one hundred percent it did. Except for the tracking device." Jed stood like a Marvel hero. A second cluster bomb dropped from the sky and detonated on Mac. Its force yo-yoed him to a galaxy far beyond the last one. His patchwork face stretched apart.

210

"Face's coming apart, boss. The Good Doc don't like malpractice suits. Better ease up."

"Keep out of this, foam brain. Speak Jed. Speak up, I can't here you!" He waved his gun like a rock star would his mic. "Speak to this here .38. *Or it'll speak to you.*" His echo carried half-way to Blanding. "What tracking device? Where? Who attached it?"

"Only one place could have done it. Gordy's. Truck was clean as a whistle at the rental yard. Gave it a thorough going over. Just like you said. Every square inch. Never thought to check for an electronic device at Gordy's. Figured he was one of us. Doesn't matter, though, he's a walking dead man until I return to Farmington. Besides, I plucked it off and stuck it on some poor sucker's delivery truck. Good thinking, huh?" He stood like a peacock in full plume, smiling his hero smile.

Mac choked as if he'd swallowed habaneras. "What are you Jed, a retard? Doesn't matter?" Dammed-up ducts burst again. His mouth reached flood stage a second time. A quart of saliva slobbered from his lips. Jed was humored by Mac's malady. He burst out laughing. Mac circled Jed, sneering and shaking his head, like Jackie Gleason after a Norton goof-up. He sopped up the mess streaming down his chin, speechless until the levy was sandbagged. His sleeve was drenched. "Of course not, you jerk. Here's exactly what it means you air-brained worthless thug-driver from Steel Town. Means our whole operation's breached for the second time today. Christ almighty, what's next?"

Jed's expression turned glacial, burying Mac under thick ice. "Thought I was doing good by finding it. Discovered it a half hour west of Shiprock. When I adhered the government decals and switched plates. All the while that sicko teen rapist stood in front of the truck taking a leak. Playing with his honker, exposing himself to Gordy's niece. Damn near jacked off right in front of her. Like I said, Mac. I ain't at fault here. You're the one who hired a registered sex offender. Not me."

Mac grunted like a sick boar. "I'll kill him myself. Today. Let's quick load this cage. We'll find that jerk after we shuttle this load." Saliva ebbed to a slow brook. "Don't you worry none about killing him. I'm going to carve out a huge chunk of his ass for myself. You can have what's left - but not until this first load is safely tucked away in our truck. From here on out we'll make do without Buzz. Leave him for the coyotes." Whitey's eyes beamed dollar signs. "We'll finish loading and clear out. Take me to that hostage woman. Damn, thought I crafted this heist perfectly. Planned it for months. Millions and millions at stake here. Now, everything's crumbling." He set the last crate in the cage and held the remote. Jed rode the cage to the rim and loaded the ATV trailer. Then, he lowered it for Mac.

THE snake lay coiled and waiting. Its heat sensor delighted at Buzz's loamy, blood-soaked body. The reptile concealed itself between the driver's seat and a cabinet. As fate would have it, Buzz's neck hung at snake level. His veins bulged through agonized breathing. Blood seeped into his lungs. His chest wheezed and gurgled. He rattled but the reptile didn't. It waited two minutes and then sprang, fully extended and hardened, clinging tenaciously to his throat, clutching his windpipe. The fanged upper jaw pierced his carotid artery. It refused to let go. Its jaws pulsated, emptying both sacs. Fangs slid from their canals into his throat. Venom swam swiftly to his brain. Some found his heart. Blood spurt from the severed artery, splattering against the van's window. His Wild West days neared the end. He convulsed profusely. Blood dribbled from his mouth. The diamondback released its hold and slithered to the sliding door.

In a delirious fit, Buzz bolted upright and clicked the door lock. It slid open. The creature with diamond patterns slithered to freedom. Buzz sat in a stupor, hallucinating, envisioning his home town, its sordid alleys and seedy nightclubs, underage prostitutes painted in gaudy makeup lining the streets. Those were the visions he carried to his maker. Judgment would be swift. He stood and hobbled from the van, took three steps, and thudded back against it, quivering violently. His color was ashen. Foam secreted from the corners of his mouth, mixing with blood. He gripped his blood-drenched leg, stiffened with early stages of gangrene, and tugged it alongside. He staggered ten feet. Spasms gripped him. He twisted sideways. Gravity tugged at him. His last words drifted quietly through foamy lips. They'd been trapped in an air pocket above his punctured windpipe. It was no plea for mercy to the heavens. "Well... slap...my...face..." He stiffened and hit the ground. Fifty feet away, the creature with a wide triangular head lay coiled tight as a deck rope. Its metabolism began equalizing after a bizarre morning.

MAC sat behind Jed, gripping his beltline like a girlfriend would. He shouted over the whirring engine for him to stop. After he cut the throttle, Mac made him an offer he couldn't refuse - that if Buzz wasn't already dead, he could go ahead and mete out his own punishment. Instead of Mac. The way he was famous for, as Steelhead Jed. To make it ten times worse if he'd raped Gordy's niece. Jed looked like he'd won the lottery. Glacial eyes receded like spring's thaw. He was a changed man, buoyant and exuberant. "Mac, you just handed me a new lease on life. Besides pulverizing that pervert's fuzz head, I earn extra money. I can pay off the Mob for good. You're like God himself, granted me eternal life."

"Think of it as a little sweetener, a bonus for discovering the tracking device."

They pressed on. The modified truck revealed itself parked beneath tall cottonwoods. Mac let go of Jed's belt and sprang upward. "Christ almighty, is that how high I told Gordy to raise it? That's too high, it won't clear nothing."

"Matched your blueprints, boss. Me and Gordy checked them twice. Before I slapped the rest of the dough in his slimy palm. Damned double-crosser."

They stopped in a cloud of dust five feet from Trixie Grebe. Mac jumped to the ground and squared-off in front of her. "Be an accomplice or be dead, lady. Your uncle too. Got that?" Her head nodded slowly. He outlined their plans and timetable. Gave her a second stern warning not to pull any shenanigans. Next, the leader turned and climbed aboard his ATV and inched forward. "Come on, can't leave Whitey alone for too long. Deviant's capable of anything."

"Hold up." Jed raced over to Trixie. He set his steel-cubed head one inch from her nose. It glistened in the sun like polished stainless steel. "Let me give you some advice, sister. A word to the wise, as they say. I don't just drive trucks for a living. I'm the munitions expert for the whole eastern seaboard. Any big demolition job comes up, they call me in. Catch my drift, sweetheart? I timed our trip here to the Mesa. Precisely 2 hours and 53 minutes from your uncle's shop. You do anything stupid and Gordy plus his derelict crew will go airborne. In small pieces. When they float back down they'll make nice little fishy food in the San Juan. Still catch my drift?" He stooped down, cocked back his head and let loose with a firm tap to her forehead, just below the scalp, about one-quarter lethal force. Trixie stumbled backward and fell to the ground, seriously dazed. Steelhead towered over her. "That's just a taste of what'll come next if you screw up. Before I high tail it to Farmington." He turned and jumped on his ATV. Trailers bounced high off the ground as he and Mac sped away.

"Was that necessary?" Mac asked.

The steel cube nodded. "She won't be as prone to switch allegiances. Or even be tempted. Temptation comes easy. Ask Adam and Eve."

"I like the way you think, Jed, gotta a good way of making a point." He hit the throttle. Twelve minutes later he pressed hard on the brakes and skidded to a stop twenty yards from the van. The side door was wide open. Jed parked next to him. Grotesque carnage lay straight ahead. Mouths agape, they stared at the inert mass laying face down. They killed their motors and ran to the tree line, guns in hand. Jed sported a Colt .45. It was a heavy powerhouse. Resembled a hand cannon. Silence prevailed, the place was deserted. Mac raced to the contorted stiff. When Buzz had collapsed, he had bulls-eyed a giant clump of prickly pear cactus. If it weren't for a body connected to a head, Mac would have mistaken it for the cactus itself. Worse, the back of his head had been seared by the blazing sun. A strange shade of rigor mortise clung to the corpse.

"How prophetic, a prick for a prick," Jed said, kicking the heap. His foot stopped like it hit a wall. "Some lucky jerk got to him before me. Hope it was an Indian. That'd serve him right." Jed accumulated a chest-full of gritty phlegm. He vacuumed it up from his bronchia; siphoning wads of viscid mucus up through his nostrils. He swirled the seedy cauldron in his mouth for nearly a minute. Then, let loose with a hocker the likes of a cesspool. It splattered on Buzz's rotten head. "Good riddance, you sick wacko!"

"Nice eulogy," Mac grunted. "Like I said, you got a good way of making a point. Looks to me like the pervert thought he could weasel his way into heaven boasting a crown of thorns. What do you suppose is up with those holes? Why'd someone nail two spikes in the poor bastard's throat? Especially after shooting him full of holes."

"Bet I know. I warned him about rattlesnakes. Bet those punctures are from a big old rattler. He was itching for an old-fashioned Western shootout. Like in the movies. Instead, turns out a reptile got him." He studied the corpse closely. "Know what? Got me a theory. Knowing that trigger-happy psycho, I'll bet he tried shooting the snake when it fanged him. Took the shots straight in his own leg and arm. Probably missed the rattler altogether or it'd be lying nearby. Dumb jerk probably did his self in. Damn rattler got the prize I wanted." He looked up at Mac. "I was wrong about one thing, though. A hat wouldn't have saved him."

Mac's grin exposed his dagger tooth. "You're entitled to your theory. Got my own. I knew Buzz better than anyone. Guy was a deviant but he sure knew how to handle a gun. Smart money says the same creep who slugged me also got Buzz." His eyes scanned the horizon. "Someone pretty conniving is onto us. Time's our enemy now, let's get a move on."

WHITEY grew impatient. He schemed a vile plot. He hated outsiders, wasn't used to sharing, or to teamwork. His loyalty to Mac was thick as mud. He figured just he and Mac should split the pot. He wanted *his* millions. Immediately. He turned and faced Inner Ruin. Like an actor on stage, he bellowed into the amphitheater: "Math by two. Works for me. I like that, a fifty-fifty split." Ancestral spirits shuddered.

He paced briskly along the ledge, picturing each crate stuffed with $100 bills instead of artifacts. His pace accelerated, his path widening to the eastern boundary of Inner Ruin. An object lying close to the cliff caught his eye. Foot and hand-holds above went undetected. The ceremonial fragment was lightly coated. Dirt particles had mushroomed upon impact and then settled. He bent over and picked it up. He blew off the dirt. It was love at first sight. It felt smooth and good to his touch. He smiled down at his palm. Incised glyphs went unnoticed. A strong bond formed. He coveted it. Clutching it tight to his chest, he declared to the cliff village, in higher, spirited octaves: "*My lucky charm.*"

THIRTY

Mac was sloppy loading the artifacts. Hurriedly, he threw crates into the cages and then into the ATV trailers. During the two mile shuttle to the truck, he bounced along the bumpy trail at full throttle. The primitive road was spiked with boulders and deep ruts. One mile overlapped with the Old Mormon Trail of 1880, nearly as harsh as virgin ground itself. When he and Jed returned for the second load, Whitey spoke up. Mac's haphazard antics could cost millions. He agreed to slow down, claiming his mind was foggy, that he'd been up too long. Fatigue overshadowed his face and he was dangerously dehydrated.

"Hey, see what I found?" Whitey boasted. "It's my lucky charm." He held up his newfound treasure. Jed gawked from above. Mac stopped breathing. "It'll bring me luck, guaranty my millions. Found it over there." He pitched it to Mac.

"You retard, *where'd* you find this? We packed several of these inside the chamber. Whole ones. Our buyer claims they're priceless. Feather holders is what he called them. Whole ones might fetch a half a million each to the right buyer. Say again, where? Did you break it?"

Whitey pointed to the eastern edge of the amphitheater. "You lost your mind? Don't remember? That fancy art dude in Mexico bought the other half."

"*New* Mexico, ignoramos, not Mexico. "Yeah, I remember. Just that finding that perverted weasel all shot up and fanged by a rattler threw me for a loop. It's clear someone's watching our every move. I've staked my entire life over this piece of broken clay." He clutched the artifact and stared into Snow Flat Canyon, eyes distant, voice evangelical, all but unrolling an orator's scroll as in ancient Rome. Jed saw it coming and eased back in his seat like he was asleep at the opera. "Picture's coming into focus now. *It's all about uranium.* Not just the millions. That's what the slick art dealer in Santa Fe must have meant when he said he'd help me if I helped him. Sounded like a square deal. Name's Wainwright. That was last November. I used the money to hire you bozos and front this venture. Guy's a slimebag barterer, that's all. I don't trust him.

"Ordered me to empty this damn cavern. Take everything we could lay our hands on. Told me his woman friend was a highfalutin, wealthy babe back East. A bigwig for the government. Carries a lot of weight. Energy Department, I think. She gave him some fairy tale about her father. Said all we gotta do is remove this crap without breaking it and drive it to the exchange. To some conveyor chute and electric train that'll be waiting near that god-awful, dirty Indian town Kay-Enta.

We'll get our fifteen million. Mr. Slick barters what he wants, and his government lady friend, itching to dump her uranium, gets this heap of old Indian junk. Said no price is too high." The orator looked up. Steelhead slumped deeply into his ATV seat. Whitey was almost asleep standing upright.

"Boss, I kill people for sermons that long. Just to shut them up. Now give me my lucky charm. It's mine."

Mac was stunned, even damaged, as he emerged from his preacher trance. "What? No applause? Weren't you bozos even listening for Christ's sake? Might as well been screaming into the canyon."

"Give me my lucky charm." His voice ran aground on a gravel bar, then scraped hard and freed itself. "Give me my lucky charm. Now. And my millions. By sunrise. Or else."

Mac wasn't frightened. Whitey's larynx sounded scarier than his threat. "Yeah, sure. Take the stupid thing. For now. I'll get it back at the exchange." He tossed it carefully to the titan. Whitey netted it with his paw and tucked it in his shirt pocket, padding it lightly against his heart.

WHEELER applauded the conference speaker and headed to his room. Time read 3:10 pm. He printed material for the evening panel discussion. Then, retrieved the e-mail draft to Parker and Windsong. "I know a heck of a lot more now than I did last night," he said, scanning portions of yesterday's draft. He tugged hard on his metaphorical thread, button poised to fly off. Parker and Windsong *had* to be told. The second they arrived home. Other than his DIA contact in Farmington, no one else knew. His conclusions bordered on lunacy.

"Ah, yes, here's where I left off. Maxine Schisslenberg's new name. Schissler, that's it. A shorter version. Still sounds very German to me. Maxine Schissler and her daughter Della Schissler. She was age six when her name changed. That was 1956.

"Guess how old Agent Coldditz was in 1956? Six, same age. Guess who met many years later, like in 1973? He just returned from his second tour in Vietnam. Nixon's troop withdrawal was real. National Security Agency recruited him immediately. Della was a young intern at the U S Department of Energy. And guess what? Coldditz and Della married. Stationed at Fort Meade, he traveled extensively overseas. They divorced twelve years later. No children.

"Husband and wife were masters at keeping secrets. Neither could talk about their work. Went with the territory. She kept her father out of the picture. He never learned of his mysterious 1disappearance in 1953. Coldditz's father worked for Immigration and Naturalization Service. He kept that secret from her, too. Many years later, after the Berlin

Wall toppled, Della's mother abandoned the scene and immigrated back to "eastern" Germany. Back to her Motherland. Della stayed on track with her career at Energy. She earned rapid promotions. She loved Washington.

"Ms. Schissler was truly a chip off the old block. Her career path paralleled that of her father's - geochemistry, mineralogy and geology. Degrees in each. Masters Degree was conferred from Massachusetts Institute of Technology. Following their divorce, she changed her name from Coldditz back to Schissler. It was never red-flagged on intel's radar.

"Word on the street says something fishy's been going on at Energy. Has been for five years. The Government Accounting Office began an investigation into crafty accounting of uranium deposits held by Uncle Sam. Particularly at top secret military installations and strategic defense stockpiles. Ambiguous accounting practices became an embarrassment after September 11. Dozens of heads lined up on Cheney's chopping block. He slay them all. Essentially, policy makers had no reliable data as to the precise number of nuclear warheads which lay vulnerable to terrorists. Well, same thing regarding uranium. No centralized inventory. No truer accountability than Hershey's knowing the number of chocolates eaten on Halloween.

"After 9/11, number crunchers got busy. More heads rolled. They exposed a bunch of phony baloney accounting, a huge hole in the dam. The leak drained uranium stockpiles. Pentagon's fingers pointed straight at Department of Energy. Our leader from Texas listens only to Cheney and Defense. So, Energy took the fall. Enter domestic surveillance without court orders. Warrantless wiretaps were born. The NSA's apparatus came to the rescue. Grabbed hold of it like you do A-1 Sauce. White House ate it up; or, allegedly, dreamed it up in the first place. Even dreamed up legislation exempting their cronies at giant telecommunication companies from prosecution. Nice guys, huh? Pays to protect the elite base that put you there in the first place.

"In recent years, Ms. Schissler amassed a fortune in art and prehistoric artifacts. Her museum-quality collection is second to none. She began appearing at pricy auctions and festive gallery openings throughout the West. During one flamboyant spree, two peas of a pod attracted each other. I liken it more as *flies to elephant shit*. A fling more or less. Neither one sought permanency. A romance forged solely through convenience. You'll never guess who it was. Horace Wainwright. Her appetite for antiquities and his rancorous bartering merged. No one got it. Until 9/11. Within months, shit started churning like the wake of a Mississippi paddlewheel.

218

"Now enter Wendell Coldditz. Conveniently dropped on stage like a prop falling from the rafters. The mole's been watching his every move. He attempts to bore out the mole. To no avail. Arrives on Cedar Mesa and schmoozes my superior, Ms. Quirk. Man's instantly promoted *charges de affairs*. Here's the tricky part. Della Schissler, career DOE bureaucrat, daughter of USGS immigrant scientist, acquirer of Southwest antiquities far beyond her government pay grade, and ex-wife of agent Wendell Coldditz, could she be the mother lode of hundreds of millions of dollars in unaccounted uranium? Could Miss Schissler be Delilah in the Delilah Project? How weird would that be! Della, *translate*, Delilah? Stockpiles easily manipulated electronically. Jet-setting at will on a buying jag with lover Horace? Could this have anything to do with looting in Snow Flat Canyon?"

Wheeler jumped from his chair and raced to the fridge. Cleansed his palette with a Snickers and slurped down a Dr. Pepper. Grabbed a second pop and flew to his laptop, blood sugar soaring. He stroked the keyboard feverishly.

"I'll leave you with this, my friend." "FBI reports dated September, 1953 earmarked *where* they believe Dietrich Schisslenberg disappeared. This was omitted from both newspaper articles. The location matches coordinates where the three tourist photographers were arrested by Navajo Police last week. Also adjacent to the mystical convergence of three mountain ranges. And, Navajo shrines. The area was actively mined from the late 1940s to 1961. Narrow shafts penetrated into weapon-grade uranium ore. That information, omitted from both newspapers, is a matter of public record, available to any citizen. So, why'd they omit it? Did Della Schissler hire people to tap one of those mine shafts? Navajo miners?

"Now I'll drop the mega-ton bomb. The picture's assembled. It's ugly. Defense Intelligence Agency hid a clue along their exit trail after hacking into the NSA's database. My buddy downloaded a file entitled: "The Delilah Project." He literally peered down into one of the NSA's supercomputer 'eyes' when the NSA itself uploaded routine updates to other intel agencies. More dangerous than a drunk racing up the off-ramp to enter a freeway. Had a sixty second window to peer through a tentacle into the NSA's database. He succeeded in the treacherous maneuver. The quintessence of counter-intel. If you ask me, he's genius. That was at lunchtime today. It won't take long for wizards at Fort Meade to trip over the tantalizing clue left behind. Soon they'll be tugging the very same thread stitched to the very same button I'm tugging on. My guess is *it'll pop before day's end*. When an emergency call comes in to our *charge de affairs*, wherever he may be, it'll start a holy bloodbath.

"Call me at 9 tonight. Until then, watch your backs like a hawk."

The small dish atop his hotel did more than send a high speed transmission to Parker and Windsong's desktop at home. In encrypted format, it delivered a high-speed death sentence. More than one. Assets in Baltimore and Washington received simultaneous instructions.

HIS left arm was numb. It slept soundly beneath Kika's weight. It was midnight. His mind raced like electricity through a cord. "To hell with government timetables," he whispered, easing away from his sleeping beauty. He fired up a pot of coffee. Then, he added six eggs to a kettle, set it atop a low flame, and grated sharp cheddar into a bowl. He diced a small wedge of green pepper for coloring; tossed in dried onion flakes and waited for the eggs. He poured water into his hydration pack and threw in a bag of almonds, one apple and four chunks of chocolate. Coffee was ready. He filled a small thermos.

"Sweetheart, how're you feeling?" He stirred her gently. "Breakfast is two minutes away. One cup of creamy coffee too." He sweetened his wakeup call with a peck to her forehead. She rose up on an elbow. "Wow! Swelling's practically gone. Your right eye opens fully. You look almost new."

"Feel much better but I'm still sore." Her lisp had disappeared too. She had full movement of her jaw. Only her upper lip was slightly restricted by the butterfly bandage. "How long did I sleep? Is it time for the showdown?"

"Not yet. I woke up wired. Came up with a plan. If you're up to it. We'll take a sneak peek into Snow Flat Canyon. See firsthand how far along those crooks are. If they're being careful." She frowned. He continued. "Don't fret. Just a quickie recon mission to the south rim. We'll distract the guard posted outside and sneak away. We'll watch those crooks through our scopes. Nothing treacherous. *A quickie.* One hour tops. Be back with time to spare. Promise." The word "quickie" aroused her.

"Glad you reminded me of the guard. I need to step outside and pee."

"That's how we'll escape. Go ahead and pee now. I'll yell for him to turn his back. Give you privacy. Then, after breakfast, when we're ready to bolt, I'll yell it again and slip out behind you. We'll vanish in a flash. Wendell promised there'd be no infrared scope. Said he's not the Peeping Tom type."

Kika brushed against him on her way to the door. It was an unintended, random act of intimacy. It sparked primal juices although neither one admitted it. After days in the canyon, it didn't take much.

She turned and planted a firm, loving kiss on his coffee flavored lips. The bandage was no impediment. "Thank you for saving my life. And healing my wounds. I'd be dead if Buzz hadn't spotted you that very instant."

"You're thanking me? *I love you.*"

She reached the camper door and turned around. "We're just going to watch them during their final loading process, right?" That's all? In and out in a flash? No shenanigans?" He nodded. "Well, Mr. Parker, what happens if we don't like what we see? What if they're willy-nilly tossing those crates around? What's your plan then?"

Howie reached for his backpack. He looked straight at his lover and fellow adventurer. "See these? The NSA's new thermal-imaging device. Plus a unique two-way transmitter. Absolutely silent. Newfangled gadgets, hot off their test farm. Cool, huh? We're doing it, Kika, we're acting out what we've always joked about. We'll act out Q and Bond when I explain their state of the art functions." He opened the door and yelled to the unseen guard. She stepped outside.

They sat at the small table where he and Coldditz had enjoyed their coffee. Howie's masterpiece eggs resembled scrumptious quiche. He surprised her with two blueberry muffins stashed for a special occasion. They ate in silence for several minutes. "I have to tell you," Howie began, wiping his chin and raising his mug, "What I've been thinking since you shared your darkest secret last night." Kika's chewing slowed, her ears perked up. She trapped a lock of hair with her finger and began curling it. His juices stirred again. Not digestive ones. Yet, he had a nervousness about him. He glanced down at his plate frequently and experienced difficulty making eye contact. He fidgeted with his silverware. Kika, on the other hand, had a precocious look, waiting for Howie to spark the ignition.

"I'm terribly in love with you," he said, still fidgeting with his fork. "Your story moved me more than I could possibly describe." He stabbed a chunk of egg. Then stirred it around his plate. "Especially the part about your fear of going to your grave before telling me your deepest secret. That's the most flattering thing anyone has ever told me. To care enough about *me* when *you* faced certain rape and death. Awe heck, Kika, I'm having a hard time saying what I'd like to say." He finished chewing. It paved the way for a genuine smile. "I believe in you 100 percent. I don't judge you for what you did as a runaway teen. You were different then. You had serious issues with your mother. Her drinking drove you out. You'd never even laid eyes on your father. Face it. You were in full flight from teenage reality. Adoption seemed natural. But, today, your values center on relationships, family, you know, your mom, cousins, uncles and the like. You're a twenty-five-year-old woman, not a young teen. And, you're *the* woman I truly want to spend the rest of my life with." Nervousness seized him. Bashfully, he looked down at his plate. Kika sipped the last drop from her mug, eyes more curious than a cat's. They reached out for him over the rim.

"Howie Parker," she said, leaning across the table and breathing into his face. "Are you asking me to marry you?" His fork landed in his lap.

"Well, er, what I think is…well…yes Kika, I am. That's what I'd like. Couldn't quite put my words in a straight line. But, yes, yes. Kika Edison Windsong, will you marry me? We'll drive to your mom's and I'll ask permission. We'll visit Uncle Lenny too. Me not being Navajo, I'll need both their blessings. How's late summer sound? Fall at the latest."

She felt lightheaded. She poured herself around the table and landed softly on his thighs. "Oh, Howie, I love you so. You mean everything to me. Everything! Yes! Yes! I will marry you." They kissed endlessly. They caressed each other's lips. Howie was gentle. He wasn't bothered by the butterfly bandage. They stayed lip to lip, kissing softly and rubbing their noses, pressing their chins firmly together, even licking each other's faces. The bandage became a symbol, not an impediment. It symbolized how they'd saved each other's lives through multiple acts of bravery - Kika's powerful dream - his zany tale about an optometrist's theory. The bandage bonded their hearts, not her lip.

"Maybe," Howie whispered into her nostrils. "Maybe we could put your name into that national registry. The one which helps adopted kids learn about their real parents. Just in case your little girl wanted to look you up someday. That's your big dream, isn't it?"

"I've been thinking a lot about that lately. Oh, Howie, what more could we ask?" Her eyes flooded. Joyful tears. Tears of promise, not despair. It was her turn to breathe words into his nostrils. Her turn to sensuously lick his lips like a playful kitten. "How long has it been, Mr. Parker? How long has your horse-like feature been corralled?" She slid back to his knees and reached for his zipper. "I'll take him out of the stable. Let him gallop around. Rear up a time or two. You game?"

Howie kissed her nose, then her neck, then between her breasts. He turned off the light and checked the curtain. His tongue massaged her lower lip. "Speaking of rearing up, why don't you turn around and face the other way."

"Yum, how lovely," she exhaled, tugging harder at his lips. "We haven't done it like that in awhile."

Howie caressed the nape of her neck, soft as a tulip petal. She breathed heavily. Within a minute they panted in unison. Forced to hide their screams from the agent outside. Like passionate young teens whose parents sat in the next room - satisfying their craving without getting caught. Deep, fulfilling thrusts, near silent orgasms, nearly simultaneous. Perhaps the guard noticed a gentle rocking. Like a land yacht anchored in a sea of sand.

A red dot next to "am" told him it was 12:14. He reached for the snooze button. The shrill repeated. And again. It wasn't the alarm. The hotel phone shook on the night stand. "Wheeler," he blurted into the corded handset. Chained to the bed by the curly cord, he couldn't stretch.

Her voice was annoyingly loud and curt for midnight. More appropriate for a 07:00 am staff meeting. "I'm ordering you back to Cedar Mesa. Back to the real world. Return by zero eight-hundred hours. Events have reached critical mass." Mozart's Serenade No. 10 in G Major drifted into his earpiece.

His head throbbed. Day-old donuts and leftover coffee perched tantalizingly on the microwave. He lunged for them, falling short of his prey. "Damn cord. Sweet Jesus, Quirk, what're you doing to me? You and your symphony. What's this about returning?" She notched up the volume. "Hold on a sec while I put the receiver down." He nuked the coffee and inhaled two donuts. Grabbed a third and his mug and raced to the handset.

"Been a rough day," she confessed, "tomorrow may prove worse. Two homicides pinned to *my* watch, damn it. *Our turf, Officer Wheeler.* He held the phone away and burped. The coffee too cold to enjoy. Quirk's black cat, Spike, rubbed hard against her leg. He begged for freedom, another nighttime prowl. She moved her leg. He was free to go. "Get more shuteye. Tomorrow's a big day. One other thing, don't forget your trip report. I'll watch for it with my first cup of tea. 5:00 am. Sharp!"

"You'll have it."

"And Wheeler, drive directly to the road leading to Brushy Mesa. Don't stop here first. I'll send a team to meet you at the fork bearing toward Snow Flat Canyon. 8:00 am. Sharp!" The click was as curt as her speech.

He stretched and ambled toward the balcony door, staring out at moonlit landscape. His eyes dropped to the hotel parking lot. "What? What's that?" A shadow darted between vehicles. Or so he thought, still not fully awake. He rubbed his eyes. "Moonlight's playing tricks on me. There it is again. Something *is* moving down there. *Someone.*"

He leaned over the metal railing. The shadow continued bobbing.

THIRTY-ONE

The call came over secure line at 12:33 am. The DOE mole spoke briefly with her lover and hung up. She clicked her mouse. Columns of figures stared back at her. She shook her head and smiled. She was certain her office door was securely locked. A digitally-controlled lock programmed by Security had been activated. It controlled four massive cylinders anchored in the jam which protruded into the heavy steel door. She rose to inspect it just to be certain. A series of LED lights blinked affirmatively. She picked up her private line and called Security.

"I'll be working late," she announced. "Preparing our secretary for a 7:00 am cabinet meeting. I'll sign out at zero three hundred hours." She sat down in her plush chair, swiveled from the screen, and stared out at D.C.'s night skyline. The view from her sixth floor office spanned beyond the intersection of 9th Street S.W. and Independence Avenue. Myriad metro lights blinked back at her.

But dazzling lights would not quell the mole's stress. Anxiety gripped her. Her call to Security was timed between bouts of panic. They'd begun at sunset. Their source was the RUSH. The same RUSH all big-scale criminals felt on the verge of their last big job. It was always one more, one last big one. One final, typically vain, attempt to procure endless streams of money, property, and prestige. Just the thought of the final countdown commencing sent nerves to their breaking point, hearts to explosive proportions. If her last Big One failed, Della Schissler, like any master criminal, would be snared in the web of her own treachery. Possibly right in her own office - her den of iniquitous dealings for five years, manipulating uranium inventories with the click of her mouse. She'd paid two million for her private software program. It kept Government books out of the loop. Once the program was fully debugged, the programmer met a suspicious death.

The call had come from Wainwright at a critical time. Her lover was parked at the Navajo trading post in Lukachukai, Arizona. He told her McAllister had advanced his timetable by several hours. The exchange would definitely occur at dawn nineteen miles west of Kayenta, Arizona, where a tall silo dropped coal into the Black Mesa and Lake Powell railcars. Thanks to state of the art hardware furnished by Ms Schissler, Wainwright's call was untraceable. Even by the NSA's cyberspace "fishing" nets. Only three people knew of the exchange site.

Uranium, not coal, would load onto the 6:00 am electric-powered train destined for the Navajo Generating Station at Page, Arizona. The distance from the silo to the coal-fired, steam generating plant spanned

80 miles. The trip took approximately three hours. The train was slated to haul 90 railcars. Its payload would include several thousand tons of uranium, some weapons-grade, some depleted. Sub-bituminous coal extracted from prodigious Black Mesa mines was transferred by conveyor chute to a silo at the rail yard. The conglomerate, Peabody Energy Group, mined it on land belonging to the Navajo Nation. The Black Mesa and Lake Powell Railway was operated by the Navajo Generating Station. Wainwright had facilitated the switch-out from coal to uranium. Handsome donations to the yard superintendent's drug habit and heaps of cash to certain Peabody employees did the trick. Della Schissler smiled a tight, Germanic smile, one that caused her eyes to shift. Her barterer boyfriend had negotiated a deal with terrorist cells. They'd pay $150 million for Della's uranium. Terms were F.O.B. delivered, Navajo Generating Station, Page, Arizona. Mac and his marauders would earn $15 million for the Indian artifacts. Barterer Wainwright would reap astronomical gains when his secret trade panned-out.

She unlocked her briefcase and withdrew a discolored envelope. Its contents had launched her career into a quagmire of dirty dealings. From her position of trust and authority, she falsified shipments to and from stockpiled uranium, delving in deadly cat and mouse games with cutthroat buyers. She was caught up with forces more powerful than the government she represented. And, in the process, had amassed a fortune held in secret bank accounts. An unequaled, private collection of southwest prehistoric artifacts added to her booty. Most were acquired and held illegally according to US laws protecting cultural resources.

The mole narrowed her window blinds and picked up her readers. Once, she had memorized the envelope's entire contents. But, that night, on the eve of her crucial mission, she sought only to internalize the *spirit* of her father's monumental expose. There were no other farewells, no goodbyes, preceding his swift disappearance. Just his expose, written from the point of view of a scientist, about the land he surveyed and mapped for the Department of Defense. Undercover, as an employee of the United States Geologic Survey. The letter included an intricately drawn map. Maps were his forte. "Ah, yes," she chimed in her sound-suppressed office, his "map of riches."

Dietrich Schisslenberg's disappearance had occurred 36 days after he'd written the letter. "Damn you, papa, you up and vanished when I was only three. I was shattered, my childhood ruined. You robbed me of it! Mama hadn't a clue where you went. She dreamt up every excuse she could think of. Men in dark suits came to our door every day and watched our house for three years. Where'd you go? Did the dusty

225

desert swallow you up? Was it supernatural forces? Witchcraft? Did Navajos have a hand in it? What about those weird gadgets you left behind in our cellar?"

She clenched the tarnished envelope and stared at international postage stamps affixed to its face. It was addressed to her father's executor in Frankfurt, West Germany, posted in Farmington, New Mexico March 20, 1953. The purple-black ink from Schisslenberg's fountain pen had survived a half century. She opened the letter. Meticulous penmanship was his trademark. She clutched it in both hands and pulled it into her chest, as though embracing his flesh. His spirit was still alive, as though inked lettering translated into genes locked in a time capsule.

She'd first read the document after her mother's passing in August, 2000. Cause of death was attributed to congenital heart failure. She had died before 9/11. Della sat loyally by her bedside for the two weeks preceding her death. Although Maxine slept most of the time, she was seized with periodic states of delirium. As she passed, she stared hauntingly into Della's eyes, begging forgiveness for an unconscionable sin. Incoherently mumbling that someday Della would learn for herself. Della's ex-husband, agent extraordinaire, Wendell Coldditz, made a bizarre appearance at his former mother-in-law's memorial service. Della was shocked. She hadn't seen him in six years, her mother, longer. The motive of his surprise visit remained a mystery, claiming he'd been attached to a diplomatic mission in Wiesbaden and decided to pay his respects.

Later that evening, in her Frankfurt hotel room, she read the letter until her eyes crossed, laying awake all night in tortuous slumber. Nighttime spilled into dawn with no sleep. Sometime before daybreak, she plunged into the bottomless abyss of "head-game" dreams. At sunrise, she ordered breakfast and a pot of tea delivered to her room. Afterwards, she adjourned to her balcony, nine floors above Frankfurt's bustling financial center. Her eyes wandered purposefully through its nerve center of wealth. Prodigious business dealings transpired on the streets below. She could practically reach out and touch the wheels of others' fortunes changing hands. Exchanges of billions, even trillions, from one fat bank account to another. It was all so close. Yet so untouchable.

Then, it clicked. An inherited gene perhaps. Staring down from the ninth floor, her mind transformed into a state of "criminal enlightenment." She rationalized each mental step of the way, yielding a great epiphany, a paradigm shift from mundane bureaucrat to mastermind white-collar criminal. Her logic seemed rational to her - that so long as she remained status quo in a civil service job, in spite of pay-grade advances, she'd spend the rest of her life staring *at* other peoples' riches. Her inbred, lifetime ambition of amassing wealth would fizzle. She'd forever daydream about it, nothing more. Greed seized her on that Frankfurt balcony. A penchant to steal imbedded itself. Just like it had grabbed her father a half century earlier while he was mapping uranium for the Department of Defense.

Treason also spawned in Ms. Schissler's mind, just like it had in her father's. Born, then visually incubated nine floors above Frankfurt's financial district, she attained "criminal enlightenment." She vowed to become filthy rich. She swore to herself that she would steal from the wealthiest nation on earth. And, she vowed to do so from her high-ranking office in the heart of the nation's capital - the office entrusted with the stewardship of decentralized uranium stockpiles. "Easy as pie," she proclaimed. "Papa did it by falsifying maps and surveys. I'll do it electronically." Thus began her legacy of betrayal, treason pure and simple on the grandest of scales, originating in 1953 and jump-started in 2000.

Semi-closed blinds diffused the city lights into slits. The pages resembled sheet music, sepia in color, inscribed in midnight ink. With the reading glasses sitting firmly upon her nose, she opened the envelope and began reading.

"20 March, 1953

"My Dear Maxine,

"No doubt you or our daughter will be reading this after I have passed. This letter will be retained by the Executor of my estate, Hans Hausman, in the Frankfurt office of Hausman, Eschenbach and Haushalter. I instructed the firm to retain this document in its original, sealed envelope until your passing, or fifty years, whichever first occurs, at which time it shall be given to you or Della.

"The enclosed map will lead you to a hidden cache of the highest grade uranium ore in the world. I am compelled to use geologic terminology to direct you. You have stood fast at my side during my illustrious career. The words will not be foreign.

"The breathtaking beauty of the Kah Bighi Valley on the Navajo Reservation is unsurpassed in the southwest of these United States. Its magnificence is likened to the charm and resplendence of the Garmisch-Partenkirchen region in our fatherland. It is enriched with a feeling of lebensraum. At the windblown convergence of three mountain ranges lies a mystical land. Its predominant geologic feature is a natural arch carved into sandstone by forces of erosion. This geologic marvel embodies a perfectly shaped arc. It spans a length of 20 meters, measures 3 meters in circumference and is approximately 6

meters above ground at its center. Its geometric symmetry will astonish you when you hike into the Kah Bihghi Valley. In close proximity to the arch there exists a natural shaft deep within the earth. That is where the uranium vein is situated. It is similar to lava tunnels that you and I visited before the birth of our daughter. It is not a mine shaft. It is a deep vent formed in the earth's mantle wedged between two geologic formations. This mystical formation evolved over 200 million years ago.

"The Navajo Indians have befriended me. They esteem me as an individual, not the government I represent. An aura of suspicion is attached to endeavors by the United States Geologic Survey. It predisposes these fine Natives to a state of extreme caution. At best, Navajo people have guarded respect for the white race. Who can blame them after a history stained with bloodshed and emaciated human rights? But, me they have come to like. My agency employs many Navajo. They escort USGS personnel throughout their reservation where our race is viewed with great suspicion. They earn a small pittance for the light duties they perform. They are my passport to safe thoroughfares.

"Navajo customs do run deep. We have come to understand each other as well as we can. Our cultural traditions are light years apart. Their dialogue is filled with humor. They are gifted orators, often alternating between Navajo tongue and broken English. A melodic chord rings with each Navajo phrase. Their words are embroidered with imaginative powers. Most landscape features and locations throughout the reservation have strange-sounding names. Many represent creatures dominant in their origin myths. They have shared certain stories with me during our long days in the desert. I am uncertain where to draw the line between oral tradition and myth. They are so passionate, and their stories are so beautiful. It is taboo for the White race to know precise details of their rituals and religious beliefs.

"Virtually every type of animal and insect are woven into their folktales. Their creation stories tell how ancestors emerged upward through an opening, or crack, out of dark worldly existences into new and brighter worlds. They can talk for hours. Navajo stories are punctuated with metaphors, hand gestures and broad smiles. They love to laugh and be happy. They are a peaceful and kind people.

"The secret shaft holding the vein of uranium is positioned 40 kilometers west of a sacred Navajo landmark. It is named Shiprock. It is a volcanic neck protruding 1,800 feet skyward. One Navajo myth tells how their People escaped from the enemy. Prayers offered by medicine men were answered when the earth rose and moved like a great wave to the east. The Navajo reached safety. The great wave

228

settled where the stunning promontory now stands. Navajo still believe that the earth nearby rumbles and is prone to magical forms of 'walking in place.' We scientists call it force fields of energy. In seismologic terms, the phenomenon does not reach proportions of an earthquake. It is in this magically moving land that the rich vein of uranium lies.

"Navajo elders advised me not to enter alone into this sacred land. It forms where the Chuska, the Carizzo and the Lukachukai mountains converge. But I have done so, and that is when I came to discover the hidden vent. I have visited the land many times secretly at night. They have warned me of supernatural, mystical powers at the point of convergence. They have a special name for it. They tell me that the meaning in Navajo does not translate precisely to English. Their name for this sacred space is 'The Land of Walking Earth'. I have also heard them call it 'The Land Where the Earth Starts to Shake'.

"You and I know the earth's mantle is prone to churning and horizontal movements. This natural shaft is the quintessential location to conceal the uranium vein. It was laid down in the Jurassic formation when soluble uranium minerals found organic matter in richly vegetated riverbeds. The beauty of my secret is that it will never be discovered by another person because it is confined to The Land of Walking Earth. It moves in unison, as one mass, with its surrounding landscape. It is perched upon a plate stretching westward toward the hogback feature known as Comb Ridge.

"My top secret, futuristic work using ground-penetrating radar prototypes led to my discovery. A stroke of luck and my mathematical genius allowed me to secretly conceal it. I have falsified official maps and survey records of The Land of Walking Earth. My dear Maxine, you and I have discussed at length the contingency of our immigration status. It is repulsive. The government coerced me to sign those appalling documents, stripping me of my genius, my inventions, and my rights to publish. Such things are inalienable rights, or so I believed, when we swore an oath to become US citizens. I will use my genius to strike back at them, for I mistrust the officials of this land. My loyalty toward the American system is mired in betrayal. I will even the score for their bedevilments. I will commit treason.

"I also cringe at the government's mistreatment of American Indians. Their arrogant, White superiors wear patronizing smiles in their presence. They are two-faced. They may think such masks ease the pain inflicted upon Indian culture. But, the Navajo and I see through their transparencies. My superiors insult them and order them around. They lie directly to their faces. It sickens me. It runs contrary to my values. American politics are predicated solely upon world domination.

229

But, we all know that Natives owned the entire continent long before the white race conquered it. I'm afraid our emigration from Hitler's fascism to America has taken us 'from the frying pan to the fire'!

"The cache concealed within the shaft is yours. Or Della's. I beseech you to recover it by means of a secret mining venture at the time of your need. Everyone has a price. I am certain your resourcefulness can locate a private enterprise when the time comes. If the price is right. As in our fatherland before the war, perhaps the value could be bartered to a consortium of foreign mining firms. It will command a fortune far beyond the limits of today's meager horizon.

"Here is the map. It is drawn to exact scale. The minute you set foot in The Land of Walking Earth the landscape will guide you. Hike directly to the natural arch and stand beneath its center. No doubt you will feel a surge of a powerful energy. Set your compass at a bearing of 321 degrees. Now, you face an abrupt terminus of the Carizzo Mountains. Proceed on this bearing of 321 degrees for precisely 75 meters. The 1,200 meter sheer rise to your left is the convergence of the Chuska and the Lukachukai Mountains. Two unmistakable landscape features lie eight kilometers before you. They are called The Thumb and Mitten Rock. At the 75 meter mark, set a bearing at 290 degrees. Walk 40 meters. You will find yourself standing besides an etching in the sandstone called Dual Castle. From that point, continue 24 meters on a bearing of..."

Della folded the letter into its envelope. Seconds later, her muse came to an abrupt end. A chilling draft passed through the room. Followed by another. She snapped to attention. "What the h - ? Air doesn't move like that unless a closed system is violated." She was correct. When a draft whisked through a room or slammed shut a door, it had to originate from a sudden opening. "Someone has compromised the sixth floor at DOE." Her words tumbled from trembling lips. Panic struck. Cold sweats. "The elevator?" she whispered. The mole leaped from her chair. LED lights blinked back at her. The door was still secure. She listened. It was too quiet.

She grabbed her cell phone and stabbed in an emergency code. Security picked up on the first ring. Her office was well soundproofed, yet she spoke softly. The guard assured her no sensors had been tripped. All doors in the sixth floor zone were secure. No movement was indicated on their security monitors. "Are you certain? I swear - ." She lowered her terror-stricken voice.

"Yes, Ms. Schissler," the duty chief of Security assured her. "But for you, I'll run a systems check. Please hold." He failed to mention that two of his officers hadn't returned from routine sweep. That was six minutes ago, decidedly against protocol. Something wasn't right, but he couldn't alert her prematurely. Three minutes dragged into eternity. Della was left hanging. The duty chief never came back on the line. Twenty seconds later the line disconnected. The click paralyzed her. She reached in her drawer and clutched a sleek, low profile 9mm. It held 17 rounds, trying desperately to steady trembling hands. She tiptoed to the door and flattened against the wall. DOE's air circulation system hummed back at her, its drone produced an eerie silence. Nervous and sweaty, she extended her arms. Clammy hands gripped the weapon. The RUSH was fully engaged.

WINCHES had glitches. Raising metal cages in primitive environs, each carrying a heavy payload, 48 feet to the rim, was a delicate process. McAllister should have planned for a third ATV and shuttle driver. He had two extra shuttles for backup, but not enough drivers. The roundtrip was consuming far more time than he'd allotted, the terrain harsher than he remembered. His dream of turning clumsy urban thugs into Indiana Joneses was a monumental blunder.

An unplanned and debilitating plight was dehydration. It crippled and fatigued them. Aside from Kane Gulch Ranger Station, they were thirty-plus miles from any potable water. Their supply of one gallon containers dwindled to two. Not bad for a Navajo or an experienced backpacker. But gangsters from the Great Lakes couldn't fathom rationing anything, much less water. It killed teamwork, placed them in competition. Whitey was hit hardest. He could've drunk Lake Erie dry. He even dreamt of being back in his death-noose and dragged behind the Mob's yacht.

They readied for another shuttle. "I'll tag a ride up on this full cage," said Jed. He aimed the remote and launched into the air. Three fourths of the way it jerked to a stop. The cage swung precariously. The winch ratcheted loudly, gears ground. It slipped two feet. Mac and Whitey lunged sideways, arms over their heads. The cage dangled. It slipped four feet further. Jed freaked. He clutched the remote and waved wildly. Then tapped its cover and pounded it hard against his thigh. A sickening whine followed. Profanities echoed in the canyon. "Damned that dealer in Bluff. I'll blow him away!"

"My cage is loaded," Mac said. "I'll go up and see if I can un-jam it. You yell up instructions."

"Just be damned careful, half-head. Or me and this whole pile of junk goes crashing down. I'll crush the other half of your skull if that happens."

Jed spelled out instructions from his precariously swaying cage. Repairs took 40 minutes. Another costly delay. Minutes later, he and

Mac raced off with loaded trailers. Whitey wandered idly in the amphitheater. He had too much time on his hands. He paused next to the gargantuan boulder. He brushed against it, even gave it a karate chop, acting out his tough guy role, acting as if he could toss it around like a beach ball. "Got me an idea," he bellowed to ancestral spirits of Inner Ruin. "Math by two is easy." Spirits cringed.

HOWIE and Kika slipped past the agent. They moved swiftly under a full moon. It took twenty-six minutes to reach the rim opposite Inner Ruin. He raised his night scope. The ruins looked all but empty. Five stacks of crates remained. Perhaps three shuttle runs would wrap it up. Kika scanned the plaza using his scope. Inner Ruin was decimated. It would never be the same. Never. No matter how well the BLM attempted to stabilize it. Ancestral spirits were forever uprooted. "Looting's just a disguised form of genocide," she said. "Ancestral genocide. Whites never let up, do they? Whether we Indians are alive or dead! They get us either way." At 1:18, she spotted faint light and movement. "Hold on, got something. Looks like a firefly. East of the ruins."

She handed over the scope. "Got it. Some firefly. It's Whitey. He's messing with boulders. Shoveling too. Destructive as a bulldozer. Not sure what he's up to." The giant mass of brawn busied himself clearing sagebrush and rocks on downward sloping terrain. He looked up at the shuttle road periodically. Suddenly, he stopped shoveling and raced back to the ledge above the ruins. He moved like a galloping elephant. Next, he put on a custom climbing harness and rigged a rappel line just to be safe. He dropped down using a set of Anasazi holds at the extreme west side of the village. They were pecked alarmingly deep. He half rappelled, half glided down the cliff.

Headlights appeared. Mac parked his ATV and lowered himself in the cage. Crates were quickly loaded. Whitey commented how nice it was that Buzz was removed from the split. He pressed on with his greediness, pushing Mac beyond his breaking point. Finally, he nailed Mac square between the eyes with his new brainstorm. It hit Mac more powerfully than the wrecking ball had years earlier. "Nicer yet if it was just us two, huh? Just you and me? Math by two."

Mac donned his death mask. He was bent over, looking sideways like a mad rhino. Gravity distorted facial patchwork beyond belief. No different than thick folds on a rhino's face. "You no-good, dimwitted mass of brain foam. What the hell you talking about? Listen, retard, you keep dropping people from the equation and we won't have enough manpower to even show up at the exchange. Then what, bozo head? We'll all come up short, nothing but one big fat goose egg, you greedy

232

ignoramus." Mac's dagger tooth was no different than a rhino's lethal horn, ready to impale without warning. "Be glad I even let you in on this job. Could have left you in Cleveland. So drop your smart-aleck epiphanies. We need Jed. We need everyone. We all need each other. Slick from Santa Fe is ruthless. Worse than you or me. He'll kill us if we're late. Keep everything for himself. He's got more riding on this scheme than we do. Juggling three or four barters at once. Thought I told you all that."

"You mean that dumb sermon? Heard every word you said, preach. It's still coming to me. I got brains, I'm just slow. Just takes me longer. You never said nothing about uranium before. I don't want no rade-dation. Only millions."

"Don't worry none about radiation." Mac looked up. He heard the drone far away. It was Jed. He'd stayed behind to rearrange the cargo and keep an eye on Trixie. As soon as Jed arrived, he and Mac loaded one trailer and rode out together. That way, Whitey and Jed could drive the final loads out after Jed returned again.

WHITEY climbed to the rim and returned to his construction site. Parker and Windsong kept him in focus. He shoveled and moved boulders at a furious pace. He didn't have much time. "Millions, millions, millions," he chanted gutturally. When he finished, the titan held his lucky charm, rubbing it over his heart in a circular motion, chanting: "Bring me luck, lucky charm."

HOWIE studied the second hand of his Chase-Durer. Time advanced by spurting to a new second mark. He wondered what the busiest hand on a dial did between one-second intervals. Did it rest until the last nanosecond and then launch confidently to its new landing? Or did it do calisthenics and then spring enthusiastically like a hiker jumping to the next rock while fording a stream? He waited sixty such spurts, then declared: "Thirteen minutes, fifty-two seconds and we're out of here. Can't miss our ride to Todie Springs." Kika nodded and munched on almonds.

Dual headlights, caked with a fresh coat of mud, blinked faintly in the distance. Impaired visibility forced Jed to muscle the handlebar with one fist and shield his eyes with the other. He'd taken a shortcut through a soggy, spring-fed arroyo. His head angled forward to gain better sight. As fate would have it, a wisp of ribbed clouds floated high overhead. It darkened the moonlight. Poor timing for the driver from Pittsburgh. He'd left his headlamp at the truck, figuring he knew the trail by heart. He'd figured wrong. One thousand feet east of Inner Ruin, Whitey had skillfully created a diversion. He formed a natural-looking trail veering into the canyon and sloping gradually down to the ledge below. Like the switchman at a rail yard, his work paid dividends. Jed steered onto the false trail. Ribbed clouds thickened. Muddy headlights were useless. The surrogate trail led him 125 feet below Inner Ruin. It was acutely wedge-shaped, unlike the broad amphitheater above. Jed was doomed. He crept forward, unable to see clearly, until the ledge narrowed to the width of a walkway. He was past the point of no return. Whitey waited 125 feet above, leaning patiently against the massive boulder.

The professional driver cursed his own stupidity. He brought both hands to his eyes and rubbed hard, then squinted and looked around. The landscape wasn't the same. He'd been duped. Engine idling, he inched forward. It proved too narrow to negotiate a turnaround. One inch of each left tire hung over the ledge. Two hundred and fifty feet below, the verdant canyon bottom beckoned his soul. He stood and used his footrests like stirrups. Profanity filled the canyon, echoing off dark sandstone walls. Across the canyon, bewilderment gripped Parker and Windsong. Parker glanced up at Whitey, forefinger pressed against the house-sized boulder. For the second time in twenty-four hours, Parker failed to scream warnings to his adversary.

Jed looked over his shoulder and lurched in reverse. The front left wheel dropped over the edge. Cloaked moonlight and muddy headlights availed him nothing. In a last-ditch attempt to build his confidence, he screamed at the top of his lungs, boasting he'd handled huge rigs in tight urban squeezes. His pep talk failed. "Oh, shit," were the last words uttered from his lips. One hundred and twenty-five feet above, Whitey cackled loudly. He peered over the ledge like a hawk about to descend upon helpless chicks in their nest. He stepped confidently behind the boulder. The giant mass of tertiary sandstone had kept vigil over Snow Flat Canyon for millennia. It had witnessed civilizations rise and fall more than once. The loss of one more human wouldn't even register.

The massif rubbed his lucky charm, greed spilling from his eyes like molten lava. He chortled in joy and scraped from the bottom of his windpipe to deliver a thundering message. The words were ringing in Jed's ears when he arrived at the gates of hell. "Head of Steel. Take this!"

Kika let go of her binoculars. They thumped against her chest. Howie lowered his scope and stared at her. A plume of dust rose to the moon. He was paralyzed. He'd witnessed his share of killing, but that one took the prize. Like watching an elephant crush an ant. The ledge below Inner Ruin broke away from the cliff and splintered into small pieces. Mysteriously, unknown forces kept the wall above from fracturing. Inner Ruin and its amphitheater ledge avoided cataclysmic demise. The dirt plume drifted upward. Fine particles began settling on Cedar Mesa. "Now we know what we're up against," Kika blurted in shock. Howie nodded slightly, unsure if Snow Flat Canyon would remain intact for long.

MAC and Trixie stood next to the rental truck. He chugged from a water jug and dumped the remainder over his head. Their entire fresh water supply had just been reduced to one gallon. After his improvised shower, he cast a vile look at Trixie, raised a finger to one nostril, and blew with all his might. Snot discharged like a fire hose. He repeated the ordeal with his other nostril. He loved demeaning women with all forms of passive-aggressive antics. He hated her uncle, Krenecke, so he hated her even more. His head jerked suddenly. "What was hell was that? You feel it? An earthquake? In these parts?"

"Don't know, Mr. Mac. A meteor?"

"Could be. Don't know. Whatever it was, I don't like it. Come on, follow me. We'll hide in the brush just in case." Ten minutes passed. Headlights came into view. "Must be Jed and Whitey," he said. "Our last shuttle. We'll make the exchange after all."

Trixie peered closer. "Only one rig's coming, Mr. Mac." She jumped from the bushes, squinting. "It's not Jed, Mr. Mac. Never seen this guy."

Mac reached for his gun and shone his flashlight. "What the hell? It's Whitey." He stepped from the brush, picking snotty residue from his nostrils. He admired his catch before popping it into his mouth as though it were caviar. "Jed right behind you?"

The human Doug fir swayed proudly. He remained silent. A minute later, he cackled. It spilled into a chuckle. That overflowed into a boisterous laugh. "Jed's crushed he couldn't make it. Yup, boss, crushed. So we're down to two. She don't count."

THIRTY-TWO

Following his emergency call at Parker's campsite, Coldditz reached his command post in fourteen minutes. The Captain greeted him without fanfare. "You have orders to connect immediately, sir." His curt tone matched the agent's disposition. "Issued four minutes ago. But first, Colonel Holmes insists you contact him at Brownie. Uplink is standing by." He cracked a five percent smile. "Didn't mean to interrupt your coffee clutch with Parker, sir. You know how fidgety the Colonel gets."

Coldditz nodded. He sat at a wireless plasma screen integrated with a sensor-touch keyboard unique to mobile applications. "The Colonel comes first. He transmitted the e-mail intercept, correct?"

"Yes, sir."

He took a deep breath. A reply formulated quickly. He appreciated Parker's love for coffee. Caffeine would keep him alert. Depending on Ft. Meade's response, another late night was in the offing. He'd only squeezed in a handful of power naps for three consecutive nights. The Captain watched his superior. He had respect and admiration for him. He'd volunteered for the Delilah Project. He'd served Coldditz on eight previous missions. He set a bottle of iced water next to him. "So," he began, eyeing the Captain, "this Officer Wheeler works for the Interior, correct? Bureau of Land Management? Been busy, hasn't he?"

"We've dealt with his type before, sir. Pain in the ass is more like it."

"Thought he was sidetracked at the archaeology conference."

"He's tenacious, sir."

"Quirk designated him moderator of the panel discussion, didn't she?"

"Yes, sir. Didn't hold him back one iota. Like I said, pain in the ass. Also has one hell of a contact at the DIA. Man's a cunning hacker. Ingenious is more like it. Covered his tracks beautifully. Almost. Left us something to nibble on when he exited. Holmes is tracking it. He'll nail him. Holmes is the best."

"Agreed. I'll transmit in five minutes. Inform our squad we'll debrief them on the takedown at Todie Springs in fifteen minutes. Final stages of the Delilah Project will commence at 02:00 hours. You're dismissed." His near-transparent screen showed 21:41:16. About the same time that Wheeler concluded his panel discussion in Moab and Kika made her confession to Howie and Mac and his crew began shuttling artifacts.

He was grateful. His team was the best. Resourceful and bright. Handpicked. After the criminals were in custody, they'd tie up loose ends until daybreak. Then he'd fly to Washington. Pay one last visit to the mole. He read Wheeler's e-mail. A printout wasn't necessary. He made a copy in his mind using a skill he'd been born with – photo-telegraphy. Slightly different than photographic memory, photo-telegraphy retained an identical facsimile of seen objects. Symbols, images, alpha characters or numbers became etched in his memory - forever - the nanosecond he saw them. It was a frequent lifesaver during covert ops.

His fingers stroked the keyboard with precision. He was a cunning intelligence officer. He would not be undermined by the tenor of Wheeler's e-mail. His response to Holmes would exonerate the NSA. "We're hours away from bringing closure to Delilah," he began. "Priceless archaeological artifacts and uranium bound for terrorists will be confiscated. Criminals will go down. I realize that allegations in said e-mail add sensitivity to the project. But *I* have to see this through. Delilah is *my* baby. I've arranged to be in Washington tomorrow morning. Ex-wife or not, I'll look the mole straight in the eyes. Call her Delilah to her face. A rare opportunity for me. Face-to-face contact with an objective is infrequent. I'll wrap up the project by zero nine-hundred hours. Therefore, do not, I repeat, *do not engage NSA assets*. We'd have one hell of a mess on our hands." The encrypted message disappeared into cyberspace. Four seconds later, Holmes watched the deciphered script materialize on his wall-sized screen.

His second transmission was to a long-time associate stationed at Andrews Air Force Base. They'd been assigned to the same station chief in North Africa in the mid-nineties. He owed Coldditz a favor. A huge one. His friend obliged within minutes. Military transport was arranged from Farmington to Washington at 04:00. Once Coldditz confronted the mole, Colonel Holmes would shut down the entire project within minutes. There would be no record of its existence. It would simply vanish. That was the plan anyway. If all went well.

"YOU imbecile! You *are* retarded." Mac shook his patchwork skull like a Lab shaking off water. He torpedoed Whitey with demeaning names. "Now what do we do? We're already late. I told Slick hours ago that we were ahead of schedule. I can't renege. Everything's in motion. Christ, why am I stifled by incompetency?" He paced like a caged tiger. "We have one more load to shuttle. What if it breaks down? Who's gonna fix it? Her?" He jerked his thumb like an umpire.

"Boss," he said, impervious to Mac's insults. "We rush outta here now. Save face. Leave the last load behind."

Mac launched into orbit. He stomped the ground and cursed loudly. The truck's fender became a punching bag. The .38 remained in his grip but didn't fire. Trixie freaked. She was excess baggage and she knew it. She retreated ten feet. "What, you delusional? I'll pretend I never heard that. Over my sorry ass, leave the last load behind. So help me God, foam-brain, if this deal is blown because you crushed Jed, I *will* kill you. Don't care if you saved my life in Cleveland. This is different. *This is millions*. Never have to work again!"

"Mr. Mac." Trixie stepped boldly in front of their fuming leader. Although cautious, she was greatly relieved that head-splitting Jed was dead. "I can help, Mr. Mac. I've worked in my uncle's heavy-duty truck shop. I'm strong, I know I can help. I don't want your money. Just let me and my uncle live. Fair exchange, isn't it? He's family. He's all I got. Promise me our lives and I'll be the best damn worker you've ever had. Let's me and you go back into the canyon. Right now. We'll hurry and make up lost time. Mr. Whitey can stay with the truck."

The scraggly-haired, unkempt ex-hostage had found her voice. It rang with confidence instead of terror. She knew Mac and Whitey were more volatile than nitro, that anything could happen. If she helped, they might keep her alive. "Really, Mr. Mac, I'm a hard worker. I hold my own at my uncle's shop. Run circles around the old-timers." She stood inches from his death mask. Foul breath spewed from his dehydrated mouth. She exhaled and swallowed hard to keep from puking.

Mac gripped his gun and strode off. His only concern was personal gain, millions in cash, not the life of someone whose uncle had double-crossed him. He stopped at the rear of the truck and looked inside, staring at crates stacked neatly by Jed. Crates worth fifteen million bucks in artifacts. He knew he couldn't stop one shuttle short. He walked back and faced off with Trixie. "OK," he said firmly. "But you better be worth your salt." Then he turned to Whitey. He raised his gun to Whitey's forehead and pantomimed shooting him between the eyes. "You stay here and keep watch, imbecile. Don't move nothing. Don't screw up. We're *this* close to splitting fifteen million," he said, squeezing his fingertips together.

He and Trixie started to leave. Whitey glared back. His voice rumbled like thunder. "Hey, boss. Don't forget who you're talking to." He pounded his chest like a gorilla. "Me Whitey. Impossible to Kill!"

THE call came at 00:19. The Captain awakened his superior. Coldditz had eked out two hours sleep. He needed ten. Half-awake, he lumbered from his tent to the secure line. Colonel Holmes spoke in a distant, hollow tone. It told the story. The agent's knees buckled. The true architect of Delilah expressed his condolences. The order had been issued by the Director's Office. They'd dispatched an asset and a clean-up crew five minutes earlier. The decision was out of the Colonel's hands. He'd been told, not consulted. "I'm sorry, but I'm ordering you to return immediately. I'll meet your transport at the base. You'll be debriefed at the usual place." He was referring to a countryside safe house nicknamed "the Farm." A battery of polygraphs would follow. Dr. Lindemann would conduct them. Coldditz despised Lindemann, principally because he knew every secret ever held by every agent employed by the NSA. He knew more about agents than their Maker. "If Lindemann determines you have no link to the mole's activities," Holmes continued, "we'll have you turned around and back on Cedar Mesa shortly after sunrise. You can wrap up the Delilah Project yourself. Then take personal leave, three months minimum. Clear the cobwebs, as they say. At full pay, of course." A conspicuous pause filled the line. "If you're debriefing goes south, then…" The line went dead.

The veteran agent had been snapped out of sound sleep before, but never with such a devastating impact. Words echoed somewhere in his head but didn't fit together. "Impersonal bastards," he yelled. "Heartless pricks. You could have at least called her by her name, not 'the mole.'" He turned to the Captain. "She's become an objective. Where's *my* phone? Assets don't waste a second. I might be able to stop it." The Captain handed him his private, emergency satellite phone. It was iridescent orange. For use in life and death emergencies only. It tripped a signal at the Situation Room in the White House.

Standing beside the gently flowing stream, he punched three successive nine-digit codes, followed by another sequence of five codes. The line rang. A Marine Honor Guard answered. He'd reached the Director's Office of the National Security Agency. In the event of a true national emergency, Director Quay would be summoned in seconds. Coldditz screamed into the orange instrument. The Honor Guard Officer handed the phone to a First Lieutenant. Coldditz begged the highly trained officer to call off the asset. He pleaded for him to awaken Director Quay and stay the execution. Despair echoed in his voice. "You *must* stay the order until I arrive tomorrow morning. I must speak directly to Ms. Schissler. *She's holding vital information. We must extract it from her. I'm the only one on earth who can do that.* She shouldn't be an objective, not tonight. Not after my 35 years of devoted service. The agency owes me that. *She's the heart of the Delilah Project, for Christ's sake!* I know you have the authority to alert Quay and rescind the order! I know how Fort Meade works. SO DO IT! NOW! It's not too late. Once the objective is in the crosshairs, an asset always awaits a final nod from Command. Stop this nonsense. It's too rushed!"

His plea fell upon deaf ears. The First Lieutenant stood stiffer than a light pole. His shiny-brimmed cap aimed down at his eyebrows. Coldditz was given a bureaucratic brush-off. As though he never existed. "It violates protocol," the Marine lied. "I'm to inform you that this office has no knowledge of such an order." The satellite link went dead.

Coldditz's knees buckled a second time. He had failed. The outer reef of Director Quay's security atoll was impenetrable. Even for a high-ranking, 35-year veteran agent, even speaking through his emergency orange phone. He slammed the instrument against his thigh. "Shit." He raced to the van and preyed upon it, circling it wildly, eyes as iridescent as the phone. The Captain kept his distance. A full moon punctuated the drama. He punched another sequence of codes into the phone, then a top-secret number. "I'll try a different approach," he shouted. "But it better happen fast. Della's life is measured in seconds." Holmes picked up on the first ring.

"Sir," the Captain said after he'd hung up, "a Cayuse chopper is six minutes out. Dispatched by Holmes from Kirtland AFB in Albuquerque. It'll pick you up in Blanding and whisk you to Farmington. The Air Force takes over from there." Coldditz threw documents relating to Delilah in a courier pouch. The Captain's voice raised one octave. "You sure know how to pull the right strings. Your buddy at Andrews has the right connections too. Claims he saw the writing on the wall. Diverted a plane at 11:30 this evening. Was en route to our friends at Peterson in Colorado Springs. Not much out of the way." He continued on an upbeat note, wanting his superior to leave in a positive mindset. "Sir, hand me that pouch, I'll carry it." They ran to a waiting SUV. "Officer Marling here is our ace driver. He'll have you in Blanding in a flash. Here's the best part, sir. Holmes ordered Marling to return to Blanding at 07:40. For your turnaround flight, sir. *Hopefully.* The Colonel's confident. So are we. Good luck. We know it'll go well. *We must have you back.* Our mission is incomplete."

Officer Marling saluted Coldditz. Coldditz sat pensively in the backseat. "Not really, Captain," the agent thought. "Our mission is far from incomplete. That bastard Quay got what he wanted all along. The NSA's prize - the mole. The Pentagon will be pleased. As for me? Back to the nest for a debriefing. What a pain in the ass."

OUTSIDE her office, city lights twinkled brightly. Inside, she shook like a leaf, flattened against her office wall behind where the door would crash open, clinging to a 9mm semi-automatic, sweating profusely, trapped in her own vile web - waiting.

THE Gulfstream IV lifted off from Four Corners Regional Airport at 01:13. The roar of its twin Rolls-Royce engines was absorbed by the desert. He stared out the small passenger window, mind searching frantically in old memory vaults. The memories had been tucked away into deep compartments, catalogued, then stacked high like tall warehouse shelving. His photo-telegraphic mind accessed one. His failed marriage. Their twelve years had seen fleeting endearment. They'd shared the same bed, delighted in ecstasy. They'd shared dreams too. But like any couple scaling ladders in professional careers, they'd experienced more than their share of ups and downs. Eventually, the "downs" claimed victory and the government-career couple buckled. Vows uniting them frayed. "United as one" echoed in the past from some previous lifetime. Both sides admitted blame. Extensive travel became the scapegoat.

The jet climbed at a rate of 4,000 feet per minute. Coldditz looked down at a glowing inferno erupting from the Four Corners Power Plant, far brighter than the lights of Farmington. A minute later, darkness prevailed. He sat numbed, thoughtless, peering into the dimly lit cabin. He had no way of knowing if "Plan B" had been activated in time. No clue if Della was still alive. His aircraft was placed under a strict communications blackout. The jet reached cruising speed as it passed over volcanic uplifts known as the Jemez Mountains. They surrounded the atomic city of Los Alamos, its National Laboratories churning out nuclear weaponry like Glock did guns. Somewhere within the 54-square-mile super-secret complex, a scientist named Dr. Lin Chao studied a prehistoric artifact from a lost civilization. He awaited the discovery of its missing half in hopes of deciphering an ideographic script. If he succeeded, it would likely alter the historical record regarding human migrations. The aircraft leveled off above the eleven-mile span of the Valles Caldera. There, the navigator set course over the grasslands of northeastern New Mexico and across the Texas border, toward Andrews AFB 1,750 miles away.

Before dozing off, his mind toyed with revenge. He thought about the paybacks associated with his trade. About assassinations. About the numerous executions he'd either personally carried out or witnessed. His mind traveled to the Casbah, the ancient quarters of Algiers. To an execution eight years ago he'd witnessed beneath its cloak of shadows. Duty had beckoned him to the maze of Algeria's mysterious and narrow passageways. He was one of three backup assets in case something went wrong. It was as painful to watch as it was to execute.

The objective did not die swiftly. His final moments were marked with torture and brutality, representing sectarian violence at its zenith. The victim was forcefully overexerted. Blood rushed through his veins until they bulged to the bursting point, fueled by his explosive heartbeat. Then, in one skillful slash, it was over. Blood exploded with the force of a cannon. Stains blended with those of centuries past, artful mosaics recording conflicts on Algerian soil.

He stayed awake long enough to make plans for Wainwright. He was as guilty as the mole herself. It was he who had facilitated the mole's demise. The agent decided to follow the template laid down in Algiers. The four-hundred-year-old alleys and narrow passageways of old Santa Fe would mimic the Casbah, its adobe dwellings and narrow streets very familiar to Coldditz. They too had seen bloodshed long before the Pueblo Revolt in 1680. And for centuries subsequent to Don Diego de Vargas's Reconquest in 1692. His head bobbed slowly, signaling approval of the plan. The hypnotic drone of turbofan engines acted as a lullaby. He lapsed into deep sleep. The Major guarding him had orders to awaken him before their descent into Andrews. And to bring him two cups of very strong coffee. Black as pitch, piping hot, very tall cups.

"WE'LL be late for the rendezvous if we don't get a move on," Kika said, tugging his arm.

"Slow down. If I know Mac, he'll return for the last load." He took a long pull of water. His hydration pack was almost empty. He reached for the special communication device Coldditz had loaned him. "I'll tell Command we've been delayed. That we'll meet his man at 2:30 am."

The Captain answered immediately. "Sorry, sir, but our leader is not available."

"What? What do you mean 'not available?' Wake him up. Tell him it's Howie Parker. I've got news that affects the operation."

"I'm well aware of who's calling, sir. Furthermore, I know all about you, Parker. But agent Coldditz is engaged in another urgent priority. I'm in charge of Delilah until he returns." His tone cut like a scythe.

"What're you talking about? When he returns? Where in the hell is he?"

"I'm not at liberty to say, sir."

"What? Does this have anything to do with the call he received outside our camper?"

"I'm not at liberty to talk about that either, sir. I'm instructed to inform you that Agent Coldditz is engaged in a top-secret, urgent priority. It affects national security."

242

Howie cringed. There they were. Those words again. The words recently demoted to a lower status. Words less meaningful to Americans than "The War on Terror." Just like Pluto had been demoted from planet to dwarf planet. "When will he return? What's more important than nabbing the monstrous fish he's been waiting to net? Huh, Captain? Artifacts up the wazoo. Scientists will pee in their pants when they get their paws on them. Huh? What could possibly be more important?" Silence cloaked the canyon just as the dirt plume had. "I know - you're not at liberty to say."

"Roger that, sir. Agent Coldditz left me in charge. The timetable is still in place. He'll return shortly after sunrise. It's still *his* operation. Our team has worked with Agent Coldditz before. He's the best in the business. We wouldn't steal his show."

"Well, Captain, what's your name, anyway?"

"I'm not at liberty to say. Just refer to me as Captain. Besides, I wouldn't tell you my real name anyway."

"Things haven't changed, have they? Same old spy games. Sure glad I didn't reenlist. Please note that the timetable has moved *back* thirty minutes. Has to do with that seismic blast ten minutes ago. Did you feel anything?"

"Negative that, but our instruments recorded it."

"I'll bet they did. Well, the epicenter was in the middle of Blizzardhead's greedy mind. He dislodged a boulder large enough to fill Oriole Park. Crushed the driver. He and his rig are at the bottom of Snow Flat Canyon. Flatter than the foreskin on your Marine pecker."

"Roger that." The Captain was in no mood for humor. "Sounds like blissful oblivion. Must have gone quick. By the way, Parker, was his rig loaded at the time?"

"Good God almighty. Are you for real? I'll pretend I didn't hear that. You guys are nothing but a bunch of insensitive dicks. Never give a rat's ass about the personal element, do you? Never have, never will." He held the radio at arm's length and squeezed it hard. "No, God damn it! His trailer was empty."

"Roger that, Parker. Two agents will meet you and Miss Windsong at 02:30. Watch your backs. Over." The radio fell silent.

Parker and Windsong were dumbfounded. Why would Coldditz leave at the climax of a mission? Kika had heard every word. Fear overcame her. She convinced Howie that something was drastically wrong. That Hollywood had taught her the basic tenets of the spy business. That it was nothing short of deceitful guessing games. That Cedar Mesa was enveloped in an ugly cloud of deceit. It reeked of it, and they'd better make plans to save their own hides. "Translate: 'double cross', Howie, and I don't mean the feather holder symbols."

243

"Roger that," Howie said, chuckling, imitating the Captain. "Seriously, honey, that being the case, I *am* searching for a hidden message in the Captain's dialogue. Perhaps the rendezvous, the shakedown itself, could all be a trap. What if Coldditz *was* reeled back into headquarters? Will we be next to disappear?" He leaned into her ear and whispered. She smiled and nodded. They began walking, cautiously, watching their backs. The veil of clouds that had doomed Jed drifted east. The moonlight was so intense they stuck to the shadows. Suddenly, they had company. Kika raised her binoculars, Howie his scope. Dim headlights appeared.

"It's our favorite villains. Well, I'll be damned, they've recruited a woman," he said, rather scornfully. She slapped his injured shoulder. "What'd you expect, another *guy* killer? Well, smarty-pants, maybe you should read the latest issue of SWAT. See what some of us babes in camo and SWAT regalia are up to these days! Precision sharpshooters, we are. *A woman's precision. A woman's touch.*" She blew air out her nostrils and grunted. "Humph."

"Whatever." The word stretched into a long sentence. Mac stopped and removed boulders that Whitey had carelessly left in the path. Soon, the true shuttle road was restored. Howie's watch read 2:06 am.

AFTER punching the snooze delay three times, BLM Officer Wheeler awoke at 2:25 am. Like agent Coldditz, he'd slept a mere two hours. He crept like a sleepwalker and targeted the microwave, nuked yesterday's coffee, and inhaled a day-old donut. Relieved that Quirk had summoned him back to the front lines, he stepped into the shower with a cold Dr. Pepper. He donned a freshly laundered law enforcement uniform, sat at his laptop and compiled a trip report. In a matter of minutes, five days worth of conference meetings would arrive in Quirk's inbox. She checked it each morning at 4:30 am. Precisely thirty minutes later each day, whether she was on duty or not, she walked 150 yards to her office in the Visitor's Center. Wheeler's report emphasized the conference's primary mandate - for Utah to implement a state-wide SiteWatch Program. Like Arizona, Colorado, New Mexico and Texas had already done. At 3:10 am, he loaded his truck and reentered the lobby to sign for his room charges. Sitting comfortably in the empty lobby, he enjoyed his first cup of real coffee.

At 3:55 am, he called Howie and Kika's home phone. Still no answer. He left a curt message. After waiting ten minutes for them to call back, he bid the night auditor farewell and walked to his truck. An engine turned over. He stopped in his tracks. A nondescript sedan inched forward with its headlights off. He couldn't read the license plate. Intuition should have raised a red flag. So should have eight plus years of law enforcement.

PARKER trotted to the canyon rim and threw Coldditz's communication gizmo as far as he could. He was certain the device's memory chip emitted a tracking signal. They were on their own again. "Your Situational Intelligence better concoct an awesome Plan B," Kika said. "One that guarantees we stay alive. One that also guarantees *us* seizing the artifacts before the government does."

Howie raised his scope and nodded, just as Mac and the woman left with their last load. "I'm not at liberty to say, Miss Windsong, but I'll come up with something," he chuckled.

AT 4:35 am, Brewster downed his second cup of coffee. A thermal carafe would allow him to revisit it later. He scanned a draft of his message. It was 7:35 am in Santiago, Chile.

"Dear Raul,

"I'm scheduled to arrive at the Sheraton Centro Historico Hotel Saturday, June 22 at 5:00pm. Let's meet for dinner. My large suite will accommodate us meeting *tête-à-tête* anytime during the conference. I propose we take advantage of that seclusion and order room service Saturday evening to privately view images of the feather holder symbols.

"I have exciting news. Two days ago, the Cedar Mesa office of the Bureau of Land Management tipped off the FBI. The Santa Fe antiquities dealer, Wainwright, the one responsible for pawning the feather holder fragment, was spotted near Kayenta, Arizona. The FBI's department in charge of art and museum illegalities has him under surveillance. As does our US Department of Homeland Security. We are told to not set high hopes. Dealers commonly visit the heart of Anasazi country. As the FBI put it, 'a farmer must inspect his crops.' Perhaps it's no more than that. However, I remain suspicious. When we excavate at Inner Ruin tomorrow, our field lab will be equipped with state-of-the-art hardware. We'll have access to the museum's data base and to the internet and e-mail. All available resources will be at our command. The possibility that shamanistic pilgrims migrated from Easter Island to the Colorado Plateau almost 20,000 years ago has…"

He completed his e-mail, ate a light breakfast and arrived at the museum at daybreak.

THIRTY-THREE

Parker and Windsong hiked parallel to Mac's ATV. Their path, not much safer than the adjacent shuttle road, was a veritable obstacle course. Jagged rocks tripped them up, moonlight cast black shadows, and eight-foot drop-offs plunged into dry waterfalls. Although it provided superb cover, it challenged Kika's weakened state. They stopped to rest, crouching low, blending into a rock fortress. The ATV inched beside them a scant thirty feet away. Mac steered with one hand gripping the brake, not risking their final load. Kika tugged Howie's sleeve, whispering: "Go ahead without me. I'm a burden. You can sneak alongside and stay hidden much easier alone. You'll want to watch them button up the last load. Overhear their *real* plans. How do we know they'll really take everything to Todie Springs? Because *Coldditz* said so?"

"Quit humoring yourself, lady. We're *not* separating ever again. Have you forgotten what happened the last time we did? Come on, now, they just passed by. Let's slide over to their path and follow at a safe distance. It'll be easier going." At that point, the shuttle path coincided with the Mormon Trail of 1880. The rig was 100 feet in front of them. Kika kept up, even quickened her pace. "With two of their crew dead, it ought to louse up Mac's timing pretty bad, huh?"

"They've got Superwoman now, so things will actually improve." She cracked a smile but not the bandage.

Distant voices closed in. Lantern light reflected off the large truck. It was parked in a broad swale with tall grasses. There was a depression in the landscape nearby that measured fifteen feet in diameter, probably the outline of a Basketmaker II pithouse or a twelfth-century kiva. Howie raised his night scope. Kika suddenly realized how close they were and froze "This is far enough, Howie. I'm not getting any closer. This is where I draw the line. I was almost killed once today. Well, yesterday, if anyone's keeping count. You watch, I'll back off and hide in those trees."

He held her arm. "Honey, wait. We've come this far. Let's sneak 50 feet closer. We'll see and hear everything. I have another super-secret gizmo from Coldditz. A new issue from the NSA's playpen. It'll record everything they say and do. We'll download it later onto my phone." He attached an object the size of a raisin to his scope. When he was done, he stared into her eyes, knowing full well he had to keep his end of the bargain - keep Blizzardhead far away.

Their new post was thirty feet from the truck. Positioned to its rear, it afforded perfect sight into the cargo box. Crates were stacked neatly, but they hadn't been cinched to grommets. Howie studied the scene.

Half of the last shuttle remained in the trailers. Commotion erupted from the passenger side. Thuds and pounding. Whitey's hoarse guffawing rang in the night.

"You're both screwed," he shouted. "Screwed big time!" A series of loud thuds rang out.

Kika's eyes queried. "What's he pounding?"

"Beats me, but I'm getting it all with this tiny gadget." A new sound erupted, like a bolt cutter snipping through metal fencing.

"I'm moving closer," he said.

"Hold up. Here he comes. What the heck's he carrying?"

The massif toted two orange objects, one over each shoulder, and rushed to the rear of the truck. He maneuvered in moonlight without lanterns. He slid both cylinders to the ground. They clanked hard. Stunned beyond belief, afraid to tell Kika, he leaned his head into hers so his lips touched her ear. He kept both eyes on Whitey. "You're not going to like this one bit. Seems Stumpman gagged and blindfolded Mac and the woman. Bound them from head to toe in orange cable. If they had an amber light on their heads, they'd look like construction barrels."

"That's *not* funny. I've had enough of this." She raced into the trees. He chased after her.

"Shush. Hold on, don't let him hear us. Where're you going? Don't panic."

"Oh? Don't panic? What am I supposed to do? Walk up and ask him for a light? Howie Parker, it's high time we cut our losses and saved our own lives. Right now! We've done our good deed, Mr. ex-Marine. We've done our volunteer work. Way, way above and beyond the call of duty. We're done observing. *Or at least I am.*" She fired him the "this is suicide" look. It was her final say.

Still, he grasped only part of what she said. The way he saw it, the crooks were still trapped. Trapped on Cedar mesa. If they escaped north, they'd be captured at Todie Springs. South, they'd likely tip over and cascade down the Moki Dugway. He glanced around for his imaginary lieutenant. He was nowhere in sight. If he had been, Howie knew damn well he'd have spit the words out venomously - *"Deadly encounters produce deadly results."* Alone, he struggled to defend himself. "OK," he began, letting out a deep breath. "You're right. Your complaints are legitimate. I've promised to protect you. To use everything in my power to keep Blizzardhead far away. We're a team, and teams stick together. Especially in combat. Look how we've bonded during the last eighteen hours. My epiphany and expelling my rage demon; you confessing your long-held secret. That's bonding with a capital B if there ever was any. So, bottom line, we have mutual goals

247

here - to stay alive and to make sure the artifacts aren't smashed to smithereens. Hell's bells, Kika, we just got engaged two hours ago. We *both* have to stay alive to see that dream come true."

Another loud roar burst from the truck. They jerked their heads. Whitey threw his mummy-like captives into the cargo box and then haphazardly heaved the remaining crates up against other crates. Lids flapped open. Mac and Trixie lay bound and helpless.

Howie cringed. Whitey climbed into the truck and kicked the bodies. They rolled into a stack of crates, teetering precariously until gravity pulled them into three other stacks. Like dominos, all crates crashed hard to the truck floor, contents spewing forth. He stomped over to Trixie and Mac, arms spread as wide as grappling hooks, lyrically humming: "Fe-fi-fo-fum…" He scooped them up and carried them like a blood-thirsty giant to the front of the cargo hold. There, he dropped them upright in separate corners and stacked crates so they wouldn't tip over.

He rushed back to the tailgate, kicking artifacts in his path. Then he jumped to the ground and carelessly threw the remaining cargo into the truck. Several artifacts fell loose. Howie counted six feather holders lying bare on the floor. Stumpman picked two of them up and began juggling, hell-bent on destruction. He hastily threw four unwrapped feather holders into a crate and dropped the other two into his tent-sized pocket.

"Enough is enough!" Howie screamed at the top of his lungs. "Before he smashes everything. I've *got* to stop this madness, Kika. No one else will. It's entirely up to us - or *we'll lose everything!*" Before she could speak, he handed her Mac's Beretta. "Cover me."

"But Howie…" Her words trailed off. She steadied the gun with both hands.

THREE specialty teams arrived at the DOE within 45 seconds of each other. A small panel truck arrived first. Two men in work overalls exited and approached an overhead door at the shipping dock. One held a clipboard containing a phony work order. Fifteen seconds later, a white utility van appeared. A woman and two men removed tool boxes and an over-sized, heavy-duty dolly. They proceeded to the main entrance. Lanyards hung from the their necks with phony ID. Precisely thirty seconds later, a step van drove slowly along the curb. It entered a service driveway at the back of the building and coasted down a ramp which led to six overhead doors. Two women and one man removed a long metal cart and wheeled it through a half-raised door. The cart was draped in black Tyvec.

248

Their ascent to the sixth floor ushered in the first draft beneath the mole's office door. It occurred when they wheeled the cart out of the service elevator. Carpeted floors, sound-suppressing construction and the whir of circulating air provided a silent atmosphere. The cart rolled silently toward Ms. Schissler's office. The team regarded their trade with dignity. They moved with a singleness of purpose. They served the government.

The second team entered the sixth floor through an emergency doorway. They created the second air flow beneath her door. The squad leader signaled by hand, ordering three long cases set next to the door. Cannon-like weapons loaded with annihilating 40mm rounds were removed. The new design was nicknamed "396-er." Essentially a 40mm bullet-turned-lethal projectile. It could pierce the hull of a battleship. A new generation of sound suppressor fit over the muzzle. Their leader hated the term "396-er" so she renamed the death piece more appropriately - "TNP," Take No Prisoners. The overall length of the sleek cannon-gun was a manageable 25 inches.

They moved in unison. The leader gripped a GPS-looking device in her gloved hand. The digital instrument was capable of seeing through walls into Della's office. Its palm-held visual monitor retrieved images recorded by hidden devices within all VIP offices. Her prey was locked in, perched in fear, exactly where 90 percent of all objectives hid waiting - against the wall behind the entry door. As though they'd read an instruction manual. Hand signals reached out to her squad. Three fingers pointed to the door hinges. Three TNP bearers nodded. Within the office, Della's sweaty grip tightened on her 9mm. The monotonous drone of circulating air drove her to the brink.

A team member approached the lock mechanism. He held a small gadget containing a nano-chip scanner. They called it a "Reverso." Essentially, its counter-electromagnetic force field could reverse the magnetic field of anything. He directed it at the lock mechanism and at each hinge. One second later, four deadbolt cylinders reversed direction and anchored into the door jam. LED lights turned red, indicating that the fiber-optically enhanced security lock had been deactivated. The team leader listened closely to a device imbedded in her ear. Director Quay had given the green light. She signaled accordingly and activated a second scanner. The new gizmo from Fort Meade was referred to as a Parallel Reduction Bombarder. It emitted intense energy waves into the mole's office. The device was powerful enough to deflect an opponent's ammunition even when fired at close range. It would not counteract their TNPs. The leader gently tapped the door with her boot. Three TNP cannon-bearers, replete with antiterrorist body armor and headgear, stepped across the threshold, swiveled and faced the solid steel door. Twelve rounds soared from each weapon at a muzzle velocity of 2,840 feet per second. Four times as fast as the Gulfstream making its final approach into Andrews.

The German immigrant's daughter never got off a shot. Her bulletproof steel door resembled Swiss cheese. Della Schissler crumpled to the carpet without another breath. She was blessed with one last image as the tea-colored rug reached up to grab her. The carpet matched the red-orange soil in The Land of Walking Earth. The Map of Riches also came hazily into view. Criminal enlightenment had failed her.

Within nine minutes, the eight professionals tidied up their mess, new door and all, and exited the building the same way they'd entered. All in another day's servitude to their government. All in the name of War on Terror. Dead security guards would be taken to a secret morgue in downtown Washington. Brownstone ops would notify next of kin. Families of the fallen would not probe deeper. The word "investigation" was not even in the NSA's vocabulary. The remains of Della Schissler-Coldditz-Schisslenberg would never be found. Just like those of her father.

HOWIE sprinted like a cheetah, gripping his Sig tightly. Kika leveled the Beretta. The giant laughed. Howie pulled the trigger and lunged through the air. Whitey stopped laughing. He was under siege and he knew it. Parker's body mass accelerated and angled 45 degrees. He propelled into Whitey like a human torpedo. Head first, he cratered into Whitey's broad face with a thunderous crack. A meteoric head shot, its epicenter above Whitey's nose where it joined the frontal bones. A perfect bull's-eye. The ghost of Steelhead Jed applauded from the sidelines. If Whitey's skull had been normal instead of an impenetrable, stump-like mass, both frontal bones would have pierced the front lobe of his brain. Convulsions and a blood-soaked brain would have led to a quickened death. A frontal lobotomy, of sorts, gangster style. Gone awry for Howie Parker because Whitey was - well, "Whitey - Impossible to Kill."

The titan reeled two steps back, tilted his head and smirked. Stretching forward, he clutched Howie's skull, squeezing it in his famous vise grip, slurping blood from his throat as though through a straw at the bottom of a milkshake. He spat the bloody glob into Howie's face. One gallon spewed out like a fountain. It destroyed his vision, leaving his head cocked to the side, eyes popping out from the steel grip. Whitey stomped forward in a death march and planted Howie upright into the ground. Next, he twirled around like an Olympic discus thrower and backhanded his skull. The impact was appalling. CSI experts would have claimed that Parker was hit by a freight train. He flew horizontally over the sagebrush and impacted against the truck. His backpack flew out of sight. His gun sailed the opposite direction. He lay as still as a cadaver.

His teammate popped up from the brush and ran toward the massif. She unloaded the full clip. Bullets did nothing. She panicked and threw the gun at him. A loud shrill burst from her lungs. As blood-curdling as a cougar's. It awoke Howie. In a starry stupor, he rolled onto his back. Eyes and throat became easy targets. Whitey raced over and straddled him, prepared to execute, finger stubs poised to bore through his eyes. Howie attempted one last maneuver. Bracing himself against the truck, he heaved both feet into Whitey's groin. Another direct hit. He heard a deep thud, like a cow dropped from the sky. Whitey's only reaction was a mild grunt, followed by two snorts and a sickening grin. Blizzardhead fixed a deadly stare. Ten lethal stubs aimed down. Death loomed seconds away. He reached into his pocket and grabbed the feather holder half. His newfound and prized possession. He forced open Howie's jaw and lowered the artifact. Laughing, he jammed the eighteen-thousand-year-old relic into Howie's open mouth like an apple in a roasting boar. He flaunted his human trophy like a big game hunter. Secrets to unlock the code to *Make-make's* energy field siphoned Parker's breath. At last, Whitey's drill-press fingers bore down with terminal intent.

Kika raced to her backpack and searched frantically for extra ammo. There was none. Her little Guardian was back at the camper. Desperation forced super-charged adrenaline to kick in, giving birth to Herculean strength. The kind of strength that had rallied on behalf of heroes since man's first battles, miraculously engaging to free humans from collapsed buildings or beneath automobiles. So it was with Kika Windsong in defense of her fiancé. Killing became her only option. She was forced to kill the beast before the beast killed Howie. An urge to kill so overwhelming, it surpassed a similar urge she'd had after Buzz Lane attacked her. Perspiration, not blood, pumped through her veins. She raced to the truck and grabbed the winch bar. It took most of her strength.

She grimaced: "Oh, Howie do you intentionally create situations that evoke deadly encounters?" Clutching the twenty-pound bar of steel, she wound up in a Barry Bond home run swing. Whitey saw it coming. He reached up with a smile and caught it one-handed. As gently as catching a birdie in badminton.

But it gave Howie the split-second break he needed. He unsheathed a combat knife strapped to his thigh and sunk it into Blizzardhead's skull. Finger stubs stopped short of their mark. His head jerked spasmodically as though yanked by a noose. But it wasn't a noose, it was a seven inch blade of hardened steel buried deep in the base of his neck-less skull. At first, it had no more effect than a nail pounded into an old-growth tree. Then he flinched, massive paws still clutching Howie's throat. Gradually, as if in slow motion, the blade cut his concentration. Nothing more. He pulled his lucky charm from Parker's mouth and stuffed it into his pocket. Then he let go entirely and reeled back. His head hung off-balance.

Howie wasn't quite finished. Weakened, he rolled away and rose groggily to his knees. He stood next to the truck, rocking sideways like a gorilla. One minute passed. Then another. Blood oozed from Whitey's skull. The knife stuck in place. Howie launched horizontally through the air, feet first, legs coiled until he was three feet from Whitey's sternum. He uncoiled like a human ramrod. A loud crunching sound rang through the air. Parker's third bull's-eye. He felt Whitey's sternum crush beneath his feet. Whitey stumbled backward, frame too square to topple over, angling Neanderthal-style and grinning. The knife stuck out from his cranium like a second penis. A jagged piece of manubrium bone splintered from his sternum and protruded from his chest like a twenty-fifth rib. He tried to shove it back in, grimacing in agony. The exposed fracture would have toppled anyone other than the killer from Cleveland. In a bizarre move, he reached into his pocket and fumbled for his lucky charm. It was still in one, blood-soaked piece. He rubbed the artifact near his heart and around the jagged bone, bellowing like a werewolf in the night: "Me Whitey, Impossible to Kill."

His opponents stood 25 feet away, mouths agape, arms akimbo. A brief respite in the battle, each combatant pausing as though a time-out had been called. Whitey's next move hung in the air. Howie looked at his Chase-Durer. Thirty seconds passed. An eternity. Their invincible foe stomped forward. Parker and Windsong stood side-by-side as a team. Easy targets. Yet they clearly understood that common desires had to face common consequences. Whitey pressed his giant paw against his chest to ease the flow of blood. Howie was too weak to mount a fourth assault. "Howie, Howie," Kika screamed, "for Christ's sake find our guns and kill him before he kills us!"

"I'm all out of weapons! Bullets from my Sig, a meteoric head-butting, a full clip from Mac's Beretta, a two-footed kick to his groin, my combat knife buried in his skull, and a crushing blow to his sternum. Nothing can stop him." Her eyes were ablaze. It was worth a thousand pep talks. "Wait, I've got it," he said, eyeing the huge bolt cutters next to the spool of cable. "Watch this, I'll…"

Suddenly, Whitey's gait changed. He ambled awkwardly, veering sideways and nearly stumbling into the sagebrush. Then he stopped in mid-stride, turned and stared into the truck. Unexpectedly, he ran to the truck. Though he was noticeably injured, he covered the distance like a raging bull. He climbed into the cargo section. One by one, he lifted Mac and Trixie and hoisted them out to the front of the truck. He maneuvered them upright in the seat so they wouldn't roll.

His opponents were stunned. They expected death. Instead, they watched as he carefully placed scattered artifacts into the crates, secured the load and closed the overhead door. He yanked the combat knife from his skull as though it were an ingrown hair. Blood coagulated. He slid the bloody weapon into his pocket beside his lucky charm. Before climbing into the driver's seat, he pivoted to face his opponents. "That round is mine. Just like the loot. Everything's mine now. All the millions is mine. Math by one. Thanks to my lucky charm." He started the truck. It lurched forward. He'd never driven any vehicle in his life. Accelerating too quickly, it teetered and bounced precariously. He aimed it toward two dirt ribbons leading through Brushy Flat. Highway 261 was two miles away; Todie Springs, four and a half.

Parker and Windsong stood in disbelief. Expecting to watch it topple over, she raised her hand to her mouth. Whitey felt danger and slowed to a crawl. "Maybe I can stop him now. Yank him from the cab and let the wheels run over him. You hop on their ATV and race to Todie for help. We're a team to the end, Kika. It's not too late. We can still stop this nonsense." He sprinted after the rig. When he caught up to it, he managed to keep pace alongside, but the driver's door was locked. He pleaded for Whitey to stop. "Don't do this," he shouted at the top of his lungs. "You don't know how to drive. The law's waiting for you. You'll be shot and killed by snipers. You have no idea who you're up against." Whitey grinned and white-knuckled the steering wheel. "You won't escape. "You'll be shot dead within minutes. You're NOT impossible to kill! *The Feds will kill you.*" Whitey rolled down the window and gave him a whale shark grin. He coughed up blood. Howie took a direct hit. He accelerated down the deeply rutted trail, rocking sideways and bobbing like a cork at sea.

THIRTY-FOUR

"Any idea why he didn't kill us?" Kika asked, blending bewilderment with gratitude. The over height truck forged through ruts and was soon out of sight.

"If I knew, I'd be a millionaire."

"I've heard enough about millions to last me a long time." They searched for their handguns and backpacks. The sagebrush was as tall as Kika. "Bet you're the first man who's ever rushed Whitey."

"Could be. Thanks, but we're a team. We both held him at bay. Ah, here's my Sig. Beretta's got to be close. And there are our packs." He set his hands on her shoulders. "Got to level with you, though. It was *your* bravery that saved us, not mine. You were the hero tonight."

"Heroine, but that's nonsense. You're the one who torpedoed him. Twice. Like I said, who's ever been crazy enough to do that? And lived to talk about it."

"Didn't even faze him. I still say it was *your* charging him, Kika. Your bravery to stand by me in the face of deadly force. He had me pinned down. You threw him off just long enough for me to knife him. *That's* when everything changed. Not all at once, it took a minute. But the whole scene changed after that. On the outside, he was still Whitey, knife sticking out from his bloody neck. But his momentum fell off. No sense in arguing, all I'm saying is that your charging him saved our lives. After that, killing us was no longer priority."

"You mean sticking out of his head, don't you? He doesn't have a neck." She giggled "You'd change too if you had a seven inch piece of steel buried in your skull. Not to mention a jagged bone sticking out of your bloody chest. You gave it your all, didn't you, Howie?"

He nodded and straightened tall. "Yeah, I did. Got to admit, though, strong as I am, I'm pretty exhausted. Still dazed. Now I know firsthand that his trademark slogan is no bullshit. What we dealt him would have easily killed anyone else ten times over again. Come on, let's get moving. Remember our secret approach to Todie Springs? Let's use it." He disconnected the trailer from the ATV. Kika sat on the seat.

"You've said nothing about the most important artifact. The feather holder half that slipped out of your pocket yesterday. At least now we know where it is. Not that it'll be easy getting it back."

Howie paused. He looked sheepish. "I know. Pisses me off. Damned humiliating, it was, having that priceless treasure *I'd lost* choking the life out of me."

"You *have* changed, Howie. How could you think of humiliation when you were seconds from death?"

He propped his foot on the ATV. Her obsidian eyes netted his blue eyes. Stubby whiskers eclipsed his smile. "Let's cut to the chase here. To the reason you and I are still on Cedar Mesa. Why we haven't bolted. *The truck's contents. That's why you and I are sticking it out, why we have repeatedly risked our lives!* They belonged to another civilization. As bizarre as it sounds, it could somehow be connected to South American cultures, Easter Island in particular. That's why I backed off during the brief repose instead of fighting it out to the bitter end. I glanced over and saw the truck's contents. Contents which may rewrite history. I figured, let the beast go. Let him have that round. He won't get very far anyway. Like I said, they're still trapped. Perhaps that's what truly separates criminals from normal people. They're always trapped, never free. Always looking behind them. Petrified of sirens. Never answer phones. Horrible way to live. A wasted life. Their only future is a gruesome death. Usually sooner than later. Oh, well, I'm rambling. Let's move out. We'll observe the Todie rendezvous from a distance. In case we're being set up."

"Oh, Howie, are we still *observing*? When can we finally call up the infantry and seize the loot?" She looked up at the full moon. For help, possibly. "I know this is going to sound insane, but please hear me out. You know, maybe you and Whitey aren't so different after all."

"What? What the hell's that supposed to mean? This better be good."

"What I mean is he easily could have killed Mac and the woman, whoever she is. Instead of wrapping them in cable. But he didn't. And he didn't kill us either. In fact, *he's* the one who stopped fighting first. My guess is he also looked at the truckload of loot. Just like you did. And realized fifteen million smackeroos was all his if he kept his cool. That he might need Mac alive to make the exchange. Who knows? What I'm suggesting is that greed outweighed killer instinct. Just like you looked over at the artifacts. Only you saw museums and academia. Preservation instead of killing. Similar motive - *preservation*, just for different reasons. Your minds are more alike than you thought, huh? Just a few degrees of separation, perhaps?" She winked. "My woman's point of view."

"I can see that marriage is going to be a whole lot more than sex! You got a strange way of thinking, Miss Windsong. Comparing me with that killer Blizzardhead. Guess I've got a lot to learn about women. I see about as much logic to that as I do to clouds passing *behind* that full moon up there instead of in front of it. After all, have you ever seen a lion quit ripping flesh in the middle of his meal? Like Whitey done?"

"Unless a fleshier meal comes along."

"Humph, now we're both rambling, and punchy. Let's hightail it to Todie. Make sure no one else stakes claim to the artifacts. Confiscate his lucky charm."

THE Major awakened Coldditz as requested. Coffee brewed to perfection, two tall cups, piping hot, dark roast. They'd begun their descent into Andrews AFB. The coffee turned his stomach. But it wasn't to blame. His digestive tract was. It reacted to a gut feeling. Visions of catastrophic events taking place on the VIP floor of the DOE's office building. He doubled over in his seat. The visions were so nauseating that small amounts of vomit rose to his mouth. His sixth sense envisioned death on the sixth floor. He sat back and tried calming himself. He swallowed hard. It was 3:43 am. Two tall scotches, straight, no ice, would be more appropriate than coffee. The practice was common among recalled agents prior to debriefing.

His life was on hold, his career too. If polygraphs so much as hinted a link to Della's treasonous acts, there was no telling what would happen. Non-Muslims weren't exempt from extraordinary rendition under Bush-Cheney. A rancid taste coated his tongue. He coughed up phlegm into his napkin. The Major removed both coffees and brought a large bottle of water. Room temperature. He placed a barf bag nearby. The agent had practically written the primer on mental torture administered in spy games. He knew the bastards at Fort Meade had timed the mole's assassination to coincide with him being in-flight and under a communication blackout. Plan B had obviously failed. He'd devise another. A payback.

The Gulfstream vectored northeast in its final approach. High-intensity guidance lights came into view. Its centerline sequence flashers guided the plane onto runway 19L. The two-mile-long runway was also used by Air Force One. A mild six-knot breeze made for a smooth touchdown. His welcoming party, led by Colonel Holmes, would escort him to one of several NSA safe houses scattered across the countryside. Holmes selected one nestled in Maryland's rolling hills 28 miles away. Debriefing and polygraph procedures would begin immediately. A tentative fight plan departing Andrews at 07:35 and returning to Farmington had been filed. *If there were no glitches.* The Delilah Project could be sealed forever by noon.

Holmes's somber face greeted him as he descended to the tarmac. Outstretched hands shook. It was very dark. They turned and stepped into a black SUV. An identical SUV led their procession away from the runway. Two others trailed behind. Placed strategically along the route, eight other vehicles, all black, idled. That's how the spy business worked. Holmes looked straight ahead rather than at his agent. Coldditz

256

stared out at strobe lights bordering the runway. His mind hadn't arrived on the same flight as his body. The Colonel broke a long silence. "I'm sorry for your loss."

Coldditz wretched within. "The friggin' news isn't even thirty minutes old," he thought to himself. "Sorry for my loss? No eye contact, no emotion, no voice inflection. Holmes is colder than an eel, regardless of circumstances. Heartless, impersonal antics of the intel trade. Bastards. In all my years as a dedicated agency operative, I've never been treated any differently than his secretary's file cabinet." After several minutes of silence, he gathered his wits. It was then that he acknowledged, deep down, *that he too was one of them*. He was no different than Holmes or any of his peer agents. He'd signed his life and soul away thirty-plus years ago when he'd executed the NSA contract.

The black caravan cut smoothly through the night. Had it not been for headlights, they would have traveled invisibly. He turned away from the window and looked at Holmes. His expression remained barren, with about as much lure as the dark countryside. Finally, Coldditz's mind reunited with his body. "It's time, Colonel," he began, "to turn our losses into gains. Time we see fewer sparks and more flames in southeast Utah. I consider the timely closure of the project my sole *raison d'être*." Holmes managed a reserved smile.

He cleared his throat. "You have my word, I'm not involved in my ex-wife's dirty dealings in any way, shape or form. I'll return to the front lines later this morning and take care of our situation. Or, should I say, *opportunity*. You'll get your uranium back. Every single nugget. Every single vial of DU. Museum curator Brewster will get his artifacts. And the case will be closed air-tight. All files deleted. Dragged clean like infield dirt during the seventh-inning stretch." A reserved smile chiseled into Holmes's cadaver face. He loved the Orioles. Coldditz leaned into his CO's ear and cupped his hand. "Now that you've got your mole, scoring the uranium is frosting on the cake. Your bonus, our little secret. Quay doesn't have to know. No one does. You're a genius at manipulating software. Counterintelligence isn't your only forte. Erase all traces of it from the face of the earth. Use it as ransom someday. As you direct your dirty little spy games from Brownie. Might come in handy maneuvering around the Korean Peninsula."

"Frankly..." the Colonel let his sentence drift off. He was cunning. The SUV's interior was filmed and recorded more adroitly than a music studio. He eked another quarter-smile instead. He was proud. Coldditz was an admirable subordinate. He'd been trained well, molded from old-school NSA. Minutes later, the black caravan approached the

257

"farmhouse." One hundred sixty-five acres also enveloped in blackness. As soon as they, or any object, crossed its perimeter, sensors triggered lights and each building lit up like a stadium. Coldditz's military "escort," the Major, who'd accompanied him since Farmington, opened the SUV door. That's how the NSA worked. One or more escorts stayed with recalled agents no matter what. Even in the bathroom. *Especially* in the bathroom. He fixed a reserved smile when Coldditz stepped out, admiring the agent's iconic reputation. Coldditz stood tall and stretched, staring at a hazy brown blanket smothering the Baltimore-DC megalopolis. Particulates choking urbanites. It would remain after sunrise. It would remain after sunset. He glanced at his doorman. "It's not Cedar Mesa, is it, Major?"

BLM Officer Wheeler stopped at a convenience mart on the southern edge of Moab. He topped off his coffee thermos and set three carb-drenched burritos in the microwave. Following a brief visit with the clerk, he drove south toward Monticello, Utah. Thirteen miles from Moab, the landscape transformed. He left a serene valley known to old-timers as Spanish Valley. Pack Creek drifted in from ridges to the east and snaked its way along the east side of Highway 191. It formed a shallow gorge along the river. Beyond that, conifer-capped peaks rose in the Manti-La Sal National Forest. To his right, stunning sandstone outcrops formed hoodoos and canyons as far as his eye could see. He traveled the route often. It was one of his favorite drives. That morning, there was heavy oncoming traffic. Trucks and large RVs ruled the pavement.

Four warning signs greeted him. The first told of deer crossings over the next four miles. The second stood at the approach to a long hill. An oversized yellow sign read: "Sharp Curves, 5% Grade, ½ Mile Ahead." A yellow beacon flashed on its top. A quarter mile beyond, a third warning sign begged caution. It too was crowned with a yellow flasher. It depicted a slanted vehicle to show that a steep downgrade lay ahead.

Wheeler considered himself a cautious driver. Particularly in his BLM Ranger pickup. He polished off the burritos and drove one-handed while sipping from his mug. A brilliant orange sun was seconds away from birthing a day. His speed matched the posted limit. He felt somewhat dozy after his road breakfast. Two hours of interrupted sleep coupled with the engine's drone exacerbated his fatigue. Drowsiness intensified. He knew from experience the Hole in the Wall rest area was three miles ahead. After the steep hill leveled off. He needed a five-minute power nap. If he could make it three more miles.

The highway dropped away where the fourth sign glared at him. It displayed a sharp curve and reduced speed limit. Amber flashers blinked above it. He gained speed on the steep grade. His was a single traffic lane directed downhill. Oncoming vehicles shared two lanes uphill. Sleepily, he fixed his eyes on the bright, double yellow lines between lanes. Suddenly, a giant fireball burst above the cliffs. Air waves shimmered. Brilliant sunlight caught him momentarily off guard. For a brief spell, he was blinded. He fumbled for his sunglasses. The raging fireball glared brighter. Too low to be shielded by his visor. He pumped the brakes. There were none. He tried again. Nothing. The limp pedal stuck to the floor. Two visions flashed before his eyes. One was a shadow darting between vehicles in the hotel parking lot. The second was a double lane of traffic racing uphill - vacationers with smiling young kids staring out the windshield. His truck fishtailed. His speed reached 80 mph.

He steered wildly into the guardrail, careening off like a billiard ball and racing toward oncoming traffic. He muscled the vehicle back to the right and smashed the guardrail a second time. Glass exploded, both passenger-side tires blew out. Chunks of sheet metal, a bumper and plastic parts launched skyward. Tires became rims. Rims became axles. Axles hugged the guardrail no matter how he steered. That was a blessing. Until drainage culverts caused long gaps in the guardrail, exposing a steep embankment into a ravine. And oblivion. He was headed right into it when, by sheer luck, he managed to jerk the steering wheel to the left. The truck tipped onto its driver side and rolled onto the roof. It slid nearly 300 feet, spinning like a top, bouncing off the guardrail, missing other gaps. As it slowed, it rolled over halfway, swayed, then continued its momentum until bouncing upright in a rocking motion. But inertia and the steep grade swallowed it up. Within seconds, it eased onto its passenger side. Then, in a macabre, slow-motion rhythm, it rolled off of its side and landed upside-down. The cab was crushed from all sides. A tangled mess of metal hissed and steamed.

Traffic in both directions stopped. Four minutes passed. People clutching cell phones raced to the catastrophe. Slowly, a man crawled through a cavity that was once a window. He hoisted himself up with one arm. Dazed and in great pain, his right shoulder sagged toward the pavement. One second later, he fell into a sea of glass shards and drifted into unconsciousness. But not before realizing that his e-mail had led to a death sentence rather than a gag order. The highway had recently been resurfaced. It was shiny black. Glass shards glittered like diamonds. Kika's dream once again proved true. It was all there. A man in uniform, new road and thousands of glass shards. Except the man in uniform wasn't standing.

PHILLIP Brewster stayed at his computer after e-mailing Dr. Fernandez. He completed an on-line Survey Proposal Form for the BLM. He sought formal approval to excavate in Snow Flat Canyon. They'd begin the next day at dawn. In the summary comments, he wrote: "This excavation is of immense global significance. We are on the verge of discovering the missing half of an artifact reputedly dating back to 18,000 – 20,000 BP. A secret cipher is incised therein. We purport that such a plume holder was used by shaman pilgrims in ceremonial rituals. If discovered, it will likely coincide with the other half held in our museum vault. Evidence predicated on research conducted through the Universidad de Chile, Santiago, Chile and Hanga Roa, Easter Island supports this postulate. Although the scope of this excavation is limited to the missing half, a cache of eleven additional plume holders accompanied a sacred shaman pilgrimage - allegedly to the Colorado Plateau nearly 18,000 years ago." He transmitted the application to Chief Ranger Quirk. He knew she'd approve it and forward it to her superior in Monticello. Even an archaeologist of Brewster's fame required approval to excavate on Public Lands.

The new mail icon flashed. The sender was Dr. Lin Chao, Los Alamos National Laboratories. Brewster was shocked. "Contrary to protocol," Chao wrote, "I'm recanting my previous hesitancy and have decided to place my professional reputation at risk. I will render an official decipherment by utilizing only one half of the feather holder. I will e-mail my interpretations to you later this afternoon. Please bear in mind that partiality of artifact may equate to partiality of decipherment." He then confirmed his attendance at the forthcoming Mexico City conference, adding:

"Our *ad hoc* committee established at the Palo Alto conference in 2004 continued its investigation into northerly and easterly trans-oceanic migration patterns parallel to the Andean spine. Under the auspices of The Institute for Advanced Cultural Studies, we now have evidence from five excavated sites which supports habitation dates along these routes clearly predating the 11,500-12,500 BP Bering Strait land bridge dates. Several South American sites have occupation dates of 16,000 BP. Our startling hypothesis continues to crystallize, strengthened largely by oral histories collected by the Institute. When certified, these oral histories will document shamanistic pilgrimages migrating north into present-day Central and North America. Dates range between 15,900 and 20,000 years ago.

"If, in fact, we rewrite the archaeological record for one of earth's major human migrations, we must be squarely on the money. Global colonization is quite complex. People keep moving. Tremors of Herculean proportion will bombard us and everything we have stood for in our careers. Aftershocks will ripple throughout laboratories and campuses for decades. Prior research will be reopened and reexamined. That is a very costly process - in terms of financial resources AND in terms of egos - egos large enough to fill your museum. Consequently, the Institute will *explain* the evidence it has gleaned rather than fit the evidence into our theory.

"Although we must have the entire feather holder to empower our evidence, I will test the water and decipher what I can from its fragment. So the heat is on. For me and for your excavation team. You have essentially one week to come up with the jewel I need. I cringe to think of the mathematical probability of your finding it. But, dear chap, that is why I've devoted my life to ancient cryptographs. And you, to digging small artifacts from buried villages. Yet perhaps our two disciplines are not so distant after all - we each search for that proverbial needle in a haystack."

HORACE Wainwright was a master exploiter. Antiquities, illegal arms, black market art and women. Didn't matter. He mined resources belonging to others for his own financial gain. He walked on the razor's edge in a business where lives were as expendable as the next breath. He wrote the primer on bartering illegal arms in the twenty-first century. His dealings were multi-tiered. Schemes often penetrated five layers deep. His mind functioned that way. Like a giant honeycomb, compartmentalized into deals and myriad prices, commodities, buyers and sellers. Multi-dimensional transactions made it difficult to pin him down. He eluded assassins' bullets and federal prosecution.

Wainwright's frame was chiseled, tall and arborescent. He stared down at his subjects. It was maddening. Most meetings occurred outdoors. He always stood with his back to the sun. His subjects stared feebly into menacing brightness, squinting and shielding their eyes. Extremely dark, virtually opaque sunglasses distracted them. His head angled upward, propped on his shoulders like a sculpted bust. Such posture aided his display of superiority. A thin-lipped smirk was engraved into the bust, as wide as the Pacific, nearly spanning from ear to ear.

Romancing the mole became Wainwright's chief strategy five years ago. She taught him about enriched, bomb-grade uranium containing over 90 percent of the U-235 isotope. And about depleted uranium, often called military uranium, or DU, dirty uranium - the class of uranium remaining after the enrichment process. His lover had unchecked access to both. Their skills complemented one another. Hers, the thrill of treason. His, the art of barter. They amassed fortunes.

On Tuesday morning, May 24, 2005, as Whitey escaped in the over height truck loaded with artifacts, Wainwright was oblivious to his lover's demise. The next move was his. He was to call her on a secure line the instant he'd inspected McAllister's contraband. The exchange would take place at the Navajo Generation Station's rail yard west of Kayenta. A stringent time frame had to be met. The inspection and call had to occur before 07:00 DC time. Then, and only then, would Della Schissler authorize the release of uranium down the conveyor chute and into the silo. And the exchange of fifteen million dollars in cash to Mac.

THREE months earlier, in February, 2005, Wainwright recruited a key worker bee for their scheme. He snared his quarry, compartmentalized him into his own honeycomb cell, then molded him like a potter would clay. His victim was a discontented Native American, a descendent of the Mountain Ute Nation with mixed native bloodlines. Tomas Two Tree Franklin had been employed by the Peabody Group for seven years. After advancing through various positions at Black Mesa's coal mines, he was promoted to Rail Yard Superintendant. Such a position was indispensable to the mole's agenda. Normally, chunks of coal traveled along a 22-mile conveyor chute spanning from the mines to the silo yard. When it reached Highway 160 west of Kayenta, it was suspended by trusses 24 feet above the roadway. The chute supplied the silo, the silo supplied the railcars and three electric powered train loads departed the yard daily to supply the coal-fired steam generating plant. The concept was simple. NGS, in turn, supplied Phoenix, Tucson, Las Vegas and Los Angeles with much of their electrical needs. Arguably a quartet composed of some of the nation's thirstiest electricity guzzlers. Two Tree's job was pivotal to keep the generating station operating.

Since the day Wainwright recruited Two Tree, he preyed upon him unmercifully. He tore at his weaknesses piece by piece. He skinned him into submission layer by layer as voraciously as a secretary bird ripped flesh from reptiles. Two Tree snorted nearly as much white powder as the silo dropped black coal. The Arborescent One made certain a free supply of the drug was delivered weekly. If Two Tree ever quit cooperating, Wainwright promised to expose his little habit. He'd also link Two Tree to a suspected terrorist plot threatening to cripple the generating plant. He'd never dream of shooting the Ute. He was smarter than that. An overdose, unintended or otherwise, would do it for him.

262

Two Tree had been bought once before. Without even realizing it. By the unscrupulous energy conglomerate Peabody Energy. His and thousands of families like his were trapped in a state of "learned dependency." They didn't know what it meant. Peabody was a subtle thief. Corporate generosities kept citizens like him from being responsible for themselves. Families grew accustomed to the money, the cost-free services and the plain old convenience of Peabody being their omnipresent provider.

"They do everything for us," Two Tree once told Wainwright. "They mend our roads, plow in the winter, dispose of our trash. They provide drinking water and remove our waste. *They are the core of our existence.* More generous than the people we elect. If anything breaks down, we simply say, 'go ask Peabody, they'll fix it.'" And so went life for families on the rez who hitched a ride on the gravy train.

The resource extraction industry was normally the culprit. Pillars of the mining industry that performed dirty deeds by plundering native lands. Unscrupulous exploitation which depleted billions of gallons of water from limited aquifers and poisoned reservations with cancer-forming agents, devastating delicate ecosystems. All the while under the guise of taking care of communal and household needs. But learned dependency took an even greater, subtler toll. The practice kept the giver in control of the receiver. In control of their sovereignty. Families were essentially held in custody, imprisoned by what they saw as free services. Occasionally, corporations crossed the line of responsible citizenry and acted like wardens dominating inmates.

Horace Wainwright had stared down into Two Tree's face when he "recruited" him in February. It was an icy-cold day. Gusty north winds eclipsed all warmth. He stood in his classic pose, back to the sun, black sunglasses forcing Two Tree's own image to stare back at him. The Ute, eyes stretched wide open, fixed a bug-eyed look of drug-induced, perpetual anxiety. Several of his front teeth were missing, both top and bottom jaws. The result of drug-related neglect, not scuffles. On most days, he donned a half-toothed grin. His friends called it a real shit-eating grin. It was ugly. He was in a prolonged state of "gimmie-gimmie," begging for someone to hear his plight. And for money. Wainwright held Two Tree in contempt. For everything. For living. *Especially for being Indian.*

"My daughter," Two Tree said, "she's four. Got birth defects. Con, con genitals, they tell us."

Wainwright shook his head. His perennial grin widened two inches. "You mean congenital. Your genitals are your friggin' *cojones.*" He laughed it off as Indian stupidity, a sinful attitude for a resident of Santa Fe, New Mexico.

"She got special needs. I need money. Not just your usual package."

"My weekly package will have to do. There'll be a big sum of cash after you uphold your end of the bargain. More than you'll ever need."

"Special needs, you know? Just like yours. You got special needs too, Horace, my man. I'm the one who knows how to make the silo do what you want when the time comes. I run it and the conveyor chute." Two Tree stared up into two dark lenses, shielding his eyes from the corona ringing Wainwright. Constant squinting plastered a drooling, half-toothed grin on the Ute's face. The voracious secretary bird ripped more flesh. His stylish sheepskin coat had deep pockets. In one, he gripped a slim, silenced .22 caliber pistol. An assassin's tool. Just in case. For the kind of stakes Wainwright dealt in, that was minimal weaponry. But his driver and bodyguards positioned twenty feet away carried assault capability at all times.

"I control the flow of coal traveling on the conveyor. It fills the silo straddling the tracks." Wainwright stood tall and silent. "I can make this work real smooth. Read me? Or I can bring it to a grinding halt. Read me now, Mr. Santa Fe Wheeler-dealer with the fancy overcoat? How much that fake sheepskin cost you anyway?" His slobbery grin began to freeze. Wainwright begged his finger from pulling the trigger. He knew the train's maintenance crew was nearby. Besides, he couldn't waste the Indian. He needed him. For Della.

The railcars were top-loaders. When they unloaded at Page, bottom doors opened as they passed slowly over a hopper. The Yard Superintendant worked twelve-hour shifts. He normally loaded two trains. It took forty seconds to fill each car, after which a complete safety inspection was conducted. "I run the whole show. I'm the man. *I'm your man.* Now you catch my drift, Mr. Wealthy Antique Dealer from Santa Fe?"

He held his hand out like a beggar. A perfect fit for Wainwright's image of Indians. "Don't forget about my little four-year-old girl. Special needs, remember? Costs lots of money. Peabody's insurance pays about half. They don't buy into that congenington crap, or whatever you called it. They should pay everything, no? Can't sue them cuz they provide everything else for us. Trouble is, nobody knows more about contaminated mining than us Indians. Close to 1,000 abandoned uranium mines on Navajo land alone. Still poisoning us. That's why my daughter got what she's got. And it ain't a pretty sight." He raised a dirty sleeve and wiped his chin before it froze solid. It joined a menagerie of frozen snot and saliva plastered to his diesel-stained Carhartt. "You think it over, Mr. Wealthy Art Dealer, Mr. Wainwright, my man. You wouldn't be wearing them fancy clothes and riding in a limo with armed guards if you weren't a smart man. So stuff this in your puffy sheepskin jacket - without me, your big-shot plan is nothing. NOTHING. Hear me?" He formed a near zero with his icy fingers.

Wainwright's grin shrunk to half his face. He stood undaunted, forcing a powerful neurological charge from his brain to his trigger finger, compelling it not to bend. He'd heard about Buzz Lane from Cleveland. A trigger-happy freak like him would have gladly blown holes in the plush sheepskin to waste the Indian. But, he kept his cool, for Della's sake. "So, what about the train engineer?" he asked. "Who else is present during loading?"

"Always two or three inspectors plus a safety engineer. Like I said, to make sure the load's buttoned up tight. On the trip back to NGS, brakes are on the last third of the way. Quite a downhill grade. Ninety-some railcars loaded with coal ain't no light load."

Horace digested the data like a gator feeding on chickens. "What about uniforms? Who wears them and what do they look like? I'll need photographs."

He laughed in Wainwright's face for a full minute. He swallowed drool before it froze. That was uglier still, like a boa swallowing a horse. He wiped an excess glob with his coattail, already stiffened from earlier wipes. "They're Navajo," he continued laughing, "that's their uniform. Couple are Ute, like me. Plus a few Apache. Other Natives tossed in from Hopi and lands west. But mostly Navajo. Indians don't need no ID tags, Mr. Santa Fe Wheeler-Dealer, in case you ain't noticed. Course, we all wear white hardhats. Maybe that'll help a rich whitey like you."

Wainwright's stomach regurgitated. He was sickened by the hideous sight facing him. It threw off his concentration. He swiveled and studied the rail yard. He photographed a half-mile loop of train track, zooming in on the tunnel where the silo dumped its burden into slow-rolling railcars. So that Las Vegas lights could be seen by space shuttles. So that fountains could spit sky-high. Even he despised such waste.

"Do inspectors ever climb into a railcar? You know, examine the load?"

Another minute of mouthy laughter. Two Tree slapped his thigh. "Ever try climbing out of a grain elevator? Or out of a grain truck? Same difference. Impossible. You sink down and suffocate. Takes only a minute. If my inspectors drop into a railcar, they go in with a climbing harness and top rope fastened to the edge. *Else they perish.*" His grin was fixed, eyes open wide enough for Lasik surgery. "If they don't suffocate, temperature gets them. When it's 95 degrees outside, railcars been known to top off near 200 degrees. Or better. A day like today? Drops way below zero. It's hell either way, Mr. Horace, my man. A frozen corpse arrives in Page nearly every week. Most time they're caught before dropping into the hopper. Better that way for next of kin. Drifters or drunks mostly. Think they'll keep warm out of the stiff winds. Dead on arrival. But heat? Heat's a thousand times worse. Ever see a person baked, Mr. All-American White Art Dealer? Baked, like half-cremated? Like in a kiln? Makes you want to puke on the spot. Practically ruins the whole railcar, it does."

Horace's thin lips parted. They matched the train tracks behind him. He turned and snapped more pics. He photographed Two Tree without his permission. His plan was fixed. In three month's time, he'd bring a battery of highly trained combatants. Plus specialists to perform the risky and delicate process of loading vials of depleted uranium. "One last thing," he said. "If I tell you precisely which day I intend to load my goods, how much lead time do you need?"

Two Tree knew the answer. Something inside told him he'd better be on the mark. "Ah, no margin for error, right?"

"Of course there is, *my man*, the margin of error is your *life*. Simple as that. Your lead time must be right on the money. Perfect. When I say we're ready to load my product, the conveyor must be empty of coal. Same with the silo. Got it? If anything goes wrong, you'll end up in the hopper at NGS. Smothered like mushrooms in manure. Very fitting for your kind. Then pulverized. Your family will be paid a visit too. Got that, you ugly, half-toothed Indian? In my business, dumbass, there's *never* any margin for error."

Two Tree stood as rigid as his name implied. He didn't yield. Words such as "uh-huh" drifted out quietly. A long silence followed. Finally, he blurted his response. "Two days. I need two day's notice. I know my job and I know it better than anyone."

"You'll get your two days, Mr. Two Tree."

"And I'll get my cash, right? Fifty grand, like you promised."

Horace's palm spread around the sound suppressed .22. "Rest assured, *Kimosabe*, you'll have more money than you'll ever need. In May. Should be the third or fourth week. Early in the day. First train. My buyers will be waiting at NGS." Both hands emerged from his sheepskin coat. He strode thirty feet to his vehicle. The driver and four heavily armed bodyguards stood next to a powerful, customized G500 Mercedes SUV. Metallic silver. It was his chariot. That was three months ago.

ON Sunday morning, May 22, Mac called Wainwright from Snow Flat Canyon. He'd deliver the artifacts before 6:00 am Tuesday morning. He immediately phoned the Ute.

"You got two days."

THIRTY-FIVE

Twin headlights guided Parker and Windsong's ATV through predawn light. Like Whitey, they reached Highway 261 in eight minutes. They turned north and accelerated on the narrow shoulder. Half the distance to Todie Springs, they coasted into a bar ditch and killed the ignition. Howie led the way on foot over a cattle path through tall sagebrush. The topography crowned ahead, allowing them to observe the government's net-dropping without being seen. They each gripped a handgun. Squatting behind a clump of mountain mahogany, they looked down to the highway. Kika gasped. She pressed her binoculars deep into her eyes and stared ahead. "What? What's that? Where's everybody? Oh, God, Howie, tell me it's not what I think it is. Please, it's too freaky. Just like my dream. Not again. I hope I never dream again." Howie studied the scene. There wasn't much to study, simply a Navajo Nation police car angled perpendicular to the highway. Emergency lights flashed.

A man in full uniform stood beside the Chevy TrailBlazer, arms folded over his chest. A friendly smile and flat-brimmed hat made him resemble Smokey the Bear. The surroundings were void of activity. Silence and peace greeted them. There was no shakedown. No sting. Nets didn't drop. No giant catch dangling in government nets. The only person within miles was the Tribal policeman. He leaned nonchalantly against the driver door.

"This is straight out of my dream," she repeated, clutching Howie's arm as though she were dangling from a cliff. They approached their friend. He wore a lightweight shell bearing the Navajo Police emblem.

"Wondered when you two would show up." His smooth voice was characterized by harmonic chords. Other than Audrey Quirk, not much rattled Blue Sky. His demeanor was the antithesis of a tough guy cop. He typified what every child would ask for in a grandpa. In action, however, he was always the hero, as gnarly as cops came.

"What's going on? Where's the Captain, Coldditz?"

"Hop in." He opened the passenger door for Kika. Howie climbed in the backseat. "Water anyone? An apple? It'll have to do for breakfast." They guzzled and crunched loudly. "We're going for a little ride in the country. Sit back and relax, get comfy."

"What *is* going on, Dudley?" Kika demanded.

"I'll explain everything." He accelerated south on Highway 261 toward the precarious switchbacks. "I arrived at 03:00. Knew immediately something was amiss. I waited two hours. Then Officer Nez radioed his description of the teeter-tottering truck veering left and barreling south toward the Moki Dugway. Said a crazed-looking beast was bent over the steering wheel, zigzagging over the entire highway. Had two orange barrels in the front seat."

"Those orange barrels are *bodies*," said Howie. "Live ones, as in Mac and a woman accomplice. Bound tight in orange cable. Gagged and blindfolded."

"Uh-huh." He accelerated to 70 mph, a safe speed for the Mesa in spite of its rollercoaster undulations. He informed them that Coldditz was scheduled to return to the *real* takedown after sunrise. That the Feds had everything under control. That he'd issued strict orders to his captain - keep the truck in their sights, but don't close in until he returned.

"Where exactly are we going?" Kika asked.

"Ground zero's the Navajo Generating Station rail yard west of Kayenta." During the next several miles, she and Howie took turns updating Blue Sky on their perilous exploits since early Sunday morning.

"Coldditz isn't taking any undue risks to prevent them from netting a grand slam, capturing *all* targets and *all* contraband. The Captain figures if Whitey hasn't crashed his top-heavy truck yet, he'll arrive safely at the rendezvous. His team is up ahead. The route is blanketed." He raised his calm voice two octaves, his tempo increased. "Here's the crux of the shakedown. *Uranium.* Archaeological looting is only part of the equation. May even take a backseat role."

Howie thrust back into the seat, then leaned forward, gripping Kika's headrest as though he were choking it. "See? I knew it. Damn, the artifacts keep slipping further and further away. What do you mean by 'a backseat role'? Coldditz was right. Uranium. Mac's way out of his league. And, that makes Whitey heading for disaster. It all seemed so nebulous at the time. But, evasive as he is, he did make a promise. He guaranteed that Brewster's museum would receive the artifacts, immediately - as well as federal grant money. Damn." He'd strangled the headrest. Dudley looked straight ahead. Kika watched for Whitey's truck. No one wanted to spar with Howie. Round two shot out from his wide-open mouth. "This whole business pisses me off more and more. Damn, we should have ended this crazy fiasco when we had the chance. Right there. At Inner Ruin. Two days ago. Crouched near the T-shaped doorway. We had them trapped, Kika. Why didn't we? Now look. They're on a collision course with terrorist cells and uranium. Damn Agent Coldditz! Damn his Delilah Project! It's much clearer now. See, Kika? We've been set up the whole time. That's his specialty. It's what spies do best. Oh, man, he's a smooth operator, alright, schmoozing me with his coffee talk. He knew damn well there wasn't going to be a shakedown at Todie Springs. That gave him time to return to Washington. But why? What's his *real* agenda? What's he got up his sleeve?" Tires whistled on the blacktop.

Kika placed a comforting hand on his forearm. "Honey, hold on a second. I totally feel your frustration. I've been with you every step of the way. Look how many times we almost got killed. Our ordeal has been brutal to say the least! And I've stuck with you because I believe in you. You've changed noticeably during these…ah…ah…deadly encounters, as you call them. You're a new man. One I always want to stick with. *We're a team.* That's why I haven't bolted. But, face it, we can't go back and change what happened. Think it through, the only thing that's different now is the location of the rendezvous. That's all. We'll still get our artifacts. I truly believe that."

"I hope you're right. I want this over with. It keeps dragging on. I'm a man of action. You know that. Wherever Dudley is taking us will be swarming with anti-terrorist forces. It'll look like Baghdad. That's what I mean when I say that the artifacts keep slipping further away." He cracked his knuckles, one by one, loudly and slowly. Another way of acting out his rage instead of punching something. "You know what terrorists do, don't you? They blow things up. They don't care what the hell's in that truck. To them, it's just an infidel target. With three bozos as expendable as the spit in their mouths." His eyes met Dudley's in the rearview mirror. He fixed a grave stare. "Here's my proposition, Dudley. Honey, see if you're with me on this. This is the bottom line, Officer, here's what'll work for us. You call headquarters, or the Captain, or Coldditz, or anyone with authority. Tell them this is the last straw for Parker and Windsong. We've risked our lives for the BLM and for the National Security Agency. We're done. Whatever our destination is, it'll be the last stop. For us and for those artifacts. We've reached the end of our rope. So everything better go slick. That's it for this gig and our involvement. The buck stops there. We take possession of the archaeological loot…or else. I'm not letting them slip away again. No matter what!"

"Roger that," she chimed, smiling boldly.

Static on Blue Sky's radio typified Howie's frustration. It played like the final chords in an operatic tragedy. Deputy Nez spoke loud and clear: "Subject's just passed the turnoff into Valley of the Gods. Bearing toward Highway 163 and Mexican Hat. Six black SUVs with high antennae are idling along the route. One's a heavy-duty Land Rover with a reinforced brush guard. Resembles a modified armored personnel carrier. The Captain's inside."

"**KAY-ENTA**, Kay-Enta!" Mac screamed through gagged and severely cracked lips. "Go to Kay-Enta." Dried blood clung to his gag. Whitey gripped the steering wheel like a gorilla. "What the hell you doing? You saved my life in Cleveland. Now you're croaking me in Utah." His gag had loosened, but he was still blindfolded. Whitey was relying on his blindfolded leader to help him drive and provide directions. Mac had only been to the region once - six months ago when he discovered the hidden chamber behind Inner Ruin. Whitey'd only driven a total of sixty minutes in his entire life. It was truly the blind leading the blind.

"Millions all for me," he choked hoarsely. "You're screwed, boss. You and the misses stay cabled. Money's all mine."

"I *will* kill you for this, you lame brained moron. Don't care if you saved me from a wrecking ball. You'll never get away with it. You ain't smart enough. Don't have the brains to pull off something this big. You're just a lousy, dimwitted killer." They passed a hitchhiker. He glimpsed through the oversized windshield. His mouth dropped in disbelief. He quickly turned and dropped his thumb, figuring Mexican Hat was hosting a carnival.

"Where's the millions?"

"Get to Kay-Enta first. Then I'll tell you."

"You're stalling."

"Take off this bullshit blindfold. How can I help when I can't see a damned thing?"

Whitey stared straight ahead. The truck rocked on at 70 mph. "Made it this far. You don't need to see nothing. You and the misses, not your lucky day. Me, I got my lucky charm. See?" Whitey pulled the feather holder from his pocket and rubbed it against Mac's cheek. It left bloodstains. They veered toward an oncoming vehicle. He jerked the wheel just in time.

"Whitey, I'm begging you. Stop this nonsense. Pull over. There must be a turnout up ahead. Untie me and the woman. If you stop right now, I won't kill you. Promise. I'll give you some of the money. How does two-thirds, one-third sound? You get the one-third. I'm begging you."

The titan laughed for a full minute. "Like I said, you and the misses both, ain't your lucky day." Mac cursed for five minutes. Trixie hadn't heard such profanity in years. The cab was a seething cesspool. None of them had bathed for days.

Mac let out a second round of expletives. When he caught his breath, he relented and gave directions to Mexican Hat. "Take the bridge across the river. There's a restaurant there. Anasazi Café, I think. I need chow badly. Hell, bet we all could use some eats. Aren't you famished? Thirsty? It'll be shady by the river. We can cool off. Let's stop. Whaddaya say?"

Whitey cranked up the air conditioner. "Too hot, huh?" His laugh sounded like a sick donkey. "Your boss man days are over, boss. I'm driving now. I decide if or when we stop. We're already late. Sun's just up. Supposed to meet the buyer *before* sunrise, no?"

"Damn you, I *will* kill you for this! I need eats. Get me out of this frigging cable suit."

"Talk's cheap, boss. If you don't shut up, I'll tighten your gag. Your mouth was nothing to look at anyway. Shoulda let that wrecking ball come around one more time. You're still stalling. In Kay-Enta. Then where?"

"Better gas up there."

"Don't care about gas. Where's the millions?"

Mac stretched his tongue and lapped blood from the corners of his mouth. He collected it with as much saliva as he could and spat the messy glob onto the dashboard. Next to the gauges. The blob spread slowly down, like an octopus inching down a piling, falling onto Whitey's boots. "I'd have spat that hocker on you, bastard, if I could've cocked my head."

"Time to teach you a lesson about who's boss now, boss." His finger stubs formed lethal projectiles. He drilled Mac in the temple. "Last time I'm asking - in Kay-Enta, then where? Or your brains'll be Swiss cheese." Mac reeled from five air hammers striking at once. Words spilled out slowly. He told Whitey what he wanted to hear. He also warned him that Slick would confiscate his lucky charm. "Ain't no one gets this, boss man. Don't care who they are. It ain't for sale." Mac cussed his stupidity. "You cussing a lot today, boss. How come?"

Mac turned his head as far as he could and thrashed furiously within the cable. "You *are* a retard. Christ almighty, you sick moron." Glands secreted through tear ducts. His blindfold resembled a wet washcloth. "Look at me. Just look at me, will you? Look at how you got me. And her. I'm cabled up tighter than my asshole. Up to my damned head. And you're judging my language? What the Christ almighty do you expect? Should I hum holy church hymns? Why not untie the lady's mouth too? And we'll harmonize a few stanzas from Onward Christian Soldiers. Sweet Jesus, you're stupid. Come on, let's all sing Sunday school tunes, why don't we? As we drive through the lovely countryside. While me and her are all friggin' wrapped up in two spools of friggin' cable. Merrily cruising through this ugly friggin' desert. On our way to exchange friggin' Indian junk for friggin' money and uranium. You are an imbecile! Christ almighty."

272

Trixie sputtered through her gag for the first time, staring over at spires within Valley of the Gods. "Rock of Ages. More fitting."

They entered Mexican Hat. Whitey jerked the truck hard to the right. They'd gas up there instead of Kayenta. The sudden movement caused a shift in the cargo. Crates crashed to the floor. He lifted an oily rag from the pedal area and re-gagged Mac. Then he tossed a smelly moving blanket over both hostages before stepping out to refuel.

THIRTY-SIX

Officer Blue Sky and his companions rode silently atop Cedar Mesa. One mile north of the Moki Dugway, the sun peeked over the horizon like a tiptoeing toddler peering into a cookie jar. As fast as the toddler reached for a stepstool, the sun stepped above the horizon. It was the same sunrise, at the exact same instant, that blinded Semlow Wheeler. Contrary to his death-defying crash, Blue Sky and his intrepid mates were graced with awe and beauty. The yellow-orange glow appeared so far below them it felt like they were airborne. Serenity climbed into the TrailBlazer as a fourth companion. It guided them to the edge of the world. To a peninsula overlook called Muley Point.

Blue Sky used a Navajo frame of reference when it came to space and time. He measured distances in terms of how they fit into the sixteen-million-acre reservation. To his way of thinking, their pursuit didn't lag far behind the over-height truck. Two minutes earlier, NTP dispatch had issued another update. Whitey's truck made a pit stop in Mexican Hat. That, he figured, would allow ample time for his quick detour. He drove as far as vehicles were permitted, to the very precipice of Muley Point. It happened to be the same area where Mac and Whitey had camped during last week's sandstorm.

The overlook afforded a 100-mile panorama into a slice of Navajo. He hoped the time would act as a cleansing for Kika, a brief "ceremony," a respite that would allow her to become grounded again, to help purify five days of homicidal hell which had embroiled her and Howie. An unencumbered view of sacred *naatsis'aan*, Navajo Mountain, fifty miles west, anchored his plan. The high, and isolated dome in western Navajoland represented the head of the sacred female in their Blessing Side stories. Honoring it could restore harmony to her feminine place in the universe. A passageway, perhaps, to guide her to a state of *hozho*...to beauty, peace of mind, goodness and health. To homogeneity. There would be time for true Navajo purification ceremonies later, time for the correct Chantway. Leonard Atcitty, her mother's brother, whom Kika referred to as Lenny, would know what was right. Until then, Blue Sky would facilitate panoramic vistas of her rez. Their timing was perfect. The sun had risen six degrees above the horizon, ushering in grandeur not often seen by human eyes. Had they arrived ten minutes later, unique shades of light would have disappeared.

They stepped from the patrol car and approached the 1,100-foot drop-off. After honoring Navajo Mountain, they turned southeast toward the intersection of four states. The Navajo term for the junction was *tse'ii'ahi*, meaning "Rocks Standing Out." The rest of the world called it Four Corners. Blue Sky chanted quietly in his native tongue. Kika stood in reverence. She found his melodic cadence refreshing. The three stood solemnly at the edge of space and time. Howie had deep respect for Kika's native beliefs. It balanced them as a couple in spite of their otherwise hectic lives.

After six minutes, Blue Sky spoke. "We better get a move on."

"Thank you, I needed this," said Kika.

Howie held her hand walking back. He stopped suddenly and turned to Dudley. "I just thought of something. Let me ask if you've ever seen this design. I haven't had much time to ask Kika. We've had our hands full."

"Oh? Life in the fast lane? In Snow Flat Canyon? Who'd have ever guessed?" A smile melted across his face.

Kika turned to Howie. He knew the look. Obsidian pupils shaped like question marks. Usually spelled trouble. Or humiliation. Dudley dangled his ignition keys impatiently, edging toward his door.

"Oh, yes, I forgot to tell you. We're engaged. Hope to marry this fall. Pretty exciting, huh? Almost forgot to tell you. Happened a couple of nights ago. Um, maybe it was even last night. Huh, Kika?"

"Six hours and fifty-three minutes to be exact. And counting. Now let's get moving. You're the one complaining about the artifacts slipping further away."

"Just a second. Back to my question. Dudley, does this symbol mean anything in Navajo ritual? Or in your origin myths?" He placed the toe of his boot in the sand and carved a deliberate pattern. His movement was exacting. When he was finished, two crosses lay side by side. Then he connected them with an arc over the top, from one sidearm to the other. It was a perfect replica of what he had seen incised on the feather holders. And what agent Coldditz had drawn with his boot next to the camper.

The Navajo policeman stared in wonder. Time was suspended. All urgency to leave vanished. For an instant, he was transported to another place and time. To a sacred space in the Dinétah where a similar symbol appeared. Etched in the landscape. He spoke quietly in his native tongue. After a spell, he looked at the design, then at Kika. He articulated in Navajo. Each phrase told a story in itself. Except for the parts relating to their origin myths, she'd never heard the story which spilled from his lips.

"I'm an officer of the law, Parker, not a *hataalni*. You must realize I know only a little, largely what I have heard and seen. Some could be speculative. This is what I can say to you, *bilagaana*. This motif may appear with star symbols. Or *sha yiikiizh*, a sun rash. Stars, sky fires, the sun - they're all spheres of fire. Certain folktales tell us the sun contains sunspots. There exists a mystical place in our land where it is safe to look up at the sun and see sunspots. Without being blinded. With no damage to our eyes." Kika snapped to attention, recalling Uncle Lenny's story.

He stepped closer to Parker. "If Miss Windsong hasn't told you, the sun and the moon and the stars are woven into our cosmology. They represent all light. It was light which guided our ancestors from darker, lower worlds to brighter, upper worlds. It was light which the First People sought when they ascended to our present Fifth World. The sun, moon and stars *are* light. Whenever I see this symbol, I see light. And celestial bodies. But, Parker, I'm bewildered. I don't understand how you, a *bilagaana*, a white person, came to scribing this motif in the dirt. *Our dirt.*"

"It's one of many symbols incised on the bottom of the feather holders. All eleven of them. Plus the half piece now confiscated by Whitey. The pattern struck me as unique because it's the only symbol which repeats itself on all twelve artifacts."

Valuable minutes slipped by. "Might I add," said Kika, "if we don't get a move on, we may never see those feather holders again."

"One more minute," replied Dudley. "There's more. Things you haven't heard." The sun, by then a blazing fireball ten degrees above the horizon, fit his lore as though the scene had been rehearsed. "To Navajos who have converted to the white man's religion, an emblem of two crosses is not such a mystery. It is *Tsin alna'asdzoh,* two Christian crosses. To Natives, the symbol may represent two dragonflies side by side. But there's so much more to it than that. I have hiked to a magical landscape setting on our Dinetah. At that site, I have seen with my own eyes an arc connecting two side-by-side crosses. It is not far from where we stand." He nodded, his lips pointing toward the southeast horizon. "Seventy miles away, past the small communities of Rock Point and Round Rock past Lukachukai and over Lukachukai Pass to Cove. To the mystical convergence of three mountain ranges. See? They are shrouded in morning haze.

"When I hiked into that mystical land, I saw a geometrically perfect sandstone arch. I stood beneath it and faced south, toward what we call *Tsé Bit'a'í,* Winged Rock. The world knows it as the Shiprock Pinnacle. I laid down on the smooth ground and cast my eyes in a semi-circle. I saw two sandstone columns supporting each side of the arch. They formed a cross, thus a double cross. A perfectly shaped arc connected what looked like two crosses. From a distance, the feature looks like any natural sandstone bridge. Lying beneath it, however, a mystical sensation came over me. When I looked up at the sun, I saw sunspots, *sha yiikiizh.* I was not blinded. One folktale, the story of

276

whirlwinds, says that sunspots are teachers, reminders of disrespectful Ancient Ones many centuries ago. More significant to our origin story are the four sunspots placed as guardians by Fire Man when he created sunlight. I saw those too.

"The three mountain ranges terminate in a cove-like area which encloses this sacred site. In our tongue it is called *ni' hidi' naah*, which means the 'The Earth Starts to Shake.' It has also been called 'The Land of Walking Earth.' I prefer the latter name. Many in my generation call it that. That is the location of the double cross connected by an arc. There is only one other landscape in Navajoland which rumbles and undulates with energy. It is what we honored minutes ago. Over there." He pointed with his lips and chin toward *naatsis'aan*, Navajo Mountain. "Navajos have felt underground rumblings on its western slopes for generations.

"One last thing. I've been told that people have disappeared in The Land of Walking Earth. Vanished without a trace. Strange, isn't it? Tradition instructs us never to climb on the sacred arc. Or its supporting crosses. For fear of being punished - by lightning, or snakes, *or whirlwinds*. Whirlwinds, especially large ones, sprout up almost daily at the convergence of the three mountains. Some believe whirlwinds are what produce the strong energy fields - and the rumbling earth. Magical, isn't it? This *ni' hidi' naah.* The Land of Walking Earth.

"Did a German scientist vanish there in the fifties?"

"Legend has it that he and others have been swallowed up by large whirlwinds. Me being an officer of the law, I don't really believe that. But I do respect our lore. A Mormon, a *gaamalii,* also perished there once. I remember the case quite well. Quite a mystery, we never found a trace of him. Most peculiar case was that scientist you asked about, the *beesh bi ch'ahli.* I'm told that the Navajo liked the man. Even helped him with his surveying and mapping work. Story goes that he frequently entered The Land of Walking Earth without permission. It was a time when *bilagaana* mined uranium. There were mine shafts everywhere. Although the money was nice, Navajos greatly resented poisonous uranium mining. Tragically, many fell sick." Kika stood like a sentinel staring at the distant mountain convergence, still shrouded in haze formed by sand particles clinging to cooler morning air, not pollution. "I think I've said too much," Blue Sky added. "This has been private talk. That's why I frequently spoke in our native tongue. I couldn't have said everything I did to your ears, Howie Parker, all due respect, of course.

He nodded approvingly. "Did Wheeler ever show you two newspaper articles?" Blue Sky shook his head.

277

Howie felt betrayed. The story he just heard was moving. But he still couldn't connect the dots. His mind always hit a brick wall, striking the same conundrum. How could an NSA agent know about a double cross-arc motif? Then it hit him. Perhaps Coldditz couldn't connect the dots either. Perhaps he really *was* fishing. And perhaps someone in Washington could connect them and wrap everything up into one nice bundle. Like the mole. He did mention something about a mole playing a key role. Was it Department of Energy? Maybe that's why Coldditz made an emergency trip there. "Of course," he said quietly. "Double-cross. That's it, Kika, I know it is. *This whole gig's a double-cross.* The damn agent himself drew it for me in plain sight. With his own boots!"

WHITEY exited the gas station and veered into a vacant lot one block away. In a half-hearted measure, he un-gagged Trixie and rubbed the soreness from her mouth. Then he held cup after cup of water to her parched lips. She slurped like a horse. He did the same for Mac, being careful of his titanium tooth. It was like spoon-feeding a rattler. Not that there was much left to bite of Whitey's fingers. Next, he sprayed a healthy dose of aerosol cheese into their mouths. He aimed it like a fire extinguisher. Then he rolled up some cold cuts and crammed them in. Chewing was difficult at best, swallowing nearly impossible. Dessert consisted of a chocolate bar stuffed into partially full mouths. When they'd finally swallowed, he poured Pepsi down their gullets. It gushed like the gas he'd just pumped. The meal was rushed in less than three minutes.

"Gotta get moving." His half a heart clamped tightly shut. He re-tied their blindfolds and re-bound their gags. Then he revved the engine and sped toward the bridge spanning the San Juan. "Not the eats you wanted. But they'll keep you alive until I'm done with you."

OFFICER Wheeler was admitted to Moab's Allen Memorial Hospital at 7:23 am. He got off lucky. A direct blow to his skull resulted in a mild traumatic brain injury. It happened to quarterbacks all the time. The concussion wasn't as debilitating as the "AC shoulder," caused when the end of the humerus dislodged from its socket. That would likely require surgery. With two cracked ribs, head lacerations and serious bruising, he looked like he'd been trampled at Pamplona's running of the bulls. Yet he was alive. The hospital insisted he remain overnight for observation. If his vitals were stable by morning, he'd be fitted with an arm sling and released at 11:00 am.

His cell phone was trashed in the wreck. Hospital policy forbade head-injury patients phone access. His wife, Ann, was no help. When

278

she slipped out for cafeteria lunch, he conned a nurse out of hers, purporting it was official law enforcement business. She insisted he make only one two-minute call. She stayed in the doorway to police him. He couldn't decide between calling Quirk, Blue Sky or Brewster. He needed to speak to all three. His career triumphed. After dispensing with protocols, he asked Quirk about his best friends.

"You needn't worry about Parker and Windsong," she said in her officious tone. "Coldditz met them at their campsite yesterday afternoon. They remained in the canyon last night to perform additional recon for him. The Feds were scheduled to drop their net at sunrise this morning. About the same time as your crash. My bet is it's already a done deal. Case's practically closed by now." She despised lying to her law enforcement officer, her pet subordinate. But she was under strict orders to do so, to keep Wheeler out of the loop. "Your two friends should be absolutely fine. Still out of cell range, but fine. By the time you arrive, we'll all enjoy one big, happy homecoming." She lied and he withheld. "Mutuality," he'd heard it called - a frequent style of communication between public servants and politicians. Mutuality, they made steady diets of it.

Bulletins issued by Utah State Police said his accident was caused by faulty brakes. Not brake tampering. Wheeler kept hush about that. According to hospital staff, he exhibited mild states of confusion, most likely post-traumatic amnesia, a hallmark sign of mild concussions. He himself wasn't certain of each detail surrounding his near-fatal crash. He almost welcomed being kept overnight. It'd give him time to sort things out. Even with his tweaked brain. He did, however, retain clarity about two events - the bobbing shadow he observed in the hotel parking lot and the alarming urgency of those who wanted him dead, presumably cyber-spies who'd intercepted his e-mail. "Hell," he mumbled quietly, "the order must have been issued before it was even saved to a flash drive. Guess I tugged one too many times on that thread."

As the night wore on, bouts of anguished thinking mixed with states of confusion. He had difficulty connecting the dots between his "accident," the two newspaper articles, Agent Coldditz, the mauled woman backpacker, Mac and Whitey's canyon looting and the corpse stuffed under the cattle guard. He knew a pattern would emerge. Sleep came in spurts. Each time he awoke, his mind seemed to focus more vividly. At one interval, he realized he had another problem - squelching an accident investigation by the Interagency Motor Pool. He'd have to handle that when he returned to work. They were, after all, federal employees; and he already knew it was the Feds who'd ordered his death. All told, Officer Wheeler's head injuries placed him worse off mentally than physically. He was confused by too many dots and too many lines to be drawn in connecting them. It was a pattern typical of patients suffering from focal neurological deficits, signs that a specific part of the brain was not working properly. By 3:00 am, he'd managed to fall asleep and stay that way until the first of many nurse interruptions occurred at 6:10 am.

At mid-morning, he passed his medical exam. While hospital bureaucracy arranged release paperwork, a man wearing casual slacks, a sport shirt and generic ball cap produced government identification papers. The nurse in charge of his section inspected the man's ID. She thought it read "Intelligence," but it could have been "Interior," as in "Department of." Either way, she handed over Wheeler's briefcase and laptop. The man politely thanked her and left through the automatic doors. In less than forty-five seconds, the Feds had gotten what they wanted.

SANDSTONE sentinels in Monument Valley angled skyward. Whitey's truck raced past the park's entrance at 70 mph. Trixie's cable-clad body angled against the passenger door. She stared out at Goulding's Trading Post. A wind sock next to the airstrip flew horizontally. Nearby, a camouflage helicopter was securely tied to its anchor. Mac's cabled body faced straight ahead. They were as rancorous as wild beasts captured for a zoo. A cacophony of cussing spewed through his wet bandana. Whitey looked at his ex-boss. His pallor was cadaverous. It matched an October sky over Cleveland. Lake Erie looked healthier.

Eight miles north of Kayenta, Whitey saw an expanse of sand reaching the horizon. It sloped downward and fused into small rock formations nine miles west of the highway. Ripple patterns resembled a Caribbean beach. Beyond that lay Nokai Mesa. Near Owl Rock, he jerked the truck onto the shoulder. He activated the flashers and ran to the passenger door. He lifted Trixie as if she were a bag of groceries and carried her upright to the rear tires. She was out of view from passersby. She trembled uncontrollably. She felt warmth in her crotch. Stricken by fright, she'd urinated a putrid yellow, foul-smelling liquid, the result of trauma and severe dehydration. Next, he hoisted Mac up, carried him against his blood-encrusted chest and dropped him in the sand with a loud thud. He returned to the front seat and removed one of the two feather holders. He stretched the bound cable from Mac's chest and stuffed the ancient artifact into his pocket.

"You might need this out there. It'll bring you luck. You'll need all the luck you can get." He laid Mac horizontally and propped both feet against him. Then he supported his massive arms against the truck and, like a ramrod, thrust his legs outward with explosive force. Mac rolled down the steep embankment. The oily cable gathered sand as it rolled off into the distance. Mac's head missed a large rock by inches. He slowed upon reaching a break in the sand, after which he gained momentum and plunged down a steep incline. The sandy abyss swallowed him whole.

A fierce gust of wind blew. Several whirlwinds sprouted up. Some were small and short-lived. Others gained strength and churned into energized twisters. Two in particular zigzagged across the desert floor. They chopped up sand like giant eggbeaters, glowing brightly at their base. Whitey wasn't dumb. He knew that the only thing that could cause air to glow was electricity. He grunted gutturally. If the electrified furies approached Mac, he knew he'd fry. The whirlwinds were only 200 feet from the orange cable. The air sizzled with electricity. It sounded like high voltage wires.

He swiveled toward Trixie and placed his lucky charm on the truck's running board. Instead of rolling her into oblivion, he loosened her gag so it dropped to her chin. Pungent urine filled the air. After several horrifying minutes, hyperventilating eased to sporadic sobs. Soon, somewhat regular breathing raised the oxygen content in her blood. Circulation improved. He touched her forehead with care. Startled, she screamed. But sounds never came out. Her vocal cords had dried up. Cracked lips bled.

"I won't kill you. All I want is the money. All for me. Didn't want to kill the boss man either. Maybe his lucky charm will keep the whirlwinds away." Gently, he rubbed her face. He moved his finger stubs from her cheek to her neck, then up again to her forehead and temples. It brought instant relief to knotted nerves. Next, he moved to her shoulders, massaging them in a semi-barbaric manner, careful not to frighten her. "I'm not molesting you. Just don't want you to die. I got plans. *I need your eyes.*" He lifted her into the front seat. Her flesh shone pink again. Although she remained in mild shock, a ray of hope lifted her spirits. She wanted to believe him, knowing full well that if he wanted her dead, he'd have killed her long ago.

He put the truck in gear and eased onto the highway. Seconds later, he slammed the brakes and veered off the pavement. He ran back to where they'd parked and paced back and forth. Nothing. He searched below the embankment. Finally, he spotted it, engulfed in sand ten feet away. Boasting a toothy whale shark grin, he climbed back in and accelerated like a rocket. He dropped the sand-covered artifact in his pocket.

THIRTY-SEVEN

Dr. Brewster composed an e-mail to Dr. Alonzo Milad de Mendoza in Santiago, Chile. The museum curator had never met the Chilean scholar. He toyed with formalities, but instead got right to the point.

"I respect Dr. Chao's courage to decipher the ideogram utilizing one half of the artifact. Therefore, my quest to discover the missing fragment takes on magnanimous proportions. Excavations of this nature rely upon calculated hunches. And, there is chance, that serendipitous moment when everything falls neatly into place. One additional factor has played a significant role during my career: Luck. Heaps and bounds of luck. You no doubt have read the works of legendary author Ernest Hemingway. Perhaps you've also heard the term 'Hemingway Luck', the iconic writer's *modus operandi.* He knew he couldn't create his own luck, but made certain he was ready whenever it came his way. It's not quite the same as being in the right place at the right time. It's a deeper state of readiness. It was written in his constitution, only today we'd call it written into his DNA, that he had the capability to embellish opportunities the instant they occurred. An 'indexical' quality, the ability to change to changing conditions.

"That's exactly how I feel about our foray into Snow Flat Canyon. I feel it in my bones. I *do* feel lucky. I envision piecing the two halves together so Lin Chao can crack the ideogram. Every so often a scientist guesses it just right and his or her data supports the hunch. Makes working in the trenches worthwhile.

"Now to a related matter. Could the discoveries in southeast Utah be juxtaposed with excavations at the site closest to Easter Island, the Monte Verde Site? If so..."

MAC'S cabled body rolled like a 55 gallon drum. It surfed through rippled sand until reaching an arroyo, where it came to rest in sand that was hotter than a frying pan. If other forces didn't kill him, he'd bake like a weenie in a corndog. The air above was shimmering. In physics, basic tenets of fluid dynamics produce "shimmering air", and also mirages. Those same forces also produce wind shear, and ultimately, air rotation. Desert air consists of miniscule electrified particles of grit. It's what gives birth to whirlwinds. Lightweight, dusty particles flow upward as negative charges, while positive, larger grit churns downward to its base. Earth's rotation does the rest. Spinning and rising air, known as the Coriolis phenomenon, transforms gleefully playing dust into electrically-charged whirlwinds, some surpassing 15 feet wide and 100 feet high. Conditions that day were perfect. The atmosphere near Nokai Mesa gave birth to embryonic swirling every few minutes. Mac lay directly in the path of two monster whirlwinds. His metal suit would conduct electricity like a lamp plugged into its outlet.

Dazed and disoriented from perpetual rolling, he had no idea where he lay. Acute dizziness caused him to vomit. Trapped by his gag, he nearly choked. Soon, his cocoon began to vibrate and a deafening roar increased to jet-like proportions. It was as if he'd been dumped on a runway. Seconds later, a vacuum produced an eerie calm. Next, a drop in air pressure compressed the cable and his ears "popped." A wave of singed air arrived, followed by a distinct buzzing sound, which became a loud crackling. One second later, the wind monster swallowed him whole. In a horrifying shriek, Mac surrendered. Electricity zapped all around him. At first it stung, and then it felt more like a Taser weapon. Swirling and churning, the dusty twister raised him up and crashed him down. He twisted and bounced and rolled like tumbleweed. After several minutes, the devil of dust skirted beside a towering cliff. There, it expunged the crook from Cleveland as fast as it had swept him up. The whirlwind met up with another one and they danced in unison toward the highway.

Mac's titanium tooth glowed iridescent. Spindly cacti protruded from exposed skin. His head felt like a pin cushion. He'd been zapped and lightly barbequed, but he endured a desert Armageddon. Six minutes total. It felt like six centuries. He looked as old. Most of his hair was gone and his skull resembled petrified wood from nearby "Forest Gump" Mesa. An extraordinary physiological transformation also occurred. It would shock those who knew him. It would baffle medical experts. Guinness would have to find a new category for it. Swirling energy known on the res as the Wind People spared him that morning. Justice would have to be meted out through jurisprudence, not forces of nature. Whirlwinds were messengers, not executioners. He, who had defaced ancestral villages, uprooted spirits and pillaged sacred artifacts, would face public prosecution.

BREWSTER'S office phone rang at 10:56am. A cryptic message followed. He recognized Chao's voice. "I have eighteen seconds to speak. Drive two miles north. Entrance to Fairfield Snow Bowl. Woman in white sedan. Go for a ride. Tell no one. Repeat, tell no one."

He raced to the museum's door forty-eight seconds later, shouting back to his staff he'd forgotten an urgent appointment. He whisked to the rendezvous. A dirt-caked, indecipherable sedan, its unreadable government license plate attached with baling wire, awaited him. The vehicle was beyond the point of sending it to the junkyard crusher. Noxious white exhaust spat from its tailpipe. The driver reached over and partially opened the door. He sat down. She drove north on Highway 180. It operated better than its appearance. At half the 76 mile distance to the Grand Canyon, she parked in a pullout at Red Horse Wash and handed him a sealed courier pouch marked: "Extremely Sensitive Material. Top Secret. For your Eyes Only".

"Hard copy," she said. "Here it is on audio." She handed him a tiny, wireless earpiece and depressed a device clipped to her belt. Chao's voice carried into his ear, and along with it, a sense of extreme urgency, as though he'd just cracked an enemy code in his previous Defense Department job.

"Phillip:

"This recording self-destructs as it plays. Listen carefully. My preliminary decipherment of the ideogram is contained in printed form just handed to you. Guard it as you would your own life. It's as valuable as the half of a feather holder retained in your museum safe. The only version I've retained was encrypted on a hard drive. It's in cryptographic code I created at Defense. The code was scrapped soon thereafter and replaced. I retained it for personal use someday. Today's the day. Positively no other person in the universe is capable of untangling it. This morning, I accessed one of our satellites used for archiving nuclear warhead test data. My complete, encrypted report is in safe-keeping there, some 640 miles above earth. All files on hard drive were swiftly obliterated utilizing a technique devised for the White House and Pentagon. Counter-intel has come a long way in cover-ups since Watergate. Ask Ashcroft or Cheney.

"Here are my 'stabbing wildly around in the dark' findings. We may be looking at a cosmological 'sign language' to interstellar travel. Subject to examining all twelve feather holders, it could also lead mankind to map the genetic code of the entire universe…and parallel universes. Please recall my previous e-mail where I indicated certain symbols are arranged to represent large monuments, or stelae, based at geographic coordinates in the Southern Hemisphere. One element of proof is NAA, Neutron Activation Analysis. As you know, NAA is nearly 100 percent successful in determining prehistoric migration routes since source materials can be fingerprinted through their chemical composition. Test results on the subject fragment were delivered to me yesterday afternoon. They were conducted under the protocol of delayed gamma-ray neutron activation analysis, whereby measurements follow radioactive decay. Indeed, they linked trace elements to Southern Pacific latitudes. The chemical composition is consistent with minerals abundant on Easter Island. This will support our air-tight theories when we decide to go public. Allow me to now highlight the credibility of Raul Fernandez's statement contained in his e-mail of two days ago. No one could have articulated it better:

'Make-make's energy field will provide the world with the theory of everything... clues to unlock secrets of the cosmos.'

"As scientists, we both comprehend the importance of this - we are on the threshold of leaping headfirst into distant galaxies. Have you ever, my friend, stood on a shoreline and wished you could instantly travel to the other side? Have you ever looked up at the stars and wished, just for a moment, you could fly to one of them to pay a quick visit? Yes, dear scholar, so have I. Nothing would be more outrageous! Frankly, I'm anxious to meet my peers in parallel universes. Aren't you?

"Until Mexico City, I bid you 'adios amigo'. Lin Chao."

"The pLIT device attached to my belt is already blank," the female agent dispatched by Los Alamos assured Brewster. "But, just to be certain..." She unclipped the secret audio device from her belt. Brewster handed her the raisin-sized ear piece removed from his ear. Next, she withdrew a small bottle from the glove box and placed three drops of green liquid on the items. Almost instantly, the pLIT and its earpiece disintegrated into a glob smaller than a grape seed. Then, vaporized and disappeared entirely. A black SUV approached out of nowhere. "That vehicle will return you to your vehicle," she said, reaching over his lap and opening his door. "Goodbye."

Stunned, the famed archaeologist sat in his car after being dropped off. He couldn't help but articulate his thoughts loudly. "By Jove, I think Chao's got it. Easter Island ceremonial artifacts on the Colorado Plateau. He's not a mad scientist after all. He's genius. Although what he described doesn't by itself prove *dating*, such as *when* the feather holders arrived. That's where I come in. We already know they were discovered *in situ*, in their natural context of a secret ceremonial chamber sealed for millennia. My field excavations will aid Chao in building a solid case. Damn, he'd also make an exceptional archaeologist. Northeasterly coastal human migration routes...shaman pilgrimages...trans-oceanic, pan-Asiatic deep water voyages...hum, let's see how Chao's hypotheses align with Fernandez's oral histories.

KIKA sprung forward and gripped the dashboard. "Over there, what's that?" They were eight miles north of Kayenta. Blue Sky hit the brakes. She stabbed the window with her finger. "Look!" He swerved onto the shoulder and activated the flasher bar. "See? That orange thing. Way out there, near those two whirlwinds."

"I know what it looks like, but no way," said Howie.

"I'm jumping out."

285

Howie laced up his boots. "Right behind you."

"Hold up, folks," said Dudley. "No one's chasing after an old construction barrel. We're closing-in on Whitey. Ground zero is twenty-two minutes away." Too late. Kika raced into the desert. Howie followed at a brisk stride. Dudley turned off the ignition and silhouetted Howie's footprints, raising his binoculars. A smile blossomed. He spoke quietly in melodic Navajo. His smile widened.

Howie watched Kika stoop over the orange object. Dudley caught up with Howie. They stood fifty yards from her. He spoke to the future newlywed on woman's intuition. How helpful it was in marriage to grasp that most women possessed a sixth sense; that they could sometimes see circumstances three dimensionally, almost halo graphically. In Kika's case, visions also came to her in dreams. He suggested Parker heed them well. That she was para-quixotic, and would sense things long before he would.

Howie smirked. "Gee, thanks dad."

Kika stood up and faced them. It wasn't a construction barrel. They darted ahead and stared down in horror. Blackened-orange cable encased McAllister. His face was badly bruised. Second-degree burns glistened in the sun. "Looks like a weenie orphaned on the grill," said Howie. Dudley unclipped his radio and called dispatch. Kika loosened Mac's blindfold. Puffy eyelids blinked up at them, his breathing was shallow and raspy. He was a crispy mess. *Nevertheless, he was alive.* Kika turned and watched two fierce whirlwinds flee the scene of the "crime," as though she eyed muggers fleeing in an alley. They swirled north and crossed the highway. A rare occurrence. "That was a mean dust devil," said Howie. "Oops, sorry. That's not what I meant. Let me rephrase that. The messengers delivered a mean message. Better, huh?"

"Not even close. In fact, quite horrible. Except that at least you referred to them as messengers instead of that other filthy name." She pointed her chin and tilted her head at the whirlwinds. "Wanna' know what I think? The Wind People have spoken to us today. Could be *both*: Persevering Badger and Trickster Coyote. Look for yourselves. There must be eight or ten whirlwinds out there. Plus two across the highway. I believe their message is quite clear. This half-melted body lying at our feet is a graphic warning. Telling us there's others up ahead even more dangerous than this *hombre*. More sinister. More evil. As much as I have feared Mac, the Wind People have delivered him for a reason. We should proceed with extreme caution, prepare for the worse. This was a *good* message, Howie Parker, not a mean message. And certainly not a mean Messen*ger!* They spared this evil man's life. They will spare our lives too." Her fiancé had no rebuttal. He looked at Blue

Sky, who was smiling one of those "I told you so; better listen to her" looks.

"Good god, Dudley, what are you doing?"

"Reading him his rights. He's alive isn't he? I'm arresting him before the EMTs haul him off. It's my duty."

"Funny," Howie said, "of all the things I pictured doing to McAllister when I finally caught up with him, reading him his rights wasn't one of them."

Dudley unclipped his radio and called dispatch. "Don't hear any sirens yet. What's up?" Sweet Voice coursed the static. Howie recognized her instantly. The same sweet-voiced woman when he called dispatch three days earlier. "Lost a unit to Tuba City twenty minutes ago," she said. "A head-on occurred at mile marker 338. Your replacement unit left four minutes ago. Ought to hear sirens any second. Over."

"Roger, out." He stooped down and checked Mac's pulse. His breathing was weak. Sporadic blinking eased their concern. CPR was out of the question. The officer reached inside the cabled mass to check for other injuries. His hand slid over Mac's chest. "Hum." He fumbled near the victim's heart. "What's this?" The three were speechless. Blue Sky held a 19,000 year old feather holder up to the sunlight. "Is this what you've been talking about? Never seen anything quite like it." He held it at an angle and studied the glyphs. He rubbed his finger across them. "You know, I see four symbols which resemble our mystical motif in The Land of Walking Earth. Not just one."

"Hand it to Kika. She hasn't seen one yet."

"Oh yes I have," she said, laughing loudly. "Not nearly as close as you, though. Like when Whitey…"

"Ya, ya ya, whatever," he said, blushing. "How long am I going to pay for that?"

She took the artifact and held it respectfully in front of her, commenting on the intricate symbols and how they were scribed clear to the edges. Side to side and top to bottom. Like a book with no margins. She asked her companions what the symbols might say and handed it back to Howie.

"Hum, interesting choice of words, Kika. What they might *'say'*. Most people would have asked what they might *'mean'*, not *'say'*. And, your analogy of a book. You're interpreting these symbols that they actually speak, as in telling a story, not just artistic etchings."

"Howie Parker, might I remind you, Mr. Avocational archaeologist, that all etchings, all rock art and all Native paintings and weavings *say* things. They communicate. They're not just stuff to look at."

Kika had him again. He took a closer look at Mac. "Holy shit, will you look at that? Haven't you noticed? Something's drastically different about his head. Besides looking like a meteorite, his features are *reversed*. Good God!" He crouched and held Mac's head like a waiter displayed a dessert tray.

Kika was aghast. She stooped down, chuckling. Her eyes darted playfully at Dudley. "I'd say the man's got a new slant on life, wouldn't you?" Howie burst into laughter and lowered Mac's head. Blue Sky joined in. They stared down at the crook. The slope of his skull, the slant of his face, angled down to the *left* instead of to the right. Truly extraordinary.

"Chalk-up another one to 'Ripley's Believe It Or Not'," said Howie. "Course, smart money says it was electromagnetic forces within the whirlwinds. They contain those too, not just electrical charges."

Kika bounced to her feet. Sirens wailed from the highway. Three paramedics jumped from their unit and raced into a sea of sand. "We good to go?" she asked. Blue Sky nodded.

THIRTY-EIGHT

Whitey removed Trixie's blindfold. Her face was no longer puffy. Its color matched that of normal flesh. Sight gave her the will to live. Hope sprouted from despair. Grateful yet baffled, she wondered why a bellicose brute who enjoyed killing would stop at her.

The truck became Whitey's new toy. Hollywood's death-defying chase scenes were galvanized in his mind. He longed to race at top speed, to outrun pursuers, to watch them in the rearview mirror, recklessly chasing and wildly shooting at him. He dreamt of driving off into the sunset. Him as the big hero, a babe at his side, maybe more than one. All he needed was Trixie Grebe's eyes. He knew she could utter a simple "uh-huh" or "uh-uh" through her gag. They entered the outskirts of Kayenta. He cruised past Navajo Nation Police headquarters and the Kayenta Medical Center. He figured he'd slipped by unnoticed since no one chased him. He turned west onto Highway 160 as Mac had instructed. "This the way?"

"Uh-huh."

Trixie was the first to spot it. The unmistakable outline of a conveyor chute spanning the highway. Stood out like the fuselage of a jet. An obtrusive feature against the majestic backdrop of Navajoland. Beyond it to their right, the terrain rose steadily to Navajo National Monument. A place so serene and so abounding in ancestral spirits that it should have been preserved a century ago as a sacred Navajo site - off-limits to visitors. But it wasn't. Instead, it's managed by the U.S. Park Service. Fortunately, the Agency has restricted visits to three ancient cliff villages more stringently than in years past. Seconds later, Peabody's towering coal silo came into view. It protruded into the pristine landscape, as ugly as the coal chute.

The massive outgrowth to their left was Black Mesa, home to Peabody Energy's three coal mines. In terms of ecological destruction, the blunt coal chute and its silo were just the tip of the horrifying iceberg - akin to the bombardier's doors on the Enola Gay. Instead of opening to release a 9,000-pound hydrogen bomb on civilians, the chute transported high-grade coal from toxic mines scarring the Mesa. Mines which delivered a bloodless form of genocide to the water table and minerals on Navajo's sacred Dinétah. Bombs versus unchecked mining. Each one represented an ugly means to an uglier end. Each brought annihilation. Each pillaged on a macro-scale what individual pot hunters destroyed on a local level.

"The chute, the chute," Whitey bellowed, stabbing his massive arm in front of Trixie. "My millions!" Words churned like waves crashing on a rocky shoreline. A mass of uneven teeth floated like kelp between thick lips.

A sign affixed to the chute warned: Clearance 23'6". Trixie sighed. As high as the cargo bed appeared, she knew her uncle had modified it for a seventeen-foot clearance. Whitey was on autopilot, fixated on nabbing $15 million in cash. He coasted into the ten-acre clearing. The 90-car train stood idle; the silo straddled several railcars. Four engines protruded like a turtle's head. Unlike diesel locomotives, electric engines were quiet. An eerie, deathly silence hung over the rail yard.

A large moving truck was parked next to a black Mercedes SUV. Both faced back toward the highway. A man stood as erect as a Roman soldier, ten feet from his SUV chariot. He was handsome and extremely tall, arborescent in stature. A foreboding line composed of thin lips spanned the width of his face. Exceptionally dark sunglasses hid his eyes. Whitey hated him at first sight. Trixie was frightened. She smelled a trap. The tall one stood statuesque in his trademark stance. He waved his arms in an arc, like an airport spotter, for Whitey to park alongside the big truck. Twelve bodyguards were positioned strategically in the yard. They made no pretense of hiding. Each muscleman weighed in excess of 350 pounds. Each gripped an assault rifle. Semiautomatic handguns were holstered at their waists. They sported protective armor over tight black shirts.

"Piece a cake," Whitey boasted. Blood soaked through his shirt. The titan was too strong to drop. A tree didn't fall with one whack from an axe. He forged ahead even with a smashed chest and protruding manubrium. "Ain't scared of that beanpole twerp. Nor the jerks protecting him. Man's lost his marbles. Looks like a thug convention. This Injun junk ain't *that* special. Ready for some fun, little lady?"

BREWSTER stood at the head of a conference table. Images of Inner Ruin projected onto a screen. Maps and diagrams covered the table. He spoke enthusiastically to his crew chiefs, those who would supervise the excavation in Snow Flat Canyon. The clock read 11:31 am. A lab assistant swung open the door. "Sir, you just received an urgent e-mail. It's from Señor Mendoza in Santiago. I think you should read it." She left the door ajar. He invited his handpicked crew to read over his shoulder.

It began like a transcontinental cable would have decades earlier: "URGENT URGENT URGENT STOP 'SMOKING GUN' DISCOVERED STOP MUST READ PRIOR TO SNOW FLAT CANYON EXPEDITION STOP MOST CONFIDENTIAL FILE ATTACHED STOP

"Dear Phillip:

"I am pleased to make your acquaintance through cyberspace. Your distinguished career is highly admired at our Institute.

"Yes, formalities will come later. What I am about to tell you is of utmost urgency. It contains an oral history interview between a centenarian resident of Easter Island and our Institute. The interview was conducted two days ago. His message is almost prophetic; its timing incredulous. It is the smoking gun we've been searching for. The words he speaks are miraculously close to the Institute's research goals. We have sought a breakthrough such as this for over a decade. I am beginning to believe in what you call Hemingway Luck.

"Now, my astute colleague, as Norte Americanos would say, 'I hope I'm not putting the cart before the horse', for we stand on the threshold of mankind's most significant revelation. You, Dr. Brewster, stand poised to liberate humans from our galaxy. The odyssey will begin when you discover the missing fragment. Physical barriers denying access to parallel universes will disintegrate as readily as the Berlin Wall.

"Consider, for example, what happens when I hold my arm up to the light. Yes, it casts a shadow. That very shadow gives the viewer an idea of *what* object cast the shadow. And its approximate dimensions. Likewise with *Make-make's* energy field. When we enter the deity's unique eye orbits, we'll cross a physical threshold. We won't simply see the shadow and guess what we're looking at. Instead, we'll see across broad spatial and temporal scales into parallel universes. We will see *multidimensionality*.

"The interview was conducted by my senior assistant, Consuela Trinidad, PhD. Her chief duties are to record the oral histories of centenarian natives residing on Easter Island. Longevity is the hallmark of rural islanders. Males particularly. Census figures taken in 2000 report the rate of centenarians to be significantly higher than in mainland Chile. The instant this particular oral history was completed, she contacted me. That evening, she transcribed it and personally delivered it to my home. It was 2:00 am. I studied it thoroughly and reviewed it with her until daybreak. She articulated the centenarian's gestures, facial expressions and the like which don't translate onto audio tape. Presently, his account is uncertified. As you know, certification is an elaborate process. It mandates a review by related scientific disciplines, not the least of which are linguistic and ethno-archaeological scholars. You have undertaken such processes during your career too. As I said, the timing here is magical. Please download this specimen of Hemingway Luck now."

Brewster's heart pounded. He looked at his four associates, eyes glued to the monitor, necks outstretched like bridling. He clicked his mouse and the file materialized before their eyes.

Date: Sunday, 22 May 2005
Interviewer: C. Trinidad, Institute for Advanced Cultural Studies, Universidad de Chile
Subject Interviewed: Nata Rapu Paoa. An Honorary Degree in Philosophy, Mathematical Sciences and Physics from the Universidad was conferred upon Señor Paoa in 1985.
Residence: A tiny hamlet, 4 kilometers southwest of Hanga Roa, Easter Island, Chile
Date of Birth: Spring, 1891
Qualification: This transcript has not been certified. His dialogue is an ancient derivative of Rapa Nui. Certain phrases contain a blend of Polynesian and Spanish languages. In the Institute's opinion, certification will not materially alter the dialect recorded or the validity of the subject's account. One additional qualification is noteworthy. Señor Paoa's great-grandson was present. His purpose was to ensure the subject understood each question. Otherwise, he remained silent. The responses are entirely those of the subject.
Institute: "Please tell us about yourself and where you live."
Paoa: "I am Nata Rapu Paoa. My life spans 114 years. I am in very good health. My vision is clear. I live in the shadows of volcano Rano Kao. In a hamlet of caves. My ancestors have lived there since the beginning of time. Generations of stone carvers have lined our caves with stone masonry. The stones interlock with stone mortise and tenon. It is art. My home is comfortable. Our hamlet is sacred. The volcano is sacred. The shadows are sacred. They protect us."
Institute: "What is, or perhaps was, your occupation, your art form?"
Paoa: "My hands carved stone. Here, observe for yourself, disfigured and scarred from creative work. My mother's ancestors were chosen by the Creator for this work. Stone carvers and stone masons are the trades of her lineage. My ancestors sculpted the massive *moai* revered the world over. They were masterful engineers. Each *moai* was crafted in honor of smaller obsidian statuettes carved nearly 20,000 years ago.

"My father's lineage is of the spiritual realm. He descended from shamans ordained by *Make-make.* My great-great-grandfather passed down spiritual legacies to me. The gifts were given to him by his great-great-grandfather. So it goes with spiritual legacies. Passed down to each generation for all of time. Twenty-five years ago, I fulfilled my obligation to my great-great-grandson. His son is seated next to me today.

"Through ceremony, my father's lineage taught universal song and dance. To manifest the divine wellbeing of all human spirits. Sacrifice and penance have no place in our teachings. Our celebrants honor all life. In matters of spirit, their wisdom transcends earth's plane and aligns with extra-spatial dimensions. That is the source...the center of all wisdom. Shamans access the source in parallel universes by entering our creator statue's eyes. Long, long ago, these teachings were inscribed as symbols on ceremonial stone objects. Only my father's clan understood these inscriptions. They became our spiritual legacy. They embodied wisdom, not spoken language as we are undertaking."

Institute: "Tell us about these writings on stone."

Paoa: "Each symbol is a picture which transmits wisdom. Our Creator, *Make-make*, anointed shamans with great talents to journey far beyond this Island. To destinations exhibiting energy frequencies identical to *Make-make's*. Each ceremony was adorned with exotic feathers placed in small, flat vessels. One, and only one, shaman pilgrimage carried with it *twelve such vessels incised with symbols forming the code*. That pilgrimage also journeyed with thirty statues carved from obsidian - spirit stones from the belly of our volcano which erupted long ago. Here, I show you a similar one, carved by my great-grandmother."

Institute: "Thank you. It's truly exquisite. Señor Paoa, please return to the writings, the symbols."

Paoa: "Yes. Symbols were inscribed on only twelve plume holders. That pilgrimage departed northeast from Isla de Pascua on a coastal migration route 18,000 years ago. Ice had retreated from the last Andean glacial epoch. To comprehend what I am saying, you have to believe in the mystic, in things unknowable and invisible, in mystery and wonder. The symbols form an ideogram. When deciphered, its code contains precise instructions on how to access *Make-make's* eyes, and thus his energy. Once accessed, it will solve riddles which have perplexed the world's greatest minds - spiritual leaders, mathematicians and astrophysicists to name a few.

"Unlocking *Make-make's* force field will also explain *why* the giant statues on our island are constructed a certain way, *why* certain ones face the directions they do, and *how* their energy lines connect to energy sources throughout this planet. Citizens of this world may not be prepared to hear this, young lady, but those energy convergences also align with vortices in parallel universes. When viewed through those dimensions, mankind will see with its own eyes the answer to hundreds of baffling puzzles. For example, lines inscribed without apparent meaning in the Peruvian desert. In fact, they align with interstellar vortices. As do our own sacred statues on Isla de Pascua. The alignment of the Stonehenge *moai* in England and the positioning of the Great Pyramids in Egypt - all are accessible through *Makemake's* mysterious eyes - eyes humans can pass through if they possess the secret code.

"The cosmos will be mapped out for all to comprehend. The spiritual realm will be embraced by all. Discord and wars could cease. You will view all this and much more through interstellar vision. You must also know this: the government of the Estados Unidos has partially developed such capability. With some degree of success. However, such brilliant scientists were hushed, isolated and locked up as lunatics. They vanished forever. Just like witnesses to extraterrestrial beings near Roswell, New Mexico and UFOs near Area 51 in Nevada. Their government guards such discoveries as top-secret. Yes, Señora Trinidad, perhaps mankind has not evolved enough to embrace this knowledge."

There was a knock on Brewster's door. "Sir, there's a Mr. Coldditz here to see you. He's downstairs in the lobby. Says it's extremely urgent."

"Ah, please tell him I'll be a few minutes."

"I can't, he's causing a scene! Extremely adamant. Even pushy. Insists on seeing you immediately. Says it's a matter of national security. His eyes keep honing-in on his laptop. That and his watch, which he looks at every other second. Says he'll keep you only five minutes."

"Tell him I'll be right down." He stood, eyes still fixed on the computer screen. "Let's read the Institute's next question and response, okay, crew? Then I'll go. You can continue reading without me. I'll remember where I left off."

Institute: "Where are these twelve sacred plume holders?"

Paoa: "Shaman migration routes are secret. Civilizations sought movement. Their capacity to travel developed more rapidly than what is believed. We learn about global migration routes by accessing multidimensional time. You will see it with your own eyes too, how cultures dispersed throughout earth's history, from the sparsely used land bridge in the Bering Strait to migrations leading from Mesopotamia, to waves of emigrants traversing Asian Steppes, to oceanic voyages by Norsemen and Polynesian cultures, including seafarers braving waters off the Kamchatka Peninsula. Indeed, Señora Trinidad, there was no *one* migration route into both Americas.

"Ancestral migrations cannot be understood using today's measurement of time. Or spatial dimensions. The Creator teaches that time too is multidimensional. That it is not linear. That time is more like holographic circles spiraling upward into extra-spatial dimensions. Events are accessible whether they occurred recently or in previous generations. If you view time in such dimensions, possessing ever-expanding cylindrical components, some of which, as I say, spiral up and outward, then you will perceive time no differently than the spiraling DNA molecule within our genes. DNA is the blueprint for life. Time follows that blueprint. Time contains its own genetic code and once that code is deciphered, mankind will access and travel in multidimensional existences. Some call it teleportation. Time has no hidden dimensions. Now, Señora Trinidad, please understand this: *spiral forms are symbolized in the twelve plume holders.* One particular symbol is repeated on each feather holder. Spiral shapes hold the key to all wisdom. You shall comprehend all this for yourself someday, Señora. *Make-make* holds the key to this wisdom."

Brewster left and returned eight minutes later, quicker than he anticipated. He joined his crew in-progress. He added that he was supposed to meet again with his visitor in thirty minutes. In his office, after he'd finished reading Mendoza's e-mail; as was the man calling himself Coldditz seated in a corner of the museum, glued to his laptop. He was reading the very same e-mail from Mendoza, compliments of Brownstone.

Brewster and his crew read on:

Institute: "But the location? Please, Señor Paoa, return to *where* the twelve artifacts may be found."

Paoa: "The pilgrimage that was dispatched 18,000 years ago vanished. Legend holds they were teleported via *Make-make* through a vortex of brilliant energy. Shamans would have cached their sacred possessions before such an event. That cache would have included the twelve incised plume holders. They have yet to be found. Mankind has been incapable of accessing parallel universes since that catastrophic event. Then, tragically, many thousands of years later, wars decimated *Make-make's* clan. Atrocities beyond your wildest imagination were committed, akin to raging and unabated cultural wildfires. By our count, those battles occurred forty generations ago. By your count, that approximates A.D. 500. Clan members were on the verge of reconstructing and deciphering the ideogram. There have been no efforts to continue their quest since that time. The lost feather holders must be found! We *must* access *Make-make's* eye orbits, our portal to the Creator's energy source. Regaining our ability to view multidimensional worlds is the **only way** to enable mankind to save Planet Earth. *If we don't, mankind will destroy this planet and all life as we know it.* That, Señora, is the magnitude of our dilemma.

"Fortuitously, last month I discovered an ancient text cleverly concealed behind a false stone wall in my great-grandfather's cave-home. I believe it contains clues concerning the location of the perished pilgrimage. I may be the only person on this plane of existence holding this knowledge. Recall the *one* symbol repeated on all twelve artifacts - an arc which connects what looks like two religious crosses. According to shamanistic teachings, the arc symbol represents the connectivity of all people through dance and ritual. Dance manifests connectivity of spirit more than any other human movement.

"However, members of *Make-make's* clan have a secret interpretation of the double cross-arc motif. The symbol is not two crosses. It replicates intersecting spirals, in other words, connectivity on multidimensional planes of existence, in all universes. It is impossible to explain these principles in four-dimensional imagery. The external world is defined by four dimensional space-time matrixes. That paradigm must be breached. NOW! Someday, perhaps, mankind will graphically illustrate DNA migratory patterns. Señora, I am tiring. Will we be much longer?"

Institute: "I have only one additional question, Señor Paoa. You may continue only if you are able to. Otherwise, we could schedule a continuation in three day's time. Where, I beseech you, astute elder, may we discover the incised plume holders and thirty small statuettes?"

Paoa:..."The...motif...provides...clues...of...location...incised vessels...must find whirlwinds...connected by...electrical...*Make-make* is the custodian of all energy...including what we call electricity. The incised plume holders are also custodians of his energy. Today we refer to *Make-make's* giant statue and other *moai*, our *oringa ora*, as 'electric ancestors.' That is not disrespectful. We do not mock ancestral heritage, Señora. It is simply the truth. Explore desert environs...you shall see whirlwinds...**you shall find electric ancestors**..."

Institute: "At this juncture, Señor Paoa's dialogue veered from the question at hand. His energy waned. Indeed, he was tiring. Reliability of his account would be compromised if he continued. The centenarian's head bobbed during episodes of drifting off. He slumped in the chair. His great-grandson stood to prop him up. Then a macabre statement flowed from his lips, even though he appeared to be sleeping."

Paoa: "Find *Make-make's* clan symbol in the landscape. Find an arch...our sacred double cross-arc symbol...an energy vortex will be close by...as will whirlwinds. Such a landscape is connected to Isla de Pascua. Both force fields are connected. The twelve plume holders will..."

Institute: "The time is 7:54 pm. The subject is sleeping peacefully. This oral history interview is concluded."

Brewster and his associates returned to the text of Mendoza's e-mail:

"By this time tomorrow, I intend to transmit one additional centenarian oral history. It elucidates a very significant historical event mentioned by Señor Paoa - the massacre during an incursion of rival clan factions. Archaeological evidence puts the date of those battles at approximately 1,500 years ago, at the end of the fifth century AD. Oral histories *do* in fact allude to *Make-make's* clan having made progress in deciphering the code prior to its decimation. If Chao is successful, the time is right to usher in a new era for our planet's 7 billion human inhabitants.

"Lastly, I encourage you to acquaint yourself with ancient teachings relative to spirals, rotating columns of energy, whirlpools or whirlwinds. And their relationship to origin myths, creation symbolism and sacred rituals. Perhaps Señor Paoa is correct. Perhaps an abundance of whirlwinds will provide clues. Clearly, Dr. Brewster, a man of your eminence must have a worldwide network of indigenous elders who can enlighten you. We sit on the edge of our seats awaiting your discovery."

Sincerely,
Alonzo Milad de Mendoza, Senior Fellow
Institute for Advanced Cultural Studies
Universidad de Chile

The readers were stupefied. No one spoke. He circled the room and came to a stop next to his massive file safe. He propped both elbows on it. "The wise old man is indeed prophetic. He could be absolutely correct. Mankind may *not* be prepared for what *Make-make* has to offer. Look back just five short years. To how anticipation of a new millennium had people, prompted by our own government, freaked out. To how it encouraged stockpiling commodities, establishing highway escape routes, and safeguarding financial and computer records beyond reasonable measures. What would happen if those same people peeked into parallel universes? What if they saw themselves in a parallel dimension? Same person, different context. What if they peered through time and saw how history really unfolded *instead of what they'd been taught?* Are people ready to view earth's 14-billion-year lifespan? What will become of life's purpose if all riddles are solved? Yes, I'm afraid very few of us are ready for all that!"

"Sir," replied a youthful crew chief, "we have our smoking gun. I'd like to petition you here and now to join your team when you visit

Easter Island. If and when we discover the missing feather holder. After Dr. Chao decodes the ideogram. I'm ready for what Señor Paoa said. *I want to visit that place he described.* Think of it. Isn't it high time we burst out of our linear existence and expanded our scope of time and life? To paraphrase Señor Paoa - it's been too many generations since mankind has had that capacity. Not since the fifth century, for God's sake. Well, I seek that wisdom. There must be vastly more to life than what's contained in our Milky Way. I, sir, am one who believes there is. Really I do. If we have the capability, we should go for it. *We must go for it.* People the centenarian cited in Roswell and Nevada and scores more throughout the globe - they are not crazy, Dr. Brewster. You know that! I want to be there when we take that first step through those white coral and red capstone eye sockets. Teleportation sounds outrageous. Please, Dr. Brewster?"

Brewster smiled. He admired her boldness. And her courage. He'd observed several heads nodding during her discourse. "Miss Turner, crew, let's find the missing artifact first. Then we'll worry about traveling to Easter Island. Like Mendoza himself said, please don't put the cart before the horse." He looked up at the clock. "Why don't we all take a thirty-minute break? I'll meet with that Coldditz man for a second time. We'll reconvene in the conference room at 1:20."

He printed two copies of Mendoza's e-mail and its attachment. He stamped them "confidential" and placed one in his laptop case. The other was placed in his file safe with the feather holder. He reached down, anxious for a sense of touch, a reality check, to cradle the ancient ceremonial artifact in his palm. Connectivity, a link to his five senses *and* to several recent e-mails.

Preparations were complete. He and his crew would leave Flagstaff later that afternoon. The drive to Mexican Hat would take five hours. Accommodations at Goosenecks Lodge adjoining the Anasazi Café were set. Tomorrow morning, they'd establish a field camp at the rim of Snow Flat Canyon. The man waiting downstairs hadn't discussed anything even remotely linked to national security. Perhaps he was waiting for their second conversation. However, Brewster had already decided one clandestine encounter was enough. He wanted out of the cloak and dagger business. Thus, he would not inform his visitor of Chao's secret message. Or Mendoza's e-mail.

Before joining him, he looked again into the Ponderosa forest surrounding the museum. The face of an acquaintance surfaced in his mind. He knew just the person who could help. Fifteen miles west of Hubbell Trading Post in Ganado, Arizona was the Chapter House at Steamboat Canyon. A certain Navajo elder named Leonard Atcitty lived nearby. He went by Lenny. His sister, Rosita Windsong, lived in

Steamboat Canyon. Atcitty lived on higher ground on Balakai Mesa. Brewster recalled that the view from his hogan was arguably more stunning than any other on Navajo land. From his elevated perch, he could see eighty miles, beyond Canyon de Chelly, to the Lukachukai Mountains. There, on practically any day, partially concealed in a veil of dust, was a vortex of energy where the Chuska and Carrizo mountains joined the Lukachukai. He knew Lenny Atcitty was a Navajo elder disciplined in ancient spiritual rituals. He was familiar with every folk tale, creation myth and origin story. He was a visionary, a crystal gazer, capable of viewing multiple planes of existence, past and future. Brewster wondered if he knew of a landscape feature alluded to by Paoa. A geological formation revered by the Navajo. And the best part - the principal reason he would detour and visit the elder - Atcitty understood the ancient teachings of whirlwinds. Better than any Native in North America. Atcitty knew. He could help.

WAINWRIGHT'S buffoons were clustered about the yard. Whitey noted the exact location of all twelve. The killer from Cleveland had faced similar scenes hundreds of times before. On Cleveland's sordid street corners, in dilapidated housing projects and abandoned warehouses. His eyes were ablaze. He drooled. The titan was ready. He looked at Trixie. She'd already bid farewell to his gentler side. The side that had nourished her and eased her aches and pains. At that moment, she only saw Monster Hyde the gladiator, readied for combat. It was a reality check - nice as he had been, her fate still clung to a deranged madman.

He swung open the door and jumped to the ground, legs spread wide. It was the moment he'd waited for. Six of Wainwright's goons stepped forward. Others adjusted their stance. Whitey scouted them again, making eye contact with each one, chuckling confidently in the process. The electric train sat silent. It would roll through the silo when the command was given. An Indian stood erect near the operations shack, bearing a half-toothed grin and glazed-over eyes, staring at nothing in particular. Whitey stepped with confidence toward the moving van, gobbling up dirt in five foot strides. The six closed in. Wainwright donned one of his masks, a thin-lipped smile spread wide. From Whitey's distance, it resembled baling wire attached to each ear.

"Might I ask who in the hell *you* are? Where's McAllister? What kind of game you playing?" Whitey was mute. The thug squadron inched closer. Wainwright stared at Whitey's blood-soaked yet energetic physique. "What the hell's that sticking out of your chest? You spill a bucket of KFC on your shirt? Where's your manners?" When Wainwright laughed, a chorus of hoarse laughs echoed from the goon choir. "I asked you a question, freak-man, where in the hell's McAllister? He's the only one I'll deal with."

Whitey's eyes bore straight through the black lenses. He sidestepped to avoid the glaring corona. "You must be Slick from Santa Fe, huh? I'm here to tell you that Mac got rolled before we reached Kay-Enta. Stepped outside to admire the sandy scenery."

"Damn Indians. Kayenta's full of them. Tried to warn him. So who in the hell are you? My deal's with McAllister, not you. Deal's off." He turned his back.

Whitey knew he was bluffing. He remembered Mac's sermon about Slick from Santa Fe. He knew a fortune had been promised to the shady antiquities dealer. He remembered that Slick had a traitorous lover working for the government. He knew she was addicted to Indian artifacts. "I'm Whitey." He stood erect and flexed his finger stubs. They transformed into lethal weapons. Wainwright hadn't walked ten feet. "You know who I am if you know Mac. Everyone who knows Mac knows me. Deal's not off. Quit bluffing, quit stalling. I want my millions. All of it. The Indian junk's in the back. Just like Mac said it'd be." He jerked his thumb over his shoulder. Trixie stiffened. All eyes pointed her way. Wainwright saw a scraggly head and bright orange.

"Where'd you get that piece of trash? Hitchhiking?" His caustic question offended Whitey. He hadn't decided what to do with Trixie, but he wanted to keep her out of harm's way. "Or is that a prison suit she's wearing?"

"None of your birdbrain business."

His piano-wire lips stretched to the snapping point. He rubbed his chin, slithering sideways to trap Whitey in the sun again. "You know? Come to think of it, I *have* heard about you. I heard you're real tough. Well, freak-man, you'll never fight off my army. Right, men?" His assault team stomped forward. Whitey moved at right angle to elude the glare. Wainwright's little game wasn't working. "On the other hand, being the nice guy I am, perhaps we could negotiate a little deal..."

"*I don't negotiate.* Quit messing around. Same deal as Mac's. Period. $15 million. Cash. Understand? Or should I start busting heads and breaking bodies right in front of you."

Horace laughed in Whitey's face, waving his goons closer. "I kill for a living, Mr. Skinnyshit." Cocky grins spread among the thugs. "You musta heard. Me Whitey, Impossible to Kill." He pounded his chest for emphasis, never flinching, even with a mangled sternum. "In case you ain't heard, Mr. Skinnyshit, I crack people in half. End up in two pieces. Don't matter how big they are. I can start right now or we can shake hands and deal. Same price as Mac's. Fifteen million bucks. What's it going to be? Choice is yours." He stood like a fairytale giant, crossing his arms and taking three steps forward. Finger stubs extended.

Horace held up an arm. "Hold on, men. Let's see your merchandise, joker. See if you're for real."

"It's all packed up. Me and Mac was careful. Hundreds and hundreds of junky old Indian pieces. Maybe a dozen of these too. Found this one lying around. It's mine now." Whitey un-pocketed the twenty-millennia-old artifact and held it in the sunlight. "Gave one to Mac for good luck before he was rolled. Didn't want to see him die." Wainwright lunged at Whitey and tried to grab it. Whitey recoiled at lightning speed. "Just for looks."

"Must be the other half of what I bought in Santa Fe last fall. I'll make sure my army keeps it in one piece before they rip you apart, limb by ugly limb. I'll get my hands back on the other half too. Both halves will fetch at least a million bucks. I promised all twelve to my lady associate."

The titan knew he was back in the game. He had everything the slimebag dealer wanted. He clutched his ante tightly. "Let's get down to business."

Wainwright signaled his flunkies. One of the brutes opened expansive moving van doors. Wainwright opened the door to the cab and removed two classy leather briefcases. Their handles were inlaid with turquoise, silver conchas laced the borders. Obviously ritzy designer goods from Santa Fe. He scraped a smooth patch in the gravel and placed both suitcases side by side. He stooped and touched a concha on each. They clicked open. $100 bills filled Whitey's vision. Neatly stacked in tight rows. "There's $7.5 million in each briefcase. That's how Mac wanted it. All in hundreds. You'll get them both when the transfer's complete." He waved his hand. Eight musclemen appeared instantly. The other four leveled their rifles. "Men, move everything from his tall truck into my moving van. Be quick about it. And be *extremely* careful. Anyone drops anything, they're cut from our deal."

THIRTY-NINE

It took fourteen minutes to transfer a vanished civilization's artifacts from one truck to the other. Crafted by artisans two hundred centuries earlier, transported by shamans two millennia later, preserved in a secret chamber in southeast Utah for 17,500 years. Fourteen minutes didn't even register as a percent on most calculators. Seemed shameful.

Wainwright selected four crates at random. His flunkies unwrapped their contents. He inspected the goods with the expert eye of an antiquities dealer. "Looks genuine. Seal them crates tight, men." Large doors at the rear of the truck swung shut. He stepped away and called Two Tree. Cell phone to cell phone. The NSA intercept was child's play. They gleaned what they needed. The Ute sat in his control shack 300 feet away. He slobbered through an ugly grin and yanked a lever to start the conveyor. He was wasted. Large bundles of cash and a huge stash of white "powder" were tucked away in a bag next to him. He planned to escape the instant the railcars were loaded. He spoke into a two-way radio. Within seconds, the train jerked. Loud metal clanks echoed as couplings between railcars responded. Like giant dominos, inch by inch at first, the 90-car train snaked through the silo until it crawled at two miles per hour. Wainwright watched as his dream materialized. Instead of sub-bituminous coal, weapons-grade uranium ore and canisters of depleted uranium began loading.

His second call was to the mole. He used a uniquely encrypted satellite phone linked to a top-secret DOE satellite. The National Security Agency, however, was one step ahead. The call was diverted to the dead mole's digital messaging service at the DOE's communication center. The NSA swooped it up high above earth. Decipherable details were instantly reviewed by Director Quay. Then Colonel Holmes. Wainwright frowned and immediately disconnected. He couldn't fathom Della not answering. They'd rehearsed that call a dozen times during the past month. It was to go off like clockwork. The instant he disconnected, the US government considered the Delilah Project consummated. Legal requirements had been met; strict protocols observed to ensure a technicality wouldn't spoil a conviction. The Captain and his force were parked one mile east on Highway 160, awaiting Coldditz's arrival. At that point, the net would drop on Peabody's Black Mesa rail yard complex.

OFFICER Blue Sky refueled in Kayenta. A cell phone was glued to his ear. "We're still awaiting his order," the Captain informed him. "Sir, I've served under Agent Coldditz on numerous missions. He's saved my life twice. If he says 'jump,' I jump. When he says 'wait,' I wait. And that's that. We *will* await his arrival! Tell Parker to cool his heels. The Gulfstream touched down in Farmington nine minutes ago. Chopper's in the air."

The NSA agent was primed and ready. His debriefing had been excruciating. Polygraph experts had dragged him over the coals. Emotionally, he was even worse off. Someone at the agency leaked details surrounding his ex-wife's preposterous assassination. He was out for blood, as gory as what he'd witnessed in the Casbah. He could practically taste it. "No one else lays hands on Wainwright before I do," he commanded from his chopper. "We're bucking a headwind silhouetting Highway 160. I'll bypass Goulding's airstrip and arrive at your convoy in 12 minutes. Lieutenant Marling will meet me. Remember, I get that skinny sleazebag first. All to myself. Let the Navajo cop go after Whitey. Parker too if he's up to it."

WHITEY stood twenty feet from Wainwright. His eyes darted beyond him to the train. It slinked forward silently. "You know," said Horace, "every kid growing up before the digital age begged for a train set." He spoke as though they were old friends. Eyes fixed on the massif, he pointed to the train by jerking his thumb. An old-fashioned umpire's signal, before television dramatized it. "Can't quite picture you as a kid, though. Bet you just sprouted up one day into the ignoramus, stump-headed freak you are now."

"Don't give a damn about kids, skinny shit. Or their dumb train sets. Deal's done. Truck's loaded. Train's rolling. You got your Indian junk. Now give me the briefcases. Fifteen million bucks." He glanced at signs above the train, reading skills rudimentary at best. Pictographic road signs cautioning drivers of dangers in descending the Moki Dugway were easy to comprehend. But oversized four-by-six-foot warning signs posted throughout Peabody's yard were unreadable. Yet, on a certain level, he knew they were important. Each sign was the same. Each painted with internationally recognizable red background and reflective white lettering. "DANGER. 50,000 KILOVOLTS OVERHEAD."

Wainwright's true motive engaged. He got down to business, shrinking his baling wire smirk to a rancorous, bent nail. His gallery of goons spewed ugly snarls. "You freak," he shouted, "you couldn't pull off a real man's job if you tried. You're just a dimwitted Cleveland bozo standing in for your boss. Trying to make a fast buck. Indians near Kayenta my ass. I'll bet you the entire truckload *you* killed your boss."

Whitey's chest swelled like a puff adder. His eyes turned molten, finger stubs forged into steel. Wainwright was impressed. He admired courageous opponents. He stepped back, raised his hand and snapped his fingers. Words shot like bullets from tight lips. "Take care of this stumpy freak, will you boys?" A swarm of bloodthirsty thugs raced toward Whitey, springing like ravenous attack dogs. The pack's leader launched first, growling in midair, mouth opened wide. "Men, when you're done felling that ugly tree, block him and stack him like firewood next to the tracks." He remained cool and calm, as though ordering from a menu at his favorite restaurant. He glanced over at the second assault team next to the tracks, yelling to the team's leader. "Antonio, on second thought, instead of stacking him like firewood, toss each piece into the last railcar. Give him an early morning excursion to Page, compliments of Horace Wainwright, all expenses paid."

Pandemonium broke loose. The leader completed his flight path with a growl. Whitey stood calmer than a bored security guard at an empty store. His grizzly paw met the thug during his final approach, infamous vise grip crushing the man's skull like a popcorn ball. A second attacker sprang for the Cleveland killer. Whitey skewered his stubs through his throat like a spear fisherman. His 360-pound catch kicked and quivered like a giant tuna. He lowered his other hand and lanced the goon's chest, piercing his heart. He tightened his grip and exhaled nauseous breath through ugly teeth. The man's blank stare met Whitey's eyes, he gurgled like a flushed toilet and keeled over backwards, dead before hitting the ground.

Three more bodyguards gave it a go. They launched into the air with legs compressed like skilled kick boxers. Their trajectory appeared graceful, almost theatrical. One massive fist and Whitey's stump-skull met each pair of feet in midair. Every bone in their feet smashed like glass. Compound fractures pierced their calves, bleeding profusely. Whitey jumped high in the air and brought down one foot on those attackers. One buffoon's chest flattened completely, his lungs and heart crushed. He died within seconds. The other man was even less fortunate. Whitey's left boot landed on his neck like a guillotine. His head rolled off to the side, eyes wide open, staring back at the rest of his body. The third lay dead, skull an oozing pulp.

A sixth muscleman turned and ran away. Whitey easily overtook him, breaking both legs in a merciless tackle. He picked up the 375-pound thug, held him horizontally, and turned to face Wainwright. The dealer, scared shitless, clung like a gecko to the moving van's door, feebly clutching his .22 caliber pistol.

"Hey, skinny shit, see this?" He yelled triumphantly, standing in the center of the clearing like a gladiator. He was in his zone, ready to take on the whole world. "You said you'd heard about me, right? Then you know what I can do. This!" Displaying supreme strength, he raised his right leg in a marching step and brought the man down with the force of an elevator. The man's spinal cord snapped in two. As did his frayed body. Victorious, Whitey separated the halves and slung each limp mass over his right arm. They hung limply like dead eels. "Six down, six to go." He dropped the two-piece corpse. "Who's next?" he asked, turning in a circle and rubbing his palms.

Four thugs sprinted from the tracks to the moving van. Seized in a deluge of self-centered fear, Wainwright cowardly climbed in and locked the doors. Next, he crawled into the rear cab where drivers bedded down. One of the men smashed the window and snatched both suitcases. A dumb move. The four warriors raced back to the tracks where the other two frightfully waited. The train inched ahead at three miles per hour. Two-thirds of the railcars were filled. Two Tree smeared his face against the window. Saliva covered the glass. His heart raced at the speed of light. It nearly cost him his life. He'd snorted cocaine and watched the action like a captivated moviegoer inhaling popcorn. He cheered the massif on, never feeling threatened himself. Wainwright still needed him and Whitey had no score to settle with him. Deep down, he hoped the thin-lipped bastard would be slaughtered too. He despised his contemptuous attitude toward Natives. And his stash was big enough to last him awhile.

Whitey snatched an FN FAL assault rifle from the closest corpse. He took aim and picked off two men before they could reach the tracks. He turned and shot out the moving truck's front tires, then shot the windshield out to keep Wainwright at bay. $15 million lay in suitcases next to a lead-filled thug. He swiveled to face the remaining gunmen - and froze - locked in the sights of *four* assault rifles.

With incredible speed, he raced to the rear of his over height truck and reached inside for the twenty-pound winch bar. The other hand clutched his favorite ally - the spool of aircraft cable. Orange. He yanked open the passenger door and laid Trixie's cabled body sideways, out of the line of fire. Then he charged the shooters, raising the spool as a shield, clutching the winch bar like a Neanderthal club. "Hey, bozos, how about a barbeque? Who's first?"

Two Tree was mesmerized. "Best flick I seen in years. What the hell you got up your sleeve next?"

Bullets ricocheted off Whitey like harmless gumballs. He reached the center of the rail yard and stood tall and proud, turning in each direction and bowing victoriously like a gladiator claiming victory. Like George Bush on the deck of an aircraft carrier weeks into the doomed Iraqi invasion. He fixed his eyes like gunnery sights, prowling like a cheetah on the Serengeti. One man made a getaway next to the tracks, arms mercifully outstretched to board the slow rolling train.

Whitey raised his weapon like an Iroquois cocking his tomahawk. He released it with the force of a missile and it flew as fast as one, end over end, with guidance-system accuracy, striking the man squarely in his back. It didn't stop there. The twenty-pound lance pierced straight through him and continued airborne, clanging like Big Ben against the railcar. Stupefied and unable to breathe, the googly-eyed victim jerked sideways. The cauterization left a hole wide enough to see through. He resembled a human clothespin, mouth gurgling, torso opened from neck to belt. Not yet dead. He stumbled in vain toward the haven of steel slipping quietly by, collapsing onto the tracks between passing wheels. Sliced clean through as though the train had been doing eighty.

Three goons remained. Whitey glided toward them, crazed grin getting exponentially creepier, beyond sick. He was on a roll and couldn't stop. From his depths, he bellowed a mantra made famous by Ed McMahon: "Heeeeeeeere's Whitey!" He glanced up at the train's electric lines. Enough juice to power four 6,000-horsepower locomotives hauling 90 railcars loaded with 100 tons each. "Well, gents, whaddaya say we string us up a tasty rotisserie?"

Catenary is the official term for the maze of electric lines that runs above train tracks. It was a giant spider web over the NGS's main rail yard in Page. But where they stood at the silo yard, the catenary was minimal. The pantograph connects the locomotive to the catenary lines. It is the train's umbilical cord. Locomotives can only travel when the pantograph makes contact with the catenary. Whitey studied the setup closely. He'd seen it before, at the rapid transit train connecting Shaker Heights to downtown Cleveland. Where he'd offed many an affluent commuter.

He looked twenty feet to his right. The severed thug lay next to the tracks. Three surviving thugs scrambled for their lives. They knew what he had in mind. It wasn't rocket science - buzzing electric lines, his invite to a barbeque and rotisserie, and his invincibility. Frantically, they scaled up a railcar ladder. When they reached the narrow edge, they balanced like trapeze artists. The sheer mass of these 375-pound hired killers proved too top-heavy, however. Rabid and panicked, two of them leapt like wild monkeys to the catenary above. Miraculously, they made it. Dangling, their legs peddled frantically in midair.

The third man jumped into the railcar. His fate forever and horrifically sealed. He'd melt like cheese smothering an omelet. Whitey looked up at both monkey-thugs clinging for their lives, safe from electrocution until contact was made with another object. Two Tree radioed the operator to keep rolling. The train was fully loaded, its last railcar emerging from the silo.

Whitey quickly tied off one end of the cable to a railcar ladder, then picked up the bottom half of the severed brute and kept pace with the train. A race against time. At four miles per hour, the cable unwound rapidly. After 100 feet, he cut it and tied that end around the corpse's torso. He hurled the corpse-counterweight high in the air. It arced over the catenary. When it came down, it triggered a light show as spectacular as any on the Fourth of July. The railcar attached to the cable glowed like the sun. A cloud of gas spewed upward. Whitey heard screams from the cargo bed. Thug number ten melted instantly. Bodies number eleven and twelve twisted furiously. They sizzled, smoldered and popped like bug zappers at a burger stand in July. The train instantly shorted out. Its brakes locked and the wheels seized with a deafening screech. Putrid fumes engulfed the rail yard. Some were toxic.

Whitey raced to the briefcases, then turned and faced the moving van. He loudly proclaimed his defining legacy: "Me Whitey...Impossible to Kill." Wainwright was not in view. He pressed the magic concha and the ritzy briefcase popped open. There it was. $7.5 million in cold hard cash. Row after row of Franklins stared up at him. He did the same with the other case. Next, he ran to his empty rental truck and lifted Trixie upright. Sirens wailed on the highway. "Hold on, sister, we're going for a joy ride. Now the fun really begins. I know how to drive. Empty, this baby ought to do 120." He stomped on the accelerator. Dust billowed.

Suddenly, the door to the moving van sprung open. Wainwright jumped to the ground. The coward raced to the train, cell phone against his ear. "God damn it, I'll give you another ten grand. It's stashed in my SUV. Help yourself after I hop on the train. Just fix the damn short. Immediately! Train's *got* to get to NGS with me on it. Hear them sirens? You got two minutes. I'll turn you in if this train isn't racing in two minutes. You'll go to prison for the rest of your life. Your family, homeless beggars. If I'm merciful. Two minutes. You decide, *Kimosabe*."

Two Tree stared at him in a stupor. Mangled corpses and severed body parts littered Whitey's coliseum. Ashes covered the ground where two bodies had hung from the catenary. It didn't take long to decide. Another $10,000 would set him up forever. Or so he figured. His crew completed the tasks quickly. He radioed the operator. The train jerked ahead and gained speed.

Wainwright sprinted alongside like an impala. Split-second timing was crucial. Sirens grew louder. He focused on jumping. Outstretched arms clamped down tight on a ladder rung. Liftoff. Arms and legs floated horizontally, lanky frame resembling a pterodactyl in flight.

307

THE chopper set down adjacent to the McDonald's parking lot in Kayenta. The team's ace driver, Lieutenant Marling, sped west with Coldditz, minutes away from Peabody's yard. The Captain's team had advanced to the entrance. Dust from Whitey's clean getaway hung over the clearing. Wainwright climbed the ladder as the train gained speed. Within minutes, four powerful locomotives reached a cruising speed of 42 mph. For the first 23 miles, its tracks ran parallel to Highway 160, a scant 100 yards west of the pavement. Then they cut a diagonal path through barren desert of the Kaibito Plateau, terminating at the Navajo Generating Station in Page, Arizona. Wainwright reached the top of the railcar and balanced on its edge. The car was empty. "That double-crossing, no good, slobbering, half-toothed Indian! He's as good as dead."

The train sped along, rocking from side to side. He looked back at Peabody's yard. Whitey's truck bounced wildly through the sagebrush until it swerved recklessly onto the highway. A fleet of official vehicles swarmed the silo complex. Wainwright tried to call the Ute. Too much electric interference from the catenary. He had to investigate the railcar in front. Perhaps it too was empty. At first, he inched forward with the delicacy of a high-wire artist. Being too tall, he lowered himself on all fours and crawled like a baby, swaying with the train's motion. An eternity passed. Finally, he reached the front of the railcar. Although he'd seen it done in movies, he didn't have the guts to stand up and leap to the car ahead. Another daring plan materialized. He'd have but one shot at it.

He climbed down four rungs, then stretched his left foot and hand out to the ladder on the front railcar. Contact. He remained spread-eagle between two railcars for a full minute, rehearsing every move, as Parker had rehearsed his escape from the diamondback. He clung for dear life by the strength in each hand. He focused hard, gaining confidence each second. Then he played a wild card gifted him at birth - his giraffe-like height. Imitating the first step of a waltz, he leaned his body to the left and joined all four limbs together. He remained paralyzed for two minutes. When he caught his breath, he ascended the ladder and straddled the top edge. Bingo! The front section of that railcar was loaded halfway to the top with uranium ore. Stacks of sealed crates occupied the rear half. He stood in wonder. Passersby on the highway gawked. Horns honked and people leaned out windows snapping pics of a madman balancing atop a speeding train.

One hundred fifty million dollars. Terrorists were waiting eighty miles away. He and Della would share endless wealth. Greed overtook him. As it had overtaken Dietrich Schisslenberg in The Land of

Walking Earth before his disappearance. And Della Schissler as she stared down at Frankfurt's financial district. He *had* to touch the ore. He *had* to peer inside one crate. Greed caused neural tissue in the cerebral cortex of his brain to dysfunction. Nanocells which normally passed signals to each other via synaptic connectors disintegrated. His neocortex became a jumbled mass of spaghetti. His genius vanished. The brilliant mastermind barterer from Santa Fe, whose mind normally functioned in complex matrices, couldn't even recall a simple warning laid out by the Ute Indian.

He gripped the edge and lowered himself into the railcar, landing with a thud on hot ore. Doomed, he may as well have leaped into a volcano. It was 11:50 am. Temperatures in northern Arizona's desert soared to 98 degrees. Air circulating above never reached the cargo depth. The ore was too hot for his feet. The soles of his city shoes melted, sticking to it like bubblegum on a hot parking lot. He clawed desperately at the rusted sides only to be burned. Temperatures at the seven-foot depth approached 170 degrees. He was entombed in a kiln. Horrifying images of a half-toothed Indian on an icy February day, grinning, drool freezing to his chin, haunted him. "You'll never be able to climb out in a million years," Tomas Two Tree had warned. "Inspectors...they go in with a harness and a top rope. Else they perish. Takes only minutes...if they don't suffocate...temperature gets them...ever see a person baked, Mr. All-American White Art Dealer? Like in a kiln?"

A procession of vehicles raced into the silo yard. Coldditz, the Captain and Blue Sky. Fourteen others trailed in their plume of dust. Streaming in single-file like the train that had just left. Appalled, no one spoke. The body-strewn war zone was not what they'd expected. "So much for the Fed's net of justice clamping down," said Howie. "All I see is mutilation."

"What *did* you expect?" Blue Sky asked. "Everyone sitting around eating Häagen-Dazs? Face it, Parker, ancient artifacts, terrorist-bound uranium and a dozen thugs aren't what you'd call party mixers." His eyes darted from body to body as though watching a tennis volley. Moving truck, scattered corpses; moving truck, more scattered corpses. Back and forth it went. He called Quirk. "What's your 10-20?"

"Four minutes out. Just passing the Anasazi Inn. What's at the silo, Officer? What can we expect?"

"Quite a blood bath, Chief Ranger. Hard to imagine how one man could be responsible for this much destruction."

Quirk raised her thermal mug. Two mouthfuls of Irish Breakfast helped. Dudley's portrayal was too graphic. Seconds later, her phone rang. A Moab number displayed. "Damn, talk about bad timing," she said to her driver. "Thought he was still in the ER." Her driver squelched the siren. "Morning again, Wheeler. Feeling better? What? Great idea. Everyone needs a good night's rest now and then. See you tomorrow around noon. Here? What's the status here?" Two more swigs of tea. "Ah, everything's fine, Semlow, just fine. We're turning into the Peabody rail yard this very second." She stared in awe at the abomination before her. "Electrifying, actually. Fill you in later. Got to go." She clicked off. Guilt strapped her tighter than the seatbelt. She'd have major explaining to do later. She despised Coldditz for keeping her best subordinate out of the loop. But she was an admirable bureaucrat who followed orders to the letter. They skidded to a halt beside Wainwright's chariot and stepped into the death zone, visibly fazed by the carnage. She walked stiff and erect to Blue Sky. The Captain and his agents were scattered about inspecting what remained of the bodies.

"Seen enough here. Come on, let's go after Whitey," Blue Sky commanded. "Can't be too far off. He opened the door for Parker and Windsong.

"Just a second," yelled Howie. "At least let me open *one* crate. Need to see some artifacts before Quirk calls Brewster to come and get them."

"Not so fast, all of you!" Coldditz shouted. "Just hold your horses. Not a single artifact is leaving this crime scene. Federal prosecutors need every ounce of evidence. As of this instant, this contraband is property of the US Department of Homeland Security."

"What? No way!" screamed Howie. "Didn't I tell you? The artifacts keep eluding our grasp, Kika. Evidence, huh? Come on, Coldditz, *you promised*. Hell, Quirk's part of the U S Government. Hand the truck over to her. I'll change the shot-out tires myself and drive it out of here. Take Highway 160 almost straight to his museum." The agent was silenced. "Don't play games here, Mr. NSA. You even promised a lot more than the artifacts, remember? Give the BLM this entire truckload. Right, Ms. Quirk?"

He passed the baton to her, but she remained stolid, as emotionless as the flat tires, still in shock over the carnage. The corpses reeked. She grew pale and nauseous. Inadequacy in times of emergency was her chief character defect. She stood stiff as a board. She should have responded with as much enthusiasm as a kid on Christmas morning. Two long minutes passed. The air was heavy with indecision. Then, out of the blue, she turned and walked gingerly to Howie's side, planting her face one foot from the agent's. "You would do your country a great service, Agent Coldditz, by transferring the entire truckload exactly as we see it. To my agency. *I'm the United States Government too, you know!* The second you've given it the once-over. Like before the sun sets today. That's all the evidence-gathering you should need. Get your fancy gadgetry over here and start documenting it at once. As soon as Parker replaces the tires, we're moving out. I'll drive it to Flagstaff myself if I have to! They absconded from *my* turf on my watch, remember?" Parker smiled. He started up the ramp and approached the crates.

Dudley never left his patrol car. He yelled out the window, head cocked uncomfortably. "Ah, not to get technical, but this here is actually *my* turf. Leased to Peabody Energy." He tapped the siren annoyingly. The light bar flashed brightly in spite of the glaring sunlight. "Come on, you two, Whitey's lead's growing."

"Have Coldditz call in one of his Sikorskys," yelled Howie. "You'll do that for us, won't you?"

Before he could reply, Blue Sky shouted the answer. "There won't be any choppers in this chase. We're doing this my way, the old-fashioned way. Nothing high-tech. Just us versus them. An old-school Indian chase across Indian country." He inched forward. "Come on. There are two dozen federal agents plus half the Navajo police force here. No one's going to steal your truck, Parker." He tapped the siren again.

Kika tugged on Howie's sleeve. "Let's go." He didn't budge. She let go and ran to the cruiser.

"Kika, wait! We're not finished here. No one's going anywhere. Not until Coldditz answers Quirk's demand and tells us he's playing ball. Willing to hand over every crate like he promised yesterday."

Coldditz walked up the ramp and met Howie. He hadn't spoken for five minutes. He stared into Howie's eyes and slowly nodded his head. Affirmative nods. Gradually, he rejoined their way of thinking. His face cracked a smile, the first gesture of any kind since they'd arrived at the massacre. "OK. I believe I can pull a few strings in Washington. The correct strings. You're right, I promised. Besides, you and Miss Windsong risked your necks to have this truck brought here. The Delilah Project is almost history. You go after your man. And those feather holders. The truck is safe with me. Remember, keep that beast alive. His partner is alive and in medical custody. Bastards will pay for what they've done."

Howie smiled and held out his hand. They shook firmly. Then he unwrapped a slender object, 18 inches long, carved from obsidian as black as Kika's eyes. It was a 20,000-year-old statuette of *Make-make*, carved by an ancient ancestor of Señor Paoa's. He carefully re-wrapped it and returned it to the crate. In a move almost as agile as his escape from the diamondback, he sprung to the ramp and sprinted behind the TrailBlazer. He never broke stride. He covered the distance in six seconds, grabbed the front door handle and climbed in. Blue Sky stomped on the accelerator. Tires spun as they fishtailed in a plume of dust. Howie had seen what he needed to see. He was ready for the chase.

HE'D run out of options. His life was slipping away as fast as the train speeding along the tracks. Attempts to breathe were futile. Unmerciful heat singed his lungs. He danced on the scalding ore like a flailing puppet tap dancing with magnetized shoes. He clutched his throat and massaged his windpipe, gasping in vain for more air. Seconds later, the slimebag dealer collapsed onto part of the $150 million payload. His miasmic sarcophagus "rocked on" at 42 mph. The staccato clickety-clack where steel wheels met rail seams played all the way to hell, providing a soundtrack for Two Tree's half-toothed, slobbering grin and bulging eyes. The Ute was right on the mark. The fancy antiquities dealer died a horrible death baked atop his treasure. The melody played on. Clickety-clack, clickety-clack.

"IF we're doing 90, then Whitey must be going faster, right?" Kika asked.

"We're gaining slightly," said Dudley. "Caught a glimpse of him a second ago. He can't escape. There's no place to go." He glanced at Howie. "He'll be all yours in a few minutes."

Trixie's uncle had followed McAllister's blueprints precisely. Besides raising its height, he swapped out the stock differential for one with a lower gear ratio and installed overdrive. The truck was capable of cruising on straightaways at 100 plus mph. Not in his wildest dreams, though, had Mac imagined Whitey as the driver. "Show me the way!" he ordered. "Just point your stupid head." Massive paws scrunched the steering wheel. She had no choice but to cooperate. She nodded her head and rocked forward. "Which way?" he repeated. "Use body language." He wove in and out of traffic, recklessly aiming his high-profile projectile at 100 mph. But he was obviously not thinking clearly. There was only one way to travel. No other highways were in sight. Only Highway 160. They were on it. Southbound. Asking twice was moronic. Tuba City was 46 miles ahead. Flagstaff, 72 miles beyond that. Interstate 40 was between the two. They'd entered a barren section of Indian country, much of it resembling the moonscape, Hopi land loomed on their left and Navajo land everywhere else.

FORTY

Whitey's truck caught up to the train. Trixie strained her eyeballs. She watched the 90-car serpent slip by slowly. Like a shipwrecked sailor watching a ship sail past, unnoticed. The operator's elbow was cocked out the window, fresh air cooling the cockpit for him and his assistant. Both men were crammed into a tiny, hot space on hard, drop-down seats. "Oh, please, please, dear God, look over here, will you? Look over here. See my condition? I'm a damn hostage. Can't you see the weirdo next to me driving like a maniac? He's hell-bent on killing us both. Look, God damn it! Open your stupid eyes!" The operator was responsible for dozens of gauges and controls. He glanced left but never gave them a second thought. He was too busy. The assistant operator was the train's lookout, closely observing rails, crossties, and catenary supports. He rarely glanced toward the highway. Whitey passed the locomotive doing 95 mph, double the train's speed. Trixie panicked. Acute nausea struck. She fixed her eyes on the landscape to avoid vomiting. Periodically, the tracks passed over drainage arroyos or gravel roads leading to Navajo homesteads. Unique tunnels supported the tracks.

It worked. Images of the landscape replaced her urge to vomit. But they also rekindled childhood memories. "*That's* what they are," she muttered in newly adopted Gag dialect. "Multiplate. Multiplate tunnels." She mused on how Uncle Gordy used to weld them for homesteaders before August monsoons. How thick sheets of galvanized steel were joined together in an arc to form the tunnel's curved roof structure. Good income when his shop was slow. Kept food on the table. She used to go with him when they were installed and play with Navajo children. Poke sticks into snake holes and chase rabbits. She had counted eight multiplate tunnels since their escape.

"Slow down, slow down, damn it," she begged in her strange dialect. "We'll crash. Kill us both. Truck's too high and empty." Whitey ignored her. He focused on the highway. May's tempests ignited fierce crosswinds. It would spell disaster if he wasn't careful. The weather service had posted strong wind advisories, warning drivers in high-profile vehicles to use extreme caution. He wrestled the steering wheel. Trixie slurred a second round of warnings. Soggy pleas fell upon deaf ears.

She screwed down her eyelids, gutless, unable to watch what was inevitable - an impending crash. She'd heard about rogue waves snatching beach walkers. She feared a rogue wind gust would blow them over. They passed four additional multiplate tunnels leading to Navajo homes. Each tunnel unmistakably warned of high-voltage power lines overhead. Large red signs with white iridescent letters: "50,000 Kilovolts Overhead."

FOUR miles behind, Blue Sky exceeded 100 mph. He'd closed the gap. Long sections of highway had been recently resurfaced. Passing lanes were added on upgrades. His driving skills were unequalled. He'd top out safely at 120 mph if he had to. Whitey's circus truck was no match for the TrailBlazer. Silence was interrupted by Sweet Voice.

"Subject Terry McAllister, rescued on Nokai Mesa," her cadence began.

"Roger."

"Sir, official report: Airlifted to Salt Lake City's burn center. Jaws of Life had to torch through cable armor. Quite a stir he's caused. Strange-looking dude. That's what the EMT said after stabilizing him. Never seen a face slanted like a rotting pumpkin before. For all intents and purposes, he suffered an extreme meltdown. Like lightning, but not lightning. Tests continue. Assume you'll want to interrogate him ASAP."

"Me and about six federal agencies. More later. Gotta drive. Over 'n out."

"Roger." Even a single word carried her melodic chime.

"I swear," said Howie, "that voice needs to be discovered by a talent agent. Maybe do national programming."

"Family tends better than a thousand sheep. Big operation. Near Kaibito. Been there since the Navajo first arrived. Wouldn't move for a million bucks." His eyes met Howie's. "We'll keep her doing what she's doing. A welcome voice during long shifts across our wide open rez." He tightened his grip on the steering wheel. Their speed hovered at 105. "There, got him in sight, see? Two miles or so."

AT the crest of each rise, Whitey saw a flashing light bar. His lead diminished. Trixie saw it too in the side mirror. Hope sparked again. "Capture us before we crash," she gurgled. Whitey's eyes darted like a trapped animal. Back and forth between side mirror and windshield. His lead kept diminishing. He fretted. He realized he was fleeing. He was the pursued, not the pursuer. He couldn't ever remember being pursued. He notched it up to 110 mph. A road sign announced Highway 98's turnoff to Page. He raced past it. To Trixie, everything was a blur. "Only one copper chasing us," he grunted. "I can lose that bum. Piece of cake." He patted his lucky charm. Then, the briefcases. He spread gargantuan lips and gave her a whale shark grin. Trixie realized how Jonah must have felt. She spoke in Gag, desperately warning him they'd crash. Or roll over. It was lost in translation. An apocalyptic ending loomed. Suddenly, Whitey acknowledged a pattern repeating itself. Their pursuer disappeared for more than a minute within each trough in the highway. Their route traversed part of the Great Basin's monotonous undulations. Signs warned motorists of flash flooding during heavy downpours. To avoid low-lying areas during such times.

He held the needle at 110 mph. The gap hadn't changed for several minutes. Like a rollercoaster, the highway dropped into a deep ravine. It bottomed out on a moist streambed and then rose steeply on the other side. It was more a shallow gorge than a simple trough in the topography. Tonalea Post Office flanked the crest on their left. The community of Red Lake sat nearby. A road sign sprang up out of nowhere. Like a running back breaking away from tacklers, his lucky break materialized before his eyes - Navajo Road 21. "Ha, 21, my lucky number. Thanks to my lucky charm. Now we lose that copper."

Cresting the opposite side, Whitey watched Blue Sky's flashers disappear like a submarine. He buried his foot on the brake and muscled the steering wheel with both arms. Trixie watched in horror. If they rolled, the highway road sign would decapitate her. Death played in slow motion before her eyes. It triggered involuntary muscular responses. Her sphincter muscle gave way, emptying her bladder. For the second time that day, streams of urine drenched her jeans, running down her legs and onto the floor mat. Pungent fumes filled her nostrils. She didn't care, death was seconds away. But death never came. Whitey miraculously pulled it off. As though he'd discovered a new law of gravity. Stunt drivers would have marveled. When they straightened out, he buried the accelerator. Super-charged fuel injectors kicked in and he reached 100 mph in thirty seconds. Navajo Road 21 welcomed them. The Great Basin swallowed them again. They vanished from sight. He boasted as loud as a ship's horn: "Me Whitey, Impossible to Kill."

"Shit, we're still alive," Trixie mumbled. "This jerk's a curse. Can't seem to die with him at the helm. I'm sick of this." Her jeans were as wet as her gag. She prayed for the nightmare to end. She wanted out. She preferred death. "Push me out. Push me hard. Don't care what happens!" Whitey didn't understand. All he saw was empty highway clear to the horizon. Utopia. No flashing light bar. The truck stopped rocking. Freshly paved blacktop sent it safely on its way.

"WHERE'D they go?" Howie yelled. He slid forward, sinking his fingers into the dashboard. Blue Sky turned white.

"Impossible!" Kika shouted from the backseat. "This is *our* turf. Thought we were closing the gap."

316

Howie pelted the officer with a verbal barrage. He turned another shade whiter. Navajo white. They raced past the turnoff to Navajo 21. The highway before them became flat and straight. Rolling landscape wouldn't resume until Tuba City. He slammed on the brakes, swerved onto the shoulder and made a U-turn doing 30 mph. Cars stopped in both directions. Stones shot out at muzzle velocity behind burning rubber. He buried the speedometer. Howie feared their engine would blow up. The veteran policeman cursed quietly. "Shit, no way," he stammered. "Couldn't have turned off. They were going too fast. We'd have seen them crashed on the roadside."

"You mean on Navajo 21?" Kika asked. "The one by Elephant's Feet? I didn't see a thing."

"It's the only turn off. Has to be. Can't just up and disappear."

"Maybe Tonalea gulch swallowed them up," she added, lightly. "I'll say one thing. Imagine how we'd feel if the artifacts were still aboard. Can't believe he hasn't rolled that skyscraper truck yet. Must be a better driver than we thought." They reached Navajo 21. He yanked a hard left and steadied the accelerator at 65 mph. New blacktop rode smooth as glass. To Howie, it felt like they'd stopped.

"What're you doing, Dudley? He's going twice this speed. We'll *never* catch him."

"Oh, yes, we will." A smile creased his soft complexion. "No sense in risking our necks too. You'll see."

"See what?" demanded Howie.

"You'll see."

"What's up your sleeve?" Kika pleaded. "Does this just drop off into Lake Powell or what?"

"It'll be a sight for sore eyes if he continues at top speed. You'll see what happens to that smart-ass driver when he hits our Navajo red. That's what my family calls it. Nothing quite like it anywhere on earth. When monsoons arrive, we sometimes rely on the National Guard for emergency supplies. Roads turn to gooey Navajo red. Grips like shallow quicksand."

"But it hasn't rained for weeks."

The Officer grinned and relaxed his grip on the wheel. He eased his foot off the gas, dropping their speed to 55. "You'll see."

THE titan raced along without a care in the world, ready to start a new life. One filled with bikinied babes dangling from each arm. White, rippled sand, rolling surf and champagne bubbling in crystal stemware. Romantic mariachis serenading him and his concubines to afternoon delight. Nothing but clear sailing all the way to the horizon. He boasted to Trixie about his nifty getaway. How he'd out-smarted the dumb copper. No more sirens. No flashing light bar. Just smooth blacktop clear to the ocean.

A series of road signs appeared. The first was a gentle nudge. It was intended for drivers who could comprehend English. It warned of road construction five miles ahead. Delays of thirty minutes or longer were possible. It directed drivers to watch for a flagman and pilot car. One mile later, a larger sign instructed all commercial trucks to stop and turn around. To return to Highway 160 and detour northbound to Highway 98 to reach Kaibito or Page. Trixie jolted. She knew Whitey couldn't read. She rocked her barrel-like physique. Movement was futile, Gag dialect indiscernible to the massif. His ears were sealed. Frustrated, he figured she had to pee again. He lost patience. She shook violently. He ignored her, already sickened by two bouts of odorous urine.

"Soon, I'll spend my millions," he bellowed through noxious breath. "Sip champagne with Mexican cuties. Smooth, brown skin. Bushy black hair." He stacked one briefcase on top of the other, dreamily staring at dollar signs through the windshield.

"I'VE heard Navajo red sand can be awfully messy," Howie said. "I've worked on pipeline projects throughout Navajo and Hopi land. Always avoided it. Figured sand's sand."

"Messy?" His tone was stern. "Miss Windsong, please remind your fiancé there's nothing *messy* about sacred Dinétah soil." He cracked a smile. "Did you know that our Nation still calls roads 'Navajo Trails?' Not highways or roads, but *trails*. Huh? Did you know that?"

"Not really," she said. "Makes me feel more Navajo, though."

"Unfortunately, the Bureau of Indian Affairs in Tuba City still has final say over our Navajo trails. A sin, isn't it?" He pointed through the windshield with his chin. "They finally decided to pave Navajo 21. Nice and smooth, huh? Long overdue. An important trail on the rez. Cuts through White Mesa and Grey Mesa. Lots of families up here. They depend on this road. Grazing, livestock, trading, Kaibito Chapter House. And most of all, unencumbered views of our *naatsis' aan,* Navajo Mountain."

WHITEY'S spontaneous escape route, Navajo 21, intersected with the Black Mesa and Lake Powell Railroad three times. Two of the crossings passed smoothly *over* the tracks with proper warning lights and bells. But the first crossing westbound was *through* a multiplate tunnel *beneath* the tracks. As fate would have it, funding had been delayed for a one-mile stretch surrounding the tunnel. It was the last section of Navajo 21 scheduled for paving. The construction crew had busied itself re-grading a stretch of road base beneath the tunnel. It resulted in loosely graded, soft Navajo red.

The final warning sign was ugly. Not to the maniac driver, but to Trixie. The message, printed in bold lettering, was short. It gave ample time to turn around. "WARNING. LOW CLEARANCE BRIDGE. 12' 6". THREE MILES AHEAD."

The horror of being squished like a bug on a windshield was unbearable. Anyone could do the math. Her uncle had raised the rig's clearance to 17 feet. She did the math. It wasn't rocket science. She calculated precisely where the razor-sharp multiplate would slice through the windshield. And their bodies, titanic strength or not, cabled mass or not. Her reaction was violent. She screamed in her own wet, muffled dialect: "I was just kidding, God. Changed my mind. I don't want to die. Not this way! PLEASE have mercy! He can't read!" She tried every possible means of communication, attempted every imaginable form of physical movement. The moronic driver was in a dream world. Her eyes bulged from their sockets. She rocked sideways into his huge frame.

Whitey was bent over the steering wheel Cro-Magnon-style, barbaric grin glued to his face. "Whiskey, champagne, Mexican cuties, bushy crops. And sand. Millions of bucks to blow. Just a few more hours."

Trixie's third and final, involuntary physiological reaction occurred. The culprit was her anus. It was common before executions. Her circumstances weren't much different. Whether he wanted to or not, Whitey was poised to execute Trixie Grebe - and himself, chest-high against the top arc of multiplate tunnel. Defecation resulted, explosively so. Fumes mushroomed like toxic gas. Whitey gagged. He couldn't breathe. The stench was excruciating. It was the last straw. He pushed her hard against the passenger door. He shoved her repeatedly, hoping she'd crash through it. She hoped she would too. All it did was smear her mess and magnify the stench. He screamed vulgarities. She screamed warnings. He kept pushing. She squirmed. Each wiggle made matters worse. He lost his cool, accelerating recklessly. It came into view, looming like a giant guillotine, arced low to the ground. Bold lettering advertising their execution: "CLEARANCE. 12' 6"." The word *mutilate* replaced *multiplate* in her mind.

Whitey dry heaved. "Bitch," he barked, spitting bile on her. "Smelly broad, you reek. Out of my truck!" He held his paw over the briefcases and slammed on the brakes. He never let up. The truck skidded to a stop. Smoldering rubber engulfed them. He jumped out and ran to her door, grabbed her cocoon and planted her upright. Except for scraggly hair, she matched other construction barrels. He jumped back into the truck and buried the accelerator. The needle struck 110 mph. He unclipped his seatbelt and relaxed, bent arm out the window. He was back in the game, music blaring, air conditioner on high. The stench was gone.

Trixie laughed and balled her eyes out at the same time. "Shit happens."

.

FORTY-ONE

"Life is good," Whitey boasted. "I did it. Picked up an easy fifteen million. Don't need that smelly broad's eyes anymore. I'm set for life. Can buy any babe, any champagne I want. Buy me a seaside villa with a whole flock of Mexican cuties. Math by one. Hate splitting anything. Except spines." He sailed ahead over smooth blacktop. Blue Sky and Parker cruised slowly, one and a half miles behind without the siren or light bar activated. Kika stayed behind and attended to Trixie until the EMTs arrived.

Whitey glanced right. "What? The same train?" The electric, uranium-laden train bound for NGS approached the tunnel overpass. Truck tires met Navajo red doing 110 mph, 161 feet per second. They smeared it like a knife spreading peanut butter. The truck slowed by only 20 mph. Inertia propelled him on a straight trajectory. Defiantly, he goosed it. His Road to Utopia ended. His flight to hell began.

The operator looked left. Horrified, he reached for levers. Too late. Four locomotives and the first 20 railcars passed before the truck struck the tunnel. Either Trixie had miscalculated or the re-grading Navajo red was incomplete. Either way, the arced multiplate sliced off the top of the cab three inches above Whitey's skull. It got the tall cargo box though. Full-on impact stopped the truck in its tracks. Experts would piece together the accident later. They were accustomed to gory, high-speed wrecks. Whitey's collision would also require specialists who dealt with satellite trajectory.

The 450-pound killer launched through the windshield still sporting his whale shark grin. G-forces exacerbated it akin to an astronaut launching into orbit. His carcass catapulted at the truck's impact velocity - 90 mph - 132 feet per second. He whistled through the air, sailing in a prone position through the shaded tunnel, easily clearing its 75-foot length, emerging in sunlight on the other side. Arms outstretched like Superman, he soared 185 feet beyond the tunnel and crashed on his pulp of a sternum before sliding another 110 feet like a plane without landing gear. When he came to rest, his limbs were tangled like a knotted octopus. He faced skyward on a bed of soft Navajo red, blizzard-white hair forming a macabre contrast.

Gordy's welding reigned supreme. The cargo box remained with the chassis. Sections of riveted paneling flew like shrapnel and struck the catenary. The train shorted instantly. One briefcase flew forward and wedged unopened below the dashboard. The other launched with Whitey and burst wide open. $7.5 million scattered in the Navajo breeze. $100 bills floated gently like goose down feathers. Blue Sky and Parker arrived. Howie swatted the currency as he ran to Whitey,

321

letting it float toward nearby Navajo homes. Blue Sky radioed Sweet Voice. When Howie caught up with the mangled beast, he knelt like a priest administering last rites. Except that priests in developed nations didn't grip a Kimber 1911 Special Forces pistol. He stared at the massif and shook his head. Blue Sky approached.

"Hit earth like a meteor. Anyone else would be in a million pieces." Howie said.

Dudley's eyes traced Whitey's flight path. "Anyone else would have been captured long ago."

"True." He holstered the Kimber. "Doesn't look much alive, does he?"

"Not sure. Going to take some convincing before I admit *he's* dead. Dude's a tough *hombre* to put down." Blue Sky knelt beside him.

"What the hell you doing? Oh, no, not again. Show some respect to the deceased. You arrested Mac when he was down too. Never skip a beat, do you?"

Blue Sky read him his rights. "Might as well, what if he's still alive? Look. Man's eyes are wide open."

"Lots of people die with their eyes open." Howie knelt to shut his eyelids. Whitey blinked. Not once, but twice. Then repeatedly. He felt for a pulse. "Son of a gun, can't believe it. 'Course, then again, with a guy this huge, it could take awhile for the organs shut down, right? Might still be dying. Anaphylactic shock or something."

"Doesn't look much dead to me. Glad I read him his rights." Whitey blinked again. Men from the highway crew one mile ahead heard the crash. Watched the train short out. Two of them ran to the crash site. One of them turned and yelled to a coworker to fetch a wheel loader. "Not so fast," said Dudley. "Man isn't dead yet."

Howie reached in each of Whitey's pants pockets. No feather holders. He raced back to the crash site to search the truck. Blue Sky couldn't resist. "Hey, Parker, is that what you archaeologists call roadside archaeology?"

"Very funny," he yelled. "Could a sworn he threw two on the front seat. Could be anywhere. I'll find them if it's the last thing I do."

The policeman's radio crackled. "Hey, Parker, you'd better come back. You're wanted on the radio. Here you go, Miss Windsong." He handed him the cordless instrument. It had a range of 100 feet.

"Howie, are you all right? Have you captured Blizzardhead? Did I miss anything? EMTs are tending to Trixie. She's in pretty good shape. Ecstatic, actually. What's so amazing is her captors never beat her up. Hardly laid a finger on her. She's one lucky woman."

"Everything's stable here. The beast is immobile. Must have flown 400 feet from the truck. Landed on his smashed chest, of all places.

He's still alive, though." He pivoted and stared through the tunnel to the crash site. He stood spellbound, holding the transmitter down at his thigh, and blurted at the top of his lungs: "Hey, Dudley, will you look at that? I'll be damned. Truly unbelievable!"

"What? What are you talking about?" Kika demanded, voice resounding from his thigh. "Look at what? Tell me, I can't see through the radio!"

Blue Sky stood and focused on Howie's line of sight. "What? What's the matter? Tunnel going to collapse?" A railroad maintenance crew worked quickly to free debris and restore power. Multiplate was strong, but it wasn't designed to bear the weight of a loaded train stopped overhead. A man in full Hazmat gear walked atop the railcars. He swept a sophisticated digital device over their contents. It detected low levels of radiation. A shoulder strap led to a square, metal box at his waist. "What're you onto, Parker?" Then he saw it. Plain as day. He'd never noticed it all the years he'd traversed the rez.

Howie shouted into the radio. "The arc of the tunnel is the identical shape, absolutely a perfect replica, of the arc connecting the double cross motif on the feather holders."

"*And* the arc of the sandstone arch in The Land of Walking Earth," Dudley added.

"Are you guys hallucinating? Sounds ridiculous. An arc is an arc. Don't read too much into it. It's just a manmade tunnel. Most arcs are about the same shape, aren't they? I'll see for myself in a minute. An officer's driving me there." She clicked off.

"She's got a point," Dudley said. "Then again, it could be for real. Could have been designed by a Navajo who's hiked into The Land of Walking Earth. Or any holy shrine. Like I said, there are several sacred shrines on Kaibito Plateau. I can even see *Naatsis'aan* from where I stand."

The man in Hazmat gear waved to the maintenance crew. They jumped aboard a "rail rider" parked in front of the engines and sped off. The short was fixed. The train inched forward. Dudley breathed a sigh of relief. Hazmat Man skillfully moved from railcar to railcar panning their contents.

Kika arrived. She surveyed the wreckage and took deliberate, two-foot strides the length of Whitey's flight path. "Wow, he flew this far? Truck's way back there."

They showed her where he'd scraped Navajo red the last 100 feet.

Whitey's breathing rattled and creaked, like a crowbar opening a crate. His eyelids opened and closed like giant clamshells. His hand twitched. He bent his left arm at the elbow and raised it triumphantly above his chest. It dangled in midair. A smirk snaked through his war-torn face. Then his arm dropped like an anchor on his gory chest. The fleshy thud turned Kaka's stomach. An object bulged through his tattered shirt. His mouth opened. Lips moved without sound. Vocal chords labored. A hoarse whisper slithered out. He pressed down on the bulge, slowly panting his legendary mantra: "Me…Whitey…Impossible…to Kill." His head dropped to the side and he slipped into unconsciousness. Still very much alive, still clutching the bulge.

Howie became a believer. Whitey had earned his iconic title. The man truly was impossible to put down for good. Like lifting a fallen tree, he raised Whitey's huge limb and reached into the bloody pocket. His face lit up like a stadium. His fingers held what he'd discovered in the ceremonial chamber several nights earlier. He held it up at an angle. It was the same half that had slipped from his pocket. He knew it. He left it blood-soaked, allowing archaeologists to clean it properly. He wasted no time placing it with the one recovered from Mac's pocket. "I swear on my life, no one's ever snatching these again."

The train gained momentum. Hazmat Man met up with the railcar that entombed Wainwright. His radiation detector emitted a loud signal. He stooped down, holding the metal box by its strap, and lowered it carefully into Wainwright's railcar. He stared in awe through his translucent shield. A gauge told him the temperature in the railcar was 200 degrees Fahrenheit. There wasn't much left of Mr. All-American White Art Dealer. He climbed down the ladder and monitored rail cars passing by.

"Whew," exclaimed Blue Sky, "weight's finally off that tunnel." They knelt down and monitored Whitey before MedVac arrived. Dudley's phone jarred them. "Blue Sky." Absolute silence. His smooth Navajo face hardened. The call ended abruptly. He could barely move his lips. "Man only identified himself as Smith," he half-slurred. "I'd say he's a spook. Said he's been conducting top-secret research for Wheeler. Helping him connect two newspaper articles. Couldn't reach Wheeler so dispatch transferred him to me. Told me his intel was a matter of life and death. *Our life and death.* Of utmost and immediate urgency - *prior to our next contact with Agent Coldditz.* Said the case officer in charge of Dietrich Schisslenberg's immigration was one Heinrich Fleming von Coldditz. Had a twenty-five year career with the US Immigration and Naturalization Service. From the fifties to the seventies. That's all he said. Exact words. Then he clicked off." Chills raced up Kika's spine. Her neck twitched. She scrunched her shoulders, shivering in the heat of day.

Hazmat Man cut through security fencing bordering the tracks. He slid down the scree as though he were riding an escalator, creating a small landslide. It eased his landing. One minute later, a black shadow enveloped the trio bent over Whitey, looming like a toxic cloud. The NSA agent unzipped his suit and withdrew a sleek cannon-gun 25 inches long. The same Take No Prisoners model used to annihilate his wife ten hours earlier. A sound suppressor fit over the muzzle. Slowly, three heads angled up, staring into the apocalyptic weapon.

Suddenly, Parker got it. The lightning bolt struck. Random events scattered over the past four days were not so random. Pieces of the puzzle fell into place. The evil towering over them cackled, a strange echoing sound through his headgear. "Damn, why didn't I see this coming earlier?" Howie cried out in despair. "A voice deep inside kept warning me. I ignored it, didn't follow my gut. Ever since you drew that symbol in the sand next to our camper, you bastard. A second alarm sounded when I radioed from our last lookout post. The Captain answered. I still let it slide. Even after my brainstorm of the double cross-arc motif and it's double meaning - symbolically warning me of a double-cross setup. Damn, damn, damn! Damn you, Howie Parker." He rose slightly. The agent tamed him with his TNP. He watched his anger reflected in Collditz's face shield. "How ironic," he continued yelling, "*I'm* the one who lectured *you* about betrayal the first day we met. Over a peaceful pot of coffee. You must have roared inside, laughed your guts out. Wheeler had it right all along. Suspected foul play since day one. There *was* a connection between the newspaper articles and the crimes on Cedar Mesa."

Hazmat Man removed his headgear. "Welcome, Parker, to my closure of the Delilah Project. You too, Miss Windsong, and you, Officer. Nice to make your acquaintance. I'll take that," he commanded. Howie clutched the feather holder half with a steel grip.

The agent smirked. "If I pull this trigger, it'll take forensics a month to figure out which pieces belong to whom. Trust me, this would open the hull of a battleship. I helped our wizards at the NSA design this weapon. I'm the one who nicknamed it 'Take No Prisoners.' Now hand it over." He waved it in circles, silencer two feet from their foreheads. Thirty seconds lapsed. A minute. Collditz angled closer. Howie crumbled. His hand slid forward. Collditz grabbed it like a viper. "Good, now keep that hand exactly where it is. Take your other hand and throw that Kimber off to the side. You too, Navajo Man, toss both weapons far away." The men cooperated. "Windsong, keep your hands raised high. Higher! That's better. Brewster cooperated too, finally, with his half. Took a healthy poke to his chin to convince him."

"Damn intel," cried Blue Sky, cynically. "It's always too late. Remind me to thank Smith, or whoever he is, for not calling earlier."

Coldditz slid a Kevlar pouch from beneath his suit. "Snatched these two from the smashed truck while you bozos tended to this ugly swine. *Now I have all twelve.* That was my objective. I orchestrated the Delilah Project from the onset, gave the mole a wide playing field at the Department of Energy. Hereditary genes did the rest. She turned on her country. I knew she would, just like her father did. Thank the US Army too, proof that psy-ops really work. I groomed a terrorist cell for seven years. Before 9/11. *The uranium deal was all mine.* Made my superior, Colonel Holmes, believe he was in the loop. Fool! I'd hoped that money-monger Wainwright would expose the mole earlier. But his greed was too intense. Got the best of him - placed him on a slow bake in his toxic crematorium."

"Then *you* set up the mole, hung her out for slaughter," Howie shouted. "You as much as killed her, Coldditz. Doesn't matter who exposed her. Or who pulled the trigger. It was *you*. You assassinated Della, your ex-wife."

"Ex-wives are always expendable, Parker. Something you should keep in mind before you up and marry your Indian lover." Howie thrust forward. Coldditz whacked him with the TNP. A line of blood slid down his forehead. "Della was just as greedy as her old man. They both got what they deserved. She should have known I could access every byte of information in her domain. The NSA got a little sloppy too, resting on their laurels. Got out of control when Bush and Cheney expanded their role to include warrantless domestic surveillance. If you ask me, the NSA's grown too big for its britches. Wheeler's friend at the DIA figured that out. I remember your warning, Parker. The NSA should be more diligent. The eye it uses to peer out is the same eye others could use to peer back in. Your quote, Parker. Paraphrased, of course."

He spit on Whitey and kicked him hard in the ribs. The splintered manubrium bone protruded farther from his chest, caked in a pasty mixture of Navajo red and blood. "This bozo spoiled everything. Brainless oaf had to slam into the tunnel and short out the train. Now I've lost the uranium. Amazing how lamebrain blokes can spoil a flawless plan - how a low-grade government guy like Wheeler could innocuously expose the mole before Wainwright could. Imagine, after my illustrious career, after thousands of cunning, deep-cover ploys, how a duo of morons could louse up a heist of this magnitude. $150 million down the drain. Someone's got to pay. So I've resorted to Plan B. Hate to mess up your rez, Blue Sky, and half the West's power supply, not to mention its water, but I'm left with no choice. Look at it as my payback to my government - Navajo Generating Station, Glen Canyon Dam and the Army Corp of Engineers all became Plan B targets. But you three won't be around anyway." He stepped back and leveled his weapon. "After you're wasted, this 40mm ammo will make compost out of the huge clump of manure lying at your feet. Guess I'll have to settle for these twelve feather holders. They'll bring in a handsome sum for my early retirement. Easier to transport than uranium anyway. I have the perfect buyers who'll fence it. In Prague. Same ruthless, black-market dicks Wainwright dealt with. They'll pay top price for these twelve. So much for academia getting their hands on them. You really fell for that one, Parker, you naïve ass."

A helicopter swooped down, kicking up curtains of Navajo red. It landed between the tunnel and the men. Its blades swooshed to a maniacal beat. The same helicopter Blue Sky saw at Goulding's airstrip three hours earlier. The camo Bell JetRanger was as nimble as a wasp. "My ticket out," he said, intoxicated with pride at his clever escape. "I'll take that briefcase too," he ordered. "A cool $7.5 million. Pocket change until I peddle the feather holders." He stepped sideways toward the swooshing blades, bent over slightly, leveling the TNP at their chests.

The chopper door opened. Three commandos launched into the air, hitting the red earth in lightning-quick summersaults and squaring off in assault stances. One was the Captain. He bore down the muzzle of his own TNP, head cocked firm, eyes sighted like lasers. The weapon was balanced over his left forearm, aimed directly at his superior's chest. No silencer. If he pulled the trigger, pieces of Coldditz would soar 12 miles to Kaibito. The other two gripped M16s. A rigid expression, part smile, part scorn, lit the Captain's face. Howie recognized it. He'd used it in combat when securing a position and capturing objectives. He'd never forget that look. Or the shocked response in the prisoner's eyes.

"What the fu--?" Coldditz screamed over the drone of blades. He weighed his options. He was no fool. He'd slithered out of numerous compromising, certain-death encounters during his career. His eyes moved to the rhythm of the blades. Howie's heartbeat did likewise, forehead dripping blood, as angry as a wounded Pamplona bull. Blue Sky remained calm. Kika was as outraged as her fiancé. Three high-powered weapons were poised to annihilate Coldditz if he so much as blinked. The Captain's expression moderated, two degrees shy of a smirk. He wore the look well. He was a superb commando, no longer subordinate to Coldditz. Coldditz stared past them at his chopper. His hands gripped a one-way ticket to freedom, seconds away from incalculable wealth. All he had to do was pull the trigger. Faster than the other three pulled theirs. The nimble Bell would whisk him away.

His life balanced on a delicate scale. Greed on one tray, common military sense on the other. It was obvious that *seven* lives were at stake, not just his. He didn't care. He knew that when bullets started popping, no one would be around to tell the story. For a second, the scales balanced. Then he felt the weight of twelve feather holders press against his chest. The drone of chopper blades allured him as the sirens' song had Ulysses. The scales tipped. Greed won. He pulled the trigger. It clicked. Nothing happened.

Parker knew why the Captain wore the look he did. He grinned. "You're done, Coldditz," said the Captain. "Drop it and surrender honorably. I want both hands high above your head." One of the Captain's soldiers kept his M16 leveled. The other subdued their former commander, rapidly hobbling and cuffing him.

"I jimmied your TNP before Marling met you in Kayenta. Minutes after a scrambled transmission arrived from Brownstone. Our genius intelligence officer, Colonel Holmes, cracked his best agent's plot. He'd been assembling pieces of the puzzle for days. This morning, he ingested every word recorded during your polygraph interrogation. Ran every syllable through the NSA's psychoanalytical software. They shredded every utterance, every breath you took since you arrived at Andrews. Had it been formatted in hard copy, it would have resembled a ticker-tape parade in Manhattan. He and his code-cracking team worked relentlessly. They processed it through VIPERD, Variable Intel Predictor of Eccentric Reverse Diagnostics. Gives analysts a predictability score based on contrary, 'devil's advocate' points of view. *That's* what cracked it. Holmes contacted me ninety minutes ago. You were in-flight. Good thing he kept my instincts in check. Issued an order I couldn't negate. Had it been up to me, I'd have ordered your friggin' plane shot down."

"Then it *was* the polygraph."

"That *and* his personal, direct link to National Reconnaissance Office spy satellites. As Holmes put it, no one was surprised you had *knowledge* of The Land of Walking Earth. After all, Ms. Schissler was your ex-wife." Howie grunted and spit a mouthful of blood at Coldditz's feet. "However, and here's the clincher, you would *not* have been privy to precise details contained in her father's Map of Riches, even if you were aware that such a map existed, unless you had turned in her favor by using her. You were always an exemplary double agent whenever Fort Meade ordered you to play that role. During Lindeman's polygraph, you were hypnotized without your knowledge. That's when you disclosed the precise, final compass coordinates to reach Schisslenberg's secret cache of high-grade uranium. The hidden vent he'd discovered in The Land of Walking Earth. Once the Colonel got that, he knew you'd staged Delilah. Crafted it to fit your deadly, profiteering agenda. Set your ex-wife up like a puppet, knowing from her genes she'd go for it. Even designed the very weapon that'd be used by the 'cleaners.' The rest is history. I hope you rot in hell. Some commander you've turned out to be, you traitorous dick!"

"Underscore that big time," said Parker, retrieving the heavy Kevlar pouch from inside the agent's protective gear. "Now, suppose you tell us where Schisslenberg's remains are. Connect the dots, spy man. If for no other reason than for Wheeler. After all, he exposed the mole for you. So others could carry out your dirty work. Might get you a lighter sentence."

"Piss off. I've no motive for telling you anything."

The Captain released the TNP's safety. He stepped in front of Coldditz and raised a hand. The chopper cut its power. Swooshing blades silenced. The Captain's eyes became slits. He nestled the TNP in the bow of his elbow, raising it three inches, directly at Wendell's heart. "Humor us."

Coldditz broke out in cold sweats, pale and stiff. "You'll find that bastard ex-Nazi's bones at the bottom of his secret mine shaft. The one recently displaced by minor tremors. My father, Heinrich, was a muckety-muck at the INS, in case you hadn't heard. He approved Schisslenberg's conditional immigration status. His office censored all mail to and from immigrants, including private couriers. Paid a small fortune to the courier hired by Schisslenberg. Before he delivered the letter to Dietrich's executors in Frankfurt, my father duplicated it. Dietrich's treasonous act, particularly his Map of Riches, totally enraged my father. Being a true-blooded, loyal American, he'd devoted his life to helping immigrants start over, begin a new life in America, an honest life, safe from Hitler's atrocities, free from tyrannical, Fascist Germany. When he discovered that Schisslenberg had betrayed his oath as a new American, that he had falsified official survey records of America's strategic mining resources, precious minerals required in the Cold War, and even bequeathed those priceless assets to his family, he decided to take matters into his own hands. So he escorted the genius scientist one moonless night into The Land of Walking Earth. At gunpoint and under threat of life imprisonment and hard labor for him and his family, he offered him an alternative. One which could someday be viewed by his wife and daughter as an honorable, albeit shocking, end to his life - to simply disappear. Conveniently entombed in his own naturally hidden vent. Let his family and authorities think what they may. Schisslenberg required no further coaxing. He'd reached the jumping-off point - literally. He hit bottom, or a ledge, so deep my father barely heard the impact. Yet, years later, he told me the faint echo still haunted him.

"So that's why you married their daughter?" Blue Sky asked.

"Yes, to keep tabs on her. And to access the Map of Riches. Practically the only reasons."

"And the woman backpacker?" Kika asked, kicking her foot in disgust, wishing she had her little Guardian .32 caliber.

"Collateral damage, I'm afraid, Miss Windsong. Mac and Whitey did a nice job, didn't they? I learned a long time ago to let brute force carry out my dirty work. Pays to hire a 450-pound keg of human dynamite, don't you think?" His sneer caused her hand to rise and pantomime shooting him. "Then the stupid Navajo Police arrested the three 'prospectors' I'd sent to photograph the exposed mine shaft and natural arch. Their damn newspaper had to report it *and* the seismic tremors. Of all the bloody luck. On the very same day the Farmington paper reported that the government had closed Schisslenberg's case. Shit! Is that stinking coincidence or what? To make matters worse, your BLM law officer had to read both articles. What are the odds of all that happening? Right then and there, the deck was stacked. Never experienced anything like it in thirty-plus years of covert ops. Caused me to become sloppy in everything. I began electronic surveillance on everyone. Raised all sorts of red flags at Fort Meade. Holmes became suspicious. Queried as to why I was continuously tapping into broad spectrums of irrelevant data. One thing about the Colonel - if you're under suspicion, you're doomed."

"You forgot one thing, ex-Agent," said the Captain. The train could be heard in the distance. "The metal box you lowered into the railcar. The railcar containing Horace Wainwright's vitrified remains."

Coldditz grinned. "Like that? Poetic justice, huh? That sleazy, no-good prick was screwing Della. But, you're too late, Captain. You'll never rise above that rank, you jerk. Know that? You'll never stop the train now. Plan B, remember? The Navajo Generating Station will make Chernobyl look like a tanning booth. Kill every living thing in a five-hundred-mile radius, including you. Contaminate all water and black out most of the Southwest. *There are no terrorists awaiting this train at NGS. I'm the terrorist.* Always have been, and as long as I keep this suit on, always will be. When I returned to DC, I blocked all communications, all satellites. Re-routed the train's electric power to auxiliary power grids. No one will stop it."

The Captain laughed. "That's nonsense. You're blinded by denial, you egomaniacal jerk. Holmes is always one step ahead of you. He tweaked VIPERD software, skewed its reverse-diagnostics spectrum of possibilities, then jammed *your* signals. Led you to believe you'd succeeded." He looked at his watch. The train will automatically power down in four minutes. Coast to a stop safely outside the perimeter of NGS. Our elite corps will dismantle that dirty bomb of yours in less than five minutes. Too bad, Coldditz, you lose." Hobbled, he was led to the Bell chopper.

Howie seized the moment. "You heartless bastard, you almost got away with it." He sprang like a cheetah and flew twelve feet though the air, legs coiled beneath him. The same airborne attack directed at Whitey one day earlier. He landed on the unarmed man's back. A thunderous crack rang out, followed by a blood-curdling screech across Kaibito Plateau. His spine bent in reverse. He slumped to the ground, paralyzed. It was a senseless, dirty act. Totally without valor for the new Howie Parker. A one-time only relapse into old behavior - held in three days of purgatorial limbo. At last his rage demon vaporized into thin air. Once and for all, flittering upward and disappearing into the Navajo sky.

"You feel something?" Blue Sky asked. "Could swear I felt something move through the air." He did a 360. Kika did too. She looked at Blue Sky. He nodded, warm Navajo eyes meeting hers.

"I *did* feel an energy force flitter through the air," she said, turning to Howie. "Like a singer passing nearby, carried by the gentle wind, chanting something like the Enemy Way chant, purging a ghost sickness." She pictured Uncle Lenny Atcitty. A whirlwind played in the desert not far from where they stood. Acceptance and hope enveloped her, atonement for Howie. She embraced her fiancé, looking him squarely in the eyes: **"Howie Parker...you're free at last."**

FORTY-TWO

Wheeler raised his napkin with one hand. Large enough to use as a beach towel, he opened it fully and positioned it to muffle a belch. It rumbled like distant thunder. He smiled apologetically, arm-sling resting against the table. The giant cloth also served as a safety net trapping fallen food. Shelters could feed the homeless from its scraps. He'd ordered two meals for himself. Five sets of eyes bulged. "Hospital food sucks," he proclaimed.

"You were only in one night," said Howie.

"A lot has gone down in one short week," Brewster said, nudging the conversation toward relevant topics. "The second I'm finished eating, I'm out the door." His words were choppy. His chin was stitched and bandaged. Facial wounds inflicted by Coldditz made life temporarily inconvenient. His museum had struck a deal with Los Alamos National Labs and the FBI to provide armored transport. Heightened security would guard eleven intact feather holders, two matching fragments and thirty obsidian figurines, one of which represented the ancient civilization's deity, *Make-make*. "I'll accompany the feather holders and statuettes. We plan to arrive in Los Alamos this evening. Scientific analysis will commence at once. The other artifacts remain intact in the same crates packed by Mac and Whitey. They'll be transported in the confiscated moving van to my museum by agents from the FBI's Art Theft Division." He felt his stitches, making certain that prolonged dialogue was okay.

"My museum, of course, will serve as a temporary repository. They'll be safeguarded under extremely tight security until proper arrangements can be finalized with the Chilean government to return the entire assemblage to their provenience - Easter Island. Arrangements are currently underway. Someday perhaps, the unique 18,000 to 20,000-year-old artifacts will be publicly displayed by a Chilean institute or museum which has been granted rights to possess and preserve them, including the ones yet to be excavated from Inner Ruin."

Kika finished eating first. She looked up. "I'll bet one thing," she said. All eyes pointed toward her. "I'll bet archeologists on future digs begin taking a laser-eyed look at the rear cliff wall of cliff villages." Her statement was digested like the food in their gullets. Her curiosity spread. "So, Dr. Brewster, what's Mexico City all about? When will we know what those symbols on the feather holders *say*?"

"Won't truly know until Lin Chao and his infinite computer amplitude crack the code," he said. "He has twenty-eight days to do so prior to the conference. Yesterday, he was yearning for the missing half. Now he'll have all twelve. Bottom line? Metaphorically, we're standing on the threshold of *Make-make's* eye orbits!" Kika leaned forward, intensely curious. "The immensity of it all is staggering. Can't wait to go public - evidence showing northerly and easterly flows of shaman pilgrimages from Easter Island. Journeys which paved the way for pan-oceanic migrations into the Americas by later masses. Someday, scientists mapping the evolution of the human genome may corroborate this. In addition, resolving mysteries of that island's colossal statues. Exposing answers to timeless riddles of the universe. **And what mankind has been holding its breath for - peering into parallel universes.** That's what Mexico City is all about. In a nutshell, I guess."

"Back on Planet Earth," Quirk began, "an update on your two adversaries, Mr. Parker. The one you call Blizzardhead is up and moving around. Been transferred to a maximum security facility at Tooele Army Depot south of Salt Lake City. Driving his guards crazy, I'm told. The other gem you call Slantface is under lock and key at a Salt Lake burn center. Unofficially, I've tallied thirty-seven laws, acts and statutes they've violated. That includes federal laws and at least three state laws. I'll give you a specific list after lunch." Parker frowned. "We'll teach *them* and the full battalion of Southwest archeologist-wonnabees that looting of cultural resources doesn't pay. That it carries severe consequences. Perhaps the events will stimulate a concentration of state budgetary *increases* favoring the presence of site watch stewards!" With her inimitable officious pretense, she cracked a rare smile and turned to Blue Sky. "Carry on from here?"

"Ah, sure. I leave for Salt Lake City this afternoon. Federal prosecutors informed me, however, that a battery of lawyers representing McAllister arrived early this morning. Endowed with bottomless pockets. Money's funneled through Mafia coffers back East. Same lawyers have weaseled Mac and Whitey out of dozens of previous slam-dunk convictions. So keep your fingers crossed. Jurisprudence is unpredictable." His soft complexion spread into a smile. "Want to hear the corny part? Trixie Grebe is in love with Whitey. Intends to visit him in jail. Claims that in spite of outward appearances, he's a softhearted creature. That he nurtured her instead of rolling her into the desert. Removed her from the truck before crashing into the tunnel. She's convinced that her cabled body mass and passenger-side trajectory would have resulted in decapitation. If he's sentenced to prison, she'll file for a prison wedding. If not, look for a Cleveland wedding." He shook his head. "Go figure."

Parker grinned. "You mean there'll be little Whitey monster-babies to contend with someday?"

Brewster grinned and looked at his watch. He sat on the edge of his seat. "Ah, permit me to switch gears again. Need to ask Parker a question before I leave. Is your schedule open this fall? I have an arrangement in mind." Incapable of a genuine smile, his blue eyes danced.

"Except for our wedding, I'm pretty open."

"Good. I've established a tentative itinerary for you and Miss Windsong to accompany me to breathtaking Easter Island. October sometime, perhaps November."

Wheeler gagged. He covered his mouth with his hand, swallowed forcefully, then smiled at the two lovebirds.

"Breathtaking?" Kika exclaimed. "Interesting choice of words, Dr. Brewster. The only thing breathtaking about it is that it's on the other side of the planet. Convenient if someone's trying to escape!" A precocious wink eased her sarcasm. "When I said I'd support Howie and this earth-shattering discovery, I didn't mean I'd travel to the ends of the earth. We'll be newlyweds for crying out loud. Instead of working 10,000 miles away, I pictured him tucked into our own backyard at Snow Flat Canyon. *Able to come home every night.* Live like real newlyweds. Breathtaking? Good God!"

Wheeler cleared his throat. He pecked away at Navajo fry bread crumbs, swirling them in puddles of honey and confectioners' sugar. "Could be a lovely destination for honeymooners," he said, lapping residue from his fingers. "Spring will abound at southern latitudes. Think of it as the lusty month of May. Fit for honeymoon ambitions."

Howie felt a light tap against his shin. "Ah, yes, sure," he stuttered. "Great place for a honeymoon, isn't it, sweetheart? I mean, what couple wouldn't want to escape to a distant island for their honeymoon? How about it Kika?" The answer came as a solid kick, not a light tap.

Her smile was forced, unbefitting for such a beautiful face. Disdain slipped out of cute lips. "Sure, Howie Parker, I've always dreamt of an island honeymoon - but at a romantic resort in the warm Caribbean. White sandy beaches. *Private and alone.* One catering to honeymooners! Thoughts of work as distant as Mars."

Brewster pointed out the window toward the bridge. Approaching Mexican Hat was the moving van. A long line of traffic crept behind it and its security escorts. He turned his eyes to Parker and Windsong. "Well, how about it?"

In spite of earlier cynicism, Kika danced on moonbeams. Their future sparkled like bright stars. Wedding, Howie's crucial archaeological assignment, recognition of their astonishing discovery, and a chance to travel half way around the globe. As newlyweds. "I'm ready," she boasted. "We'll simply have to marry sooner."

"Little for me to add, is there?" Future groom leaned over and kissed her cheek.

Wheeler broke the romantic interlude. "What's in store for Agent Coldditz?"

Blue Sky perked up. "You mean after his spine is surgically fused in six places and he undergoes extensive PT? Well, he's not headed for the Ritz-Carlton, I'll guarantee you that. PT is a waste of taxpayer money if you ask me. He'll be locked up in a four-by-six-foot isolation chamber indefinitely. That Holmes is a cunning sleuth. Nothing will ever penetrate his intellectual firewall. It took his genius to defrag Coldditz's real agenda. And not a second too soon either. Any longer and the dirty bomb would have exploded at NGS. And his escape wouldn't have been foiled. Turns out Coldditz arranged military transport to Tyndall AFB near Panama City, Florida. He forged paperwork to join a diplomatic delegation en route to Montevideo, Uruguay. No one would have suspected a thing. He'd accompanied countless missions of that sort during his career. If you ask me, he *almost* nailed the perfect crime."

The server brought their bill. Brewster stood abruptly and snatched it. "Museum's picking up this tab." He turned to face Parker and Windsong, bowing slightly. "Thank you for the truckload of artifacts. You're an extraordinary team. The adventure of our lifetimes begins now."

Outside, the thermometer read 91 degrees. A dry wind swayed tall cottonwoods. Everyone scurried to the shade lining the San Juan. Hands were shook and commitments were made. Brewster was met by the armored truck departing for Los Alamos. Six white Chevy Tahoes flanked it. Decals on either side read: "Los Alamos National Laboratories Security Police." Occupants wore camo uniforms and chest armor. He climbed inside. Eight additional black, unmarked SUVs flanked them. A larger fleet accompanied the moving van.

Parker and Windsong turned to Blue Sky. The men shook hands firmly. Dudley delivered a warm Navajo smile. His eyes spoke a thousand words. "You'll be respected and trusted by my people, brave *bilagaana.*"

Tears welled in Kika's eyes. She embraced her fellow Navajo, leaned her head back and stared into his eyes. "I don't know how to thank you, Dudley. It's been one hell of a week. You saved our lives. We'll be ready Sunday morning. Ready to hike into..." He held his finger to her lips. "Let me help you. First in our tongue "Into...*Ni' hidi'naah*... Now, in Parker's tongue...Into...**The Land of Walking Earth**."

THE END

ABOUT THE AUTHOR

The author, recruited as a civilian employee by two intelligence agencies during his senior year at the University of Wisconsin, Madison, experienced a thwarted intelligence career when President Richard M. Nixon slashed the federal workforce by 37,000 employees with one stroke of his pen. Upon leaving the intelligence arena, he joined ranks with an international Fortune 100 company. One decade later, he relocated to a Colorado ski town, and then, five years afterwards to his penultimate dreamland, the mountains of northern New Mexico. There, Mr. Sagemiller pursues two lifelong passions---anthropology and alpine skiing. While employed seasonally at a northern New Mexico ski resort, he found ample time to continue educational pursuits in southwest archaeological studies at a community college and at University of New Mexico-Taos. He also enjoys personally enriching volunteer archaeological assignments, including countless hours of field survey and excavation work, laboratory analysis and rock art recording projects.

Greg Sagemiller has served several three year terms as Trustee of the oldest archaeological society in North America - the Archaeological Society of New Mexico, presided as its President for two terms, currently serves as its Scholarship Chairperson and has attended its summer field school near Gallup, New Mexico. He is also past President and Program Chair of the Taos Archaeological Society. He resides with his wife in their passive solar home utilizing renewable-resource components at the foot of the Sangre de Cristo Mountains in northern New Mexico.

To learn more about the author and the evolving series "Walking Earth" please visit

www.walkingearthseries.com

Made in the USA
Charleston, SC
27 July 2012